Elena *Undone*

by

Nicole Conn

Bella
BOOKS

2011

Bella Books, Inc.
P.O. Box 10543
Tallahassee, FL 32302

Printed in the United States of America on acid-free paper
First published 2011

Editor: Katherine V. Forrest
Cover Designer: Judy Fellows

ISBN 13: 978-1-59493-254-0

For *my* Soulmate...Marina
...my love, my life, my laughter...

Acknowledgments

Thank you to the following:

First and foremost to Katherine V. Forrest who is the kindest, and Most lovely editor I've ever worked with—who always Challenges me to be better, dear and wonderful friend.

And to my family who had to live with me while I was on deadline:
Daisha – fellow book lover & "processor"
Alex – fellow poet & romantic
Lauren – fellow writer & over-achiever
David (DVD!) - fellow-philisopher & playmate
Gabrielle – my fellow artist & BiBi BoBo
& "little man" Nicholas… my fellow cuddler

About The Author

Nicole Conn has been a die-hard romantic and black and white film fan from the age of ten.

Her penchant for adult and dramatic story telling is evident in latest feature film, Elena Undone touted as "sexy and smart and smoldering." This classic romance with a twist, also hosts the Longest Kiss in Cinema History, a claim veteran lesbian writer Nicole Conn's (Claire of the Moon, little man) is thrilled to be held by two women.

Conn's previous venture, little man, is a documentary she wrote, directed and produced about her own premature son born 100 days early and only weighing one pound. The feature documentary went on to win 12 Best Documentary Awards, along with the prestigious Cedar Sinai's Courageous Beginnings Award and Family Pride's Family Tree Award. The film made three TOP TEN FILMS OF 2005 list and Showtime picked up the feature and ran an Emmy campaign on this hard-hitting story about Conn's son's premature birth and subsequent 5-month hospital stay in a Neo-natal Intensive Care Unit.

In efforts to continue her support of other parents who find themselves thrust into the insanity of the NICU, Ms Conn collaborated with Preemie Magazine Founder Deborah Discenza in creating the The Preemie Parent's NICU Survival Guide: How to Maintain Your Sanity and Create a New Normal published in January, 2010.

Conn's passion for film carried her through her first feature in which she raised the money, wrote, directed and produced Claire of the Moon, the maverick film about a woman's journey to her sexual identity. The film garnered rave reviews and paved the way for lesbian themed cinema in 1991. Conn also created a FIRST for lesbian cinema: ancillary in the form of a novelization (in its 15th reprint and 10 Year Anniversary Republish) a making-of documentary MOMENTS (best-selling lesbian documentary ever made), soundtracks, posters, t-shirts, etc. She followed these projects with the award winning short film, Cynara...Poetry in Motion.

A two book deal with Simon Schuster produced the novels, Passion's Shadow (1995) & Angel Wings (1997), a new age love story. The script adaptation for Angel Wings won the 2001 Telluride Film Festival's Best Screenplay Award. In another pioneering effort, The Wedding Dress was chosen by AOL Time Warner for its new internet endeavor ipublish, which debuted in June 2001. She Walks in Beauty was published in September, 2001 and is currently in development as a feature film along with several other original screenplays Conn has penned.

Conn achieved industry recognition with her film Claire of the Moon and was a finalist in the prestigious Academy of Motion Picture Arts and Science's Nicholl Fellowships in Screenwriting. She believes in giving back to the community and sponsored the Claire of the Moon Scholarship in 1998, awarding second time novelists through the ASTRAEA Foundation.

Well known for her speed, quality and prolific ability to write in many genres, Conn has written five novels, a parent's guide, two teleplays, eleven screenplays, and has produced four soundtracks.

She is currently in pre-production on "A Perfect Ending," her next feature which she wrote and will direct this film, based on a story idea from her life and film partner, Marina Rice Bader. Bader and Conn are partners of Soul Kiss Films (Empowering Women One Film at a Time). Conn resides with her life partner, Marina and their family of six (wonderful if precocious) children in Los Angeles.

Best Feature—"Elena Undone"—Audience Award, Reel Pride, Fresno

Best Feature—"Elena Undone" Tampa GLFF

Best Documentary Audience Award, Los Angeles Outfest—"little man"

Best Documentary Jury Award, New York NewFest—"little man"

Best Documentary Audience Award, San Diego Film Festival —"little man"

Best Documentary Jury Award, Chicago Indiefest—"little man"

Best Feature hbo Audience Award, Miami GLFF—"little man"

Best Documentary Jury Award, Philadelphia Int"l GLFF Film Festival—"little man"

Best of the Fest Award, Indianapolis G&L Film Festival —"little man"

Best Documentary—Jury Award Chicago Reeling Film Festival—"little man"

Best Documentary—Glitter Award – LA—"little man"

Best Documentary—Long Island G&L Film Festival— "little man"

Best Documentary—WA DC—Reel Affirmations—"little man"

Palme D'Or—Reel Pride—"little man"

Telluride Film Festival's Best Screenplay Award—"Angel Wings"

Courageous Beginnings Award—Cedars Sinai, Los Angeles Santa Barbara Social Justice Award Nominee

Academy of Motion Picture Arts and Science's Nicholl Fellowships in Screenwriting.

Elena—a Sunday in July…

Elena Winters sat in the stifling heat and wondered if this particular day could possess any less meaning for her than, say, the day before, the Sunday before this one, or any Sunday a month or even a year before now. She then had to force herself to stop retrieving all the other meaningless days she could summon up for comparison. What was the point of delineation without the distinction of preference? Or desire?

Stop thinking. She shook her head. *It always takes you there and you cannot go there today…you have too much to do.*

The heat was always oppressive this time of year, but even more so now because the aging church's air-conditioning was on the blink yet again during LA's third and most blistering heat wave of the summer. Instead of fixing the air conditioner Barry had spent the last of the month's budget on new flyers, blazoning his picture all over the Holy Church of Light's publications, flaunting his eager countenance in an endless supply of pamphlets that littered every nook and cranny of the church.

The church, from the outside, looked the part with its beautiful stonework, arches and meticulous landscaping. But it was the inside, once you got past the newly retouched stained glass windows, where the long years of wear showed the daily erosion in chipped pews, stained runners—and the back offices,

1

well, they were a joke with peeling paint, broken floorboards and crammed with junk from the past several decades.

Elena was all too familiar with the manner in which the budget was spread; "Presentation is everything," Millie would tsk, "we're not going to sweat the small stuff, but we always want to give the impression that God has truly blessed us." The air-conditioning had been a bone of contention. Elena and several of the congregants felt it was nonnegotiable, but Millie and Barry had decided otherwise. They had already fought about it twice, and she knew it was pointless to discuss it any further, so she fanned herself with one of his brand-new flyers, glancing over to see how her son Nash was handling this suffocating heat and was delighted to find that he had fallen asleep on his girlfriend's shoulder. Tori nudged him, until she saw Elena shake her head and mouth, *Let him sleep.*

God knew she wished she could catch a nap as she vaguely listened to Barry's rich baritone lull his adoring parishioners into a sustained state of worship. Elena would give him that: He did have a way with words. His cadence was flawless. Between his Georgian southern boy fire-and-brimstone upbringing, his Royal Academy training in London, his years of dogging the theater circuit in New York, his performances had become pitch perfect for the sinner, the ritualist, the fundraiser, and of course Millie, the grand doyenne of The Holy Church of Light, and their most zealously committed leader.

Before Elena's mind could go into any further restricted territory, she quickly put together a grocery list for dinner. Now that Nash was one of the city league's star soccer players she planned menus with a genteel balance of protein, carbs and vegetables. She enjoyed feeding her son, not only because his lean and lanky frame seemed to require nutrition every half hour, but because she took great pleasure in watching her fifteen- year-old wolf down every new recipe she could find. Even when she occasionally saw in his square jaw line and deep piercing blue eyes (clearly from Barry as hers were a dark charcoal brown) the signs of manhood, he was still her boy. Her darling sweet moppy-headed boy with his tousled blond locks (another sign of Barry) with curls that were all Elena—along with his heart, body and soul. Her son was the same fierce warrior in the face of the bland and the tepid, except Nash had found a way out, had found a way to save himself from the ordinary by falling in love with the extraordinary: Tori.

She forced her mind back to the menu, which was interrupted by the nagging reminder that the church's fundraiser was being held the following week. This meant she would have to gird herself for a slew of meetings with Millie Percival, the omnipresent arbiter of all things Holy Church, and right hand to Barry. If Elena were not so secure in the knowledge that Barry was in love with her, she might find some need for concern over Millie's obvious schoolgirl crush on Barry. After all, Millie was actually quite attractive, in a beauty queen turned socialite kind of way, her long brown hair always coiffed into a perfect chignon, her finely toned figure clad in chic, if conservative form-fitting suits, and she always laid her pristinely manicured fingers topped with cherry red polish upon Barry's arm whenever possible. Elena had watched with equal parts amusement and annoyance. Millie's attraction had grown ever more fervent as the years had passed since Barry had taken over as pastor. Almost a decade ago now. But as with everything Millie had her fingers in, Elena could not take seriously the shy giggles, the overt caretaking because it all seemed so shallow, so gutless, so void of true intention. And though Millie was fond of chatting endlessly about her husband Miles, and his "extremely high position" and "hugely important corporate exploits," always sighing, "Why, heck, he's traveling 'round the world like a globetrotter," Elena knew that meant Miles was out of Millie's hair, and she was free to do as she pleased. This mostly consisted of her "duty to God" and "taking care of others." "I was just born selfless," she constantly extolled, as if it were a curse she had to bear. But what Millie was most fond of reminding everyone, daily, was that "M&M—Millie & Miles—make no mistake" were not only the largest contributors to the church, but their single annual gift out-summed the entire congregation's tithes put together.

Elena had to give Barry his props. Her husband had a true gift with people. It wasn't just that he was tall, handsome and pleasant, with his twinkling blue eyes and sandy-brown hair. He possessed a smile that defied objections, sweetened negotiations, and he was always able to fully engage Millie without truly flirting back, capable of moving right through her as if she weren't there, even when he paid a great deal of attention to what she said. He just had a way of dealing with her. He was actually more involved with Miles the few moments they spent together. The two men golfed occasionally, even shared drinks and probably resigned conversations about "the spouse," Elena suspected, and yet Millie continued to buzz around Elena's husband with an endless flair for drama and the constant need to run something by him. Barry, always politic, met Millie head-on, taking the high road while getting all his needs met and Millie always came back for more. Elena wondered if that was the draw—she could have her cake and almost eat it too. Perhaps the ability only to gaze admiringly, to touch, smell, admire...but never actually take a bite, fueled many an unrequited fantasy.

Back to the shopping—Focus Elena. Yes, and the supplies for Tori's new experiment. Elena turned to watch Tori gently shift her shoulder below Nash's head so he could find a comfortable pillow to sleep through the rest of his father's sermon. Ahhh, Tori...she couldn't have asked for a better daughter-in-law. Without question she and Nash belonged to one another.

Elena glanced at her husband. Sighed.

Peyton—the same Sunday in July...

Peyton Lombard walked to her house with cell phone balancing against her shoulder, mail and manuscripts piled haphazardly in her arms as she waited for a human voice on the other side of a phone conversation she was desperate to have. She had been dressed for a meeting in her black jeans, a long sleeved pinstriped Façonnable shirt and vest, and she was now sweltering from the heat.

What was with the endless incompetence, she wondered. For weeks she had been dealing with the transfer of her mother from the nursing home to their own family home. She had begun to believe she could no longer be surprised by how insanely screwed up the insurance and paperwork had become throughout the process, but each day came an even more outlandish mistake.

She shifted the weight of all the materials in her arms, crooked her neck as far as it would go to keep the phone in place between her neck and shoulder as she pleaded, "No please don't put me on hold again. I beg of you. I've already talked to four different departments—no!" She almost cried when a vacuous rendition of "Lucy in the Sky with Diamonds" buzzed into her ear.

"CHRIST!" She hung up, almost dropped the phone, and stalked down the front slate stone steps into her home.

The moment she entered she felt the usual deep calming that the quiet but spacious living room offered. No matter where she had been, how much traffic she had to battle, a slew of pitch meetings, endless lunches and dinner meetings with agents, editors and publishers—when she returned to her home she felt an immediate transition back to balance and sanity. The large, ranch-style house with its massive burnished wood beams and vaulted floor to ceiling windows that overlooked a spacious pool and then an endless sea of green—maple, oak and pine—was her sanctuary.

The peace was short-lived. She heard the commotion from the back room. She knew before she entered what used to be her mother's sewing room that Sylvia, the new day nurse, would be tussling with her mom, trying to keep her in the hospital bed they had rented because of her mother's broken hip. In frustration Peyton tossed all the stuff from her arms onto a side table as she rushed to help the aging but wonderful RN.

Her mother calmed, and actually took note of Peyton for the first time in a week, connecting with her eyes, studying her daughter's face. For a brief moment, Peyton saw her mother as she used to look, the handsome if tight features, a Joan Crawford beauty stained by bitterness and now years of ill health. Her thin, dry lips curled to form a smile. Peyton's heart lifted as she bent to embrace her mother, and when they parted her mother's smile turned coy.

"I pee-peed!"

Peyton's jaw tightened.

"I pee-peed. I'm a good girl."

Peyton glanced at Sylvia. They both sighed, then smiled.

What else could they do? Humor, at this juncture, truly was the only medicine.

"Well you are a good girl, aren't you?" Peyton concurred.

But her mother had already gone back into the void, staring into a world of memories, perhaps an entirely different universe they could only guess at.

Peyton began the ritual of changing the bedding with Sylvia, wondering if what she had witnessed had actually been a flash of lucidity. Her mother's eyes had been so focused, so green, that same emerald intensity she had gifted to her own daughter. As Peyton busied herself she decided to give them both the benefit of the doubt and then remembered that she had just promised her editor the pages for her deadline.

"Sylvia, are you okay here?"

"Sure am...this is *my* job. Now you get outta here and get to *your* job." Sylvia grinned.

Peyton fluttered her eyes with gratitude as she walked back down the hallway into the living room, so happy that she had replaced the last nurse with Sylvia, a middle-aged Hispanic caretaker who was sturdy, calm and always pleasant. Unlike the previous nurse (Peyton had to wonder who screened these RNs—Sylvia had been the sixth she had interviewed!) Clara, a large-boned, extremely bleached blonde with the brightest red lipstick Peyton had ever seen, Sylvia was a godsend. The bloody imprint of Clara's lips had had to be scrubbed from endless coffee cups from which Clara had sipped her "special healing tea."

Peyton discovered, inadvertently, that the woman she had hired to care for her mother was singing, and "performing a healing" on her mother. She'd tiptoed down the hall to decipher the bizarre incantations she had been hearing from her mother's bedroom, stood outside the door, and then heard Clara begin to share with her mother her incessant obsession with the First World Order taking over the universe.

Peyton had told Clara, very firmly, that under no circumstances was she to do any such healings on her mother, but the Clydesdale-like nurse begged Peyton to allow her to do ablutions on Peyton's mother to prevent the "illuminati from taking over her body. You know, the aliens have already taken over earth, and their intention is to kill every last one of us until there are only five hundred thousand left."

"And why do you suppose they want any of us left," asked Wave, Peyton's best friend, whom Peyton had asked over to see if Clara was safe to be with her mother. "I mean, why not off the lot of us?"

Wave's offhanded remark only provoked Clara into a never-ending conspiracy theory that began and ended somewhere around the fact that Peyton's mother had been a victim. "Don't let this 'Alzheimer's' thing fool you. She's been taken over." Peyton was not to believe for a minute that her mother suffered from the last and most dangerous stages of Alzheimer's.

Wave told Peyton in her deeply rich South Manchester Queen's English, "You do realize you have a total loon tendin' to dear Mum. You gotta sack her. Stat."

Peyton had had her replaced the next day.

Before Peyton could even get to her desk, which she had set up in the huge living room, so that she could enjoy the most beautiful and peaceful view her family home afforded, her agent, Emily called.

"Do you want to lose the job I spent weeks finding for you?" she screamed.

She tried to toss in a sympathetic tone that she was absolutely understanding about Peyton's situation with her mother, "But, Peyton, the magazine you're freelancing for could care less."

Peyton replied, "I'll get it done if I have to work all night."

"Good because I have you up for a big project with Cosmo, you know that."

Peyton didn't much care, but she did have bills to pay. "I'm aware…look, I'm grateful Emily, it's just that there are only so many hours in the day and you know—"

"Yes, and I think you're a hero…I just don't want you screwing up a brilliant career."

"Got it."

Elena—two Sundays later...

"I'm not going!" Nash's voice was tense and exasperated.

Barry stood with his wife amongst the congregants who were gathered on the long sloping front lawn of the church. Dressed in one of his four dark-toned Brooks Brothers suits, his navy blue shirt and one of the many ties Tori and Nash had gifted him with over the years, Barry could as easily have been a politician as a pastor, able to keep everyone chattering excitedly, and create a certain urgency buzzing through the crowd. In contrast to Barry's stylish clothing, Elena's had conformed to the code; conservative hues of peach, rose and beige, pastel floral summer dresses. Barry had insisted she keep her hair in the traditional Indian braid, or pulled back, as he warned her, "when your hair's let free, El—you just look too damn sexy." He had winked at her when he said it, admiring what he always referred to her as her "exotic sultriness—we can't have that. You look nice and traditional with the braid, and that way you won't threaten the wives!"

"You did hear they're protesting downtown!" Garret, a mid-forties parishioner piped up. He was Millie's right-hand minion and never far from her side.

"The nerve of those people," Millie sighed dramatically. "We'll all be there. All of us, Pastor Barry, won't we?" she asked of the folks standing by.

Nods of affirmation and plenty of eager "Don't worry, we'll all be there" came from one congregant after another. If nothing else, this was one flock of geese that always traveled together.

Barry turned to Elena who was vaguely caught up in the fervor, but, as usual had other things on her mind. "El, make sure you get extra food and drinks for us to take."

Nash gently tugged as his mother's elbow, hissed below his breath: "There's no way I'm going with them, Mom. He can't make me."

Elena tried to move them both out of earshot. "Please watch your tone. That's your father's decision."

Nash's jaw clamped. Elena saw in his eyes the surprise he

couldn't hide at what he felt was betrayal from her. He too was dressed in his Sunday best, slacks, shirt and tie, which he always jumped out of the second he got home into what he called his "real clothes," a variation of jeans, T-shirts and hoodies. "Are you kidding me? Do you even know what they're talking about here?"

Tori walked up from behind them. "Don't these people know that being loud cannot compete with being clear? And Nash is clear he doesn't want to be involved with this protest. How in the heck can this benefit him or them, for that matter, if he is in complete disagreement with his dad on this?"

"It doesn't matter, Mom." Nash's voice grew louder. "Because there is no way I'm going!"

Before she could even respond another congregant came up to request the Kinder class calendar. Elena tried to divide her attention, but the woman was chattering so enthusiastically she began to glaze over, attempting to listen dutifully, but also trying to keep tabs on the situation with Nash. All this while she continued to shake the hands of the same congregants that she'd shaken hands with every Sunday for the past ten years. She knew the pulp, flesh and feel of every hand, but they still felt all the same. Undifferentiated.

Nash's displeasure with the church, attending services and now even Barry's message were becoming more and more of a problem. She kept an eye on Nash as he shoved his hands deep into his pockets, as Barry well-wished other congregants outside the doors of the church.

Barry shot a glance at Elena: *Get your son under control.*

Even when it was just the last of the folks who were involved in another one of their "God is love campaigns," the last thing Elena wanted was for the two of them to clash in front of Barry's parishioners, here outside the church. The rumor mill was a nano-second away at all times and Millie's face was already pinched with displeasure at Nash's open display of impertinence.

"Nash," Barry intoned.

"Whatever—"

"Young man," Millie interjected with a superior tone, "that is no way to speak near the church, and it certainly is no way to speak to your father."

9

"That's fine, Millie—" Barry tried to take back the reins but before he could, Nash stomped off across the sanctuary lawn. Elena watched nervously as Tori ran to join him, but Nash shrugged her off, trying to distance himself from everyone.

Elena could just make out Nash's words, "You have no idea what it's like to live in that house—"

"You seem to forget—" Tori stood in front of him now and Elena could not help but smile at Tori's absolute knowing of Nash. "I spend most of my waking hours there."

Elena shook her head, taking in Tori, who was the strangest mix of absolutely gorgeous in a sort of Disney-gone-quirky display of glam curls meets funky retro stylizing. Pieces of clothing that had no business being in the same closet somehow made sense the way Tori tossed together her ensembles, a frilly skirt with a businessman's vest, a bohemian shirt belted by an Indian scarf. And she would not be caught dead, anywhere, without one of her ties. Tori owned the most extensive collection of ties Elena had ever seen and had the most brilliant manner in which she affixed them to herself—sash, headband, belt and tie. She might appear to be nothing more than a dumb pretty blonde but Tori was the most brilliant child Elena had ever met, an absolutely stunning font of fascinating trivia, insight and wisdom.

"Yes, they're crazy—but you know my parents make yours look like a walk in the park—" Tori stopped to consider her surroundings, the church grounds edging up to the children's park next door. "Yeah...like a walk in the park." Then Tori returned to the issue at hand and mollifying Nash. She suggested, "You know, Nash, if there were such a thing as minutes kept of all the myriad circumstances and events regarding family dysfunction I believe it would rival all the sands in the ocean."

"Save it."

Nash stormed to the car, waiting for them to leave.

"Thank you so much for all your help with the food drive," Elena intoned as she continued to watch her son and Tori. "We'll see you next Sunday."

"Pastor Barry, we've got all the buses lined up for the march. We're all going to be there. Every last one of us," Elena heard

Millie profess earnestly as she chattered endlessly about their anti-gay protest. Apparently they were protesting a protest. Elena couldn't really follow what it was all about, she already had so much on her plate, and she couldn't get herself really worked up about every new cause du jour Millie pursued. Half of them petered out and were simply a framework for her histrionics. The other half Millie drove with a passion. Either way, Elena tried to stay out of them.

"Hey El." Barry walked up to Elena. He said, watching his son in frustration, "Sounds like we're going to have to have a family chat tonight at dinner when I get home."

"Barry—"

"Don't Barry me. He cannot behave like that at church."

"Maybe we shouldn't force—"

"Coming to church isn't an option, Elena, so don't even start."

"But we've always encouraged him to think for himself. Maybe this just doesn't speak to him."

"No, he's just being a fifteen-year-old who's used to getting his own way, thanks to you, and him not attending my services will simply not be tolerated."

Elena realized it was a losing battle. "I...I'm going to get the kids home so I can start dinner. Anything special you want?"

It took Barry a moment to move beyond his anger toward their son, but when he refocused on Elena, his eyes warmed, and he smiled. "How 'bout your famous meatloaf."

"Yes, well..." They both laughed. Elena's last new meatloaf recipe had been a "disaster of epic portions" Tori had quipped, even if it had been at the expense of her own idea to try every known version of meatloaf as a "truly valued experiment—the very insight into the American soul through one of its most classic dishes."

Elena smiled back. "I'll see you at home."

Barry kissed her forehead, then sighed. "Would you talk to him?"

"You know I will."

Peyton—that same Sunday in July

Peyton sat in her most comfy sweats and a dark blue muscle T as she flipped the day calendar page back and forth; back and forth, yet it was still there: "Women's Pay Scale Article Due!" circled in big red marker.

Feeling overwhelmed, she returned to her work. Then noticed that the pens and pencils in her Franklin Day Planner cup holder had been messed with. Must have been one of the nurses borrowing a pen. She knew precisely where and how each pen and pencil fit into the holder on her massive reclaimed pine dining room table that she used as her desk, and now stringently went to work to set the world straight.

As she fussed endlessly, in the back of her mind she ran the rather pointless equation that every moment she devoted to her OCD was a minute lost to her deadline, but nevertheless, in this particular instance her OCD was winning out.

Living with her obsessive compulsive disorder or "relentless brain drain," as she referred to it, had been a ceaseless, and for the most part, unwinnable battle since she had turned seventeen and had had her first full-blown panic attack. Convinced she was having a heart attack she had driven herself straight to the ER, crumpling the front end of her Toyota into a garbage dumpster on the way, so shaken was she by her racing heart and inability to breathe.

For the next eight years, she battled this disorder by white-knuckling a cure. Sometimes she drank away her attacks, only to find them worse the next day. Doctor after doctor informed her that she was not only healthy, but inordinately fit. Her obsessive need to swim one hundred laps a day along with her rigorous workout regime had prompted one doctor to fawn, "Your body is like a work of art. Your arms couldn't be more sculpted. I find women with arms so defined, hmm, quite beautiful. Please just don't overdo it." The obsequious doctor had smiled at her a little too sweetly and Peyton found a new doctor.

She had seen specialist after specialist consumed with the idea of inoperable brain tumors, an as yet undiscovered rare blood disease, an electrical malfunction within her heart—it had to be something. Because even when her mother noted with jarring coldness, "This is all in your head and you need to stop it," she knew whatever she had was real. If her heart could pummel out of her chest in the middle of the night during a deep sleep, it wasn't her imagination. Either that or her body had a mind of its own.

One day as she walked by the front of a bookstore she saw a book that literally popped out at her: *The Good News about Panic Attacks, Anxiety and Agoraphobia.* The sales clerk had stumbled as she was putting up the display and the book flew into the front of the window toppling all the other books in its path.

Peyton walked in, bought the book, started reading it before she even left the store, and didn't put it down until she had gulped it all down, sitting at the first Starbucks she encountered, swallowing every word whole, the very sustenance she had needed all these many years to finally bring comprehension to what she believed had become insanity. She did not return to work that day. After she finished the book, she walked to her car, drove to her favorite park, sat at a bench overlooking the vast and beautiful view—not the high-rise buildings of the city, but the endless stretch of Baldwin Hills, a vista of sagebrush, green and open skies. As the sun was beginning to set she cried.

She cried for hours over finally being able to put a name to all her strange brain ruminations and her physical body attacks that made her feel an utter loss of control. Not to mention exhausted by the severity of her clamoring heart, her inability to breathe, her feeling utterly outside of her own skin. The physical aspects were daunting, but it was the surreal and bizarre thought process that had taken more out of her than anything. Her do-or-die need for ritual and the fanatical compulsion to follow random thought patterns as if they had any meaning or bearing of any kind on reality had completely devastated any confidence she had in the ability to be normal. Although, as time had gone by, all her daily rituals had *become* her reality and a great deal of her rational mind had finally come to the conclusion that she truly had gone insane. Yet, here she was, on the printed page. She finally knew herself. A person who had severe and chronic OCD.

Breathing deeply, she finally owned her disorder or condition—what it was didn't even matter to her any longer. Because now she could understand it.

The next day she made an appointment with one of the psychiatrists listed in the back of the book who all specialized in OCD and Panic Disorders. She met with the rather slight and strange little fellow by the name of Dr. James at the very first appointment he could give her. But within moments the kindness in his eyes, the warmth of his smile put her at ease. Unlike any doctor she had ever known, this gentle man called her daily to check in with her and he made her feel immediately safe with his thorough knowledge and guidance. He was used to patients dropping their medication due to the side effects, which Peyton had to agree were onerous. "The pills can't do anything for you in the bottle," Dr. James stated a number of times when he called to check on her progress. But along with medication, and the next year in therapy, Peyton finally began to fully understand the mechanics of her OCD. She felt like a new woman—the best version of herself she could be. She had lived for eight long years crippled by this disorder, narrowing her life experience to a pure subsistence of writing and swimming maniacally, rarely going out, joining her best friend Wave for rare social outings, but mostly holed up inside, reading in the few free moments her rigid schedule allowed. And then she had found freedom.

It was during her second year of adjusting to life in a more normal manner that she decided to tackle the project of writing her personal memoir. Her agent had said it was sort of like the new AA—everyone seemed to be coming out of the closet and baring their soul about one syndrome or another. Regardless of Emily's crass pitch, Peyton wrote the book to speak to all the other people out there who had been suffering as she had, so they would know there was a way out—and if there was anyone she could keep from suffering even a second longer, she was determined to do so. For Peyton, taking care of her OCD was as life-affirming as a drunk quitting the bottle.

Her memoir, *Trust, Who Needs It?—An Agoraphobic's Memoir* hit number two on the Self-Help Book List the first week it was out and soon thereafter number one. Peyton won numerous awards and a bit of notoriety, she dated another well-known out lesbian in the entertainment industry and within the worlds of OCD junkies and lesbians she had a weird melting pot of fans, and was noted in *Curve* as a "celesbian on the rise."

The fact was that OCD was a condition one learned to live with. Medication helped Peyton's remarkably intense panic attacks to all but vanish. Her OCD, however, flared up on a regular basis depending on how much stress she had to endure and at this juncture, she had learned when to give in and let the ritual double-checking take over…sometimes it just was easier to cave, get it over with and get on with life. As she did now, lining up the pens for the ninth time. Nine was her number and she always performed her rituals in three sets of three. As she was finalizing this last set of three she heard the silky voice.

She knew before she even turned around that Margaret would be dressed in something seductive. As she began to swivel, very slowly to resist what she knew was coming, she saw her in the corner of her eye. Sure enough, the svelte and exceedingly attractive Margaret was clad in lacy attire. With her Marilyn Monroe tousled blond hair, her eerily transparent blue eyes, Peyton could feel before she saw Margaret's *come-fuck-me* leer. Margaret was known to be assertive, or "a bloody hounddog!" noted Wave, and was used to getting what she wanted.

"Hey…stranger," Margaret purred. "I've been waiting…"

"God baby, I'm so sorry—but I can't."

"Oh, but I think you can." Margaret came up behind her, seductively slid her fingers down the front of Peyton's T, stopping to gently cup Peyton's right breast. She bent over her, kissing the edge of Peyton's neck. The chill that ran down Peyton's spine was not desire. As Peyton was about to turn to convince Margaret to wait, Margaret leaned closer still to reveal her secret weapon: a frozen vial of sperm.

Peyton smiled, bargaining, "Babe, I know I said I'd be home early…but I have to get this article to Emily…how 'bout in an hour or two. Three tops?"

Margaret's smile slid from her face. She slammed the baby-making paraphernalia on the desk. "Right! You know what, Peyton? If it's not a deadline, it's your mom. Or your mom.

Or your mom! Any normal person would have kept her in that home. Where she belonged. I don't even know if it's that safe for her to be here with all the loony tune nurses you've got running around this house."

Peyton clammed up.

"I'm so over it, Peyton. Really. I know you think you're some sort of goddamn saint, but you're a martyr—"

"Trust me, she won't be a problem for much longer."

"Look, don't make me the villain here. This was your goddamn idea. I'm ovulating now." Margaret pursed her lips. "You have your schedule—I have mine."

"Margaret—"

"You don't have to fuck me, okay Peyton? Just squeeze this slime up my uterus."

*

"Now that's what I call high seas romance," Wave Fontaine remarked to Peyton, as she refilled her coffee cup, having been told in mini-segments, between Wave waiting upon other customers, the series of events that let up to their "kind of royally fecked up evenin'."

Wave's vernacular was unique as it comes and when people often asked where she came from, she'd respond "specifically South Manchester, but with twelve years of Glasgow thrown in for good measure. But I'd get kneecapped if I was to describe it as Scottish." With burnished red hair, fair faced and freckles, "God sprinkled 'em all over me—even my arse for God's sake!" Wave was an entity unto her own, with her boho-chic style, her genuine sweetness and "sincerely codependent" persona. And Peyton loved every ounce of her.

As Wave continued on her appointed rounds of coffee pouring, she returned and gently bowed and with the most elegant turn of the hand, she filled up one of regular Pinot Latte customers she was serving. "It's all in the wrist. Yeah, I spent years at university perfecting just this move."

Peyton watched her dearest friend in the world with admiration. She didn't know how anyone could be so inordinately friendly, bubbly and bright all the time, but that was Wave. She was a spectacular mix of bawdy stage performer who'd spew out the most random crass offerings in one moment and in the next be the wisest, softest, most nurturing and loving soul Peyton had the great fortune to know. It didn't matter what was going on, Wave was all over it, snappy, good-natured, fiercely loyal and protective.

Peyton had seen her best friend through some rough spells after high school, and after Peyton returned from college, helped her nurse plenty "a wicked arse love 'angovers." But Wave's huge light was on pretty much all the many long hours Pinot Latte —Wave's thriving coffee and wine house—was open, serving up "a libation for every possible mood."

Wave's extraordinary person was the one thing Peyton could count on in a world where most things teetered one way or the other, where you could never be certain, and even if you felt you could, you could talk yourself out of it soon enough. Trust, always Peyton's keenest issue with everything and everyone, did not exist with Wave. Because with Wave, Peyton felt safety. Certainty.

Wave was as pedigreed as they came—from the same private girl school, Campbell Hall in Studio City that Peyton had attended. That's where they had met. Only Wave had the "hurly balls," as she put it, "to strike out on me own and make me wee shell of a space in which to entertain all the lovely ladies." She skipped college, waited tables from the bottom up, took a portion of her inheritance and created Pinot Latte, the medium-sized coffeehouse that reflected Wave's personality, an eclectic blend of paintings from starving artists, oodles of old paperbacks, B movie posters plastered upon the walls, an inordinate amount of bric-a-brac, all of which made you forget you were in Pinot Latte, which was, as often as not, filled with regulars who made the establishment a second home. Wave didn't care a whit if people thought it was speculative or risky. Wave was absolute. About everything. Except love.

"Yep, you just don't get a cuppa joe like this any day. Trust me, my friend. No better brew on this side of…well, Silverlake anyway." She filled up another cup at the bar and then made her way back to Peyton.

"Don't know why you want to have a kid with Margaret anyway," Wave shook her head and rolled her eyes. "She's about as a warm and cozy as a crisp in a pool."

At that moment Wave's latest girlfriend, Erin, brash young eye candy, clad in baggy shorts, a muscle T and sporting half-purple, half-green hair ("well you know it's prerequisite to look like a TeleTubbie when you're in a garage band," Wave defended), walked up from behind them, and sat next to Peyton. Wave leaned over to kiss Erin, but Erin gently shoved a coffee cup between them. "Need coffee. Loooong night."

"Bit hung are we?"

"Is that what you think I've been doing? Partying?"

"Well, have you?"

"We played last night. Not that you would know, since you didn't come." Erin pouted.

"Well, I'm sorry if I have to make a livin', love, but it doesn't seem to bother you a jot when it comes to payin' for your bike, now, does it."

"Just the coffee, please. I've had my fill of drama."

Erin was referring to the other "cooks" in the band. Wave proceeded to fill Erin in on Peyton's terrible night with Margaret.

Erin grimaced, then turned and cocked a conspicuous eye at Peyton. "I thought you two were off baby making for now. You know, 'cuz of your sick mother an' all."

"Yeah," Peyton grimly concurred, "so did I."

"You been tryin' a lot?"

Both Peyton and Wave exchanged confused glances.

"I don't really know that that's any of our business." Wave frowned. "Even though I find it all rather fascinating spewing some dude's sperm up one's Vjay-jay, takin' it out like a hamburger, thawin' it and havin' a go. Strange times we live in."

Erin dumped her coffee into a to-go cup, dismissing Wave altogether, then shot a parting glance at Peyton as she abruptly left their company.

"Wrong side of the futon, I take it," Wave mused.

"Wave, I don't want to—"

"Then don't. Think I didn't know what I was getting into with that one?"

Wave grinned bravely, but underneath it all, Peyton knew Wave was hurt. And worried.

*

Elena whirled around their tiny, cramped kitchen, fixing dinner, unloading groceries, sorting bills, folding the last of the laundry as she chatted on the phone. "Yes...the church fund-raiser is the fifteenth. Yeah...no—and the retreat is on the twenty-second. Yes, I'm sending out an e-mail regarding Barry's new Bible study. No problem. See you Sunday."

A huge calendar riddled with appointments and church functions took over half the walnut dining room table that alongside her mini built-in desk served as Elena Central, which pretty much summed up the dining room, other than several religious paintings and a wooden cross that took up half a wall. Elena had hung the cross there because Nash had made it with Barry in a woodshop project the church had showcased. It was the only cross, of which there were many, in the house that Elena felt held true spiritual meaning—even if it was more about a father and son working on a project together than a sacred icon of prayer.

She sighed as she glanced about the chaos. True. It wasn't the most optimal spot to have a home office, but it was the only place in the very small three-bedroom Craftsman that Elena had to attempt to create some sort of order out of the chaos of running the house, keeping Nash's and Barry's schedules as well as the multitude of church functions for which Elena was responsible or involved in.

She negotiated all the many tasks without ever disturbing Nash and Tori who sat with an elaborate science project, working on the other half of the dining room table.

"Mom, did you get the baking powder for our models?"

"Oh, yes, it's in here somewhere." Elena began to search through the remainder of the half-put away groceries. Tori jumped up to help find the baking powder and gestured at the onions and green peppers she pulled out of the bag.

Tori held the onions before them, as if a sight to behold.

"Did you know ancient Egyptians used to place their right hand on onions when taking an oath?"

Barry entered the dining room through the pass door from the kitchen, several congregants following him, all holding their Bibles.

"Sweetie, can you put on some coffee?"

Elena glanced over, nodded politely at Barry and his followers. "Sure."

"Do you have any idea why?" Tori continued, looking at the onions.

"Thanks babe." Barry squeezed in a quick kiss. "Sorry I didn't call first, but you know how it goes."

Sure she did. She glanced around the room. This is how it always went. Her serving the needs of others, which she was happy to do. *It's just...it's just what?*

"Do you know why?" Tori asked for what must have been the third time.

Elena shook her head acting interested.

"It was a symbol for eternity."

Elena glanced around her. God forbid this was her eternity.

*

Peyton sat in glorious hues of sunset gold as she held her mother's hand. She was sleeping peacefully. She was about to nod off herself when Margaret entered the room, dressed in an indigo blue cocktail dress and her diamond studs, blond hair up in a classy chignon, holding her favorite "to die for clutch." She had made her grand entrance, about to do a twirl about when she stopped and the effervescent smile disappeared from her face.

She took one look at Peyton, shook her head. "Oh, God. You've got to be kidding me!"

"Didn't you get my messages? I texted you three times," Peyton returned.

"Right."

"I told you if she wasn't doing well I wouldn't be able to go." Peyton glanced at her mother. "Look at her."

"Yeah, I've heard it all before." Margaret was about to stomp off, but stopped, and actually looked at Peyton's mother. Her face softened at what she saw. "Well, part of me thinks you had no desire to go in the first place...I know how much you love these social events."

Peyton grinned ruefully. "I just want to be near her...for as long as..."

"I'm not sure why...she gave you so much grief."

"Maybe," Peyton sighed, "maybe that's just all part of it... but she also gave me..."

"What?...What did she give to you that was so damn wonderful, Peyton?"

Margaret walked to Peyton put a hand on her shoulder. They shared a moment of silence, Margaret smiled in sympathy, then latched onto Peyton's watch, twisted it toward her so that she could see. "Well, I suppose this means I'm escorting myself to the fundraiser. You know Peyton, people are going to begin to wonder if I'm available."

Peyton stood up, absentmindedly kissed Margaret goodbye. "I'll make it up to you. In the meantime, do your best to put the rumor to rest."

*

Elena walked down the winding trail of the large and endless park, meandering as slowly as she could. She had found the Russian Gardens park many years ago, shortly after she had Nash. It was a bit of a drive, but because the park was apparently not well known, very few people ever seemed to gather at a time, it was never overcrowded. Elena used to bring Nash daily and wheel him about in the stroller. Yes, it was off a difficult turn and she had only found it because she had gotten lost one day, but she had considered it a small bit of luck, almost sort of like it was fate, finding this park, because it had been a day when she and Barry had had one of their most furious squabbles and finding this place was like a sign that as long as she could sort out her thoughts, come to grips with her reality through the wooded paths, long open fields and extraordinary views, she could get through anything.

She sighed. This was her one place of refuge. She didn't want her stroll to end. When it did it meant she would have to return to the house.

*

Peyton sat on a bench near a tree. She simply needed a place where she could be alone. No mom. No nurse. No Margaret. She read a few pages of *Understanding Alzheimer's*, put the book down, closed her eyes.

A shiver crawled up her spine. She suddenly felt very uncomfortable. Almost panic-stricken. She wondered if her mother was okay.

She got up to get rid of whatever was threatening to envelop her, and left her book behind.

*

Elena had strolled to the far end of the park. She saw the book on the bench. No one was nearby. She wandered over to it. Looked down, saw the title *Understanding Alzheimer's*.

She glanced around, then picked it up. She held it for a long moment. She didn't know why, but she was certain the person who had left it would return. She set it back upon the bench, straightened it out, frowned a moment wondering if the owner was coming up from behind her, but when she turned she saw nothing. No one.

As she continued to walk out of the park and to her car, she felt a chill go up her spine.

"...We were caught together as young boys. Outcasts, ridiculed. Where we come from, Gay will not be tolerated. It is punishable by death." Rashid, a middle-aged Middle Eastern man, looks sympathetically at his lover, a younger, gentle-faced man who shares his ethnicity. Iranians.

"Our families...they kept us apart for ten years..." The younger of the two chokes back tears as he remembers. "We lost one another, lost track. Each of us tried to move on with our lives—later when we shared stories, we both discovered we had promised in our heads that we would forget, but would then quickly promise afterwards—in our hearts—we would not."

They glance at each other. The deep love that fills the space between them is palpable.

"Then one day, I'm in the airport, heading to London to go to school. I see the back of Rashid's head—from across an entire airport. But I know—I know it is him."

"I turned as if I had no control over my body. I turned and saw..." The younger Iranian looks to his lover, his eyes well up with tears, "...him...this beautiful man who I...love."

"We left everything." Rashid brushes a hand over his lover's. "Our lives started that day, fifteen years ago. And we've never looked back."

Tyler stops his camera. Walks up to the one of the Iranians leans down to face him and looks into his eyes, with tears in his own.

September 19

As Barry fucked her Elena wondered about hoping too much, hoping too hard. That maybe you couldn't force things, that maybe people were only allotted the children in life they were meant to have, and to complicate it by using fertility methods, to try as hard as she and Barry had been trying to have another baby, simply was fighting the impossible. Fighting against what was right or meant to be. And maybe, it was simply a righting of wrongs.

She shook herself back into her reality, opened her eyes briefly and watched Barry's face, saw his jaw line tethered in concentration as he continued to move himself closer to orgasm, and then wondered vaguely whether she would enjoy sex more with another man, but immediately dismissed the idea. She did care for Barry. He was a kind and gentle man, and even now, while he rutted her, she could tell by the way he was preparing to come that he wanted her to be with him. She put a gentle hand to his shoulder as he climaxed, felt his saliva near her ear as he came saying the same thing he had said a thousand times, until it stung her ear, "I love you, El..."

Panting he shifted his weight upon her, and she felt him withdraw, felt the driplets of semen against her thigh and hoped that whatever essence had withdrawn with him wasn't supposed to make a baby.

"Think that'll do it?" Barry rolled off her, lifted his muscular physique to the side. She made herself touch the tufts of hair at his chest, feeling a soft sadness for him that his beauty, his strong, healthy man's body wasn't more appreciated by her; that while she could notice other women eyeing Barry salaciously at the beach, watching his rippling muscles, for her it was simply flesh. His blondish, now graying hair, his taut nipples—none of it moved her in the way it seemed to move others. She had long since stopped wondering about her confusion...she just let it be. She had accepted after the first few years with Barry that she simply was defective in that department. But it didn't need to ruin Barry's enjoyment and she tried to be as connected to him as she could, given that her body always seemed outside of his reach. She was only thankful that Barry's sex drive seemed nowhere near that of her friends' spouses. The few times she had allowed herself to have conversations with Diana and some of her old college friends, she had to consider herself extremely lucky hearing about all the constant pawing and not so subtle hints to "do it," and if they didn't, well, then their partners couldn't complain if they roamed elsewhere.

"Ahhhh." Barry propped himself on his elbow, leaned over, nibbled Elena's neck in postcoital bliss, then chuckled. "Maybe that'll do the trick...what do you think?"

"Maybe." And again she consciously touched his arm, stroking him gently, trying to convey a sense of warmth and love.

"God knows, it would be the best thing in the world for Nash to have a baby sister or brother. Get that kid out of his own self-absorbed universe."

"Nash is not self-absorbed," Elena stated categorically. More and more, Elena felt that her son was actually a brilliant but troubled teen who every day was finding their universe ever smaller, ever more filled with contradiction, growing ever more claustrophobic for him and his idealistic mind.

"El, every teenager is self-absorbed—it's a qualification." He was in a good mood, and nothing was going to take him out of it.

"Maybe," Elena responded, then they both laughed.

"Except Tori," they stated in unison.

"Well, Tori is the exception to the rule," Barry observed, "thank God she found Nash—or Nash found her. Either way, we couldn't do any better."

Elena smiled. Whatever else, they both always agreed about Tori.

Elena was about to turn to get ready for sleep when Barry stopped her. "What about..." He didn't finish.

"I'm fine...really," Elena responded and before he could protest any further she snuck in a quick kiss. "Goodnight."

She turned over. She could feel his body, waiting, a heavy waiting, and when he finally turned to go to sleep she breathed easily.

*

Peyton tasted her, felt her wetness in her mouth, felt the hardening, the early tremble and knew that Margaret, like clockwork, was about to come. As a matter of her own need for perfection, her desire to be the best at everything she undertook, she tried to tease Margaret a little longer, hoping that her orgasm would be better, stronger, and found a dim sort of satisfaction in feeling the thudding throbbing in her mouth about her chin and cheeks, hearing Margaret hiss that low throaty growl when she came and waited just the precise amount of time before she moved alongside of Margaret and held her, because that was what Margaret liked after lovemaking, for Peyton to hold her "so that I feel cherished."

Later, Peyton lay staring at the ceiling in the bedroom, what had been her mother's master bedroom, that Peyton had allowed Margaret to "spruce up," because for her the room was "sparse and, well, ugly, Peyton." When Peyton's mother had turned over the house to Peyton and moved to her condo, Peyton had already determined that the room was going to be stripped of any fussiness and had decorated the extremely large room with nothing more than a small antique writer's desk, and a triptych of paintings over her California King bed. These exquisite line paintings of three nude women in different states of languid repose rested strategically above the bed against the spackled gold walls. Other than that, a few bookcases and some office supplies completed the room. But Margaret felt the room was "too male" with Peyton's dark blue bedding and "girly shots on the walls—penis envy much?" she had teased Peyton as she placed ferns, silk flowers and a multicolored Asian screen, one at a time after each returning visit, until Peyton almost felt like the room had been taken over, and the nights Margaret wasn't there, Peyton preferred to sleep on her chaise lounge in the living room.

Margaret had semi-lived with Peyton for the past three years, subletting her own condo that she had bought as an investment, but also to keep as a safe haven. Margaret wasn't like most lesbians Peyton knew. She traveled for her work an inordinate amount of time and she was firm about maintaining a sense of autonomy. This suited Peyton just fine as being a loner was her preferred status, which Peyton was pining for just as Margaret returned with a bottle of wine and two glasses.

"I really don't care for any, but thanks Margaret."

"Oh come on, Peyton. Live a little. It's so grim here I could suffocate."

"I just don't feel like it."

Long sigh.

"Come on, it'll loosen you up. Let go of the stress of your mom for one night. Can you just do that?" Margaret poured a glass and handed it to Peyton. "Come on, a little sip…"

Peyton decided, what the hell, held out her hand—

KA-THUMP!

Peyton jumped immediately. Ran down the hall to her mother's room where the nurse was struggling to pick up Peyton's mom from the floor.

September 23

She was there and then she wasn't.

Just like that. The finality of it was simply too much for Peyton to take in. She tried like hell to integrate the information into some kind of workable pattern in her head, but every time she thought it through her head started hurting.

She had almost fallen asleep, when she felt it. Something in the room. It wasn't Margaret because she had already told Peyton she was going to a mutual friend's birthday party "and since you won't come with me, don't expect me to be home early. I want to have some fun."

It had been ten days since Peyton's mother had fallen from the bed and broken her hip. She had been rushed to the hospital and after surgery, even though Margaret had begged to have her kept at the hospital, Peyton insisted on bringing her home. The doctor told her she wasn't likely to hang on much longer, her systems were failing. Peyton was damned if she was going to let her mother die in the hospital and brought her back, spending most every moment that she could with her mother until Margaret had exploded two days earlier, "I can't live like this!"

Peyton had looked at her then, and wondered if Margaret possessed an empathic bone in her body, but then realized it was she who was putting Margaret through an ordeal she hadn't asked for and certainly hadn't been prepared to undertake. Instead of yelling at her, she tried to let her off the hook. "No one's asking you to."

"Well you've sort of made the decision for me, Peyton, since I live here with you!"

"Christ, can you let it go?" Peyton blurted.

"Yeah, I'll let it go. I'm happy to let it go, believe you me!" Margaret had spent the night with a friend, returned the next day, apologetic.

"Look, I'm sorry. I overreacted. I'm just so...so damn tired. And look at you. You're exhausted Peyton...this is like some crazy kind of weird reverse punishment? I don't know what you're doing. Your mom was so terrible to you and I don't know what you're trying to prove."

"I'm not trying to prove anything...I just don't want...I just don't want her to die alone...or afraid."

Peyton woke from a dream. And she knew.

She knew before she got up, before she walked down the hall very slowly to her mother's room, that when she got there something had changed.

It was almost midnight and the night nurse was already dozing off. Peyton had long since given up getting any of them to actually stay awake—hell, most of them worked double shifts to make ends meet, and the pragmatic side of Peyton knew that when her mother's time came, it came.

As she approached her mother, she could feel her rustling about, but not in one of her maniacal attempts at escaping whatever was going on in her head. Her movements were deliberate, purposeful. And as Peyton leaned to her mother to ask what was wrong, her mother turned to her and in the dim glow of the table lamp, Peyton could see that she was absolutely lucid. She had something in her hand, and with what energy she had left pulled Peyton close to her.

28

"I...want you to have this..." Her voice was but a whisper. "Sit here with me..."

Peyton sat, even more dumbfounded when her mother grasped her hand. Her mother had rarely been affectionate with Peyton her entire life. Peyton held the dry hand in her own.

"Pey...Peyton...you...you were my...my sweetie girl... Always so brave. So controlled. I know...I know I made you that way, Pey...I know it was me..." Trembling and weak, Peyton's mother transferred the object into Peyton's hand.

"Mom..."

"Peyton...don't...don't make my mistakes...all the things I've told you..." Her mother began to shake her head, a glimmer of tears in her red runny eyes. "Don't listen to me...what did I know...I just want...just want you to...be..."

She smiled painfully, closed her eyes, and her body slumped into the bed frame, peacefully. Quiet. Done.

*

Elena tidied up the dining room, then had sat to compose e-mails to the church staff about the new budget when Nash lumbered in to nab a glass of milk in the kitchen. She watched him through the arched pass way, took in his omnipresent skinny jeans that outlined his lanky body, his favorite blue hoody, that mass of curls she never tired of looking at, and his square-jawed face, and thought that more and more, every day, he was growing into a handsome boy-man, and that even though father and son did not see eye to eye on many things, much of Barry existed in their son. She watched as Nash mimicked the precise gesture of Barry's when he was concentrating; a quick graze of thumb against an eyebrow, as if that motion were part of his DNA.

If Elena introduced Nash as her son and Barry wasn't in the mix, she would always be met with a confused glance—how in the world did a boy so fair, so blond and blue-eyed come from her Indian-Spanish heritage? The only thing she had in common with Nash was that she was also tall and svelte, but he had none of her olive skin, nor her deep brown eyes, and chocolate brown hair. And as "vanilla" as Nash appeared, Elena was very clearly from Indian descent. But when Barry, who was tall, blond and blue-eyed, stood next to them, it became quite clear. Nash did have her full head of thick wavy hair, however, and she comforted herself that he surely had her heart. Before he could return to his room she called out to him.

Nash walked in, nibbling on a cookie, gave his mom a quick hug.

"Sit with me."

"Mom, I've got to finish my homework."

"Just for a moment."

He considered, pulled up a chair, munching on his cookie. She put a hand to his hair and he leaned over and laid his head in her lap. He was still very affectionate with her as long as no one was around. They sat in companionable silence.

He finally said, "I know Dad's asked you to talk to me, but I'm still not going."

"Hmmm?"

"Do you even know what they're doing?"

"Nash," Elena sighed, "you know I can't keep up with it all… if it isn't one thing it's another. What I'm asking you to do is to go, not for you—but for your father's sake—"

"God, Mom…" Nash was about to get up, but Elena's hand kept pressure on his head. He cleared his throat and then asked very seriously. "What about you, Mom? What's your excuse for this sham…you don't believe even half the crap Dad preaches."

She let the pressure from her hand ease, allowed him to sit back up. She didn't have an answer. She tried to put her faith in her god, not certain at all they come from the same heaven.

Nash saw Barry's world in black and white. But she knew, in the larger scheme of things, that Barry could have done worse. At least he had found a way to keep himself happy and while he was at it, he was doing good things for those around him, for the world. Mostly. It was just so hard to remember who he had actually been in the beginning, divorced from the church and all its trappings. Who he had been when she first saw him, how she had felt about him back all those years ago in London, when she first laid eyes on him at the Royal Academy.

He had been cast as King Lear in one of the spring

30

productions. She had sat in the third row of the tiny theater with a girlfriend who had a royal crush on him. As her friend prattled about all his "terribly attractive attributes" she began to actually notice him, his handsomeness, his powerful delivery, his gentle blue eyes, that he was the "perfect mix of virile manliness and gentle Southern boy yumminess," as her friend had described.

It wouldn't have been how she herself would have described him, but it was true. He *was* powerful in the role of the beleaguered king, but not because he truly held the depth of emotion poor Lear felt at all the betrayal around him and his despair, but because he connected well with his audience, he projected in a way that drew you in, and made you *want* to believe him. And in that desire to connect, the palpable feel of him wanting his audience to believe in him, Elena found a certain vulnerability in his performance both on and off stage that drew her to him.

Coerced by her friend to attend the after party, Elena had no intention of staying any later than she could get away with. The small, dank, smoke-filled pub offended her sensibilities, and she reminded herself that she was being too self-conscious. This was where people her age got together. Her Indian father's strict code of ethics and her Spanish mother's extreme Catholicism informed almost every move and decision she made and she was petrified when she realized her friend had left and she had no way back to her dorm. As if on cue, Barry came to rescue her. Out of his costume, Barry was dressed nicely in corduroys and a nice gray-blue crew sweater. She hoped she looked casual and that she belonged, but she realized, looking over the crowd mostly clad in jeans and raggedy sweatshirts, that her attempts to be sophisticated in her chic cream colored dress that highlighted her dark looks had been a mistake.

"Hey there." He offered an extra drink he had in his hand. "This was supposed to be for Janet."

He glanced about for her, then turned to Elena and smiled. "Guess she got lucky."

Elena wasn't used to small talk and was too shy to engage in banter. "Uhmm…actually, I think she went out to get a bite—"

"It's okay—you don't have to salve my ego."

"But it's true—they said they were going out for steaks. I'm sure you can catch them..." She petered out as she watched him studying her, clearly not remotely interested in where Janet had ended up. He smiled. Sweet. Genuine.

"Can I tell you how much I love your accent... You're?"

It took her a moment and then she realized he was asking her where she was from.

"Oh...yes, well I'm Indian. Half Spanish."

"It's beautiful. I heard you when you were reciting Wordsworth in Hamilton's class."

That was strange, she hadn't remembered him from the class, and he could see her confusion.

"I audited a couple of days." He sipped his drink. "I can't tell you what the heck the poem was about...but, I'll tell you this...I remembered your voice..."

Elena blushed. She didn't know what to do. She felt...

"You seem...well, a little out of place." He again offered her the extra drink. She quickly took it and downed half the cup, hoping to find some calm amidst the raging debate in her head where one side of her argued vehemently that she should not be at this party, that this was no place for serious students, that her father would be ashamed, humiliated to see her here with all the drinking and dancing—and the other part of her, this new young adult part of her that was just as passionately committed to the concept that she was now on her own, making her own grown-up decisions for her life. She was no longer under the unyielding hand of her father and why couldn't she just enjoy herself?

As the bad wine wound its way to her limbs and began to smooth her jagged nerves and relax the anxiety she felt speaking to this strange but good-looking man, she looked more carefully at him; the ragtag beard he had grown for the Lear role, his intensely shining blue eyes, and his beautiful smile. The more wine she had the more she agreed with her friend that he was all the verbiage she had tagged on him and then some.

A bottle of wine and a hasty dinner later she found herself back in Barry's dorm, making out on a cheap mattress with akimbo sheets she knew had not been properly affixed to the bed in weeks. He kept kissing her, his tongue deep inside her and while there was an element of thrill and excitement to it, when she felt him growing hard against her skirted legs, she heard alarm bells, confusion, terror, guilt and dread. She had only kissed one other boy and that had been in India when she was nine. She had been caught by her mother, whipped by her father, and after feeling such shame and humiliation had never considered touching another boy.

But with Barry she found herself swept into a trajectory that felt beyond her control. In her dizzying desire to be adult and generational, she kept kissing him until she knew they had gone beyond a point of no return. When he took her hand, sliding it beneath his pants and placing it upon the aching bulge, she recoiled instinctively, but when he apologized so sweetly, she felt sorry for him, gritted her jaw, swallowed hard and decided this was the night she was going to lose her virginity.

This was her life. *Her life*. Not her father's or mother's. She had a right to make these kind of decisions. Yes, she was no longer constrained by her insanely strict father and prudish mother. She was living in the now and the now was happening. She put her hand back upon him, stroking him with what she knew was insufficient finesse; she had no idea what in heaven she was doing. But he took over for her, moving very gently above her, pulling up her skirt and entering her so very slowly that she knew what might have been a very painful and humiliating experience with anyone else was only mildly discomforting with Barry.

She shut her eyes, and held her breath. She was caught by surprise. The entire affair only took a matter of moments as he shuddered above her in what appeared to be some sort of physical ecstasy. Although she felt nothing bordering on pleasure, she did experience a sense of power she had never known; knowing she was desirable and that this is what a man looked like that wanted her. She held him in her arms afterward and reveled in this newfound freedom. And in her mind, Barry hadn't only saved her from the party, he had saved her from her past and her parents, and that night had given her the independence to claim who she was going to be.

She had not the remotest idea that her freedom would be so

short-lived. A mere six weeks later she discovered she was pregnant.

"Are you even listening to me, Mom?" And now here was Nash, her boy, fifteen years later, living in America, as far away from all of it as she could have imagined.

"Yes, sweetie...you don't want to go. Well, let me talk to your dad."

"Good luck with that."

"You might be surprised."

"Doubt it."

"Nash..."

But he lifted his head, smirked at her. He would not give Barry an inch. He got up, walked from the room.

*

Peyton drove through the night, the traffic dwindling as she continued to race her Lexus from one LA freeway to the next, driving dangerously fast, hoping she would get caught, knowing she wouldn't, careful that she would put no one else at risk, but at the same time imagining over and over how freeing it would be to obliterate her car and her consciousness into a freeway median. It would be a glorious letting go, she thought, as she saw her car float off the entry ramp off the 134 to the foothills—a ramp so high off the ground that the moment the car and her body made impact she would literally break into a hundred pieces. What luxury that would be.

She picked up her cell phone, tried to call Margaret again, but again got her annoyingly sexy answer "Not here...you know what to do."

"Margaret...I've been trying to reach you all night! Where the hell are you? It's about Mom...please call me right away."

Then she tossed her cell phone behind to the backseat. What was the point?

Wave.

Wave would be home by now. It was ten past two, just the time that Wave closed Pinot Latte. Peyton would go over and see her, have some wine. Hell, get shit-faced. Obliteration was obliteration after all.

34

By the time Peyton arrived at Pinot Latte the lights were already out. Peyton dug for her keys, let herself in. She stood in the darkness, let out a long sigh. And then heard Wave from down the hall. Laughter? Oh my God, were Wave and Erin doing it?

But when she turned to leave, Wave was standing right beside her. She'd just come home.

"Blimey, you scared me tits off!" Wave hissed.

"What are you doing?"

"I live here."

"Christ you scared me."

"Why are we whispering?"

"I don't know?"

"And who the hell's back there?" Wave jerked her head toward rear of the café.

"I have no idea. Wave...I..."

"Peyton?" Wave stopped when she saw Peyton's face. "Oh, Peyton, what is it?"

"Mom."

Wave scooped Peyton up in a big hug. And then they both heard more laughter. Wave glanced at Peyton, and Peyton saw the look. She'd seen it so often before, Wave being screwed over by any number of girlfriends.

"Not again. Not this time. That little tart'll get a piece of my mind!" Wave stormed down the hallway, Peyton right behind her, hoping to calm the angry beast.

Wave threw open the door.

They both stopped short.

Erin was naked, fucking the woman below her. Hard.

And when she jumped in surprise, Peyton saw the woman she was fucking.

Margaret.

Peyton lifted a tired eyebrow. *Really?* And with barely a flicker of emotion she closed the door, walked back out.

October 1

Clad in a crisp black suit, Peyton followed the long line of well-wishers to her mother's gravesite. She stood, numb and detached, listening to the meandering sermon provided by her mother's favorite pastor, who, Wave insisted, "is almost as daft as your mum," when they could still joke about such things.

Now it was simply annoying to hear his inept recounting of Peyton's mother's life, her mother's kindness and generosity; only he got her charities wrong, regaling the listeners with a mutated version of her mom; the conservative and respected Carolyn who fought with steely resolve for the underprivileged, who in the absence of Peyton's father raised this "bright young lady who ventured into self-help books, and uhmm...had the courage to be with OCD, a group dedicated to...yes, well, then, and it was Carolyn who gave her the moral fiber..."

"This twit needs good fiber to get the bloomin' fart out of his head," Wave whispered, disgusted that he had gotten it all so wrong, but also knowing along with Peyton that this was "Mum's wishes, God knows why," and Wave was here to help Peyton facilitate and honor Carolyn's precise instructions as to how she wanted her burial service to be performed. On the priest ran, extolling Carolyn's wealth, as if it were a trait to be honored, endlessly recounting all the great works she had achieved on behalf of the church, how she ran everything with equal parts grandeur and grace.

Peyton felt nauseous. This "twit"—she had to agree with Wave—rambling incessantly, her mother's death, the naked image of Margaret being fucked with such passion, the joke her life had become, the sudden cessation of baby making which was more cause for alarm to Peyton than losing Margaret—"which should bloody well tell you she was the wrong fit!" Wave admonished. It was almost more loss than she could bear.

Thank God Wave had been there for her—even after "tossin' the devil's spawn out in the gutter where she belongs." Peyton's head swam with the details of funeral preparations, packing up her mother's belongings, sorting out Margaret's stuff she boxed up the same night she had found her with Erin, and calling her agent to tell her she needed some time off, even if it wasn't the best time in her career. It was too much, too chaotic, Peyton's OCD was in overdrive at the insult to her sense of perfection and balance.

Finally, after shaking interminable hands, listening to endless platitudes, there remained only a few close friends and Wave, who came up and put an arm about her dear friend.

"As funerals go, Lombard, even with ol' dafty over there, really, not too shabby," Wave soothed as they walked to her car. She had insisted on "safely squiring" Peyton about as she had been medicated for panic the past few days.

Peyton surveyed the now empty graveyard. "Yeah. I think even Mom would have approved."

"Positively."

They walked on in silence for a few moments.

"Tellin' ya Lombard, we could have made her a Democrat if we had a few more years."

But when they looked at one another, they both categorically agreed, "Nahhh!"

*

Elena stretched for the umpteenth time that Saturday afternoon. She was trying to get through the piles of paperwork in Barry's office, an old pantry that had been revamped and crammed with three desks—hers, Millie's and Barry's. Over the years the room had become more and more constricted, filled to the gills with all of Barry's marketing paraphernalia. Even worse were the endless angels, each and every one handpicked by Millie over the years from kitschy stores, garage sales, and "all the gifts I seem to get from everyone. You know, Elena, I feel so very blessed that I am so appreciated." Yet, Millie's desk sat empty most of the time, because Millie was "always on the go, attending to God's daily 'to-do' list," leaving the more arcane tasks of opening the mail, paying bills, scheduling and organizing to Elena.

Barry had long ago asked her to help him keep the bills up

to date and to maintain all the events and scheduling so that he could spend most of his time doing his "real work" which he insisted was "serving." What Elena knew that to really mean was *performing* his role as pastor. She reminded herself daily that in the end if the work he did on behalf of others was all to the good, was it such a crime that he enjoyed his job? Even if it was for reasons other than the simple passion of serving God? How many people could claim that they loved their work with a passion and that their passion served others? She had long ago squared this with the blazing image of Elmer Gantry preying on the innocent with zealous promises of being saved. Barry was not a crusader nor a televangelist. His sermonizing was quiet, nuanced and extremely convincing. And in the end, so what that he had made some compromises.

They had both discussed this endlessly in the beginning. "This is about having to be realistic about making a living," Barry suggested. "And it doesn't mean that I can't move on from here, El ...Just let's get established, find a home, a nice place to raise Nash and in the meantime, we're doing good things for people. And isn't that what it's all about in the final analysis? Doing things for others? Acting is such a selfish profession." They couldn't really look one another in the eye as they continued to dull the edges of idealism with the pragmatism of compromise.

"Hey there." Diana popped her head in the door. She was the one congregant whom Elena had come to rely on. Diana had become her closest friend involved in her church world. Tyler was her absolute dearest friend, but he would have nothing to do with the church and told them both square on: "If you do this, know it will come with a price. Maybe not now...but it *will* come at a price."

The conversation had taken place while they were having barbecue with Tyler, shortly after he had met Lily and transitioned into his new world of "Soulemetry." Barry had scoffed at Tyler's new work, and Tyler, not insulted, very forcefully had told Barry, "What you're doing will come back and bite you. You can't fake it, Barry. It's not right."

"You know what? I don't need advice from someone who's hearing spirits and doing woo-woo whack advising me, okay Ty?"

It was at that point that Barry and Tyler's relationship ended, not that the two of them had ever been particularly fond of one another. But Elena and Tyler had been "hooked at the heart," as Tyler always described their union, after the three of them had all met in school, and he had told her any number of times, "Regardless of what ridiculousness Barry may be up to, our union can never be eroded."

But here, at the church, where she spent most of her waking hours, Elena found that Diana, though a fervent observer, also saw through the hypocrisy, shared the same distaste for Millie's need to be the center of attention, and was the first one to come to Elena and suggest, "Millie's not fooling me for a second. She's hot for your husband."

They soon became fast friends and confidantes. Over the years Elena had seen Diana through five pregnancies, a miscarriage, a premature infant, and now Diana was looking at another pregnancy. Each pregnancy took its toll on what was once a cherubic strawberry blond. Now the mother of scrambling toddlers and pre-teens, Diana never lost her pregnancy gains, a constant stripe of gray made her beautiful hair fall flat, and the attempts to raise five kids, mostly on her own, showed in every frazzled new worry line on her face. It seemed that as often as Elena had tried to get pregnant with Barry, Diana ended up doing the job for her. She and her husband Rich, who was one of Barry's right-hand Elders and best golf buddy, spent considerable time together—both around the church and on social occasions. Both families had even vacationed together.

Diana was a genuinely good and kind person and one of the few parishioners who did not border on zealotry. Elena always appreciated that Diana was the first to say and often remind Millie, "The Bible's on the dated side, and we clearly need to take some things with a grain of salt, especially if you intend to serve shrimp at the Divine Dinner fundraiser!" Diana had chuckled as she'd had a fierce craving for the evil shellfish throughout her last pregnancy.

"Hey there." Elena looked her over. "How are you feeling? Still nauseous?"

"Finally getting over that, thank God." Diana furtively

glanced behind her then said, "Elena, I know you're not exactly wild about this march."

"No, I'm not." Elena returned to her paperwork. She was already so behind schedule. "Live and let live..."

"Yeah...I sort of agree with you. I mean, come on, so they get married. Why should we care when our divorce rate is so shockingly high?"

"Exactly. Like we have some claim to knowing how to do it right?"

"That's just it," Diana said. "We can't sit in judgment. That's not what God wants us to do. But I must confess. I don't get why it has to be marriage. You know. What's wrong with just having a civil union? Why do they have to call it the same thing? If they get the same rights."

Elena had not been paying attention to the argument at hand because she rarely allowed herself to get involved in the actual movements the church participated in. She was there to take care of the grunt work, and if she did her job well, it allowed Barry to take care of the global picture. She was well aware that on a deeper level her lack of involvement and detachment was a cop-out. But it was the only way she could survive this particular playing field. Although, she had noticed for weeks now, something about this whole marriage discussion disturbed her, a sense of injustice struck her as clearly as a slap across the cheek. "But why wouldn't they want exactly the same rights?"

Diana stared at her friend with a confused frown, but before she could respond she heard a ruckus down the hall.

"Heads up," Diana hissed, "Millie's on her way over."

Seconds later Millie butted through the doorway, barely glancing at Diana. They had had their own set of run-ins about what Millie perceived as Diana's "incessant need to have children—not that it wasn't part of God's plan, but with all the starving and unwanted children in the world, did Diana really have to contribute to the problem of overpopulation?" To others, Millie was a bit more coarse: "Rich can't keep it in his pants. They need another little brat running around like we all need more reality TV!"

"Elena." Millie cocked her head to the side, as if she'd heard something that was giving her quite the case of "devlies"—her too cute by half combo of devil and gnarlies.

"I heard a little rumor that you were skipping the protest. That can't be true, now, can it, Elena?"

Elena appeared distracted as much for effect as for real. "I... I'm not sure."

"It's not enough to support Barry on the sidelines, Elena."

"Millie," Diana interjected, "Elena does so much for the church, I don't think it's fair—"

"Oh, it's very clear God's got your back, Elena," she said, then, turning to Diana, "and that he shines a special light on Elena to keep this place running so smoothly." Then back to Elena, "But there comes a time you have to commit your faith and put it to real work."

Elena glanced uncertainly from Millie to Diana who valiantly jumped in for her. "Millie, you know Elena runs the Kinder program Saturday mornings."

But Elena didn't want Diana to bear Millie's wrath later and piped in, "It's not just that I've already got commitments this Saturday, Millie."

Elena stood at the desk to give herself more confidence. "To be honest, I...I'm not sure if your interpretation is correct on this."

"Are you doubting the very word of our Bible, Mrs. Winters?"

More people were gathering in the hallway, sensing a catfight. Elena did not want to engage Millie, but she also refused to be bowled over by her. "Well, you know as well as I do that the Bible was written thousands of years ago, from a man's point of view—I mean—somehow we have to look at these passages with some kind of context to the times—"

"That's just the kind of mealy-mouthed thinking that's got us into this place—" Garret, Millie's favorite minion, had joined in Millie's fight.

Diana confronted Garret. "Elena is entitled to her opinion."

But Millie walked past them and got right up into Elena's face. "Not when it's at the expense of our safety! You are the wife of a pastor. Your husband works every day to spread God's fine word and what do you do? You put 'interpretation' into question? That's the oldest trick in the book."

Elena stood, trying to back her way out of the room but Millie, sensing weakness, went in for the kill. "They are tearing us apart with all their marriage talk and liberal judges ruling willy-nilly in their favor. Oh, no! We are not going to stand by and allow it, Mrs. Winters. Shame on you. Shame on you for undermining—"

But Elena could not bear to hear another word because all she saw was crazy. She was vaguely aware that Barry was just outside in the hall and was now jumping in as well.

"Millie, please—I appreciate your support...thank you." And then moving to Elena, "Come here, dear."

But the room had started to spin.

"I...I think I need some air." She cleared the huddle of congregants as she heard Barry continue to apologize for her. "You know she's been so tired and overworked lately. I'm sorry if she's offended anyone...Diana, can you help the ladies get squared away?"

*

Peyton sat in her black slacks, her blouse sleeves rolled up, blazer crumpled off the side of Wave's couch, and deep into her second glass of wine.

"I don't think staying shit-faced is the answer here," Peyton decided.

"I know, my dear, but at least it'll ease the pain for the time being."

"No...no more." She raised a hand against Wave's attempt to refill her glass. "I want to clear my head."

"Whatever for?"

"I...I need some air, okay?"

"Sure. Let's go for a drive."

"Alone."

"Why don't I go with you?"

"Wave, you know how much I love you...but I just need... just need to get my thoughts in order...or just out of my head altogether. I need some time alone."

Wave wrinkled her nose in dissatisfaction. "Okay then, but as soon as you get home, call me?"

"Sure."

*

Elena was packing the remainder of the filing boxes in her car outside the church when she heard Barry walking up behind her.

"That was quite a performance."

Elena kept her back to him.

"You know better than to tangle with Millie—"

But when he moved so that he could see her face, his own face fell and he quickly changed topic.

"Elena...sweetie...did you..."

Elena nodded, put her head down in shame. Barry came to her, put an arm around her.

"When?"

"I...started." She cleared her throat in an effort not to cry. She would not have any of these people see any sign of weakness in her. "This morning."

Barry took her in his arms, held her tightly, sighed, "Oh sweetheart." He continued to hold her gently, kissed her forehead.

"I...I don't know how much more of this—"

"Shhhh...come here." He held her close to him and she knew he was trying to take charge and be there for her.

"Look Barry," Elena said, "I know how much you want this— but do you think we're trying too hard? Maybe...after Sar...you know...maybe this is just not meant to be."

He raised his voice ever so slightly. "Maybe we should pray together—really pray to God about bringing us our baby—"

Elena pushed him away, her eyes angry as she looked into him, trying to understand what he was doing. Had he not heard a word of what she had just said? And then she felt it. Sensed Millie's presence, glimpsed her watching them from the open door of the sanctuary, and she got it. How dare he perform at her expense. She pushed him aside and walked from the church, got into the car and drove away.

*

"Rarely do we get the opportunity to witness the art in love... but that is what we all desire...not just to be loved, but to be loved in that all-encompassing, Heathcliff on-the-moors one-true-love, soul mate way... And rarely are we prepared for it when it happens to come by."

Tyler Montague, stylish and striking in a dapper white suit, organza cravat, and several bejeweled accessories (the assumption could easily be made that he was gay), spoke with absolute conviction into his flip camera, performing with panache his sermon of love. He considered a moment, then turned his camera back on.

"Perhaps you've been trying to inject meaning into your life, endlessly jamming your day planner full. Some of you are downright fortunate, and already understand what I'm telling you—perhaps you are one of those rare and fortunate few who find it very early in life. For others of you, your life might be at its most grim." He wagged a finger. "Fear not. It will come. Soul mates find one another. And, while many kinds of soul mates exist, what we're all really looking for is the Twin Flame. The ultimate love connection—"

As if to confirm random and unlikely, Lily, a handsome, Armani-clad executive, entered Tyler's studio cum Soulemetry store at that moment. Even though she looked completely out of place when she walked in, she owned the room, and strolled very deliberately to Tyler, took his head in her hands and planted a deeply soulful kiss upon his mouth.

"Babe...I'm about to snap up that Internet company that's been cut off at its knees." Lily spoke with pride and relish. "Wish me luck."

"If they only knew what a pussycat you really are." Tyler gazed at his wife with adoration. She nuzzled him endearingly, softly, then quickly put her game face back on—and went off to win.

Tyler returned to his editing bay where he was narrating another of his many soul mate stories for his weekly Soulemetry webisode when Elena walked in.

"He's all yours." Lily patted Elena's arm as she walked out.

Tyler jumped up dramatically. "Gorgeous! Wait till you hear this story—" but stopped as soon as he saw Elena's forlorn expression.

"Or maybe not. Let's go, kitten. You need a drink."

Elena loved seeing Tyler's face. He wasn't only handsome, his face was endlessly pleasant with his square jaw, always perfect close-cropped hair, and his blue-gray eyes that radiated love, warmth and humor, and were constantly twinkling as if he had a joke he'd just recalled. No matter what was going on in her life at the moment, when she was with her dearest friend in the world she felt a loosening of all the barriers, as if all the roles she played in her life, wife, mother, pastor's right-hand, church administrator—fell away, and she could simply be Elena.

Tyler led Elena to his favorite part of his courtyard garden, what he referred to as his sanctuary—for his beloved religion—Soulemetry, which he had founded ten years ago.

"Soulemetry," Tyler had informed both her and Barry all those many years ago, "is a philosophy—a religion, if you will—based on the premise that there is a soul mate for everyone out there and it is my calling to help people find theirs. What's more important than love, Elena?" he had asked her back then. "True love."

She had met Tyler right after she and Barry had started dating, fifteen years ago now. Tyler had also attended the Royal Academy on scholarship. He was extremely well known on campus, and had a universal reputation for excellence in academics and likeability. Everyone seemed to know him, and all who knew him loved him, or so it seemed to Elena. She had been thrilled to be cast in a supporting role in a contemporary play Tyler was directing. Within days she, along with everyone else, found Tyler to be a genius. He was easily the most talented student in their circles, a brilliant actor, phenomenal singer and the best director any of them had worked with. He had the fire, passion and desire to make it big.

So it was almost devastating, to both Elena and Barry, when they met up with him several years later in Los Angeles after having relocated from New York to discover that Tyler had decided to give it all up.

Tyler had moved west two years before Elena and Barry. Within months he had figured out a way onto the inside track of the LA entertainment machine, and had once again established himself seemingly overnight with a noteworthy amount of success in very little time.

It was clear to Elena that Barry couldn't help but begrudge Tyler his success, even though he tried to act as graciously as he could manage about Tyler's good fortune. Barry's career amounted to little more than one unrequited audition after another, while Elena worked part time and took care of Nash, hoping Barry would get a paying role. Scrimping and saving from the beginning, Elena learned the fine art of budgeting their household and living expenses within the constraints of very little. She took her joy in Nash and tried to stay as positive as she could with Barry about his career. Even after Tyler gave Barry all his contacts, Barry couldn't seem to hit his stride. Tyler was just the opposite. It was effortless for him. Roles, offers— everything an entertainer aspired to simply fell in his lap.

So when Tyler sat them down over one long dinner and several bottles of wine to explain that he had had an "epiphany" and that this "entertainment stuff simply didn't fulfill him," that it didn't speak to him in any way, and that he could no longer make his life's work be about all this "utterly ridiculous, overwrought, take-one's-self-with-waay-too-much-seriousness BS..." they couldn't help but be stunned.

"But what will you do?" Elena had asked.

"Yeah," Barry added, although Elena had noticed a marked sharpness to his tone. "How in the hell you going to put food on the table, Ty?"

"Soulemetry." Tyler had answered simply but with complete conviction. "The religion of love."

They were both taken aback.

Within weeks, Tyler had begun the practice of his Soulemetry religion in the basement of his house and ten years later he had a client list that rivaled any studio head's Rolodex along with the most beautifully crafted and serene setting for his Soul-Blim-In-Nation Store; the interior of which was covered in every conceivable soul mate artifact from ancient runes and intricately carved statues to emblems Tyler had created. The exterior was every bit as idyllic, filled with roses—the rose being "the flower of love"—of every breed, strain and variety, along with marble pillars, ornately tiled trellises and billowy fabrics, all artfully chosen to create a sense of harmony, peace and serenity, for Tyler was fond of reminding everyone, "It was only when the heart stilled itself that it could prepare to allow love in."

It was equally striking that Tyler, whom everyone believed to be gay, came back from Paris—the city of love—on one of his many "love treks" with the extremely tough and fully unexpected love of his life: Lily Aubergine. The tall, slender, endlessly elegant Lily was of French descent but with a very American if not heavily arched north Maine accent. She was as cold as Tyler was warm, as competitive as Tyler was generous. While Tyler's eyes beamed warmth, hers seared with an intensity born of the need to win.

Equally baffling for both Elena and Barry was that Lily did not want children. Tyler's only other obsession in life was to have a child. Since Nash's birth it had been the one other constant that Tyler had spoken about, until Lily informed them all at Nash's two-year birthday celebration that she planned to consider Nash the son she'd never have. It had been well after all the other guests had left, Nash had been tucked into bed, and the four of them were finishing champagne that Lily informed Tyler, as if presenting a board report: "I have no intention of ever ruining my figure with childbearing. Besides I have no time for squalling infants. I deal with them all day long at the office."

Barry and Elena left that night terrified Lily would "claw out his heart," as Barry put it, but whatever was in their union, it brought out the best of them both. Sure she was as tough as a street boxer when negotiating contracts, but whenever she was around Tyler she softened to the point that she appeared to be an altogether different person. And Lily brought out of Tyler an insanely "unquenchable love" as he described it—"My need to be with Lily supersedes anything I've ever known. Go figure."

Elena never could fully believe in Tyler's Soulemetry. As Barry put it, it was a bit too "out there love-child hippy dippy." And had it been anyone but her dearest friend, she probably would have thought it was just so much hooey. But she found herself always mystified by the transformation in her when she sat within Tyler's sanctuary. Her feeling of exaltation probably rivaled what most people would refer to as a religious experience, and she certainly felt more spiritual in the Soulemetry Gardens than she did in Barry's church.

That always held almost too much irony for her, but she had long since given up trying to figure out what precisely it was, or why it was. Perhaps she would never understand it. But like Tyler, she accepted these warm and very inviting feelings as a gift and accepted Tyler and his trappings at face value. It was utterly mystifying to her that the two most important men in her life were both preachers of a kind, but at such opposite ends of the holy spectrum.

"Beautiful woman," Tyler said, taking her hand, "I am so sorry."

She glanced up at him, trying not to cry.

"I know how painful this is for you."

"Tyler, you know—I just feel like…I feel like…" Elena blew her nose. "I've got to be doing something wrong—"

"Now stop that!" Tyler shook his head, furious. "This isn't your fault."

He stopped, breathed in deeply, exhaled. "I think I may have said this a time or two before—but, maybe—just maybe—it's a sign."

Elena smiled ruefully. "Well, that is the reason we've decided to pursue adopting. But don't worry, Tyler. We'll keep trying."

He looked at her, smiled wistfully, then shook his head. "Please, don't think you have to."

"But, of course we will. Just…you know, just in case," she said, her tone resigned, "whatever it takes."

"Well, you know, my love, I'm always at your disposal." Tyler smiled sweetly, then leaned in to give her a gentle hug. When they parted she could see he was getting emotional. "Look, I want what's best for you, my exquisite angel."

"Thank you."

They sat in silence for a moment, both reflecting on their own wishes for the future, until Tyler snapped them both out of it.

"I know better than anyone, yes?" He looked deeply into her eyes. "Everything you've been through...My Lord, between your unforgiving parents and Barry's crusades du jour—"

Elena shot Tyler a sharp look. He put up his hands— "Okay—won't go there.

"I swear to God, though, Elena, it's a testament to your strength—or complete insanity! Either way—"

"Tyler, please. Besides, Nash needs—"

"Nash is fifteen, he's going to be fine. Barry's got what he's always needed out of the church—utter adulation. So what I want to know is: what's in it for you?"

He winked at her. Elena smiled.

"Come on...give me your hand." She resisted at first, but he gently took one of Elena's hands, held it for a long moment. He closed his eyes, began to tune in, but before he had completely connected with his "committee" as he referred to his communing spirits, he stated, "I've told you a thousand times if I've told you once, he is NOT your Twin Flame with his silly little congregation—"

Tyler stopped quite suddenly. Eyes still closed, he traced a finger over her palm, then bolted upright. "Well, I'll be...this adoption thing may be the ticket...someone's definitely coming into your life." He shook his head again in wonderment, opened his eyes and pegged her own. "In a big way."

Elena nabbed her hand back and responded wryly, "Yes. A...a baby! Oh, Tyler, I love that you do all this—you know that I do... but I'm just not sure I—"

"Oh, but there's no denying what I see here. Your destiny is going to happen whether you like it or not, sugar plum. Even you, Elena the Intractable, are no match for your own fate."

*

Elena had walked through the park for some time, finally releasing all the pent up emotion, all the anger at Millie, Barry—all of it. It had done her a world of good to see Tyler. It always did. But after she had left him, the last thing she wanted to do was go back to the house. She didn't want to see Barry. Nor did she care to go back to the church, even if she had a pile of paperwork waiting for her there. She was sick of it. Sick of it all.

She really needed to tell Barry she needed to be done with it. She hated the desperate machination of the fertility cycles, having to have sex when she was ovulating, racing against her clock, hoping that Barry's low sperm count would somehow be overcome by taking drugs, shots. And then there was Tyler. As he said, this had to be what was best for her. And every time she had her period she felt overcome with grief. It was simply too much to endure after...after everything they had been through. After already losing so much. She couldn't bear to think about it another moment. She couldn't put herself through this any longer.

Now she simply breathed in the beauty of the park. How she loved this place. Thank God she had found it several years ago and had been coming here ever since. It was the only place she could hear her own mind think, feel what she was feeling without having to confront a need, a question, a must-have, a constant picking at her for everything. Why couldn't they all grow up and simply take care of themselves—at least a few moments a day?

*

She sat, took a deep breath, and allowed her breathing to calm. A beautiful sunset was on its way. A peach tint laced the edges of indigo blue. Another day finally passing, gave Peyton goose bumps. It was so beautiful. So healing and peaceful.

She glanced down at her palm, and looked again, for the hundredth time at the item her mother had handed her the night she passed away. She still didn't understand what it was supposed to mean.

Staring back at her was an extraordinarily ornate ring in a setting of gold with a large light blue sapphire glistening in the setting sun. She had never seen it, had never heard her mother even speak about it. She knew every single item of her mother's jewelry because Carolyn loved to talk about the value in things and had taught Peyton that lesson early in life—"My dear, the only manner in which to judge anything successfully is to apply some sort of value to it." Having value was an essential for

50

Peyton's mother, and try as Peyton might to resist this equation, it had been imprinted in her mind.

Suddenly she realized she wasn't alone in this section of the park. She could barely make out the russet color of the sweater, but someone was sitting at her other favorite bench.

*

Did she hear something? What was it? Elena didn't know why, but felt compelled to turn. It almost frightened her at first, but then she realized it was a person sitting on her other favorite bench. A woman in a dark coat was sitting there. She wondered what had brought her here to this park, this very moment. If it was another lone person come here to escape her life.

Peyton could barely make out the features of the woman. Ethnic, somehow. Middle Eastern? Indian? Whatever nationality, Peyton could read pain, frustration, a perturbation with the world. Where had she seen her...something familiar. Could the woman see that Peyton was looking at her? Peyton realized she had been studying her for some time.

As if answering, the woman's head moved slightly in acknowledgment.

Elena looked into the woman's eyes as much as she was able to in the quickly growing dusk.

Their gaze held for an awkwardly long moment. Elena felt somehow as if time had stopped. Peyton herself felt as if she were on a different level of consciousness. Shook her head and thought she really needed to get more rest.

Did she even know she was looking at her, Elena wondered.

Peyton wasn't sure the woman was looking at her or beyond her, but she suddenly felt very uncomfortable. She got up and prepared to leave. She began to walk the opposite direction, but for some reason she had to look back at that woman again. Something about her.

Peyton turned. The last of the sun flared into her eyes.

Elena stood up and watched the woman turn her direction, but she put her hand up to her eyes and Elena could not make out anything else in her face.

Peyton shielded her eyes. Apparently the woman had already gone.

Peyton turned and walked away.

Elena watched the woman's retreating figure until she could no longer see her.

"We spent our entire lives working in the same company."

Edith, a spry eighty-five-year-old, sits next to her husband, Milton, eighty-nine. "Passing one another every day for thirty-seven years. Never said a word to each other. He'd just nod and smile. Always so pleasant..."

"Then I had a heart attack." Milton's hand shakes as he takes Edith's in his. "Thought, I don't have much more time to let things pass me by. I'm not going to waste another minute."

"When he came back to work he walks right up to me and says 'I'm not willing to waste another minute. I'm no Fred Astaire, but I'd like to take you dancing.'"

"Well, I'm not," Milton concurred, shaking his head. "But you came anyway."

Edith smiles tenderly. "It was the best date of my life. We married exactly three weeks later in City Hall. And right after, back we went to dance some more."

Milton's upper lip quivers as he announces, "And we haven't spent a moment apart since."

Edith puts her hand over his.

"The heart knows what the heart knows."

A year later

Peyton sat tapping her pen, feeling inordinately bored as the Adoption Orientation Instructor droned on and on about all the state's rules and regulations. The instructor was tall, angular and spoke in a clipped cadence, making the information even more difficult to digest in the community service room annexed to the Women's Foster Services Building. Following her words, it seemed to Peyton, who sat in the stifling heat in jeans and a gray sweater, that the system made adoption as difficult as humanly possible—and it was that kind of meaningless counterintuitive behavior that drove Peyton to distraction as she sat amongst twenty some odd strangers all sharing the general concept that adopting a child was the most important thing they could do in their lives.

Her mother's death and what Wave described as "Margaret's totally and doubly despicable betrayal" had taken their toll. Her patience was almost nonexistent. She felt tired most days, exhausted the rest of the time. It had only been the past two months that she felt some of the fog lift, felt some mornings like getting out of the bed might not be the worst thing after all. She rarely looked at herself in the mirror these days and when she did, what she saw reflected back scared her enough that she put more effort into her appearance. She knew she appeared haggard, tired and unkempt. She fidgeted a bit self-consciously as she glanced about the other people around her.

Shuffling about in her seat, Peyton recognized the need for all these rules and regulations and for understanding how the system worked, but it was almost too much to take in on a single day. She felt her mind shutting down from the endless facts and figures, but then found herself alarmed to hear the stringent care the state took to reconnect birth families with children put into the foster care system.

She could not handle the concept of falling in love with a beautiful little baby, only to have him or her taken away within the eighteen month time frame the state was entitled to in order to restore these abandoned children to someone in their birth family. Not only that, they applied rigorous attempts to do so. She simply could not handle any more loss. She had even asked the instructor during the lunch break if by chance she would have a better chance of keeping a baby if she were to adopt a disabled child. And was thrilled and sickened to hear that the disabled children rarely were reunited with their families.

"Now I'd like to know why each of you would like to adopt," the instructor urged. "We'll go around the room."

A quite attractive woman in her mid-fifties sat with her husband who looked glazed over by their shared experience: "My husband and I lost our son in the war last spring and we have a big house...and we have all this space...you know lots of space..." She trailed off into silence.

"My husband and I have been trying to have a baby for the past three years."

Hearing the beautiful lilt of an Indian accent with English undertones, Peyton looked up. She was instantly struck by the woman's exotic Indian features, the aquiline nose, the deep lush eyebrows and dark brown eyes that appeared both vulnerable and weary. Around her shoulder curled a thick mahogany braid. Frowning, she wondered why she hadn't noticed this woman earlier...there was something about her. Or maybe it was just having seen her outside during the lunch break. No...Peyton felt as if she knew her and she listened closely as the woman continued, "We tried the whole fertility route with no luck and, quite honestly, I'm exhausted. So, we thought maybe we needed to try a new approach."

Expressions of sympathy traveled about the room.

"How about you?" The instructor caught Peyton off guard.

"Oh, well..." Peyton cleared her throat. "I've wanted to have a family for as long as I can remember...I'm single but I'm a writer and can be home all hours of the day for a child...and I...I really believe I can make a good home for an unwanted child."

Elena considered Peyton as she spoke. She had wondered all morning how she knew this woman, this woman who looked so different than most of the women she knew. She had an air about her. Commanding, almost masculine, but she was also womanly with her wavy brown shoulder-length hair. Something about her was quite striking, even though she appeared sad, tired. But why did she seem so familiar? Had she met her at the church? A church function? Then Elena realized the woman was looking right at her and she quickly glanced away.

"I've just wanted a baby forever..." One of the last women spoke, a woman who looked as hopeless as so many of them felt. "Oh God...they are just full of so much promise. Isn't that what we're all here for...a promise for a better tomorrow?"

Everyone glanced about, uncomfortable at the raw truth and desperation in the room. Elena, beginning to tear up, quickly gathered her purse and walked from the room.

*

Peyton walked to her car, but as she passed a red Sierra van, she noticed the same tall and quite beautiful Indian woman working on trying to find her keys. She stopped a moment, and was about to just keep moving on when she heard the woman's voice, low and frustrated.

"Damn!"

Peyton offered, "Everything okay?"

When the woman turned Peyton could see that her eyes were red and a bit swollen.

"Hey...I'm sorry. I didn't mean to scare you."

Elena tried to collect herself. She felt humiliated. She had spent the last twenty minutes in the women's restroom crying. All of this felt so desperate, and it made her feel her own loss. It took every bit of strength to stop herself from going down that path—she simply couldn't—or she would hit a paralyzing depression. As soon as she had been able to collect herself, she had rushed to her car, but then...

"I...I can't find my keys."

Peyton gingerly pointed over Elena's shoulder to keys that were sitting on the roof of Elena's van.

Elena, realizing she had inadvertently left them there, shook her head, turned back to Peyton, shrugged and smiled.

"Happens to me all the time." Peyton grinned

56

sympathetically, then cleared her throat, shy but concerned. "Don't mean to pry...but are you okay?"

"Uhmm...yeah. I'm..." She sighed. "It's all just a little overwhelming."

"Yeah...I know."

Their eyes caught. Elena smiled shyly and then they stood awkwardly, both wondering where to take the conversation or if to just leave it. Peyton began to leave but Elena stopped her with, "I hope you don't mind my asking...I overheard you earlier...why do you want to do this alone?"

"Well, it hadn't been the plan." Peyton shuffled, uncertain how much to share. "I thought I could make a difference...in some small way...you know what, it's a really long story."

"That's right—you're the writer."

Peyton grinned. "Yeah... What about you?"

"I'm...well, I used to be a photographer. I mean I still am..." Elena realized how uncertain and silly she must sound. She cleared her throat. "I just started doing some pickup work."

Elena looked at Peyton a moment, was about to ask something, but didn't. Peyton found herself getting nervous. She wasn't sure what to say, but managed to ask, "So...do you have a card?"

Elena felt shy suddenly. "Yes, well I do in fact. It's somewhere in here." She scrambled around in her purse, found a card that appeared crumpled and possibly like it could be the last business card on the planet.

"It's kind of old." They both grinned. Peyton gingerly took it from Elena and handed her one in return.

Elena's phone rang. "Oh gosh, duty calls. I...I really should be getting home."

"Yeah...me too."

Elena held out her hand but decided that felt too formal but just as she went to hug Peyton, Peyton put out a hand to shake Elena's. Neither knew what was appropriate, and both grinned awkwardly and hastily made their exit.

*

Peyton walked in from work, moved to her desk to look through the mail and suddenly realized she was not alone. She turned to see Margaret slinking in, looking very attractive in tight black jeans and a low-cut forest green top. She was made up, and her eyes sparkled as she held up two tickets. "Bonnie Raitt."

Peyton's jaw tightened.

"And...special passes to the after party," she purred.

Peyton continued to take off her jacket, walked to the mail sitting on her desk and glanced through it. She felt Margaret come up from behind her.

"I know I'm still on probation...but what can a little..." Margaret wound a finger down Peyton's neck, then moved in for a kiss, "...hurt?"

Peyton's lack of engagement did not discourage Margaret's seduction in the least.

*

Barry kissed Elena, long and hard as he tried to make love to her. She felt his strong hands move gently to the sides of her face, tried to avoid his eyes as he continued to kiss her cheeks, her eyelids, working so diligently to woo her. She knew he was trying, trying his best to connect with her. Why couldn't she just give him what he wanted? Why did it feel so vile to force some kind of passion? She gently touched his cheek, but all she felt was inertia. Numbness.

"Babe...El?"

Elena looked into his intent blue eyes.

"Should we not?"

"I'm sorry."

"Hey...if you're not into it..."

And then he followed her gaze to the picture frame of a newborn baby. Sarah.

"Oh, God, El! I'm so sorry..." He quickly dismounted, moved to her side. "Christ, I can't believe I forgot what day it is."

He shook his head, and in his eyes she saw the same pain she felt reflected back to her. After all, they had both lost her. They had both felt the enormous grief. This pain didn't belong to just her. And as she felt the sudden urge to blot out the agony of memories, she also felt the strong need to comfort him. She pulled him back. They looked at one another for a long moment.

"Are you…are you sure, El?" Barry whispered, but she could hear the plaintive need in his voice.

She nodded slightly. She felt him hard against her, like she had for so many years, felt him enter her, knew precisely the way in which he would mount her, knew the exact rhythm, the roughly five to seven minutes it took for him to achieve climax and knew from the way his legs trembled the second he would come. Something was comforting about knowing someone that completely. She did not consider this to be intimacy. It was more akin to wounded soldiers together, trapped in an empty foxhole; their camaraderie their only link to survival. Whatever else they were to one another, they were in this together. They were bound by more than this life. They were bound by death as well.

As his breathing became ragged, she closed her eyes and after he came and slumped against her, she stroked his head until she felt the calm breathing of his sleep.

*

Margaret's voice was husky silk. "I really don't know why we can't make another go of this. I've told you I'm sorry. I've told you over and over, again…I made a mistake."

Peyton tried to remove herself from Margaret's clutches.

"You know I loved your mom…but I begged you to let her go. And you wouldn't. Dammit Peyton, I…I was lonely."

"Lonely I understand. Erin's another matter. Wave's been trashed too."

"Christ, Peyton, you're kidding right? Wave had no business being with Erin—" Margaret shook her head, reprised her sardonic look. "How many times does it take for her to get that she shouldn't sleep with the hired help?"

Peyton sighed.

"Just because they're done, doesn't mean we are. We've had six good—okay mostly good—years." Margaret slowly but smoothly began to undress Peyton, leaned in to kiss her. "Look. You still want a baby...and I still want you."

Peyton softened momentarily. She was lonely too. It had been so long since anyone had touched her and well, at least with Margaret, she knew what she was getting into. Maybe...maybe just for old time's sake...

Three weeks later

"Off, off, off," Peyton whispered under her breath, "off, off, off."

And on it went. She had been checking, double-and-triple checking the stove knobs for the last twenty minutes—

Oh and there was a smudge of dirt on the counter—

Peyton walked to her three pairs of rubber gloves (the green for the dishes, the blue for counter work, and the yellow—well, because they reminded her of her mother) carefully pulled them on so as not to get any wet inside (if she did she had to take that pair off and start with a new pair) and grabbed a sponge. She furiously began scrubbing. Scrubbing, mashing, tearing at the dirt; real or imagined until—

"Hello? It's me, where are you?"

"Thank God," Peyton yelled back, even as she continued to persevere, "I'm in here—in the kitchen."

Wave walked in with a bottle of wine she sat on the granite counter, then she moved directly in front of Peyton. She grabbed her by the shoulders, straightened her up then snapped off each glove with finesse.

"Damn it!" Peyton smiled bleakly. "I've been so stuck in a loop."

Wave smiled back with compassion, held up the wine. "For medicinal purposes, naturally."

*

Elena was just finishing the dishes when Tori ambled in, looking a little lost.

"Nash would like a snack—actually a pound of chocolate chip

cookies was the actual order—as apparently his brain requires them to function at maximum capacity."

Elena considered Tori as she heaved herself up on the counter, grabbed a banana, but did not peel it. Garbed in a plaid skirt, striped vest, pleated knuckle gloves and her ubiquitous tie, she was, well, all Tori. Elena was the last one to understand American fashion in the teen universe as most of it looked ridiculous and an overwrought attempt at individualism. But, somehow Tori pulled it off. She was definitely one of a kind.

"Did you realize the average human utters around 124,000,000 words in their lifetime...just wondering how many of them are empty promises."

But Elena saw through Tori's shtick.

"Your dad?"

"Promises next weekend. Promises last weekend. All I got to say is he should just stop opening his mouth. Foot taking over."

"Sweetie...I'm sorry." Elena hugged Tori, then lifted Tori's chin to see her puppy-dog brown eyes. "And your mom?"

"Doin' her whole staying-up-all-night-mania thing."

It had been months since Elena had actually seen either of Tori's parents, but that wasn't unusual. Her dad was, in Tori's own vernacular, "a megageek—that's where I get my aptitude for retention" and worked as a sound technician for what Tori referred to as "really bad white boy's music." But for whatever reason, they were a hugely popular rock band, and he was rarely home. Tori's mom looked very much like her daughter, beautiful, but fragile and highly strung. She was a painter who was known to spend three days solid locked up in her attic, forgetting she even had a child. When she was present, she was a lovely and very entertaining woman, even with her constant nervous habits and ticks, but both Elena and Barry worried that she was potentially borderline and heading straight toward serious mental illness.

Early on both Elena and Barry considered Tori's options when she had become best pals with Nash when they were six, when Tori had defended Nash from a schoolyard bully, not by violence, but by talking so hard, so fast and furiously at the kid-thug that he ran from the schoolyard, humiliated. Back then

Tori's father was working locally and when he was home he was a great father. But when he took the road job, they didn't know whether to go to Children's Services, do an intervention for Tori's mom or some other action—until one day Nash made the decision for them, at nine, when he simply stated. "Tori's my very best friend. She should just live here."

Because the two were already inseparable, it truly was the most workable solution and the one that caused the least amount of pain and transition. Tori simply became part of the family and engaged with her own family when they were available to her. She still slept at her home half the time, which was just several blocks away, and half the time she slept in what was once Sarah's room, that had lain dormant for years. Elena found it healing to create a sweet girl's room for Tori, because for Elena, Tori practically was her daughter and yet they also had a wonderful friendship, sharing fashion, "girlie things" as Nash referred to them, and many long discussions. Tori made her laugh more than anyone else she knew and she loved the ease in their relationship, even if there were times that Elena wondered if Tori, with her innate wisdom, wasn't really the wiser and older of the two.

"You know this is your home," Elena now told her. "For as long as you need it, yeah?"

"Thanks Momma Bear." Tori snuggled in for another hug, then jumped up and grabbed some cookies. "Well, gotta get these to Nash, you know how he gets. Like a fix!" Tori slapped two fingers against her veins at her inner elbow for emphasis.

Elena grinned as she continued tidying up. She picked up a stack of old papers, tossed them into the garbage can. A lone card fell out, onto the floor. Elena leaned down to pick it up.

It took her a moment, but then she remembered. She stood a long while, studying the card, then found herself still grinning. She was about to toss it back in the garbage can, but at the last moment stopped and placed it beside her laptop.

*

Peyton and Wave sat with their wine, poolside, by the gazebo relaxing in the dusk. They had talked for hours, and the sun had just set and Peyton was only now beginning to feel a sense of release.

"Do you think it's worse because of all the extra stress you've been under?"

"What extra stress?"

"Oh...I don't know, your mum's memorial, Margaret's continuing bullshit, this huge deadline you've been under, and you keep yammering about doing the project you want to do... but can never get to it. It's all stress."

"Fuck, I hate this. You'd think I'd know how to beat it." Peyton smirked. "Since I wrote the book on it and all."

"Physician heal thyself," Wave mumbled. "Sweetie, I think it's brilliant that you wrote your memoirs, but that's just half the battle. Living, struggling with OCD doesn't go away once you realize you have it. You said it yourself, it's an ongoing condition—some days are better, some days are worse...and it's your job now to find the best way to live with it. But I've known you forever, and even if you go into remission now and again..."

"Yeah, but—"

"No, really, Lombard. At your mum's memorial you were like stone—I knew the minute I saw you—the unwavering Ms Granite—it was only a matter of time before you were going to crack. And in my book, even considering psycho chick who cheated on you with my girlfriend—well, even entertaining for a nanosecond having anything more to do with her is rid—"

"Wave, look." Peyton sighed, uncertain of how she felt herself about the reengagement with Margaret. "Nothing's set in stone...and you know full well it wasn't all her fault. I was completely MIA once my mom got sick."

"You're far too forgiving." Wave considered her good friend. "Don't know why you were trying to procreate with her anyway. You have seen Rosemary's Baby."

"Why do you think I'm adopting... Oh my God, you saw how crazy I got with the fertility shots."

"For the love of sweet chocolate please don't make me go through that again."

"That's what I'm saying. With my OCD I don't dare get pregnant...and with Margaret—at least...well, we were compatible."

"Compatible... Right! Like Tom Cruise and Katie Holmes? Like Keith Olberman and Bill-O!" Wave was really disgusted. "Lombard, I've known you since high school. You were with her because she was safe. There was about as much passion between you and devil woman as a bloody rice cracker. Rice crackers are very nice, but I don't want one in my vagina and I don't think you do either—"

Peyton couldn't help herself, she laughed and pointed at Wave.

"I know, I know... so I may run through them like socks in a drawer." Wave took another sip of wine. "But at least I get to feel. High, low, schmucky, and all good and fucky. And someday, you are going to have to put your heart out there so you get to feel all those wonderful feelings too."

Peyton was not convinced.

Peyton leaned into the crook of her dear friend's arm. Felt safe for the first time that evening.

"Blimey...what am I goin' to do with you."

*

Hi Peyton, I met you at the
Elena considered, deleted and started over.

Hi Peyton,
I was the one you were so kind to at the adoption orientation. Thanks for helping out a perfect stranger. Hope you're well.
Elena Winters

Elena took a moment, tried to think of a single good reason why she might want to reach out to this woman. She daydreamed a moment, thinking back to the woman who was so imposing, yet so kind in the same breath. Yes, it was that she was so engaging, Elena decided. But what was she thinking? Did her life even have enough room for a smidgeon of an acquaintanceship? The chances of her returning to that adoption organization were slim to none—she had already found another organization connected to their church closer to her home, and she—well, really there was no reason to send this e-mail whatsoever.

Elena was a little curious, wondering why she felt so....well, strongly that she should send the e-mail. Maybe it was that the woman had been so sweet to her and she had meant to thank her that day for her warmth and kindness. But, what was the point—it was almost a month ago now, and this did seem pretty random to be thanking her this much later. The woman probably wouldn't even remember her.

She heard Nash and Tori coming in from the movies.

She glanced back at her e-mail, was going to delete it but instead hit Send.

*

Peyton stood on the stepladder in the middle of her huge walk in closet digging through clothes, junk and tchotchkes as she searched and rummaged for the box she had specifically been hunting for the last hour. She had thought she had so clearly organized everything last year, glancing over the closed up cartons labeled Mom's Photos, Mom's Records, Salvation Army, Memorabilia, but now she realized she had been so grief stricken she had done all that cleaning on automatic pilot and only now was she beginning to remember where things actually lived. She also knew she hadn't come to look before now, because she couldn't have handled it.

Peyton finally saw the box marked, WOMEN'S GLORY PROJECT, but before she pulled it down, she saw the special handmade pine crate that held her mom's Biltmore Vanderbilt Teapot set. Now why had she put it away? She should really put it out in the dining room and actually use it. Even if it was a bit refined for Peyton's taste, the cobalt blue and gold etchings were beautiful. Besides, her mother would have wanted that, not for it to be cooped up in the closet here along with the beautiful Grecian urn.

She had finally spread her mother's ashes back east, near her childhood home in Maine, at the coast, her favorite summering vacation spot where she used to take Peyton every August. Peyton had been especially fond of the lovely little cabin with its rustic interior, homey and lived in. It always smelled of the sea and a bit of must, but that was what was so wonderful about it. It felt lived in and it was the only time her mother did not feel uptight to her.

The only other times Peyton could recall her mother seemingly able to relax were during the times they drank tea together. The only time that Peyton would see the pinched edges at her mother's mouth begin to relax. As if tea, or perhaps the ceremony of drinking it, created a calm for her mother.

Peyton pulled down the wooden crate and removed and unwrapped the beautiful bone china teapot and remembered that day so long ago when they were playing with Peyton's miniature tea service.

Why do people drink tea?

Peyton's mother stopped a moment to consider. Well, it's been around forever and it's a very nice and civilized way of people sharing time.

Young Peyton pretended to be very civilized as she sipped the tea out of the half-inch teacup.

But I drink tea, Peyton, because there isn't anything a good cup of tea can't make better.

Peyton thought that was a life lesson her mother had been right about. A cup of tea certainly always made things better.

*

Elena finished the church calendar at the dining room table. She sensed her laptop behind her. She turned. Checked her e-mails. Again. So many of them—always more requests from the church, but her eye scanned to see if there were any return e-mails.

Nothing.

*

Peyton rubbed her forehead, trying to erase the constant memories of her mother.

She was certain her relationship with her mother was no less neurotic than most, but because her father had died so early in her life, and she had literally no memory of him, her mother had become everything to her, even when she disapproved of pretty much everything Peyton undertook: *Ladies don't 'do' sports. Young lady, get out of those jeans right now and into a dress! Peyton, get your head out of that book—you don't live life by reading about it…you live it by doing it. Do something useful!*

Peyton's mother didn't speak to her for nearly a year when she heard of her decision to become a writer: *What kind of nonsense is that when you have gotten a four point average all through college, to throw it away on this silly dream when you could be a big success in business?* Theoretically to follow in her mother's footsteps, as she had herself become the President of International Commerce for the high-end cosmetics corporation to which she had devoted her entire life, finding all her affirmation from the praise of colleagues as opposed to the love of another human.

And when Peyton came out to her mother, Carolyn simply spat: *I cannot bear to look at you. It's evil—what you do…what you… what you crave is evil, Peyton. You need to get it fixed.*

Getting it fixed was two years of therapy and her mother's gradual if reluctant acceptance. For some reason, Carolyn could handle that Wave was, *All right, one of those kind of women—she's different, she's crazy—but you!* And it was Wave's endless patience and nurturing that helped Peyton and her mother find a way back to one another—even if it was a voiceless narrative of grudging acquiescence. Finally it was simply never mentioned again. It was tolerated. Carolyn barely got to know Margaret and Margaret was as uninterested in Peyton's mother as Peyton's mother was in Margaret. Within their mutual indifference toward one another lay peace.

After Peyton's father passed away, which she could barely even recall, the only person she could remember her mother even semi-dating was Dennis, an account executive at the company. At best it was sporadic and occasionally Peyton remembered watching her mother dress up and would feel giddy when Carolyn would ask her opinion: *Which dress do you think, Pey? This red one that goes with my new lipstick? Or this one that's more flattering to my hips?* And, of course, Peyton had no idea what she was talking about but jumped up saying "The red one, the red one" because it made her mother's face happier, shinier than she had ever seen it. And in those moments she saw her mother as beautiful, like a starlet out of a black-and-white movie. The rest of the times she simply appeared tight and bitter.

But soon Dennis's visits became fewer and fewer and eventually he left the scene altogether, except for the occasional popping over during the holidays—usually very late at night and sometimes on Sunday mornings. Peyton was mystified that he would always schlep his golf clubs along for the visit when her mother rarely golfed. It was only much later that Peyton realized that Dennis had been married and that their visits were explained to his wife as "golf dates" and that her mother's need for some companionship but no involvement was well served by having an affair with a married man.

She brought the beautiful teapot into the kitchen, washed it carefully, then retrieved the WOMEN'S GLORY PROJECT box and carried it to her desk. She spread all the papers, research and photos about her desk in the living room—another thing she knew her mother would have objected to. Peyton practically lived in the cavernous vaulted beamed living room, had transformed her mother's huge dining room table to be her enormous desk so that she could have all her projects out and at her fingertips in a moment's notice. But more than that, so that Peyton could feel safe in her womb. She often made a makeshift bed out of the chaise that cut the living room in half separating the couch and living area from her office space and she could hole up for days in that single room, making stops into the kitchen for coffee, tea and her meals, which she would also eat in the living room. Wave always teased her, "You know you have another two thousand square feet here you could be enjoying...other rooms might be feeling rejected."

Peyton spread the photos, articles, clippings before her, feeling a sense of calm wash over her. Her work had become her salvation. Since her mother's death and Margaret's betrayal, and with her OCD lurking around every corner, the few moments she felt some release and a sense of losing herself were when she buried herself in her work. And now, now that she was considering adopting, she felt renewed faith that life held promise, like that poor woman said at the adoption orientation.

Hours later, she finished mulling over and rereading all the research papers she had gathered for this project during the several years after she had written her best-selling memoir. She had pitched the idea, relentlessly, this great coffee-table book she had coined the *Women's Glory Project* which was devoted to really exploring in depth all the things that made women so wonderful. Emily, who Wave always described as, "One part performer, one part angel and eight parts killer shark," had been Peyton's agent since the start of her career. Though she lived in LA, she was still all Brooklyn and at times her bedside manner left Peyton feeling bruised. "You mean shredded!" Wave corrected. It had been touchy with this project as Emily had barked at her: "What's the hook?"

"Hook? It's not like selling a Toyota, Emily," Peyton had remarked.

"It's gotta have some kind of angle."

"How about women are amazing and we never take enough time to see who they really are—their flaws, their strengths, everything that makes them so—"

Emily yawned with feigned exaggeration. "Whatever. It's so Seventies—no one cares anymore about what makes a woman. We've gained our independence, our freedom. We fuck who we want. Give me a hook…celebrity women, or a cause—breast cancer—something. I can't sell it on just 'women.' No one gives a shit."

So while Peyton made her money on freelance articles and ghostwriting, she kept gathering all the materials to do this coffee-table book which would be not only a verbal ode to women, but a visual one as well. She could never really find the time to work on it, and as her mother became more ill, she only spent moments daydreaming about the structure, whether it should be about women of all ages, women of fame, women who worked, and then decided it should be about all of them. All women. That's what made the project so wonderful. She had oodles of ideas and research sucked away in her brain for fodder, and was always meaning to get to it, and after her mother died, she didn't have any extra energy for anything other than what she had to get done. Now she felt it was time. Time to really pursue this—

PING—an e-mail popped up from an ewintersholylight@mail.com. Who the hell was that? Some religious nut? Peyton dumped it into her spam file and went back to work.

*

Elena brought in the groceries and set them down. She wandered over to her laptop, checked her inbox, then shook her head, and headed straight back into the kitchen. She put everything away and began to pull out the hamburger meat for the burgers she had promised Nash earlier. She meticulously put together the special ingredients she and Nash had concocted for "the best burger on a bun" as Nash had nicknamed it and then remembered she had to send an e-mail to Millie.

Back to her computer. She sent the e-mail to Millie and sat there a moment. She checked her Send box. Yes, the e-mail had gone out.

*

Peyton's phone rang. It was her agent asking her to look at the e-mail they had just gotten from the women's magazine, *MORE*, offering her a recurring op-ed position. Emily was hugely excited and Peyton knew this was a great opportunity so she sat down, opened up the e-mail and had to agree that the offer was generous, wouldn't take too much time from this project she was committed to working on, and sent off her CV and clippings.

As she sat and read other incoming mail, something nagged at her. Nagged and nagged that she'd missed something. She looked through all her e-mail trying to decipher what was niggling at her and finally checked her spam folder. She opened the one from ewintersholylight@mail.com

Hi Peyton,
I was the one you were so kind to at the

adoption orientation. Thanks for helping out a
perfect stranger. Hope you're well.
      Elena Winters

Peyton read the e-mail a couple more times and then smiled.
That's right, the poor woman with the lost keys. She began an
e-mail back:

      Hi Elena, glad you wrote

Now what? She had no idea what to say to this person. What
was the point? But she didn't want to be rude. She started again.
Backspaced. Wrote something truly innocuous. Backspaced
again. She started a third time, and tried to figure out what it was
she was trying to say. When she finally finished she read it aloud,
then shook her head. "Yeah…some brilliant writer, Peyton."
      She was giving it one last go, when the doorbell rang. She
wondered if it was Wave, but Wave would just walk right in.
      Peyton made her way to the door, opened it and there stood
Margaret.

                            *

"…and then Tyler said it would be cool if I did my Amazing
Person paper on him so I've actually been getting into all this
soul mate research, which at first you know I thought was just so
much hokum." Tori was helping Elena clean up the dishes after
dinner as she charmingly went on with one of her informational
riffs. "You know, cuz, I'm all about the facts and the data, but, ya
know, now that I've done a bit more digging on the whole thing,
it's pretty amazing how some of these soul mates have met—like
with the kind of randomness no mathematical algorithm can
explain, and ya know what else is sort of whack, is how enduringly
it's existed within our consciousness."
      "Hmmm." Elena half listened as she always did because she
always had a million things on her mind and she simply couldn't
take in all the information that Tori offered up, even when Tori
was at her most absolutely charming. The huge databanks in

Tori's brain were truly a feat. She never provided information in a show-offey manner, nor was she even remotely annoying about it. It was all delivered as off-handed matter-of-fact knowledge, but also with a sweet conviction that what she was telling you was very much meant for your own well being. And, everyone agreed, it was often quite fascinating.

"I mean we're talkin' as early as Plato where he explained in this megasymposium that humans were first identified as a body with four legs and four arms but only had one head but—get this—one head that had two faces. Zeus wasn't havin' it because he believed that this being was too powerful so he ripped it in two—yeah right down the middle which left these two halves disembodied and endlessly on the prowl for the other half so they could become unified and whole. Isn't that wild?"

"Yes, Tori...yes, it is." Elena smiled, put the last dish away. "Okay, sweetie, as always—"

"Get this, it was a mystic Hindu belief, and I memorized this, that man 'yearned for a second. He became as large as a man and a woman locked in close embrace. This self he split into two; hence arose husband and wife...Oneself is like half of a split pea.' Isn't that crazy? I mean people think soul mates are relatively new—but Tyler's entire Soulemetry religion goes as far back as the origins of mankind."

"Okay, Tori, I understand...it's been around forever and please do not start harping on the ultimate flame—or whatever it is that Tyler's always going on about."

"That would be the Twin Flame, Momma Bear, and you already got that in Poppa Bear."

But even as she said it, Tori's voice got quiet. They glanced at one another.

"Well, gotta get back to Nash. Help him with that science."

Tori left Elena in the middle of the kitchen. Sighing, she looked at this kitchen she stood in every single day. Suddenly it seemed far more drab than she remembered. Maybe new wallpaper. A splash of paint... Whatever she was going to do, she had already decided she was not, NOT under any circumstances, going to look at her e-mail again tonight. But within moments she returned to her laptop.

She sat there. Sighed. What was wrong with her? Why did she even care? She was never going to see this person again. Well, she thought, the reality is that she just wanted to make sure that the nice woman knew that Elena was grateful for her help. She shook her head, closed her laptop. Done.

*

Peyton sat at the counter at Pinot Latte the next morning as Wave finished with a customer then joined her friend.

"Lombard, I'm not sure what language you need to hear it in, but you are NOT—I repeat NOT—going back to that psycho."

"Look, I know it's easy to make her the villain...and what Erin did to you was really crappy. But Wave, Erin was—"

"Look, you think I didn't know Erin was a momentary lapse in judgment? You think I don't know I'm like...like the lesbian Jennifer Aniston—without the looks or the hair. So—I'm lousy awful picking girlfriends...what can I say?" Wave furiously wiped the counters.

"Wave." Peyton put a hand to Wave's arm to stop her. "I'm not excusing what she did to either of us. It's just I have to take some of the blame."

"So that doesn't mean you have to sacrifice your happiness to make it up to her." Wave stopped then, sat next to her friend and coyly moved into the fold of her arm. Peyton looked at her as if to say, *What's up with you?*

"Now don't think I've gone and lost my last burner here Peyton." Wave seemed a bit sheepish which was completely out of character. "But there's this love guru who does these amazing readings that's helping people find their one true love."

Peyton laughed.

"And we're going, Saturday night."

Peyton just shook her head, didn't take Wave seriously.

"I mean it. I've already got us tickets."

"Wave, I'm not going."

"Come on. What have you got to lose?"

Another customer entered. Wave got up, leaned into Peyton's face. "In the meantime—can you skip the I'm-just-dandy diet and all-I-need-is-my-work distractions? And under no circumstances are you to have anything to do with Mata Hari."

Wave scribbled hastily upon her pad. "Listen to me. You are under strict orders to only do things that make you feel good. Good. Not bad. Good. Very simple instructions to follow."

Wave set the order down before her: *You just need to do stuff that makes you feel good. Good. Not bad.* Peyton smiled and picked up her prescription, folded it and put it in her pocket.

*

Elena's hope for getting a response from Peyton soon faded. It had now been nearly a week since she had sent the e-mail. She found herself usually checking at night, before she went to bed, but then decided this last night she was done. She looked for the final time.

"So, oh God, this was like, so random." Erika, a twenty-seven-year-old Italian bank manager shakes her head like she still can't believe it. "I was supposed to be babysitting my niece, but my sister gets sick and asks if I'd fill in at the PTA. I'm like are you kidding me? What am I going to do at a PTA. I don't know the first thing about kids and school, and…"

"And my mom is the niece's teacher," Bruce adds, smiling. He's in his early thirties and as tall and slender as Erica is petite and chubby. "I had to go pick her up because her car broke down. I got there early, thought, oh well, I'll go check out her classroom."

"I'm standing outside," Erika continues, "trying to get my nerve up to go inside when this football—"

"—Yeah out of nowhere completely mashes into her, knocking her over and this casserole she's got like totally spews all over everything—"

"I would have totally freaked if Bruce hadn't run over and saved the day. The minute I looked into his worried eyes I had this flash— I'm going to marry this man." She looks astounded, laughs sort of shocked, like it's just happening again. "I mean it. No shit—it just literally flashed through my head as if I knew it for absolute certain."

"And I just took one look at her and I was like… I'm in love." Bruce stares at her adoringly. "It really did happen that fast."

"We were both somewhere neither of us remotely planned to be—"

Both finish at the same time: "Some things are just meant to be—"

"Yeah…," Erika sighs, "even when you try like hell to un be them!"

Twinkling lights completely enveloped Tyler's Soul-Blim-In-Nation gardens to celebrate his "A Night Under the Stars" event in the courtyard surrounding his sanctuary. Tyler fastidiously lit candles, refinessed their placement, humming "Dancing Queen" as he moved about in lyrical anticipation.

Lily approached and placed a large platter of crudites on the food table as Tyler fussed about. Wearing her chicest Armani, Lily walked right in front of him, stopped him a moment, and looked directly into his eyes.

"It's going to be stellar, honey." She planted a gentle, yet passion-filled kiss to settle him. "Because you are!"

*

Elena completed the final touches on her wardrobe. She stood in front of the mirror, clad in one of the few dressy outfits she owned, her sleek Diana Von Furstenburg; the shape accentuated her slender figure, the pearl black tone highlighted her dark features. She tied a red floral scarf around her neck as a subtle accent, finished her lipstick and went to the kitchen to put a casserole in the oven for everyone's dinner.

As she made her way into the dining room, she bumped into Tori who was clad in black tights, a black turtleneck and semi-assembled all over her body was a half-baked Halloween design filled with data, research components, bits and numbers.

"Information," Tori announced to Elena, "that's what I'm going as."

Elena admired Tori's creative design and knew all the hard work she had put into the scientific attire to make the statement of her most sacred passion. "Tori—you're a genius. That costume is priceless."

"Thanks Momma Bear. I'm not nearly finished." Tori smiled proudly at her achievement. "Now I just gotta figure out what Nash is going as. A professor, a mad scientist—"

"Mad scientist, please." Nash walked in, checked out his mom. "You and Dad goin' out tonight or what?"

"Oh yeah, Momma Bear, you're lookin' *fine*," Tori chimed in.

Barry walked in at that moment, stopped to admire his wife. "Whoa... Where are you going so dolled up?"

Nash and Tori began to giggle. "We'll give you two some privacy."

Elena smirked. They ran out being silly and Elena shook her head. Barry tilted his head, admiring her, his eyes burning over her body. "Anything I should know?"

"You know very well I'm going to Tyler's event."

Barry shook his head. She realized he had completely forgotten, as he did most things that were on *her* calendar. He nabbed a beer from the refrigerator, then settled against a counter, took a swig and then grimaced in appreciation as he got a much better vantage point to view his wife.

"God, Tyler was on his way to being one of the most amazing directors in film school and gave it all up for this nonsense."

"Now the casserole takes about forty-five minutes." Elena continued to buzz around the kitchen readying everything for her departure. "Don't forget while you're watching the game. You'll burn it and the kids are really hungry."

"He had it all, El...I just don't get it."

"Come on, Barry, you know he lives for this."

Elena moved to him, pecked him on the cheek, but he set his beer down, and pulled her to him. "And I live for," he eyed her with absolute appreciation, "...this."

He held her a second, nuzzled into her neck, whispered, "Maybe you can wear this next date night."

"If you're lucky, maybe I'll be home early."

He was about to make a rejoinder, when she popped the rest of a cookie into his mouth. She winked at him and strolled out seductively for his benefit.

*

Peyton felt paralyzed sitting in Wave's car as Wave examined the finishing touches to her makeup in the visor mirror. How Peyton loathed having to get dressed up. She'd much rather be attending this event in jeans and a T-shirt, instead of wearing her black slacks, turquoise silk top and black brocaded light wool duster. Wave had pestered her to wear her hair up, which she did on occasion, but now she wished she hadn't. She just was not comfortable in public forums like this, her OCD was easily agitated and thrown into hyper-drive. She could do the small talk, but it took work and she wasn't fond of large social gatherings involving people that she knew, much less one where the only person she could count on was Wave. That's why she had always been such a loner.

"That chick I went out with Friday?" Wave was curling her eyelashes and brought Peyton back to the moment. "Yeah, that bugger was dating Erin and my ex."

Peyton rolled her eyes. "Look you knew she was a player and you said your eyes were wide open."

Wave stopped what she was doing and stared at Peyton. "Yeah, well—I'm legally blind in my left eye—"

"You're...you're defenseless-hopeless." Peyton couldn't help but laugh.

"Why the hell do you think we're going to this thing?" Wave joined her, laughing at herself, and then turned mock serious. "Lombard, look—just so we're clear, this so isn't desperation speaking here—this 'love guru' is supposed to be the absolute best there is."

"Yes, you've said that several times now." Peyton shook her head in futility.

"And the wholly undesperate part of me is willing to try anything at this point."

"And why is it that I have to be here?"

"Because, if I meet my soul mate—you MUST approve. And I figured, we could find you one as well, while we're at it."

Peyton opened her car door. "This isn't a Macy's two-for-one sale."

As Peyton and Wave walked through the thick crowd, the event had moved into full swing. Wave immediately dragged Peyton to the cocktail table and they both downed a flute of champagne.

"Much better then!" Wave announced. "Let's mill."

"You mill. I think I'm going to sit right here at this table and have another drink."

"Good idea, but don't get too snockered or your soul mate might not recognize you."

"Just go." Peyton made a shooing motion to urge Wave to leave her be. She stood and watched people, one of her favorite things anyway.

A chime rang three times and suddenly Peyton heard the most beautiful male voice sing, "In love, one and one are one…"

She was riveted by his extraordinary tone and soon forgot she was in this ridiculous place that seemed to her to be full of desperate people. Love came when love came. You couldn't force it. She had learned to be very pragmatic about such things.

Tyler, dressed in a rich blue paisley shirt covered by a beautiful camel suede jacket, was fairly beaming when he turned to the crowd, as he lit two matches, pulled them together to ignite into one flame and from that lit one candle in symbolism. "It's so unpredictable, yet as certain as the sun coming up every day—love."

He smiled in celebration at the word, waited a moment, glancing over his audience. "Simple. Complex. Pure. Frenzied. All those many expressions we apply to this intangible thing… this thing we all want so desperately—always trying to explain the inexplicable. You cannot quantify or qualify love. It just is. But there are many kinds of love…what we all yearn for is that highest form of love. The soul mate…"

Peyton was only half listening. She was more amused by watching Wave scope out the women in the crowd. She knew Wave had "me system, which is pretty infallible. I look 'em over, gauge the gaydar, sniff out the psychos, and head straight for the most dysfunctional one of the bunch."

"Your soul mate could be standing right next to you," Tyler continued, "and you wouldn't know it…"

Wave continued to check out the possibilities as Peyton nursed her drink.

"…this is because you have your true self, and what I call your 'celebrity self'—the one that's obsessed with ego, the one that wants that hunk, the thick brown hair, another 'celebrity self.'"

Wave nudged Peyton in the arm and whispered, "See? This is good stuff."

Peyton nodded, unconvinced, and then saw that Wave was actually referring to the gorgeous blonde standing across the way next to a tall dark haired woman whose back was turned to them both and that Wave, was, in fact, arching her best flirty eyebrow toward the slick-dressed blonde.

"These pairings never last and after each one, you wonder the same thing with your broken heart and bruised ego."

Wave nodded vehemently. She definitely had this one down.

"Don't confuse the attraction to the physical with the yearning of the soul. Your higher self, the soul-self, will always break through that and find its true soul partner—and, trust me—" he winked at Wave's current target, the blonde, "it could well be the last person in the world you'd think of!"

Across the courtyard, Elena crooked her neck as she studied the hors d'oeurves, then checked her watch trying to figure out how long she had to stay for Tyler's feelings not to be hurt, and considered how early she would need to be back home to fulfill her suggestion to Barry, and whether she really wanted to get home *that* early. Neither direction was particularly appealing.

Maybe she would just hang out here. She shook her head, angry with herself. She was near ovulation. She might as well be with Barry tonight and make him happy. She really needed to give him more affection in that way. She knew she held back— *Oooh*, a shiver went up her neck. It was getting cold. Maybe she should find her coat. Or better yet, another drink.

Peyton turned to look her way as Elena moved to get a drink. Elena suddenly felt that strange time shift, like weeks ago in the park. She turned. Looked around, confused. But before she could pursue it more fully, Lily smashed up against her.

"Oh my God, some of the crazies Tyler draws to these events."

Elena smiled sympathetically. She knew that if she thought Tyler's world was a bit on the woo-woo side, Lily with her sharp-as-a-tack corporate raider personality had no patience for it at all. Surprisingly, she had always been completely supportive of everything Tyler did, and if she was annoyed at times with Tyler's incessant need to share his philosophy of love and to examine the elements of Soulemetry at every turn, she was also his most ardent and determined advocate.

Lily glanced behind her then whispered, "There's a woman over there trying to hit on me."

Elena gulped on her drink, smiled a bit uncomfortably, and then saw the woman with the flaming red hair saunter toward them.

"Seriously. Oh my God, she isn't coming over here!"

But when Elena turned to really check her out she no longer saw the redhead at all.

Peyton.

There stood Peyton, the woman from the adoption orientation, the woman she had sent her silly e-mail to, the woman who had not answered it. She was struck again, by how attractive Peyton was, but in that uniquely authoritative manner. It unsettled her momentarily. She tried to figure out whether to go to her or to absolutely avoid her.

Peyton had been engaged in small talk when she felt a pull so strong that literally without even thinking she turned, and the moment she did, she saw her.

Elena. The woman from the adoption orientation. She looked different. Peyton recalled from the orientation that she was exotic, but she hadn't remembered her being so...so, well, stunning. Oh my God, she had sent that e-mail and Peyton had never written back. God, she felt so stupid now. Why hadn't she just sent something—anything—back to her?

They both held one another's eyes for a long moment. Smiled.

As if she didn't know what possessed her, Peyton moved toward Elena at the same time Tyler was joining her.

"Hey...I got your e-mail." Peyton shrugged apologetically. "Sorry I didn't get back to you."

Elena shook the gentle hand she extended: no problem.

"Hello gorgeous." Tyler embraced Elena, then pulling away, looked her up and down. Tyler turned to Peyton, as if he knew her. "Could she be any more dazzling? I ask you!"

Elena stood embarrassed, and Peyton nodded in the affirmative but before Tyler could go on, Elena stuttered, "Uhmm, you'll never believe this Tyler...," she indicated Peyton. "I met Peyton at the adoption orientation."

"Yeah," Peyton chimed in. "Small world."

"What does that even mean?" Tyler arched an eyebrow, tsked a finger knowingly at them while Elena and Peyton considered one another. "Small world, six degrees of separation. Coincidence. I love how people just try to explain all of this away...with this delusion of accidents."

Peyton shook her head, uncertain of how to respond to Tyler's comments, especially when he seemed to be a gay man yet also seemed to be giving her a very thorough once over.

"Interesting," Tyler remarked, then glanced from Peyton to Elena. "Okay, girls. I'm going to start my readings. I'll check in with you," he indicated Elena, "later."

He dashed away, leaving them standing uncertain of what to do. The silence became deafening.

"Well..." Elena cleared her throat. "Since this was clearly preordained...want to get a drink?"

*

Very few stragglers remained at Tyler's event. Wave had been talking so long to Tyler that her head was now upon his lap as she lamented her terrible history of love.

"Do you think I'm a player?"

"Of course you're a player," Tyler laughed. "After all, let's call a spade a spade."

"I suppose," Wave conceded. "It's just that I feel like I'm at the races, always picking the wrong horse."

"That's just it. You're picking—you're on the prowl. Stop forcing it. Has it ever occurred to you to let love find you?"

Wave considered a moment. "Feck no!"

"Feck?"

"Yeah, you know, fuck, feck—it's all the same to me. I thought if I waited I'd be an eighty-eight-year-old bag of bones before anyone even took a shine. If I pick, then I only have myself to blame if it—"

"There's no blame here, Wave. Love doesn't work that way."

"Okay, do your magic, Doc. I'll follow all your rules, promise."

*

Peyton and Elena had made their way through several drinks and hours of conversation, sitting isolated from the crowd at a small intimate table, with a waning candle between them in the corner of Tyler's courtyard.

"Peyton...you're so brave. To want to have a baby on your own...and after everything you've been through with your mother." Elena gently touched Peyton's arm, leaving it there as she continued to speak. "And you never...well, thought about getting married?"

Peyton moved her arm. "Oh, I was married."

"I thought you said you were single...or that's what I thought I heard you say at the adoption orientation."

"I am. Now."

"Oh...I'm sorry. How long were you married?"

"Six years." Peyton took a sip. "How 'bout you?"

"Fifteen." But Elena did not want to focus on her marriage. "Can I ask you what happened?"

"Oh, I guess all the predictable stuff. My partner couldn't handle all the time I spent with my ailing mother, slept around, same old, same old."

"Your business partner?" Elena was confused, looked at Peyton, who frowned as she looked back.

"Your uhmm, partner," Elena said, and as she was saying it, it dawned on her what it meant. "Your *partner*. You're uhmm— "

"Gay." They both said it at the same time.

"Oh, well, I think that is absolutely fine." Elena's voice sounded strained and forced. "It's so not an issue for me," she gushed and then rambled on. "I voted no on Prop 8—I mean yes, maybe—it was no right? I can't remember, it was all so confusing. But I know I voted the right way. I mean—you know I voted *your* way."

Peyton watched her struggling, and smiled.

"I just didn't want you to think that it was a problem. I mean why would it be? Gosh, do I just keep sounding more and more ridiculous?"

83

"No… It's fine," Peyton reassured her. "You're fine."

Elena took a quick sip of champagne, set down her glass and then looked at Peyton with the most curious stare until Peyton had to look away and was quickly saved by Wave who walked over with notes in hand.

"Apparently I was the inspiration for looking for love in all the wrong places…" Then she stopped as she checked out Elena and Peyton, and smiled, clearly intrigued. "Well, I see this was a bust for me…but looks like you two—"

Elena looked completely confused. Peyton shut Wave down with a chilly, "Wave, this is Elena Winters."

Wave shook Elena's hand.

"Pleased to meet you." Elena began to gather her belongings. "I'd love to stay but I…I've got to run. My husband has early services tomorrow—"

Peyton did a double take as Wave practically choked.

Elena realized she had surprised them and explained, "Barry's a pastor."

Now it was Peyton's turn to be flabbergasted. Both Wave and Peyton tried to regain their composure as Elena stood.

"Uh, yeah." Wave tried to act naturally. "That's cool."

"Well, uhmm." Peyton felt unusually awkward. "It was great running into to you."

"Nice meeting you, Wave. Goodbye Peyton."

Elena waved to them both as she left. Wave turned to Peyton with a "what the fuck was that?" expression on her face, and sat beside her. "A pastor's wife? Blimey."

*

By the time Elena got home, everyone was fast asleep and she had so much energy she didn't know what to do with herself. She folded all the laundry, undressed, took a long shower, and yet, she was still completely wide-eyed and awake. She was usually so tired at the end of the day and it was almost two a.m.

She sat at her laptop, finished all the church e-mails she had planned to send out the next day, cleaned up her calendar, reorganized her desk and came upon Peyton's card. She picked it up, hesitated for several long moments, then began to type.

*

"Damn!" Peyton mumbled under her breath as she realized she had been reading the same page for the last half hour. Again, that intrusive thinking. Part of it she was used to. Dr. James always used to say, when the "garbage talk" gets into your head you just have to shut it down. And for the most part, Peyton had finessed the skill of rechanneling silly OCD ruminations. But she had been going back over the conversation with Elena, hoping she hadn't said anything to offend her, realizing how shocked she had been to hear that Peyton was gay, then mad at herself for caring, trying to toss her own homophobia aside. So what if she had surprised her? It was this kind of thinking that she still hadn't conquered, and it was as if her OCD took great delight in tormenting her.

She didn't know what to think. She had been reading for several hours now. She just couldn't get to sleep. She had been researching all these incredible women and maybe all that crisp nighttime air had invigorated her. She picked up another book and realized there was a folded piece of paper serving as a bookmark. She opened it up and read Wave's prescription: *You just need to do stuff that makes you feel good. Good. Not bad.*

She grinned, folded up the paper, then hopped out of bed and dashed to her laptop. She found the old e-mail from Elena and typed.

```
Hi Elena...it was great seeing you at your
friend's event tonight.
```

But as she was sitting, mulling over what to say, an e-mail came in from Elena.

```
        Hi Peyton, ...so great to see you again.
Would you like to get together for lunch? I
don't know what your schedule is like, but
maybe tomorrow? Elena
```

Peyton thought it was pretty uncanny that Elena's e-mail had come in the same time she was about to send her one. She smiled and was about to write a response when a flicker of anxiety ran over her. She considered the e-mail for the next couple of minutes, and finally wrote:

Hi Elena, yes it was great to see you too. Lunch sounds fine. Let me know when and where...Peyton.

*

Peyton proceeded to spend the rest of the night hurling her guts out. She had the worst stomach flu she could remember. She was loath to throw up—it was a component of her OCD—even when she drank too much. She never EVER threw up, because she simply willed herself not to. It completely freaked her out. Wave, who easily chucked, always said, "Ahh, much better—you don't know what you're missin'!" To which Peyton replied that she'd rather be miserable a whole day than have to go through that kind of bodily anguish.

"You're just a big baby," Wave would say.

"No, it's against the natural order of things."

"Keeping it in is, sister, make no mistake!"

They had just had this very conversation in the last few days, although now Peyton was reconsidering her position. Maybe Wave was right, because she felt like she was going to die and the only relief she had was throwing up.

The phone rang. Peyton couldn't move. She lay in a fetal position upon her large California King bed. She let the call go to the answering machine.

"Hi Peyton." It was Elena's voice. Peyton moved her head so she could hear a little better. "Oh, you sounded awful on your message. I'm so sorry you don't feel well. Don't worry about lunch—maybe another time?" A long pause. "Do you need anything? I'd be happy to drop something by..."

Wave entered the bedroom bearing a tray with clear broth, ginger ale and aspirin and stood listening along with Peyton.

"You know, no one likes to be sick on their own. I could bring you something—well anything, actually. You know what I could bring you? Soup! Soup…or…whatever you need. Uhmm, okay…let me know. Goodbye."

"Soup?" Wave arched an eyebrow. "Seriously? Oh…now that's smooth."

*

Elena checked her voice mail and then returned to the kitchen to continue dinner. She wondered if Peyton had even gotten her message, wondered if she were sick with the flu, wondered if she had made up the excuse. No, she wouldn't do that, right? Why would she do that? Was she just being nice the other night? Simply too busy? All these things kept running through her mind when Tori popped in, a blue silk tie wrapped about her forehead like an old hippie. She dipped a finger into her casserole, smiled yummy.

"Did you know a snail can sleep for three years?" Tori snatched another bite and Elena pretended to slap her hand. "Yeah, I think Nash may very well be trying to beat that record. God, can you imagine not being able to get out of a sleep—like a coma—like this guy who has one of the longest recorded comas in history for—get this—twenty years! He's like nineteen, has some random car accident and wakes up when he's thirty-nine. Can you even, like, get down with how that would feel? Man, just an ordinary Friday you, like, wake up only to discover that you'd literally slept half your life away?"

Something about Tori's words struck a nerve. As Elena considered them the phone rang. Tori moved to get the phone because she was always the one to pick it up and suddenly Elena was lunging for it. Tori arched an eyebrow as Elena answered too eagerly.

"Yes?" Breathless and then Elena's mouth tightened. "Yes? Oh…hi, Millie."

Tori made a face at her. *See, that's what you get for picking up the phone!*

"Hey you know, we're in the middle of dinner, Millie. May I call you back?"

Elena hung up, nonchalant, as Tori watched her with the eagle eye. Before Tori could pry, Nash entered all bed head and yawning, in gray sweats and a striped rugby shirt. Elena turned to her son, gently ruffled his hair.

"Nap much?" Tori teased. Nash ignored her and then Barry joined them through the opposite kitchen door.

Tori quickly jumped up to pour Barry a glass of iced tea, handed it to him along with a quick hug.

"Hey peanut, thanks." He took a sip, set it down, considered Tori a moment. "Tori, you know we love you—but can you tell your folks we plan to take you as a deduction this year on our taxes?"

"Actually Poppa Bear, you could deduct the cost of babysitting me as a charitable deduction—that's actually allowed given the fact that Elena spends so much time volunteering."

"So now you're reading the tax code?" Barry was floored.

"Yeah, workin' on a project for school. Plus it's a stunning fix for insomnia."

Elena smiled, pulled Tori into a big hug. "Please tell me it worked."

"Well, I didn't find it endlessly fascinating, but it had good structure, narrative…I laughed, I cried…"

*

Several hours later, Elena gently tapped on Nash's bedroom door while everyone else was getting ready for bed. She tiptoed in. Nash was sprawled out over the double bed playing on one of his perennial DES games. She pushed aside some of his homework, sat on the side of the bed.

"Is everything okay at Tori's? She's been here even more than usual."

"Nope. Not really." Nash sighed, finishing the last strokes of a virtual golf game. "He's back out on the road and she's back into her weirdo mania thing she does—working all night, sleeping during the day. I don't think Tori's even seen her mom since last week."

"She just seems a little more, I don't know…overwrought with even more information than she usually has…"

"You know how she gets." Nash barely looked up as he continued thumb-thumping on his game. "When she's depressed, she digs even deeper—and, man, I gotta tell ya, some of the stuff she comes up with—"

Elena gently took Nash's game from him. "Well, God bless her...I hope she knows how loved she is here."

"Of course she does." Nash looked skeptically at his mother, as he scrunched up his knees to give her more room on the bed. "Okay...so what's this really about?"

"Well...I heard you skipped Bible study yesterday—"

"Yeah, Mom, I sure did," Nash responded proudly and then added ruefully, "those people are all a bunch of wingnuts over there. I don't care what they're crusading against. And Dad really doesn't either...he's just playing to his fawning flock—"

"Your dad—"

"Got the role of a lifetime, Mom. Playing pastor was the only gig he could actually book. Come on, Mom. You know it. We both know it, so don't even..."

Elena shook her head, pursed her lips. She did not want either of them to speak badly about Nash's father, but of course she knew it. It was simply a matter of loyalty that kept her silent and the fact that while Nash might understand on some level how his dad had sold out she also knew it was a much more complex compromise than Nash was capable of understanding.

Unfortunately, Nash could not understand how the pressure to keep both herself and Nash well taken care of worked into that compromise. Even when she tried to explain to him that the nature of his father's work—no matter how Nash might feel about it—was good works that helped many different people, Nash still would reply, skeptically, "Yeah whatever. You can call it whatever you want, or think that because the church does good work, it's all okay. But on some level, Mom, he's lying. In my book, that's wrong."

So it was black and white for Nash, and she really couldn't expect him to understand all the vagaries of gray that might exist in Barry's situation. Barry really did much of this work with an open heart and for that she respected him. She just wasn't sure how much longer she could keep Nash pacified, since he had become so keenly aware that Barry's world, while filled with good deeds, was composed of smoke and mirrors.

"Shhhh." Elena shut down this conversation as Tori entered the room. Although Tori shared the general sentiment that the church was full of contradictions, she was also fiercely loyal to Poppa Bear as she had fondly nicknamed him from the very beginning. He was the only father Tori had, in many ways, and whatever concessions he may have made in life did not keep Tori from absolutely adoring him.

Tori popped herself up on the bed. "Oh yippee, slumber party."

She made herself comfortable, drew one of Nash's blankets over her knees, then glanced back and forth between the two. "Oops...did I just crash a private party here?"

Nash scooped her up in a bear hug. "Never crashing, babe. You're always welcome. Mom and I were finished anyway, weren't we." Nash informed his mother more than asked her.

Elena sighed, picked up one of Nash's shirts and began to fold it. Nash cocked his head one way, then another, studying his mom with a thoroughness that began to make her feel uncomfortable.

"Nash!" she finally snapped.

"Mom...don't take this the wrong way or anything...but you know you're still really pretty."

"Well, thanks. I think." Elena shook her head, self-conscious. "What brought that on?"

"Uhmm...so, well, Tori was telling me women hit their—you know..." But as Elena glanced at her son in surprise he clammed up and then blurted, "Peak?...well when they...well, you know what I mean..."

Elena was blushing, but turned her body so that he could not really see her. "No. I'm not sure I do." Elena collected herself and turned back to Nash. "Look son, I know our dear Tori here is a font of never-ending information—"

"Tell her, Tori," Nash insisted.

"Yes, 'tell her Tori.'" Elena turned to Tori with a mock menacing look.

"Pleading the Fifth?"

"Mom, don't freak or anything. It's just we were wondering

what your life would be like if you had married a real actor. You know. Someone like—like well, Daniel Craig or Brad Pitt—or even like a Gerard Butler instead of...well, Dad."

Elena, struggling not to laugh, had no intention of continuing this line of discussion, and simply replied, "Well, sweetie, if I hadn't married your dad I wouldn't have you."

Barry butted his head in the door.

They all sat in guilty silence. Nash looked like he'd swallowed the canary.

"What's up in here?" Barry teased. "Planning a bank heist?"

Nobody spoke. Barry shook his head. "Okay, well you have a phone call, El...and you two should be getting to bed."

As he handed her the phone he exchanged places with his wife. "Hey guys...how 'bout a quick bowl of ice cream...then let's all hit the sack."

Elena watched as Tori hugged Poppa Bear, snuggling him close, as if to make up for their transgression. She walked out of Nash's bedroom and into the living room, lifted the phone.

"It's Peyton..." Peyton's voice was very congested. "Peyton Lombard."

"Oh, Peyton." Elena smiled and then said with genuine concern, "You sound terrible. Oh my gosh, how are you feeling?"

"Better, actually."

"Oh, I'm so glad to hear that."

Long pause.

"So, you know that project I was talking about?" Peyton asked.

"Yes...yes, the one you spoke about at Tyler's, right?"

"I'm getting ready to start fleshing it out. I was wondering, you know, if you're interested...if I could see some samples of your work—see if this would be a fit."

"Oh, sure. Yes." Elena found herself feeling very nervous, put a hand to her hair to smooth it, as if anyone could see her. How could she show such old work? Would this professional writer think she was a joke? I mean, did she really want to humiliate herself? But before she could think further about the implications she heard herself saying, "If you'd like I could bring by my portfolio. I could even do it tomorrow." And then to try and cover up, "We could meet for lunch..."

Another long pause and Elena felt her heart thudding. "That is, if you feel well enough. Or coffee. Just coffee is fine."

"Yeah, sure," Peyton responded. "I know just the place."

*

The next morning Peyton sat, dressed in her black jeans, a black muscle shirt and covering her for warmth a teal Façonnable that was as soft as it was cozy. She sat at one of three concrete picnic tables not far from a gorgeous mini-waterfall at her favorite park. She liked the tables here because while they were all near the cascading water, they were far enough apart for privacy and set amidst a huge clearing of yawning gentle slopes of green, terraced to contour the edges of a brook that ran through the entire length of the park and emptied into a small lake at the bottom.

Even with the ducks clamoring endlessly she was deeply engrossed answering e-mails on her BlackBerry as she waited and was unaware, at first, that Elena had shown up, until she heard a bag plopped on the table.

"Oh hi," she said.

"Hey there. Sorry I'm a little late. I..." But she let it go as she rummaged through the bags, pulled out a gourmet bottle of lemonade, several containers filled with salads, desserts, even a couple of flowers.

Again, Peyton was aware that Elena was a beautiful woman, but here, in the daylight, she could see even more clearly her flawless olive skin, those deeply piercing brown eyes, and when she turned to her to smile uncertainly, Peyton realized she was staring, cleared her throat. "You didn't have to go to all this trouble."

"It's no trouble, really," Elena answered. Their eyes met. "I... You know when you're sick you just want things to make you feel better. Besides...I sort of feel like no one's been taking care of you."

Elena felt flustered as she pulled items together. Seeing Peyton in this new setting threw her for some reason. A glow radiated about Peyton she hadn't noticed before, and she found herself drawn to this woman in a strange but fascinating manner.

Peyton had such charm and warmth about her. Elena shrugged, continued her task. "Maybe it's the mom in me?"

Peyton blushed. "I look that bad, huh?"

"No...no, I mean, with everything you've been through—your mother, all the stuff your ex put you through—who sounds like a real piece of work—no offense. It's like, what about you? Who is taking care of Peyton?"

"Believe me I'm not a saint...and I'm not a martyr either. Just not a great time in my life."

"This project and I are going to change all that," Elena announced as if it were a foregone conclusion that Peyton would naturally pick her as the photographer, then realizing how presumptuous that sounded, shifted. "Can I pour you some lemonade?"

"Yeah, lemonade sounds great."

"How are you feeling, anyway?"

"I'm fine. Really." Peyton watched Elena as she fussed about and then eyed the brown leather portfolio, pulled it toward her. "May I?"

Elena stopped, then nodded. "Just remember—it's been years since I've been *really* working." She sat down next to her, touching the portfolio almost as if she wanted to take it back, then settling in, she sighed. "Well, I guess...at least you can see my style."

Peyton opened the portfolio, and slowly began to look through the work, taking her time to appreciate the framing, lighting and what she could see was a very elegant eye in Elena's photos.

"You know these are really very good." Peyton's voice was laced with genuine appreciation. "I'm impressed."

Elena turned to her, smiled modestly, suddenly felt very shy. "Well, you start out thinking you'll be Annie Liebowitz...and then..."

Peyton leaned over to examine the photos more closely. Elena moved next to her, pointed at a shot, their bodies pressed together as Peyton studied a child's photo, then turned to Elena.

"She's so beautiful... What a great setup."

"Children are my favorite subjects. They're still so innocent, no pretense... They show everything they're feeling."

Peyton was about to respond, but when she turned the page she saw what appeared to be a naked woman in a sensually evocative silhouette.

"Wow." Peyton shook her head. "I love this one..."

"Oh." Elena cleared her throat, then laughed off-handedly. "That's me actually..."

Peyton turned to look at her, surprised. It seemed so out of character.

"I shot that after Nash was born. I had an idea, lit it...and thought I might as well."

Peyton suddenly became aware of the fact that they were way too close, cleared her throat. "It's...great. They're all...really good."

But when she turned Elena was looking right at her with those eyes—those unwavering eyes.

Peyton got up and returned to the other side of the picnic table and then, covering, asked, "Why didn't you keep it up?"

"Oh...you know, the usual things. My family. Responsibilities...life."

Their eyes met. Again. And Peyton became uncomfortably aware that Elena was one of the few people she had ever encountered who had absolutely no problem holding a gaze.

"You know this is one of my favorite parks," Elena announced to break the silence.

"Really? It's one of mine too. Isn't it a little far from where you live?"

"I make the drive because it's so beautiful." Elena's smile was revealing, vulnerable. "My sanctuary."

"Look." Peyton cleared her throat, and attempted a businesslike tone, "I, uh, think you'd be great for this. If you're interested."

"Yes, Peyton. I'm definitely interested." Elena studied Peyton carefully a moment. "So, uhmm, what's—where did this idea come from?"

"Oh, I've had this project on the back burner for—well, forever. My agent kept telling me no one was interested and that I could do it on my own time. But then, while my mother was sick, we really ended up connecting."

Elena smiled sympathetically.

"She and I had had a really rocky relationship—you know, she's very conservative, wasn't excited about my lifestyle choices… very Emily Gilmore. But underneath it all, I realized she was so much more interesting than I ever gave her credit for."

Elena found herself riveted by Peyton's story, her history. "Go on."

"It's just that women are so complex, so multidimensional… I want to dig below, show all our colors…everything that is indelibly female and makes women so…so delicious."

Elena had never heard women spoken about like this before and she wasn't sure if she felt awkward, uncomfortable or simply unsophisticated. "Oh…okay."

"Maybe I'm thinking too broadly. Just you know…the extraordinary essence that makes up woman in all her glory from A to Z."

"It's a wonderful project, Peyton."

Peyton looked at Elena. Smiled. And then Elena's phone rang. She wanted to ignore it but duty called.

"I'm sorry—I've really got to run. Pick up Nash from soccer practice."

They both sat for a moment longer, and then both started talking at the same time, then laughed.

"But, you know, I think I can get together Thursday afternoon. To, you know…keep moving things forward."

"Sure. That'd be great."

"Okay then." Elena stood a moment longer, then awkwardly lifted a hand to wave. "Bye."

"Goodbye."

*

Over the next several weeks Peyton and Elena found themselves meeting briefly for coffee at Pinot Latte, a quick lunch here and there, even several more times at the park, all in an effort to move the Women's Glory Project forward. Even if they both began to notice that they spent less time actually working on the project and more time talking, enjoying one another's company, sitting in the park and feeding the ducks, sharing history and stories, neither seemed to be overly concerned.

It soon became routine for Elena to call Peyton after she had sent Barry off to the church and got Nash and Tori settled at school, to check in and see what her day was like. They'd spend at least a half hour on the phone chatting about pretty much everything and nothing, and then, depending on Peyton's meetings and Elena's family schedule, would invariably find a chunk of time to connect.

"Blimey, Lombard, has it occurred to you that you've gotten literally nothing accomplished and are spending more and more time with this chick?"

"She's not a 'chick' A, and B, we've gotten a lot accomplished," Peyton stated emphatically, even while knowing just as emphatically that more often than not the research she intended to go over with Elena invariably sat on the table between them, whether it was at Pinot Latte, or the park, and several times had never even made its way out of her briefcase as they sat endlessly chatting about other things, exploring their backgrounds, sharing their day, problems, anecdotes.

At almost precisely the same moment across town, Nash noted to his mother, "You realize I haven't seen you when I get home from school for like the last three weeks?"

Elena had been mindlessly folding laundry and suddenly realized she had absolutely no idea what kind of photos she was actually going to take for the project.

"Damn," she whispered under her breath.

"What?" Nash asked, taken aback. "It's not like a crime or anything, just you're never home anymore."

"Well, I guess I've just gotten so busy working on this new project."

"And that's great, Mom. Can't a fella miss his mom?" He peered at her, charming her and she gave him a hug, then ruffled his hair.

"I'm sorry, honey. I'll try not to be gone so much." She had just remembered while folding Barry's T-shirts that she had forgotten yet again to pick up his dress shirts from the dry cleaner.

"Where the hell have you been?" demanded a peeved

Margaret when Peyton picked up the last of her messages as she drove home. "Did you forget we were supposed to get together for dinner Friday at eight? Orson's? Please don't bail. We really need to talk."

It hadn't occurred to either Elena or Peyton that they were spending *too* much time together. And it was only now dawning on them because those around them were making note. The time they spent together rushed by so quickly. What they both knew was that meeting with one another was the one thing they both looked forward to during their day. And, they both also knew, it was the one thing that made them look forward to tomorrow.

We met—of all places—at the dog groomer's," Delilah giggles, her bouffant hair jiggling right along with her. In her mid-sixties Delilah is all frill and jiggle, an aging beauty queen from the South. "We'd both been going there for at least five years—probably even ran into one another a time or two. We both showed dogs in competition—and became fast friends. But we were both married."

"Delilah and I were attracted to one another from the first moment," remarks Gary, mid-fifties, very distinguished, very Stewart Granger. "For years we did the shows together —never acted on it—never even told one another."

"Married almost thirty years and I discover the day my husband passed away that he had been seeing Gary's wife for half of them! Can you even imagine?"

"Yeah, they'd hook up while we were traveling to the shows." Gary glances at Delilah as if to say how could they not have known it, but shrugs. "Don't even waste time resenting it. We had the best time just being together, doing our favorite thing together..."

"And now darling..." Delilah snuggles their Cavalier Spaniel. "Gary and I are happier than we could ever dream possible."

Peyton opened the door and Elena stood there. She was dressed a bit more casually this visit. Rather than wearing her drab plain church wear, Elena was in jeans, and a sky-blue sweater. Instead of her hair being in "the severe Indian braid," as Wave had quipped, adding, "Hell, she looks like bloody Pocahontas! You ever think she lets that thing free?" Elena's hair was now pulled up in a clip, her full thick brown hair falling softly at her shoulders.

"Hey." Peyton realized she was standing there rather foolishly.

"You have a beautiful house, Peyton," Elena remarked, trying to understand Peyton's confused expression.

"Oh…oh thank you. Please, come in."

Peyton gave Elena a brief tour of her family home, explaining that her mother had left her the house, and she had always loved living out in La Canada, far enough away from Los Angeles so she could feel like she was up in the woods, secluded, but close enough to get to meetings and all the stuff that was required for her work.

Elena was impressed with the beautiful home, struck by how differently Peyton had decorated her environment, how masculine the wood tones were, the huge dining room table, the artistic prints, the sage green walls. It was in stark contrast to her own home, which was very plain, very simple, if cluttered. Peyton's home was cluttered in a different way; instead of laundry, books littered the corners. Instead of what Elena always referred to in her head as domestic drab dailyness, Peyton's house bordered on exotic. But not uncomfortably so. It was a completely different kind of "lived in" feel than Elena was used to, but Peyton's style intrigued her.

Peyton nabbed a bottle of wine and two glasses and then directed Elena out to the gazebo where all the work was laid out for them to discuss.

Several hours later, with the sun just beginning to fall, Elena and Peyton lounged comfortably on the outside minicouch as they started a fresh bottle of wine. True to form they had completed remarkably little work, speaking about their families, one story winding to the next, filling in the blanks, exploring one another's universes, eagerly gathering details.

Elena noticed that after several glasses of wine Peyton

had become more relaxed, her body more comfortably settled against one side of the poolside settee, while she sat at the other. She noticed Peyton's hands. Her fingers were long and lean, masculine almost. Strong. She used her hands when she spoke, and Elena found them mesmerizing. "...I thought she'd be good to raise a child with you know...make a family..." Peyton mused. "Guess I was wrong..."

"Trust me, I do understand." Elena looked at Peyton with sympathy. "Barry and I really only have one thing in common and that's our son, so, I know how people get to a place where it's more about the children than about...them."

Peyton glanced at Elena as she took a sip of wine. She seemed so carefree here, it was delightful watching her unwind. Elena sat across from her, and Peyton noted Elena mindlessly playing with the thread upon the throw that covered both their legs as the evening had grown cool. "Sometimes I think I only married Barry to rebel against my parents."

Peyton looked confused. "My father's very old school. Very Indian with a quiet but stern hand. My mother's from Spain, and very Catholic."

"Now that's a lethal combination." Peyton grinned.

"Yes it is!" Elena laughed. "For years I felt like...like a mummy." Elena clasped a hand to her throat. "I felt like I was going to suffocate from their inflexibility—their extreme dedication to ritual and tradition. They even spoke of marrying me off to a distant cousin when I turned eighteen. I couldn't bear it." Elena looked down, sadly. "So...I began to stage my great revolt and—let me tell you when I was accepted at the Academy in London it was almost more than they could handle. What could be worse for my parents than for me to be an actress and marry an actor of all things?"

They both shared a laugh, and Peyton refilled their wineglasses.

"That's where I met him." Elena glanced over to the pool, and Peyton was struck again by how deeply brown and intense Elena's eyes were. "At first I thought I was happy with Barry... he offered me freedom for the first time in my life. We got married...almost right away...actually I got pregnant."

"Ohhhh." Peyton wasn't sure how to acknowledge this intimate detail in Elena's life.

"Yes, shortly after we discovered we were going to have a baby we quickly got married, moved to New York, and it was all very exciting. Nash became my sole focus and he brought me so much joy. Barry was struggling with his acting, and even when we had so very little—my family cut me off until they visited and met their grandchild a few years later—I still felt, well, as happy as I believed possible."

Elena sighed. "But as the years went by, I kept wondering, what's wrong with me? Why don't I feel what everyone else seems to feel? Why was it all so empty? I...I tried to talk to Barry about it...I even asked him once if he wanted a divorce but by then we had moved to LA, Barry had become a pastor and we were already so involved in the church. And, then we lost..."

Elena began to tear up, but quickly covered. "I hit a rough patch..."

Peyton felt Elena's sadness, saw the serious grief in her eyes and knew there was more to this. She looked away and gave Elena the space she needed to continue.

"I don't know...sometimes I think marriage is just a series of mutual compromises that simply become the glue..." Elena sighed again, and then looked directly at Peyton. "But I've never been in love with him."

Peyton could only hold Elena's gaze for so long. She glanced down, then asked, "But he's in love with you?"

"I guess so...I don't know," Elena sighed. "He's in love with the picture."

They both turned to look at the shimmering pool and then Elena turned back to her, stared right into her and said, "I've never been in love."

Again, Peyton found it difficult to deflect Elena's intensity. "You've never been in love?"

"No. I'm nearly forty and it's never happened...I told Tyler I've come to peace with it." They sat in silence for a moment. "Maybe some of us aren't meant to find those soul mates Tyler believes are out there. That we're not destined to find a soul mate this time around," Elena summed up and then touched Peyton's knee. "Oh my gosh…I've just gone on and on. Enough about me. What about you?"

Peyton watched Elena carefully and noted her fragility at the trembling corners of her mouth.

"Come on, Peyton…please, I didn't mean to monopolize the conversation…it's just been so long since I felt…" She looked at her again, direct, "safe I suppose safe is the right word—enough to share this with anyone."

Peyton shook her head. She didn't want the focus shifted. "Don't know about soul mates, but after Margaret…after that…" She tried Southern bravado. "Frankly, my dear, I never want to see another lesbian as long as I live."

Elena laughed and grazed Peyton's hand, holding her fingers there for some time.

"All I really want is a baby." Peyton removed her hand. "To make a family…"

Peyton picked up her wine and after some time glanced at Elena, who was looking directly at her, but with something new, a sort of revelation.

"I feel like I've known you forever."

This time Peyton did not turn from Elena's direct gaze.

"I was a nun for years, with the Sisters of Charity, working at the soup kitchen...and in she comes, looking like the bad side of awful..."

Amelia turns to Jackie. The delicate white nun, Amelia, and the solidly butch and dark African American, Jackie, are a study in absolute opposites. Amelia appears even more pale as she leans toward the dark, tattooed Jackie, who smiles now, but in contrast to Amelia's confidence, appears timid, diffident.

"I got Jackie into treatment, found her a welding job, and got her back on her feet...and somewhere in all of that I fell deeply in love with her." Amelia turns to Jackie, looks at her with deep affection. "But it was against everything I believed in. I prayed, I went into seclusion but nothing, nothing could take her from my mind."

Amelia shakes head, and then speaks so softly she is barely audible. "And then one morning I woke, in the hospital."

"God, I was scared," Jackie pipes in. "You were so pale."

"I had apparently passed out from dehydration. When I came to, there was Jackie. Sitting there, like an angel."

"The janitor at the hospital was in recovery with me. Called me and let me know Amelia was there. I never thought I would see her again...when I did I..." Jackie is overtaken with emotion. Amelia helps her regain composure.

"In that moment, even though my entire life had been devoted to church and the Catholic scripture, I knew my God loved Jackie." Amelia speaks with utter commitment "...And loved me loving Jackie."

Tyler, ensconced in his small but very professional editing bay where he cut all of the stories that he aired as his Soulemetry webisodes, edited this beautiful material together. He was astonished at the physical difference between the two women. There could be no better example of opposites attracting than these two and he found it ironic that the dark Jackie was far more shy and deferential while the pale and slender nun was defiant and confident. Well, he thought, that's what love does. Brings out the best in everyone. As he continued his work he noted out of the corner of his eye that Elena was watching him. When he turned to her, he saw a new and gentle light in her eyes.

Elena had been watching her sweet, wonderful friend, sitting in what he referred to as his "drabs"—jeans and his favorite old alma mater sweatshirt from the Royal Academy. He always dressed so elegantly for the public, but when he worked in production he told her, "I like to play the part. And I do adore comfort." When he looked up at her she smiled, feeling a burst of affection for him.

"If I didn't know you better, I would be asking who this Greek Adonis is who's keeping you from us morning, noon and night."

"It's not a guy, silly," Elena laughed. "It's a woman—you know Peyton—the woman I met at the adoption center? You remember—she showed up at your event."

"Out of thin air, presumably…" He winked.

Elena paid little attention, running on. "She's just so much fun, Tyler. She's interesting, she's got such a different perspective than anyone I've ever known, she's literate, intellectual, but you know, doesn't put on airs or anything. She makes me laugh, and oh, well, Tyler, she makes me forget all the stuff that's so everyday, you know? I think…I think I've met a new best friend."

"Careful glam-puss—I'm your BFF."

"Yes, you will always be my very, very dearest friend, Tyler. It's just with women, you know, it's a little different and I haven't had a good girlfriend in ages."

"So what am I? Chopped liver?"

Elena knew he was teasing her. Tyler nabbed a half-filled wineglass, poured Elena one and grabbed her hand. They headed to their favorite spot in his courtyard. "Now tell me all about her."

As Elena filled Tyler in over the better part of a glass of Merlot, she found herself chattering nonstop, more and more giddy as she described every single thing she and Peyton had done, adding in all the little details, all the fun, the easy laughter, the things they shared in common, how Peyton was so "...she's, I don't know. It's like a very strange mix of vulnerable and yet she seems so strong and self-assured. Confident, like she really knows herself, you know? She's feminine but not like all the other women I know—"

"Yes, she's NOT like all the other women you know," Tyler stated in an *are you kidding me?* voice.

"I mean she's sooo...so sensitive and smart and intellectual—"

"Yes, you've said all of those things any number of times, angel!"

Elena shook her head, "And she's got the best taste—I love for instance the way she's designed and decorated her house, it's bold and interesting, with a sort of I don't know, I just feel so comfortable there—"

"And Martha Stewart to boot."

Elena shook her head at him, at which point Lily showed up.

"Well, then...speaking of exquisite taste in women..."

Lily, in her crisp Doris Day skirt, and black lace shirt, that strategically exposed her cleavage, walked directly up to the effete Tyler and lip-smacked him aggressively right on his lips. She asked without turning to Elena, "Are you getting my man inebriated, Elena?"

"Maybe just a little."

"Good. I'll take advantage of *that* later!"

Elena watched Tyler unable to take his eyes off his woman and she wistfully yearned for just such a connection. She decided to leave them, as they clearly only had eyes for one another.

Elena got up and patted them both on the shoulders. "Don't forget the picnic tomorrow."

"…and the Egyptians actually kissed with noses—I suppose sort of Eskimo fashion—while the Romans kissed one another on the eyes." Tori's eyes were lit with enthusiasm. "Yeah, I just love doing all this research for Tyler, and he said whatever I could get him for his new Soulemetry Calendar—you know, just little trivia bits he'd use and give me like a credit for it on the back of the calendar. Me. Tori Ambrose. I'm going to have a sidebar. I might even be able to get extra credit from school for it!"

Elena nodded without really taking in much of Tori's rambling while Nash sat up and listened to his girlfriend, proud of her prowess.

"Oh and get this, babe." Tori leaned to Nash and gave him a nice long kiss. "Now that roughly burned off three calories, since in the span of a minute you lose twenty-six calories," she motored on, "anyway—the neurotransmitters released during exercise are the same as those released during the state of kissing…so while it might take a long time to lose weight, can you think of a better exercise?"

Nash liked this concept. "Now that's some aerobics I can get behind."

As Tori pondered, a deep frown creased her forehead. "Now the flip side of this whole kissing as exercise thing is that, like, hundreds of bacteria are exchanged in a kiss—so you know…" she extended her hands in a balancing gesture, "…it's all risk-benefit and yeah, all in the name of philematology—that's the actual scientific term used for the study of kissing. Oh and get this, a woman has usually kissed about seventy-nine men before she finally settles and gets married."

"Wonder what it is for men?" Nash considered.

"I don't know but it better not be more than one set of lips for you!"

As the next half hour passed, Nash, clad in his ever-present jeans and long-sleeved blue T which Tori said "brings out your eyes" and Tori, in a multicolored jumpsuit only she could pull off, belted by a tie, lounged on a blanket with a picnic basket, while Elena kept glancing around, setting things just so, then resetting them, checking over her shoulder, full of nervous energy. She too had dressed casually, enjoying wearing jeans, which she simply could not do at the church. She always had to wear what Tori referred to as "church lady couture—one half, conservative, one half drab, one hundred percent BORING!" she'd tease almost every time they headed to services.

But today Elena felt alive, fresh, and she even wore a new shirt she had purchased, a rich lilac, and just as they left the house she had even unbuttoned the top two buttons so that the silk material could fall easily at her chest.

"Wow, risqué," Tori had quipped.

"What's up with her?" Nash glanced at Tori as he watched his mom wiping the picnic blanket, yet again, of invisible debris. Tori shrugged, she had no idea, but was clearly about to offer up more factoids when Peyton walked up with several shopping bags.

"There you are. I was afraid you weren't going to make it." Elena jumped up the moment she saw Peyton, gave her a quick hug. Peyton was dressed casually too, or as Elena thought of Peyton's style in her mind. Peyton dressed in masculine clothing, but it looked so much better on her than a man. It was all part of that look of confidence and a sense of strength, which looked so natural and good on Peyton.

"Sorry I'm late." Peyton put the sacks down and glanced at everyone.

Elena grabbed Nash and practically lifted him to a standing position and Tori popped up as well.

"Peyton this is my son, Nash."

Peyton shook his hand and then turned to Tori. "And you must be Tori."

Tori seemed pleased to have been part of conversation between Elena and Peyton. "And you must be the writer."

Peyton nodded.

"I know everyone on the planet wants to be a writer, and God knows everyone in this town has a script they're peddling. Not me. You know what my perfect job would be?" Tori glanced from Peyton to Elena and back to Peyton again and pronounced in exultation: "The research assistant. I'd do the meanest, deepest, most intimate statistical research on ANY topic and then I would correlate, extrapolate, assign levels of meaning to each and every—"

"And she'd be brilliant at it," Elena interrupted and motioned for Peyton to sit down.

"I'll keep you in mind for my next project," Peyton assured her.

"Really?" Tori was smitten. Nash was checking Peyton over, and Elena caught his grimace. Elena could tell by Nash's face that he planned to reserve judgment about his mother's new friend, even though she'd overheard him say to Tori, "She seems cool."

As the afternoon shifted to early evening, Peyton and Elena discussed different women they believed should be part of the project, each woman representing different traits they both thought were important representations of women at their best. Nash played an informal game of soccer with some other kids. Tori, her head deep into her books, would occasionally offer some germane information about the women that Peyton and Elena were discussing.

"What about firsts?" Peyton asked Elena. "You know, first woman to run for president—"

"That would be Victoria Woodhill—who, by the way, was also the first woman to run a brokerage firm on Wall Street," Tori proudly offered.

Elena grinned. "It might be nice to have a section providing women's firsts."

"Or Sally Ride, the first woman to go into space—can you even imagine? Or Elizabeth Blackwell, the first woman doctor in America, or get this, the first person born in America was Virginia Dare—what a great name for a first! Dare...dare to be..." Tori was caught up in a delirium of facts. "Or the first woman who rode a bicycle around the world—like in the late eighteen hundreds–and she did it like in fifteen months. Can you even get over that?"

"Now how'd she ride a bike on the ocean?" Nash asked mischievously.

"Clearly she couldn't pedal on water, but she did what no one else had ever done, a woman boldly journeying across the world on a bike, mind you, in a man's world. That's pretty incredible."

"It must have taken so much courage," Elena mused.

"Yeah, she apparently left her three kids and husband behind. According to what I could find on the Internet, there was a wager that if she could do it, she'd earn five thousand bucks, which if you equate it to today's dollar, it would be like—well, I'd have to have my calc to figure in all the cost of living and inflationary equivalents—but suffice it to say, a LOT of money in those days. And she had never even ridden a bicycle. The sheer gumption alone!"

"Wow." Elena truly was impressed by this woman's courage, leaving her family behind and merely striking out without any idea of what she might run into—what an adventurer. It was… well, it was inspiring.

Peyton watched Elena as she eagerly learned more about Annie Londonderry—saw the light of intrigue and adventure burn in her eyes, saw a resigned wistfulness in her face that saddened Peyton a bit.

"That was sort of her riding name." Tori said, continuing to regale them with more facts. "She was apparently amazing at self-promotion and wrote the most fascinating recounts of her expedition…"

Peyton felt relaxed and at ease sitting among Elena and her family, thinking that she should spend more time like this, out in the world, doing things instead of—as Wave pointed out a few weeks earlier—being endlessly "holed up like a little spider in her web, all wrapped up with no one's company—lovely company mind you, but face it, even you have a limit." She felt comfortable with Elena and her lovely family and it made her wonder even more about how they all worked together, what their family dynamics were like. And then she wondered what the pastor might be like and it suddenly occurred to her that no one seemed to think it odd that he wasn't present.

As if Elena knew Peyton was thinking all these things, she turned to look at her and Peyton felt the pull of her look, the full impact of the exchange in Elena's tender smile. Deep. Sweet.

Tyler came up from behind and whooshed the startled Elena up into his arms.

"Told you we'd make it! Miss Thang here just had to do some last-minute contracts, but better late than never."

Lily, clad in park-wear Prada, shook Peyton's hand, claiming to remember her from Tyler's Soulemetry event, and then plopped herself beside Tori and pulled out her traveling chess game. Tori was thrilled. "Set 'em up. You're goin' down this time!"

As the sun began to fall, Tyler opened a bottle of wine, poured glasses for the grownups and allowed Nash a little sip, to which Elena shook her head, but allowed, "Just one." And then Elena's son, lying next to his mom, took out his DES game and began to play while Lily and Tori were deeply engaged in their chess game and verbal sparring.

"Did you know that chess is the only board game that the International Olympic Committee recognizes as a mind sport?" Tori mused.

"What I know," Lily thought carefully before she moved her next piece, "is that chess is the one game that prepares you for the boardroom, disciplines takeover strategies and keeps you razor sharp."

"Ahhh, I love when you get poetic, darling," Tyler teased, and then continued to regale Peyton with Elena's past: "Yeah, she'd walk through the halls and the seas would split. People were mesmerized by her very presence and all the guys, well they would be silly fools, trying to be clever, dashing, intellectual— whatever they thought might appeal to her."

"Tyler, you're exaggerating!" Elena interjected.

"Hardly, my dear, you have to admit you caused quite a stir with your stunning exoticness, that inspiring accent and then, of course, Elena doesn't seem to have any idea how incredibly gorgeous she is—"

Peyton turned to Elena, who became quite flustered.

"—and, of course, that was half the draw. We were doing *Same Time, Next Year* and Elena was simply off the charts playing—oh, what's her name...oh yeah, Doris. She was so funny. Who knew? Right? Everyone thought she was so austere, so forbidden and here she was not only dramatically carrying the play but funny as hell."

Tyler looked at his dear friend and then back to Peyton. "She

110

really had some chops—a genuine chemistry that really held the audience captive—but the moment 'the mysterious Indian woman' was off stage, she'd retreat —so quiet and graceful in her allure because she was so unaware of her own beauty."

Peyton saw the genuine care and affection Tyler felt for Elena as she shoved him gently to stop. "Okay, that's enough, Tyler. Really!" He put his arm around her, gave her a quick squeeze.

"I second that," Lily snorted. "Although, Elena, you know I totally agree!"

Nash, tired of his game, rolled over and scooted his way toward Tori, who was in deep concentration. But Nash couldn't help himself, began to play with her hair, nuzzled her cheek and finally went in for a quick kiss.

"Checkmate!" Lily pounced "I win!"

"Ughhghg..."

"That, my dear," Lily informed, sharp and incisive, "is what happens when you take your eyes off the ball."

"Please, darling, don't eviscerate the poor child."

Tyler turned to Tori, hugged her with paternal affection. Peyton soon realized he was the father figure for all. How and where did Barry fit in?

"I'm fine..." Tori's voice was small. "Just, you know, possibly damaged for life..." Then she snuggled deep into Tyler's arms and glanced from Tyler to Peyton. "Hey Ty...tell Peyton the story."

"Yeah," Nash joined enthusiastically, "tell her the story."

Peyton looked confused. Elena smiled. Tyler looked around, eager. Lily was in a great mood. After all, she'd just won.

"Tyler has all these soul mate stories that he's been collecting for years," Elena explained. "Even when we were in school together, he'd ask couples how they met. I think he kept this grand catalogue of every love story he's ever heard."

"I have indeed," Tyler agreed proudly.

"And he does these wonderful webisodes with them on the Internet," Tori piped in.

"As soon as I make enough money," Lily joined in, "I'm going to buy him his own little network. Then we're going to monetize this sucker. Soulemetry is not just his religion—I believe it could be very lucrative."

"Sweetheart, you can run numbers and budgets all you like, but love is not for sale."

"Go ahead, silk pie," Lily purred, "...it's one of my favorites too."

"Okay then." It was clear Tyler was as eager to tell the story as they were to hear him tell it. "So, this earnest young writer comes to Hollywood to make his mark—you know, all very Youngblood Hawk, and rather soon, he realizes real life is seldom the thing of novels. To wash away the grime of his day he drives up to the Mulholland overlook..."

Tyler paused dramatically, acting out the story with his own inimitable gesturing. "It's gorgeous...the view is stunning, but every single time he drives up to his special spot, he sees this ridiculously disenfranchised vehicle—an ancient VW—a real eyesore to his epic ambitions. Well, he thought it had been simply left in the dust for history to dispense with it, that's how ugly it was."

Elena turned to watch Peyton listen to the story, noticed the gentle smile in her eyes, how intense they were, and realized that was one of the things she so liked about Peyton. Her intensity.

"Fast forward ten years. He's at a dinner party. Host is a good friend of his. By now he's been married and divorced twice since his meditation days. Host introduces him to this woman who—get this—turns out to be the agent's assistant that shoved the hero's script through the slush pile."

They're all focused on him in rapt attention.

"He thanks her profusely, tells her he almost gave up. And would have if not for this great site on Mulholland that renewed him. But the one thing that ruined it for him was this clunker VW. The woman stops him in the middle of the story. Did he, by chance, drive a green Lexus?"

"No..." Peyton started to get the picture. "No. Don't even say it."

"Yes." Tyler nodded. "The owner of the clunker VW was the very assistant who gave him his start. She used to drive to the overlook to get away from her overbearing boss." He smacked his head. "They both drove up to the overlook as their only solace from this meat grinder of a city—and all these years later they meet, their fortunes already entwined. Five weeks later—"

"Married," Elena said in unison with Tyler. They all laughed as they good-naturedly watched Peyton's amazement at this favorite story.

"Wow...how amazing is that?" Peyton was blown away by the bizarre occurrences and coincidences in the story.

"He's got a million more like it," Elena offered.

"So, what do you think?" Peyton asked Elena, then quickly turned to Tyler.

"She just thinks I'm a big ol' sap, given to romantic daydreaming. But I tell you, you cannot dream up coincidences like that one. Nope, when it's meant to be..." he glanced at Lily, "...it's meant to be."

"A coincidence is when God performs a miracle and decides to remain anonymous," Tori informed them all, breaking the silence.

"Actually it's when we are given choices and choose the right one—that's the miracle!"

Elena glanced at Peyton, and was unable to take her eyes off her. Peyton caught Elena's gaze, and could not deny its sheer intensity. She felt the flush up her neck and was happy that dusk had fallen. She quickly glanced away.

*

That night when Peyton got home she felt deliciously tired. She had had so much fun with Elena and her family. She thought Nash and Tori were adorable and it was clear how much Tyler and Lily all belonged as a family unit. Maybe that's why she felt so good. Just being with a family, having a sense of family. Of belonging.

She yawned, stretched then thought she might as well check her e-mails. There were sure to be some details she needed from her agent, but the second she saw the ewintersholylight@mail.com she immediately opened it.

Hey Peyton... I just wanted to tell you how fun it was to have you meet my family. And to

say...I feel so blessed to have met you. For the
first time in a long time I feel I'm on the path
I'm supposed to be on. I'm so thrilled to be
taking pictures again!

Peyton felt a rush of warmth spread over her as she read
Elena's e-mail. Then, just as quickly she tried to ignore the
quelling in her chest, the dampening of her spirits. *Don't even
go there...* Shook her head, and instead of responding to Elena's
e-mail, deleted it.

*

"What's with you, ants-in-your-pants?" Wave walked across
the street from her house with a baggie of coffee. "How in the
hell did you of all people run out of coffee?"

"Didn't quite make it to the store this morning." But Wave
wasn't listening nor was she buying whatever Peyton was selling
her as she took in Peyton's appearance, the elegant and refined
pants and silk shirt she was wearing. Peyton's thick, naturally
wavy hair, which she always wore loose and easy just past her
shoulders, was put up in a loose chignon. With a quite attractive
barrette, no less.

"Sooo, what's with the Rachel Zoe makeover?"

Peyton shook her head. "I...you need to go. I have a business
meeting."

Wave cocked her head and asked in a more serious tone,
"Business meeting? Here? On a Sunday?"

"Yes, now love you, mean it...GO!"

At that moment a red van pulled up and Elena emerged.

Wave glanced at Peyton then back to Elena.

"Hi. It's Wave, isn't it?" Elena extended her hand graciously.

"Yes, that would be me." Wave peered at Elena, then, "Oh,
so you must be the business...*meeting...* Got it."

Elena looked a bit flustered as Peyton pushed Wave to go, then
turned to Elena. "Why don't you go in, make yourself at home."

Elena nodded to Wave and uncertainly made her way into
Peyton's house. Before Peyton could move Wave put her hands

on her shoulders and stopped her in her tracks. "When I said do stuff that feels good I didn't mean do married straight stuff!"

"Don't," Peyton warned, nudging Wave to go already.

"Blimey Peyton." Wave shook her head. "You are to call me the second she leaves!"

When Peyton entered the house she saw that Elena was glancing through her book, *Trust, Who Needs It?—An Agoraphobic's Memoir*. Elena turned it over, studying the back cover author's photo and reading the jacket copy.

Peyton walked up, politely but firmly nabbed the book from Elena's hands.

"Is that you—I mean your story?"

Peyton cleared her throat, nodded. "Yes, that would be me."

"Wow...I would never have imagined. After all this time we've spent together."

Elena looked at Peyton, assessing her. She looked so lovely with her hair up, and it was interesting that Elena was quite suddenly aware that Peyton was a woman. She seemed so—not masculine—but so not overtly girlish, that it took a moment for Elena to get used to this new look, get her bearings. She also wondered how she could have been around Peyton all this time and not known something to be so inherently part of her makeup.

Peyton shifted uncomfortably, feeling like she was under inspection, then angry at herself for overdressing. She had just wanted to feel professional, and capable, when she woke, earlier, and realized Elena would be meeting her later that morning. But now she felt a bit foolish. She cleared her throat and Elena walked closer.

"I guess I've always thought of an agoraphobic like somebody in *Grey Gardens*—you know—huddled up in a dark room with a bunch of cats."

"Yeah, well." Peyton's voice was deprecating. "All the new meds make us far more acceptable."

"So..." Elena peered at Peyton as if trying to figure it all out and add this new piece into the mix. "How does it affect you?"

"Trust me, you don't want to know."

"I do though. It's fascinating."

"Not so much." But Peyton could see that Elena was not going to accept her response. "Okay…I'm a little OCD, a little germ phobic, toss in a couple of other things…but mostly I need to do rituals to feel comfortable…uhmm—not like satanic stuff, or anything—I…uhmm…" Peyton found herself completely self-conscious.

Elena moved closer yet, put a gentle hand to Peyton's forearm. "Really I would never have known. Clearly!" Elena smiled, as evidence that she didn't know.

Peyton smiled bleakly. Dead silence. They both became uncomfortable. Then Elena smiled again, considering her. "Can I make a suggestion? You need a new author's photo. That," Elena gestured to the one on the book, "does you no justice."

"It's not what I look like in my line of work. It's my words."

"Nonsense. I'm going to do a new author's photo for you. My gift."

Peyton grinned. *Okay…I'm game.* Elena smiled back, fully.

"Uhmm, why don't we get to work. I have all the research right in these files."

Several hours later, while they were deep into a stack of articles and photos, they were both surprised by a sharp knock at the door. Before Peyton could get up to answer it, Margaret breezed through the front door with Chinese takeout in hand. Peyton could see that she had dressed for this impromptu visit in very snug jeans, and a soft and extremely low-cut forest green blouse which accentuated her blond hair and blue eyes.

"Sorry I'm late, traffic was a nightmare—" She broke off as she saw Elena and Peyton sitting closely together on the floor. "I'm sorry. Am I interrupting?"

Peyton looked stunned. Elena glanced from her to Margaret, noting the familiarity with which this woman entered, that she was quite attractive, and like Peyton, nothing like the women she was used to dealing with. Suddenly Elena felt like a small child in a world of grownups. She wasn't certain what the protocol was here and the silence had become deafening. Elena stood, eager to meet another of Peyton's friends. "Hi. I'm Elena."

"Margaret."

Elena's face fell momentarily, then she recovered nicely,

116

reverted to her role as pastor's wife and shook Margaret's hand as if she were one of the faceless congregants. "Oh, Margaret. So nice to meet you."

Margaret turned to Peyton. "And this is Peyton I presume?" The tone was light, but with an edge.

"What are you doing here?" Peyton could not hide the irritation in her voice as she got up, grabbing some of the files with her.

"I know how crazy you've been and on deadline, so I brought you dinner."

Elena began to gather her things. "I...I've got to get going anyway."

"Oh, don't let me bother you two. I'll hang in the bedroom," Margaret said with faux graciousness, "until you're done. Take your time. I brought a book." And then looking at Elena she conspiratorily added, "She's always working...so I've learned how to entertain myself until she comes out of her writer's cloud."

"Oh, I thought we were..." Peyton's voice was thin as she questioned Elena, who was scheduled to be there until seven.

"No. I mean Nash will be home soon, so, well..." Elena put a stack of papers into her briefcase, gathered her purse and with a brief glance to Margaret, said, "Nice to meet you. Peyton, I'll call you."

She gave Peyton a quick hug, but as they parted, Peyton could see the confusion, and hurt in Elena's eyes.

*

Elena picked at her dinner, deep in thought as Nash wolfed down his burger, Tori waxed poetic on one of her rambles and Barry sat proofing the church's newsletter. *Why? Why was that woman there? Were they seeing one another again? And if so, why hadn't Peyton told her?*

"...and take Julia Child. I mean, we had to do a report on famous chefs, and here's the thing I bet you don't know about Ms. 'let's slice the chicken so it looks like a reindeer,'" Tori mimicked the high frequency dialogue of the infamous culinary star. "But while she ended up being famous for her gastronomic genius she was actually once a spy. Yeah, worked in the Office of Strategic Services."

Tori's voice drilled into her consciousness while she attempted to understand what had happened earlier at Peyton's. But once again Tori was at it, "...so naturally I had to look up other folks that were leading double lives. I mean how cool would that be... you know, because on some level, I sort of lead a double life. Anyway, there are the big ones, Benedict Arnold, Mata Hari, et cetera, et cetera—but it's the ordinary people I was fascinated by. What would make Mr. Joe Average become a spy or lead a double life—what would compel their actions? I really wanted to get into their heads..."

Elena knew that Tori was unlikely to stop and began to feel the food congeal in her stomach. A wave of nausea washed over her. It simply did not make sense to her. Was Peyton keeping secrets from her? Or was it the simple fact that it was none of her business? Elena sighed as Tori's voice continued to plague her, realizing that what Peyton did with her emotional life had nothing to do with her.

"...Well, greed for one...in my research I found a number of men, naturally—"

"Hey, we're not all bad!" Nash broke in.

"I don't think greed is a specifically male issue, Nash," Tori resumed, "it's just that women didn't hold those high-end government positions, so they didn't get the chance to sell classified info to the KGB. And, you'll be happy to note that the other reason for leading a double life was love."

Elena stopped to listen. "Like this dude who was a geologist by profession, Clarence King, who actually convinced this African American woman, Ada Copeland—who happened to be a former slave, mind you, but had moved north to New York—that he was, in fact, black. They got married, he led this life as an African American railroad worker and gave himself a completely new identity as James Todd, and when he'd go back home, he'd return to his old life as Clarence King, geologist at large—roaming from Wyoming to California. He had like five kids with Ada and it was only on his deathbed that he wrote her a letter telling her the truth."

They had all stopped eating, stunned by this revelation. Tori glanced at their surprised expressions, then smiled. "See? Tyler's right. When you find true love, you'll pretty much believe anything!"

"That was…" Elena's felt like she might be getting sick, "uhmm…interesting, Tori. I'm sorry, I need to excuse myself."

"You okay, El?" Barry asked.

"Yeah, just a little light-headed."

"Where were you today? I tried to reach you all afternoon." Barry barely glanced up from the newsletter.

"I…I've been working on the project."

"Hmmm?"

"You know, Mom's doing her photography." Nash jumped in to bolster his mom. "Isn't that great, Dad? That Mom has a project that's just for her?"

Barry looked up from his work, now, glanced about at them all. Then smiled. "Absolutely. I think your mom should have her hobbies—and as long as everything's humming along smoothly, I think it's great."

Nash frowned and was about to say something more, but Elena had no desire for further discussion about a project she was no longer sure about at this very moment. "You need to get to your homework. Tori, can you help him out with his history?"

Tori smiled. "Sure Momma Bear. No problemo."

The two kids left the kitchen and Elena began to clean up. She felt Barry watching her, waiting for him to say something, but when she turned he had buried his head back into the newsletter. She sighed. Back to it.

*

Peyton sat at Pinot Latte wondering if Elena was going to show up. They had previously arranged a time to go over some chapter break ideas, but after Margaret had shown up, unexpectedly there had been a silence that felt like estrangement. None of the usual daily e-mails back and forth, no phone calls for the past three days. Elena was a half hour late, so Peyton had to assume she wasn't going to show. She was just finishing the last of her coffee when she saw Elena's van parking across the street. She watched her sit for a moment before she exited the car. Peyton watched as Elena made her way to the café. She was wearing one of her "church outfits," which Peyton hadn't seen for the last few weeks. Even in her drab clothing, Peyton saw Elena's beauty, and it suddenly made her feel as if a whole other person lived inside the Elena that was presented to the world, a whole other life she could have had, then stopped herself from thinking any further.

Elena walked up slowly, almost diffidently, and sat down. "Sorry I'm late... I..."

"Sure. No problem." Peyton cleared her throat, played with her teaspoon.

Elena toyed with a napkin. "Sorry, I probably should have called this meeting off. I didn't have time to do the research we talked about. Got caught up in a big fundraiser for the church and Nash has had soccer practice three times this week and... they're in the playoffs and..." Elena's conversation slowly lost steam.

Elena glanced up at Peyton who was looking off out the window. The handsome jawline that Elena always found intriguing was tightening, as if Peyton was stressed. She so badly wanted to see that smile of Peyton's that made Elena feel like everything was going to be okay, but she appeared as ill at ease as Elena felt, but when she turned to her her expression was unreadable.

"If you're too busy, that's fine," Peyton replied. "Look, Elena, if there is too much going on in your life, don't worry about it. I...I totally know how it is when you just have too much—"

"No!" Elena pounced back, then stopped. "It's just...well, I guess I don't understand."

"I'm just saying if you don't have time for this project, it's totally okay. Look, I don't have kids, or a husband and a life outside of my work right now—I can't expect you to have the kind of time..."

"It looks very much like you have a life outside of this project," Elena interjected.

Peyton looked at her confused. "What?"

"It's none of my business, really."

They sat a moment in silence. "It's just...I just thought..." Elena tugged at her braid. "She hurt you so badly."

"Oh..." Peyton finally realized they were talking about Margaret. "Oh, God, Elena. I'm sorry she interrupted us the other day."

"I don't understand. Are you seeing her, now?"

"Seeing her?" Peyton wasn't quite sure how to explain the intricacies and multiple levels of dysfunction of previous lesbian relationships to Elena. "It's not that. She's been wanting to try again and I...I've been on the fence. But I..."

Elena waited eagerly.

"I just don't want anything to get in the way of my adopting. I...I just need to stay focused on that."

"Well, sure. That's exactly right. You should stay focused on that." Elena responded. "So, how is that going?"

Awkward silence. The truth of the matter was Peyton had skipped several of the adoption class meetings in order to connect with Elena. She had been so busy otherwise, she hadn't returned, even though her desire for a child was still every bit as strong as it had been from the start.

"Well, I guess I—we," she smiled, "have been busy. I thought you had found another agency. Any luck?"

"Yes and no. I found an agency through our church, but... well, I haven't really followed up." She suddenly felt guilty.

"You okay?" Peyton asked. Elena looked at her, into her, as only she seemed to be able to do, and suddenly they both laughed.

"I guess we've both been so busy with this," Elena put out her hands to express their connection and project, "that we've been letting other things...slide?"

"I'm sorry, that's the last thing I wanted this to do."

"Are you kidding, Peyton?" Elena spoke fervently, "This has been one of the best things that's ever happened to me. I feel... feel alive. Being with you," she searched for the right way to put it, "makes me feel good. Happy. And I probably needed a break from all that other stuff anyway."

Elena smiled and Peyton took a long breath, smiled too.

"I'm so hungry," Elena stammered. "Do you want to get something to eat?"

Sometime later they finished a late lunch, sharing more laughter, the previous awkwardness gone.

"My husband never likes to spend time like this."

"Like…what?"

"Just being. Being silly. Giggling. We're like that couple over there." Elena turned to a couple in their mid-fifties sitting completely uninvolved with one another. "You know…where they've lived their entire lives together but they have nothing to say to one another."

"Hmmmm." Peyton pursed her lips in sympathy.

"Is it different with you?"

Peyton was still confused.

"You and Margaret? Or women?"

Peyton smiled bleakly and Elena ran on, "It's just that I never really thought about what it would be like to be in a relationship with a woman. You know women are so much more talkative anyway. I mean I have a really good friend, Diana, from the church, and she and I spend all our time chattering away, so I'm just wondering, is that part of the draw? Having someone to talk to?"

Peyton smiled. "Just because it's a relationship between two women doesn't mean it isn't necessarily dysfunctional, Elena."

"Not mutually exclusive, hmmm?" Elena smiled back.

"Well, when I was young and idealistic I believed in the premise that the pairing between two women who are driven by emotion rather than sexual conquest would make their coupling somehow more 'worthy.'"

"I can see that. Women just feel things differently."

"Apparently not. Lesbians are just like everyone else. Trust me, they have absolutely no claim to morality."

"So…what about you and…*her?*"

But before Peyton could answer, Wave walked up while they were absorbed in their conversation. She cleared her throat to make her presence known. "Ladies!"

"Oh, hi, Wave."

"Elena…" Wave surveyed the situation and with a subtle

smirk added, "I'd ask if you need anything, but it looks like your cups runneth over."

As an awkwardness ensued, Elena's phone rang, Barry on the other end.

Both Wave and Peyton tried to act nonchalant as it was clear Elena had lost track of time and was being chastised by the bellowing voice on the other end, "...over an hour and now he has no way to get home!"

"Oh my gosh, Barry—I'm so sorry. No, I just completely forgot. I'll be right over." Elena began to gather her things and then looked up at them both apologetically. "I'm so bad. I completely forgot Barry was bringing his mentee for dinner, and I thought Nash had a way home from soccer practice, but his pal didn't show up..." She realized she was babbling. "I'm so sorry... I have to run. I'll see you Tuesday," Elena added as she got up, waved cursorily to both of them and dashed out the door.

Wave watched as Elena left and then turned to Peyton, shook her head.

"It's not like that."

"You, my friend, are playing the oldest and most tragic game in the book." Wave pushed Peyton aside and sat next to her in the booth, put a hand on her dear friend's arm. "Lonely housewife meets interesting and quite wonderful lesbo to take a midlife walk on the wild side."

"My God, Wave can you say ultra straight? Can't a girl have friends for God's sake?"

"Trust me, doll, you two are heading for that fork in the road —and once you hit the road less traveled there's going to be one hell of a tarry mess."

*

Elena sat with a group of the church women at their Church of Holy Light's annual planning retreat. Every year she had girded herself for the full weekend of meetings dedicated to the following year's activities, fundraisers and special classes, which ended up being meeting after meeting of endless chatter with very little resolution. This year it seemed doubly difficult to prepare herself mentally and to attend all the sundry and picayune topics.

Millie was yattering at such velocity and volume that Elena found herself with a spinning headache. Millie was in her three-piece Ann Taylor suit. It was a deep crimson, what she called her "battle suit," which she wore during the most important meetings. She continued to issue orders to various of her henchmen, then returned to the "central and most global need for funding. All our efforts must lead to one goal. We must support the most important work we have been blessed to do for God, our father. And all this should culminate in our largest tithing event—our annual fall fundraiser to support whoever's leading the charge on banning gay marriage."

"But I thought we had voted to stay away from the political elements of this battle," Diana pleaded.

"I know we have a strict policy and a politics protocol—after all, I'm the one that designed our policy points. But this is just too big of a fight and we have to be there to help those in the trenches fighting on our behalf. This is the one issue where we must all band together, gather all our resources. Do you have any idea how wealthy...the...those well, the men are, anyway?"

Elena's head swiveled to her as all the other women excitedly jumped in.

"Do you have any idea what they refer to themselves as?" Millie continued, her eyes too wide, her voice too shrill. "The Purple Mafia." This was followed by a whisper, "You know...the Gay Mafia. Now why do you think they use a term like that? Why, they know themselves that they're evil!"

Elena quietly excused herself. She couldn't even take in the words Millie was spouting—she just knew for the sake of her head not exploding off her shoulders that she had to exit.

She found a nice lonely willow tree to sit by, removed her phone from her purse, looked to see if she had any messages. She was about to pop the phone back into the purse, but glanced back at Millie's rigid back as she organized her minions. She retrieved her phone and began to text.

*

Peyton lounged on her sofa at the gazebo, looking at the last proofs of the photos she and Elena had taken, a variety of 8 x 10s, not only going over the shots, but the events around photographing several of the women Peyton had interviewed for the book. One was a serious bodybuilder and aerialist whose musculature was sculpted of the most exquisite lines; another was a pregnant mom; and the third was a series of photos Elena had taken of an eighty-seven-year-old spiritualist/healer who worked with disabled children.

Elena had taken photos of this master healer teaching these adorable children by utilizing a sort of gentle laying on of hands, a new way to move their knobbled knees and palsied limbs. What made all this more amazing is that the woman had been blind since she was four and was now in her late eighties. Elena had captured the gritty beauty of the woman's arthritic and gnarled hands upon the soft children's flesh. The entire photo shoot held a spirituality and a poignancy that Peyton had never witnessed before. Elena had revealed so much of her own self in the manner in which she had depicted the older woman's vocation with her own avocation and it truly impressed Peyton.

Peyton thought back to the previous week when Elena had taken the shots. "You were so good with her and the kids," she had told her.

"Oh my gosh, Peyton. They were such a joy to shoot."

And Peyton remembered the electric excitement in Elena's eyes, and wondered how she could ever have given up something that she so loved.

Peyton glanced through the photos one more time, laid them to one side, sighed and closed her eyes momentarily.

Peyton's phone buzzed. She shook off sleep, trying to clear her head. She picked up the phone and read the text:

Oh my god...I feel so out of place here. Elena.

Peyton stretched, trying to clear the bugs from her head, stared at the text a moment.

R U Ok? Peyton texted her back.
These people feel like strangers.

Is it possible for u to go home? Peyton shot back.

No. :(But looking forward to R photo shoot Friday.

For the next half hour Peyton tried to support Elena's efforts at the retreat, giving her as much positive feedback as she could, and then suddenly Elena's texts stopped, no goodbye even.

*

"Where the heck have you *been?*" Barry walked up behind Elena, terrifying her. "I've been trying to find you everywhere. We're supposed to be hosting cocktails in ten minutes. You're not even changed."

Elena looked up at him, exasperated.

"What?" he asked, exasperated right back. "What's with you?"

He sat next to her and studied her for a moment, then said, his voice calm and proficient, as if he were addressing one of his parishioners, "Everything okay here? Tell me what you're feeling. Break it down for me."

"Ughhh…."

"I'm sorry." Barry cleared his throat, studied his wife. "Okay…what's going on, El?"

"Don't you ever get…get *sick* of all this?"

Taken aback, he took some moments to consider her question. "Well, sure I do. We all do. But, it's just temporary." He put a hand on her arm. "We all have our bad days."

She shrugged him off her, then felt badly, took his hand in hers. "I'm sorry…guess I'm missing Nash."

"Trust me, he's not missing us." He winked at her. She smiled back. He was probably right about that. Nash and Tori had gone off to spend the weekend with Tyler and Lily. Tyler had purchased tickets to take the kids to *Wicked* presumably to give Elena and Barry a bit of a break. When Elena had dropped the kids off, Tyler had made a sarcastic comment about her "mysterious disappearance." Tori had jumped in to explain that "Momma Bear is on a project. She's shooting again."

"Do tell!" Tyler insisted, his tone teasing, as, of course, he already knew she had been spending copious amounts of time with Peyton "working on the Women's Glory Project." Lily had arched a brow. Tyler smiled enthusiastically and Nash summed everything up with "Yeah, this is a great opportunity for mom to have something of her own."

"Isn't that the truth!" Tyler heartily agreed.

Elena was thrilled that Tyler and Lily had the kids this weekend. It was an opportunity for Nash to have a break from all the zealotry. She wasn't sure how long it was going to be before Nash and Barry arrived at an unresolvable stalemate around the church, Barry's role in it, and the resentments Nash harbored toward all the hypocrisy he rebelled more and more against. She feared a huge falling out in the not too distant future.

"Elena!" Barry snapped. She shook her head, rubbed her throbbing temples as Barry's voice grew tight. "Look, I've got to lead the evening prayer now, and then we have to host this thing, so are you able to do this?"

He looked intently at her, his expression not quite pleading. She nodded silently.

After the endless cocktail hour, an even more endless banquet dinner, Elena was completely exhausted from all the smiling, idle chitchat, earnestness and fanaticism that had all but echoed from the walls. She had a teeming headache.

Now she and Barry were in bed, and as he read his notes for his sermon the following Sunday morning, Elena got out of bed and escaped into the bathroom.

She felt a little guilty that she had put the phone in the bathroom to charge because she had done so with the express purpose of being able to text Peyton later:

Sorry I had to dash—unexpected interruption... But I want to thank you, P... U make me feel like I can get through anything.

She waited a moment. Then hit Send.

*

127

Peyton walked up to the front door, glanced about, uncertain. Was she really doing this? Before she could knock, or decide not to, Elena opened the door. Peyton smiled.

They both felt a bit awkward. After all, Peyton had never seen Elena's world. Almost all of their exchanges had taken place at Peyton's home, Pinot Latte, at the park or a photo shoot.

"Hey." Peyton shuffled.

"Please, come in."

Elena gave her an extremely brief tour. There wasn't much to show. Nash's very fifteen-year-old-boy room cluttered with posters of soccer players, the occasional band photo and a collage of photos Elena apparently had taken as a walk down memory lane for him and Tori. Down the hall was Tori's guest room, feminine, the bed piled with Tori's clothes, but when they reached the closed master bedroom door Elena merely pointed at it, and then they were quickly in the kitchen, which was separated only by an arch from the dining room and conjoined living room.

On the dining room table, Elena had placed a variety of Danish, which she offered Peyton. "Wasn't sure if you'd be hungry before the shoot."

Peyton tried to be polite. "Nah...I'm fine. Really. I just finished swimming and had a big lunch. But thank you. For going to all this trouble."

"Well, then..." Elena looked expectantly at Peyton. "We should begin."

Elena's garage/studio was cramped, but served its purpose. In the space existed two universes. One side was comprised of the usual garage paraphernalia, shelves of hammers, bolts, a room fan, boxes, clutter. And on the other side, a sheer set of drapes had been set up to cover both corners of the wall, one serving as a backdrop, the other as a framing wall, where many beautiful shots had been hung—photos of Nash, Tori, scenic and artistic shots.

Elena finished setting up her lights as Peyton milled around studying the photos. Barry was only in a couple of family photos. He seemed to be absent from Elena's world. Peyton wondered how that must feel. Then realized that her relationship with Margaret wasn't all that different. You just sort of walked through the day, or as Wave had described it in a droll robotic tone, "…on autopilot, spread legs, insert fingers. Come. Now."

"Okay you," Elena interrupted Peyton's thoughts and stated with finality. "Sit."

On her turf Elena felt more confident, more in control. For the first time, perhaps, she felt equal to Peyton, not just like a mom, or an ordinary housewife in comparison with a professional writer who traveled and saw exotic sites and lived in an entirely different world than she, who did not have to mind the mundane—the church meetings, trips to the dry cleaners, sack lunches. Finally, she felt as if she could offer something to Peyton that was more exceptional than all that and it made her feel a little giddy.

She stopped for a moment, considering her subject, returned to Peyton, bent to unbutton her shirt, loosening it to expose more of her neck. She reflected on her handiwork. Yes, better.

But something still was bothering her. Gently Elena curled the hair about Peyton's face.

Peyton's jaw tightened. She slowly looked up. Elena's eyes lasered into her own, but Peyton did not drop the gaze.

Elena swallowed, then backed away, frowning, busying herself with the shoot.

"Do you mind if I ask you something?" Elena asked as she brushed on finishing touches of makeup. "It's rather personal."

"Oh-oh." Peyton mocked terror.

"How…well, how did you know you were gay?"

"How did you know you were straight?" Peyton crisply snapped back her collar.

"No!" Elena commanded. Shrugging, Peyton left the shirt open. Elena considered her lighting, then Peyton. "Well…did you know from the very beginning?"

"No…not really. I did the whole straight thing until my early twenties. But then, I fell head over heels for a…a photographer actually."

KA-THUMP! The lamp stand slid from Elena's fingers, making a loud clatter which scared them both. She giggled nervously, then recovering, responded wryly, "Hmmm. Yes, well…we can be very deep."

Elena slowly moved back to Peyton, cleared her throat, then swept a makeup brush over Peyton's forehead, bent to look closer at Peyton's face.

"What about you..." Peyton murmured.

Their eyes locked a moment then Elena dropped the gaze quickly, reset a bounce flag. "I didn't know I was supposed to be anything but straight."

"No schoolgirl crushes?" Peyton affected an upper English accent. "No Royal Academy theatrical experimentation?"

"No. Nothing." Elena leaned over to gently tousle Peyton's hair, and again, their eyes wove a gentle dance of hide-and-seek.

"I never even kissed a girl. With my upbringing...well, it really never occurred to me," Elena offered, then, challenging, "guess I'm a square."

"Maybe you're just straight."

Elena was struck by those words, losing her balance, and then regained her footing. "Would you turn your head to the light, yes, no, a little to the left. Just there. Good. Now relax."

Elena looked through her lens. Suddenly Peyton looked different to her. She didn't know why, perhaps it was the safety of being behind the camera, but Peyton appeared even more attractive, more handsomely beautiful, with those piercing green eyes, the square jaw, those perfectly shaped lips...

Elena realized she was not breathing. Her heart thudded in her chest. She nearly dropped her camera as it dawned on her, very clearly and remarkably, that she found Peyton very attractive. Magnetic. Radiant even.

To settle herself, Elena adjusted the lighting.

"Do you mind if I move around a little?" Peyton asked, feeling uncomfortable. She hated having the focus on her, and was keenly aware of the camera. And Elena.

As Elena turned to respond, Peyton saw Elena bathed in the halo of her own lighting, not unlike the sun flare in the park.

But Elena wasn't clear what Peyton had said, because she was still mesmerized by this new way in which she was seeing the woman before her.

"Pardon me?"

But Peyton literally could not speak. Because in that very moment she too saw Elena in a new light, her compelling beauty, felt the sweet twist in her stomach and she knew—it was not a light she was going to allow in.

As the shoot gathered speed and momentum, Peyton became more and more stiff, because every moment that Elena came close to her Peyton could feel what she did not want to feel. And as Elena snapped shot after shot, she could not tell why she felt such compulsion toward this woman. But it was undeniable. The draw. Elena kept trying to push it from her, unable to understand what she was experiencing. And Peyton couldn't believe she had fallen into this self-imposed trap.

*

Elena whistled as she fixed dinner. Tori walked in and picked up a banana, watching Elena continue to warble away.

"Uh, Momma Bear..." Elena held up the teapot. Tori nodded yes, and Elena continued whistling away as she put on water for them both, pointing to a freshly baked batch of cookies. "Momma Bear, are you aware the entire time I've crashed here at your house I have never once heard you whistle—a non-verbal expression of happiness or pleasure—by the way...so, what's up with that?"

"Oh, come on! I'm sure I've whistled before...I must have." Elena shook her head, wondering how long ago she actually had whistled, now that Tori had brought it to her attention. As she continued to fix tea, she broached to Tori off-handedly, "Tori... do you know any....well, gay kids at school?"

"Yeah, Chance is gay. You know, the gymnast that goes to Nash's karate classes."

"Nash never told us he was gay," Elena remarked.

"That's because he thinks you and Poppa Bear are completely provincial and without any awareness of the real world. I've told him that you couldn't be any less judgmental and his dad's prudishness is merely the product of method acting."

Elena gave Tori a curt frown, then returned to fixing dinner.

"And, well…do you or Nash know any…well, gay girls?"

"What, you mean lesbians?" Looking incredulous, Tori put her banana on the counter so she could place both hands on her hips. "Excuse me, but the last time I looked you were hanging out with one named Peyton."

"Yes…but she—she doesn't…she—" Elena rushed on, not really knowing what she meant or what she was saying.

"Yeah, I know. She passes. She could pass for straight."

Elena felt like she was becoming educated.

"Anyway, here's where things are as senseless as doughnut holes. A normal person engages in the pursuit of kissing a mere twenty-one thousand, plus or minus, minutes in their sorry little lives—which boils down to a lousy month when you add it all up. Heck, over the lifespan of an average eighty year old? They're only havin' sex six times a year."

Elena found this information discomfiting on several levels. At that moment Nash walked in, twirled Tori's hair, then nabbed an apple.

"Yeah," Tori pontificated onward, "we take more baths and eat more chocolate bars and yet this gay thing's got everyone's knickers in a twist—including Poppa Bear." Tori popped a bite of banana into her mouth and then added, "FYI, he's no fan of your new friend either."

"What?" Elena wondered if her voice suddenly sounded louder to them, as it did to her.

"Don't worry, Mom." Nash comforted her. "Dad's just grumbling about how much time you spend together. But I personally think it makes ya kinda cool, not all caught up in the church. Besides which, with her you get to do something you like to do for a change. You deserve to have something that's not all about the church, and so what if she's a lesbian? She's pretty cool and after all the stuff you put up with—and I include yours truly," he mock-bowed, "you deserve to have a good pal you can have fun with. And it just proves you're open-minded, which makes me proud."

"Just so you're completely informed, Nash, according to this specialist, who was on Queen Oprah the other day, straight women everywhere are suddenly wanting to be with other women to experience their newfound—" Tori offered up air quotes, "—sexual fluidity."

Elena's stomach suddenly felt queasy. Just as she was drawn to each and every word that sprang from Tori's mouth, she also was terrified by them.

"Here's the Kinsey Scale, zero to six. If you score zero you're straight-straight. If you score six you're gay-gay." Tori nabbed a pair of dice from the junk drawer, rolled them for effect. "But unlike men, women scored all over the board—twos, threes, fours—because they experience relationships with less boundaries...more gray. And that's Lesbo 101 in a nutshell."

"You trying to tell me something?" Nash inquired, munching on his apple.

"Nash...you are, and always will be, the only one for me."

Elena smiled at them both.

"Yeah, but that's not the case for my mother."

Elena felt a rush of heat spread over her chest, suddenly feeling as if the air in the room had escaped.

"Of course it's not, Momma Bear," Tori said easily. "Don't get so defensive."

Elena shook her head, fanned herself with the dish towel. "I believe you two are what Tyler calls Twin Flames!" She walked over to them, held them both in her arms. "And you found each other so early in life. Just think of all the time you have to endlessly bicker."

*

Elena found herself whistling once again as she drove up to Peyton's house. She smiled at her good mood, got out of the car and walked up to Peyton's door. She was about to place a nicely wrapped package for her at the side of the front door, when she heard a voice from behind.

"Oh my!"

Elena jumped, scared out of her wits.

"Well, hello there." It was Margaret watching her as Elena was about to place the package at the front step. Margaret's face showed nothing of the hospitality from the other day. Dressed in a severe black business suit, hair pulled tightly back, Margaret appeared cool, aloof and clearly piqued.

"You're the photographer, right?"

"Yes...uhm, I...I was just leaving some proofs for Peyton."

Margaret observed the beautiful wrapping. "Uh, yeah. Special delivery, eh?"

"No. I was just...I happened to be in the—"

"Oyyy, you *are* a newbie! That's original."

"You know...I've...really got to be going." Elena tucked the package beneath her arm and began to walk from the house.

Margaret purposefully stood in front of her, arms crossed. "I'm not sure how much Elena has told you about us...but we're working on our relationship. Trying to have a baby. I think you know she's been through a lot."

"Yes, I know she's been through a lot." Elena was not going to shrink from her. In her mind "a lot" happened to include Margaret's cheating on Peyton.

"And it doesn't help her to give her all kinds of false hope for something you and I both know will never happen."

Elena cleared her throat, flustered. "I'm not sure what you're insinuating—"

"Oh you know very well what I'm insinuating."

"I...I only want what's best for her."

Margaret smiled. "So glad to hear that. I'll let her know you stopped by." She cavalierly brushed past Elena, pulled out her keys and let herself into Peyton's house.

As Elena watched Margaret take ownership she stood a solid moment, uncertain what to think. She didn't like the feeling that spread through her, that somehow she was less than entitled, and, suddenly, quite surprisingly, another feeling became ascendant. This last inflamed her limbs like wildfire. She was sure she'd never experienced this particular feeling until now, but here it was, in all its savage glory: Jealousy.

*

The young girl runs in crying, crying desperately in pain. But as she keeps trying to talk to her mother, all her mother will do is offer up tea. The girl keeps saying things, yelling them to her mother, but the mother simply does not hear, just keeps smiling as she says, "There's nothing that a good cup of tea cannot fix."

"But Mommy," young Peyton continues to wail. "It...it's Molly. She—she's moving....and I love her so...so much. She's my best friend."

Suddenly Peyton's mother looks directly at her daughter, her eyes the color of coal as she assesses her daughter. "Haven't I always told you a young lady dresses for tea—"

"But Mom...Molly, she's leaving...I'll never see her again..."

Peyton's mom takes her napkin and wipes away the tears, not gruffly, but not with great gentleness either. Peyton continues to sniffle.

"Now get a hold of yourself. I suppose now is as good a time as any to learn this lesson. When you love—expect disappointment."

Peyton's eyes are large with disbelief.

Peyton's mother cannot handle the pain she sees, nor the pain in herself, and grabs her daughter to her. "It's just what happens."

Peyton kept thinking of the dream as she sat at her front steps until Wave snapped her out of her memories by sitting next to her. Wave was in one of her favorite jumpsuits that only Wave could pull off, a tattering quilt dress made of countless snatches of fabric topped by a huge pair of sunglasses. Wave cocked her head, then, lowering her sunglasses, she looked at her good friend.

"Soooooooooup," Wave hissed in her sexiest voice.

"What?" At first Peyton didn't understand, then realized Wave was teasing her, as she had done so for days about "soup" referring to Elena's offer to bring her some while she had been sick. Wave had decided it was the code word for Elena and all the presumptions Wave attached to their relationship.

"Oh for God's sake."

Wave laughed at her friend, then became serious. "Gotta tell ya, Lombard, this thing is gettin' way out of control: the unbuttoning the shirt, the wanting to take care of you when you're sick—and how 'bout all the eye blazing that goes on between the two of you...who does that?"

"Eye blazing? Really."

"You're the writer! Call it what you want!" Wave sighed, shaking her head. Peyton also shook her head.

135

"You gotta grow some mini-cajones STAT and tell her what's going on."

"No, no no…" Peyton shook her head emphatically.

"She's straight, Lombard. Married to a pastor. Not to mention she's culturally challenged…" Wave shivered. "It's kinda twisted how much you've got goin' against you here."

"You belabor the obvious. You know what—I have to go out of town for an assignment, and I've already decided, when I come back I'll just be less available," she declared, reassuring herself as much as Wave. "Actually, Unavailable."

"Oh, the I'm too busy, I'm too much of a chickenshit to tell you what's really going on treatment, fade into the woodwork action?"

"Yep." Peyton gazed at nothing in particular. "That's the plan."

The next morning Peyton woke much earlier than she liked, unable to sleep, thinking endlessly about her latest dream, what it meant, and that Elena had already called several times since she had attempted to drop off the proofs that Margaret had unceremoniously, contemptuously informed her of the night before.

"Oh yeah, Peyton—she stopped by, all primped and ready to impress you with her 'special delivery,'" Margaret had taunted. "You are playing with dynamite, sweetheart, and you know what happens when girls do that don't you?"

Peyton had begged off their dinner, which had made Margaret even meaner than usual. She'd pouted, cajoled, pulled every trick in the book, and it was at that moment that Peyton realized she was in real trouble. Margaret was no longer even a consideration in her mind. She was ancient history. Because Elena was all that she could think about.

She'd done everything, swum laps thinking about how to purge this straight woman from her mind. How to rid herself of the face that constantly loomed in her thinking. No matter what she was doing, Elena intruded, capturing her from whatever her mind was on, compelling her to replay every moment they spent together, thinking about the shape of her hands, the way she moved so deliberately, gracefully, thinking of her hair, her eyes, the way they seared into her with a simple glance, how she held

136

Peyton's gaze with intensity and thorough confidence; and yet, nothing, nothing whatsoever had transpired between them.

"But it has," Margaret warned. "Don't play stupid, Peyton. Don't play like you have no clue what's up here."

"What do you want?"

"I've told you over and over again. I want to give us another go. Come on, before Church Lady ever showed up you know you were considering it…and if you think you stand a chance in hell with her, Peyton, you're seriously delusional."

"You're right, Margaret. I have been delusional." Peyton stood up from her desk, held out her hand.

"What?" Margaret stood there.

"Your keys, Margaret. I'd like them back."

Margaret stood unmoving, stolid, implacable. She glanced down, and when she returned her gaze to Peyton, she had her game face on, her saucy you-don't-really-want-me-to-leave-smile, but it was quivering in uncertainty.

"Your keys." Peyton only waited a moment. "It's over."

Margaret swallowed. Shook her head. Picked up her purse, dug out her keys, and tossed them on Peyton's desk. She walked to the door, then turned. "You are so going to get burnt, Peyton. I kind of feel sorry for you."

"Goodbye Margaret."

And more laps, Peyton continued to swim, getting rid of Margaret, exhausting her anxiety, and if it still wouldn't go away, she'd just swim laps until she could no longer breathe.

She finally got close to utter fatigue, her legs shaking as she slowly removed herself from the pool. She felt like jelly as she flopped into her deck chair, her breathing heavy and labored as she let the water dry in the sun. Finally, finally, she felt a bit of relaxation ooze through her limbs. She was just shutting her eyes when the doorbell rang.

God, if Margaret was trying any more of her maneuvers, Peyton was going to seriously lose her temper. She was already close to doing so as she opened the door and she was ready to let her have it. But it wasn't Margaret. It was Elena.

Peyton stood with her mouth in mid-motion. She could not have been more surprised to see Elena, standing there, looking utterly enchanting in her jeans and soft deep blue cashmere sweater, the jewel tone enhancing her already exotic features. Elena's hair was loosely pinned, allowing the lush wavy thickness to fall about her shoulders. Peyton realized she was staring.

Elena glanced over Peyton, looking very sleek in her bikini, noticing the lean muscular build of her body, how finely toned Peyton's body was, how strong and athletic. They both stood, frozen.

"I...I stopped by earlier but you weren't here."

"Oh...okay."

"I'm sorry, I just couldn't wait—I wanted you to see your photos." Elena removed a couple of them from the special packaging she was carrying. Peyton, still trying to catch her breath, looked a bit queasy. Elena blustered along, proudly presenting her favorite headshot, bursting with a sort of parental pride, but at the same time feeling a bit shy.

"You look amazing, Peyton..." Elena glanced at her and then down at the pictures.

"Yeah...they're—wow..."

Elena now felt a bit foolish and uncomfortable. "I...I should have called first."

"No...it's fine. You just didn't need to come all the way over... here."

Elena considered this, shook her head. "Yeah, well I guess this isn't a good time—"

"No. NO! I...I...actually—" Peyton's eyes darted about as she tried to figure out what to do. Feeling like a caged animal, but knowing that if she didn't do this, and do it now, she'd have to live with the gnawing anxiety even longer. "This...this is as good a time as any. Uh...do you think you could give me a sec?"

Elena nodded uncertainly. Peyton grimaced, put up a hand, and then as she was about to dash back in, quickly turned to Elena. "Just come in...I'll be out in a sec."

Peyton raced around her bedroom, frantic, trying to get dressed, attempting to quell her panic, lamenting under her breath, "It's okay, it's okay, it's okay..."

She tried on one shirt, another. Scrambling, picked up a third shirt, silk, and accidentally tore it in her haste. "Shit!"

She ran into her closet, grabbed the nearest shirt she could find, stopped to catch her breath. Her pants! Where were her jeans?

"It's okay, it's okay, it's okay!" But nothing was working. She stared in the mirror, saw how pale she looked. "Oh my God!... Oh for chrissakes, just tell her..."

When Peyton reappeared in the living room, awkward and self-conscious, she noticed that Elena looked about as uncomfortable as she felt. She motioned her to sit.

They both did so, stiff and formal. Peyton turned to face Elena, but that made her even more nervous, so she turned away, not looking at her.

"So look," Peyton began, clearing her throat. "Elena..."

"I really should have called first." Elena shook her head, feeling terribly off-kilter.

Peyton took a deep breath. "I...I have to talk to you about something."

"Sure. Are you okay?"

"Uhmm...actually no. I mean nothing seriously is wrong, it's just that...well...," Peyton stood up and changed tack. "Would you like some Breakfast Eng...I mean English Breakfast? Because I have some in the kit—"

"For God's sake, Peyton. What's going on?"

Peyton let out a deep breath, scratched her forearm, started, then stopped, then started again, not quite certain how to deliver the information she needed to give. "Christ...this is ridiculous... first of all...you're straight. Second of all, you're straight—AND married—and, oh my God, I so didn't want this to happen—" Peyton furtively glanced at Elena to see how she was taking it, but she simply sat on the chaise, silent, inscrutable.

Peyton sat back down, and as if summing up her case. "Because well...you know I'm a lesbian."

"Uhmm...yes." Elena responded, a bit offended.

"So...well, that's it."

"That's what?"

"What I just said."

"Which is..." Elena's amazing brown eyes pierced through Peyton until she could no longer even look at her.

"That...that I'm—" Then under her breath, "Oh for God's sake..." Then aloud, "I...I like you, Elena."

"I like you too," Elena blurted.

"No," Peyton was now frustrated. "More than I should."

A long silence followed. Elena didn't move. She was starting to get it.

"So...we don't have to—you know—talk about it any further...I'm fine with that...let's just take some space, not spend so much time—"

"No! NO!...no oh GOD!"

Peyton and Elena were both equally surprised at her outburst.

"No...I don't want for us not to spend time together. " Elena's voice was laced with pain.

"But you heard what I just said—"

"Yes, but I just found you..." Elena looked about, startled at herself, scared. "We need to be in each others' lives," she continued as if it were self-evident, followed by yet another burst of incredulity. "Oh God, no! No!"

They sat, neither moving.

"Peyton—look..." Elena began to bargain. "I just feel like you are my absolute best friend...I just know we can get around this. I don't want to not be with you. And you can have," she said with all the affirmation in her she could summon, "all of me..."

Peyton glanced up at her and stared, nonplussed. Elena looked as confused as she did, momentarily trying to regain her bearings, as they both grappled with the discussion, what it meant for each of them.

"I mean...all of it—all of me except for *that*. All of me..."

"Just so you understand." Peyton put out her hands as if trying to explain to a child. "For a lesbian *that* is a big deal."

Elena laughed, realizing how ridiculous she sounded.

Peyton tried to diffuse the tension. "Well, at least in the beginning."

"Let's have some wine." Elena put her hand back on Peyton's forearm, this time leaving it there. "We'll make a plan. Just please...please don't take you away from me."

For the first time, Elena looked small and scared, and Peyton found that she could not deny her. She nodded, reassuring.

140

"I'll get the wine."

*

"Yes, these are God's children but they have lost their way." Barry's voice held the same rich tone, luxuriant and lulling, that it always had. Part of his charm and success with his congregants was his ability to make his listeners want to believe everything that came out of his mouth. Not the content necessarily, but the convincing and inviting manner in which it was conveyed. "And we do not reward a deviant course by allowing it the sacred sacrament and gift of marriage."

Elena sat in her usual pew, Nash next to her and Tori next to him, all dressed in their church wear, sitting as they all had sat for years, Elena listening as she had listened countless Sundays, half in and out, spending most of her time checking off and making new lists of the tasks and prioritizing them in the ways which were necessary to run their lives. But now, now Barry was talking about an issue, yes, which she had scarcely paid attention to before, but now held meaning because it pertained to Peyton. Elena could not square the fact that she had not only at times fully disagreed with the merits of Barry's service, but for years she had been complicit in his words by sitting in the same pew, week after week, never saying a word. Doing nothing. Just being there as the words were allowed to float out into the world and do whatever harm they might.

She couldn't take it anymore. Her eyes met Barry's. She saw in them a certain resolve, a steely kind of patronizing she had never before seen. She wasn't sure how much of it was performance and how much of it was reality. Either one scared her.

"They think if they twist enough arms in the political arena they will win this prize." His eyes did not leave hers. "But marriage is the most precious right we hold."

Elena's jaw tightened. It was not something that ever had occurred to her to do, or that she had the right to do. But she got up and walked out of the service.

Barry's voice rose. "It must not be tarnished."

141

To Elena's astonishment, some of congregation followed her exit. Among them, Nash and Tori.

Behind her, Barry thundered, "It WILL NOT be tarnished!"

"Amen," came the response from those remaining in the church.

*

Elena had been waiting for hours, knowing that at some point Barry would have finished up the last of his paperwork and parish visits and would come through the front door. And would do what he was doing now. Slam the door and walk right up to where Elena sat at her computer.

"What the hell is going on with you?" His face was red, angry. "Do you know what it looks like when my *family* walks out of a sermon?"

Elena glanced at both Tori and Nash, who both peeked up from their books in the living room.

"Barry—don't."

"You know there's a certain amount of this stuff I just have to do. We've talked about this before."

"Yes, Barry, I'm very familiar with the 'greater good' speech."

"And these compromises used to be fine for you—until now. What the—"

Nash closed his book, shook his head. "You really amaze me, Dad. I know you don't even believe that crap. You've had gay friends. Back in your grand 'theah-tah' days."

Barry glanced at his son then back to Elena.

"Look, Nash, I just think it's important for people to understand that they cannot be rewarded for bad behavior."

"'Bad behavior?'" Nash jumped up from the couch and approached his father. "Get real, Dad. Selling your soul is bad behavior. Loving someone isn't."

Fuming, Nash shook his head in unveiled disgust and stormed from the room.

"Yeah and ya know, Poppa Bear, the whole abomination thing—my gosh, the Bible also says it's—" Tori dropped her air quotes again, "an abomination to eat rabbit or shrimp. Heck, it says that if you work on the Sabbath—which you do all the time, Poppa Bear, you should be put to death. Talk about your uber-literalism—"

"Tori, that's enough!"

"Well..." Tori shrugged. "The reality is, the gays are here to stay. I don't know anyone who doesn't know or have a gay friend, brother, uncle, sister. It's only a matter of time before this whole marriage discussion is so yesterday's french fries!"

Elena got up and, trying to end the conversation by means of distraction, began to tidy.

"Look, Tori, you and Nash are going to have to trust my judgment on this and keep your opinions to yourself. I need to keep this church running, and that's all there is to it."

Elena saw Barry's body tense, then he too stormed from the room. Elena was about to go after him, but Tori stopped her with a gesture, and began to assist with the clean up.

"Let me help." Tori began to bus some meal remnants. "You know Nash needs," she glanced at her watch, "roughly another nine and a half minutes before he cools down and Poppa Bear probably another half hour, so it's sort of pointless to try and reason with them now."

They both entered the kitchen and cleaned side by side in silence for several minutes until Elena began to wipe the dishes and put them away. Tori stopped her mid-stride, gently extracted the dish towel.

"Did you know between the Utah Mormons, who funded Prop 8, and the Church of Latter-day Saints here in California, those propagandist crazies raised over thirty-eight million dollars—altogether the money raised for and against was three times more than for any other kind of—" Again Tori used air quotes, "—social issue brought to ballot. But Momma Bear, the Latter-day Saints is the home of Millie's best friend and everyone knows Millie's the money at Poppa Bear's church. I guess we should cut him some slack—cuz he's pretty screwed if he doesn't toe the line."

Elena listened intently. She hated injustice, but while she was vaguely aware that injustice happened on a global scale, daily, she knew she had for years been paying very little attention. At this point she was so tired she did not want to delve any deeper into what all of this might mean, or continue this conversation. She tried misdirection.

"Tori, does it ever hurt to carry all that information in that head of yours?"

"Like a horse to water, gotta drink...gotta think."

"Well, you will never bore anyone, that's for sure."

"It might not just be pandering, though, Momma Bear. It might be that he's afraid the gays are going to destroy the fabric of his own marriage."

As Tori handed Elena a plate, her sweet eyes pegged Elena's with the unspoken question.

*

The next afternoon Elena was supposed to have a meeting with Millie, but she told Elena, "We have a serious, and I mean serious to the toenails, crisis with one of the board members, she's electing to reduce the altar shrubs! We voted on that if you recall, and I'm not putting my hard-earned money into reducing all that beautiful altar work I had done, Elena. No sirree. So, I'm sorry to do this to you at the last minute, but I knew you'd understand. I just can't make our fundraising meeting—but we can reschedule to Tuesday evening, we'll squeeze it in, like everything else we do. The Good Lord give us strength Elena—how else do we manage?" Millie asked but then answered herself, "By choosing, us, Elena. We were blessed, Elena, do you understand that? Chosen by the Divine Power to do his bidding. I know you're just married to the man, but your support of Barry's work is just as critical—maybe not as important, certainly—but without it Barry wouldn't have the hours he needs to do his good works. And God blessed me with the resources to get on out there and fund the good fight. Okay, glory be, sister." Millie laughed good naturedly at her hipster talk. "We'll sing God's praises another day!"

Elena couldn't get off the phone fast enough. But one thing kept rankling her long after the conversation had ended. The concept of being chosen. Chosen by anyone. Chosen for what?

And wasn't that akin to being trapped? And what was her purpose here if she *had* been chosen?

She would never be able to sever her connection to a spiritual life, a belief in the divine, but she certainly would like to exorcise the entire cultish dogma of the church to which she now found herself enslaved. She had begun to feel a purpose, lately. A new purpose. Working with Peyton, extolling the virtues of women who had made grand strides in their lives—either through their wonderful role-modeling of what women could do when they put their mind to it—the Amelia Earharts, the Madame Curies, the breakthrough women like Martina Navra—whatever that tennis star's name was—she had broken barriers and then even more by her brave stance on coming out.

The excitement Elena felt around the Women's Glory Project injected through her like a jolt suddenly, and she knew what she felt might be akin to what Tyler felt about his pathway in life. Working on this book and being a part of something bigger, outside of herself, even exploring the softer, less "sexy" stories of mothers who adopted multiple disabled children, of teachers who gave up Harvard professorships to teach in the inner city, of female Navy Seals serving their country—all of it gave Elena the first sense of purpose she had had since she became a mother to her young baby Nash, when taking care of his needs made her feel useful. But after…after Sarah, it was still so difficult to think of her without falling apart. Elena knew it was from that point forward that she had felt so little purpose in life. As if by losing her own daughter she was nothing more than a failure. She had felt the only job left to her in life was to support Barry so he could function at maximum capacity, and to make sure Nash got his needs met too, however small or insignificant any of it was—whether it was picking up Barry's dry cleaning or getting Nash to soccer practice on time, she had made sure she did every meaningless errand with as much attention and focus she could put onto it. To make up for it…for Sarah. Sure these things were important to running her family smoothly—and to the happiness of those she loved but what did any of that have to do with the grander scheme of things, any contribution beyond that? The Women's Glory Project and working with Peyton made her feel special. Important. Fueled by the fire this realization ignited in her, Elena grabbed her camera and decided not to waste a moment afforded by this cancellation of Millie's. She was going to turn around what would have been most certainly a waste of time and go out and shoot. Shoot anything and everything.

Elena wandered through the park. She shot frame after frame, and each time it felt so good to feel that spark of passion she had always had for her work. This was what she had studied, all those years ago, yes, along with the acting, which had just been an inhibited young girl's pipedream. Even then she did not like to be in front of a camera. She was much happier behind it as she had discovered when they'd needed someone to take the still photography for one of the school plays.

Everyone had commented on how spectacular her work had been, the old black-and-white grainy prints somehow capturing the real essence of the performers. And just like back then, she felt a natural kinship to the frame, the concept of still storytelling. It energized her.

As she continued walking through the park, she wondered what Peyton would think of these shots, then shook her head. *Don't be silly, she's not going to be interested in these nature shots— what do they have to do with The Glory Project?* Yet, Elena knew Peyton would look at each one and comment on it, and she could see her as she did so, how the sinewy muscles in her forearm would move as she held them in her hands and at the same time how gentle and strong those hands were. She had allowed herself to come to terms with the fact that she found Peyton attractive. Actually, she found in her a handsomeness born of the most basic qualities; the sweet vulnerability that came out of Peyton even when she tried to mask it with a gruff nonchalance. And that face...unlike any other face she had studied. When she photographed, she did study every aspect of a person's composition. With Peyton's face she hadn't so much studied as memorized how the slight curl line formed along the side of her lip and coiled so sweetly when she smiled, the way her eyes looked hazel one moment, turning a spirited brilliant green when Peyton got excited, how the shape of Peyton's strong square jawline met a perfect dimpled chin, the exact triumphant arch of her upper lip, those lips...she had beautiful soft...

Oh my God! She stopped herself, suddenly realizing she had been standing in the same position taking the same picture of the riverbed the entire time she had been daydreaming about Peyton.

She shivered, turned and walked to her car.

*

Peyton sat with Wave long after Pinot Latte had closed, as they killed the last of some of Wave's scotch.

"Why her?"

"Trust me...if I had any way for it not to be..."

"You know..." Wave pursed her lips, then smacked them heartily as she savored the scotch. "Maybe we're lettin' our pessimism get the better of us. I suppose everything doesn't *have* to be so black and white. Whatya think?"

"It's black and white."

"Why?"

"Because when it's not, I seem to get decimated."

Wave mused, professorially. "Maybe there's a gray somewhere in here— hell, there are any number of colors between black and white. Blimey, the other day I thought I'd gone daft looking at paint chips with all the endless possibilities of green. After all, me love, we do live in a rainbow world, you and I, and there should be no end of color outcome in the rainbow spectrum. Maybe you aren't passion pink...maybe you're...watermelon— what—could have been?"

Peyton glanced at her friend. *Seriously?*

*

Elena spoke with Tyler and Lily at the same time, in his courtyard, drinking one of his latest "love wines" composed of dandelion, rose and hibiscus.

"Not bad, silk pie." Lily squelched a grimace at the aftertaste. "But not quite as good as your last, I'm afraid. I'm telling you if

147

you let me get a real sommelier—I did this great deal for the Vineyard Tasting in Sonoma—I could find you an expert to make this stuff sing!" Lily snapped her fingers, excited by the idea. "Yeah, and then we could start our own label—we could call it Drunk on Love or something like that—"

"Oh Lily, this wine isn't about money—it's about feeling."

Lily smirked.

"Back to our girl here. And then what happened?" Tyler asked eagerly. Elena had begun to tell them of the conversation she and Peyton had had three days ago. "But the thing is this, I don't want her to go away, or take space—"

"Of course you don't," Tyler sympathized.

"Come on though," Lily interjected pragmatically, "you've got to give the girl a break."

"I'm telling you, I've never met anyone I've felt so comfortable with and just plain like...I don't know why or how, but we were meant to be."

"Meant to be?" Lily blurted, "you mean—"

"Sweetheart," Tyler turned to Lily, "you need to play well with others. What I think our girl is saying is she's found a soul mate."

*

Peyton stared at Wave. "Watermelon?"

"It's a color. They showed me on that wand thingy. I'm just sayin' maybe this doesn't all have to end with a...a bloody hanging."

*

"I don't know what I'm saying," Elena countered, "I thought you'd explain it to me."

"I think it's fairly evident." Lily's tone had turned brisk, businesslike.

"It's so strange. I just feel like we need to be with each other. I know that sounds crazy—like, well, we are *supposed* to be with one another..."

"Yeah, that sounded much less crazy." Lily's voice was laced with irony.

"Well, ladies." Tyler cleared his throat in theatrical suggestiveness, then said with more than a tinge of sarcasm, "As I may have mentioned before, sweetie, there are infinite kinds of soul mates. But she probably falls into one of three general kinds of soul mates: The Karmic soul mate, you know—someone you've got unfinished business with, like a frightened secretary and her scurrilous boss, or where there is major business that needs to be worked out from a previous life, a mentor and his student, a killer and his victim. Also the common garden variety soul mate that is an intense kinship—like two sisters, a dog and its guardian, business partners, a comedy team. The last but ultimate of soul mates is the Twin Flame—a connection of such irrefutable togetherness that no one can explain it or defy it. It is, quite simply, meant to be."

"Meant to be. That's the ticket," Lily concurred.

*

"Has it occurred to you that she might feel the same way?" Wave offered.

"Come on, Wave. She's never even experimented with women in college. Never even thought about so much as a kiss, for chrissake. Even her best friend's kissed another woman. It's never occurred to her because she's as straight as they get."

"You never know. Maybe she's never considered kissing another woman because she hasn't met a woman she's wanted to kiss. Up till now."

"Don't even—"

"I'm just saying, maybe you need to keep an open mind." Wave took another sip. "Even if I can't."

*

Lily turned very serious very suddenly "So, what are you actually doing, Elena?"

Elena shook her head. "I'm not certain."

"Just remember," Lily stated, as she stood up to take her leave, "this isn't a world you can just visit. It's not fair to her."

*

Peyton left for New York the next day. She was just about to leave her Manhattan hotel for a meeting when Elena called. She looked at the number, swore she wasn't going to answer it, but picked it up nonetheless.

"Hey, Peyton!" Elena's voice was full of excitement. "How are you?"

"Fine."

"How was your trip?"

"Okay. Flight was a little rough." She was now on the street signaling for a cab, and did not bother to soften the curtness in her tone.

Silence.

"So when are you back in town?" Elena asked, her voice a little less certain.

"Uhmm...well...I think Tuesday."

"Oh...that's great, actually. Tuesday Barry's got a prayer meeting and Nash is studying for finals. I'll be free."

Peyton thought quickly. "Well, you know I think I'm having dinner with my agent when I get back. To go over all the contracts."

"Oh." Elena's voice sounded small and hurt.

Peyton gritted her teeth. "Well, maybe I'll have time before. I...I think we'll have to play it by ear."

Another silence.

"Peyton?" Elena asked quietly.

"Yeah."

"Why don't I see you when you get back...when you have the time."

"Sure... You know, I think you forgot a pair of your earrings at the house."

"Not for the earrings, silly."

"Well...in case you were looking for them I mean."

That night Elena found her mind wandering as she responded

to all her Holy Church of Light e-mails. She glanced around. Everyone appeared to be in bed. She considered a moment longer, then typed in the letters l-e-s-b-i-a-n in the Google search. The search page flooded with results.

She swallowed, got up, walked around the house quietly, surreptitiously, making sure everyone was indeed in bed. Back in her office she paced momentarily, then sighed heavily. She sat back down at her desk and studied the sites. Was she really going to do this?

She clicked on a site. And then she Googled to another site. She went to search lesbian lifestyle and then followed up with lesbian books, lesbian movies.

What was that? A creak on a floorboard? Elena slammed her laptop shut. She held very still for quite some time, then realized she was being utterly ridiculous. If she wanted to make sure she wasn't going to get caught, she needed to go somewhere where no one could catch her.

She grabbed her laptop and headed to the bathroom. She locked the door behind her, then sat on her makeup bench and pulled up YouTube; pulled up lesbian kisses, watched scenes from *Claire of the Moon, Desert Hearts,* and clips from so many other movies she couldn't keep the names straight.

Safely sequestered, she eagerly digested the information before her. As she watched lesbian love scene after lesbian love scene, a myriad of emotions overcame her, intrigue, awkwardness, embarrassment, fascination—but none gave her the feeling that she had expected.

The next morning, she sat at the dining room table, tired from her late-night research, sipping Earl Grey tea. She picked up the phone, called Peyton's land line, a phone she knew would be answered by a machine. "Yeah, Peyton, it's me. You know, I don't have to get those earrings—I know you're going to be tired when you get home. I'll call you later in the week. Hope you are having a great trip."

*

Flying back to Los Angeles, Peyton sat tapping her seatbelt

with two fingers in series of threes that equaled nine. Over and over again as she peered through the window and the endless sky and knew, had known even when she had promised Elena that they could continue to see one another, pretend to be "pals, BFF's, whatever," the reality was that the situation was not going to work. Not even remotely.

Peyton continued to tap as she stared out the window.

When Peyton returned and heard Elena's voice telling her that she couldn't meet after all, and hoping she had had a nice trip, she was relieved. But then she played the message again. Again. And again. She sensed an air of finality in the words. And the tone.

A day passed, then another. Peyton didn't know what to think. She was getting exactly what she wanted: space. Only it wasn't working all that well for her.

The following evening Elena called while she was out, and when Peyton returned she listened three times to the message: *"Hi Peyton. It's me. Elena. So...I'm hoping you've had some time to settle back in...and...well, I, I wanted to know if we could get together. You know, to talk—to talk about the project. Okay then. Call me. If... well, when you get this."*

Peyton paced. Listened to it again.

"What are you doing? You idiot!" she screamed at herself. She went 'round and 'round about not calling her, but then, thinking she was just being petty and small-minded, and that she should just tell her this really wasn't going to work at this point. But every time she picked up the phone, she couldn't make the call.

"You are some kinda chickenshit!" Peyton walked away from the phone yet again, but as she did it rang. She waited a second, picked it up.

"Hi."

The second she heard that voice, the liquid, beautifully accented voice, Peyton felt her chest tighten. "Hey there."

"Hey." Elena's voice was soft, sweet, almost curious. "Peyton...I...I—"

"Look, you don't have to say anything—"

"Yes. I do."

An agonizing silence ensued.

"You aren't the only one…Peyton…"

Peyton clenched her jaw, eyes shut. "What…what do you mean."

"You aren't the only one."

"The only one what?"

"That is confused." A long pause, and Peyton could hear Elena struggling. "I—I am so confused."

"Confused about what I said?"

"Yes."

Oh, crap! Peyton wasn't really sure how much clearer she could have been.

"About what I said?"

"Yes…well, no…I understood what you told me…" Elena paused. "I just wasn't sure why I was responding the way I was… and as long as you didn't bring anything up I didn't need to look at what was going on for me."

"I'm sorry, Elena, now I'm confused." Peyton felt exasperated and anxious.

"What I'm saying is it didn't make any sense. I mean even before you told me how you were feeling, I felt as if I needed to see you. Be with you. Why did I feel the need to see you—so strongly? Why did I check my e-mails, a hundred times a day? Why did I feel so disappointed if we couldn't get together? I felt like a child who couldn't put two and two together."

Peyton paced.

"I felt silly, you know?"

"I think so?" Peyton wasn't quite sure what Elena was trying to say.

"It's just that—" Elena stopped. "Oh, my God. Nash just walked in…I'm going to have to call you back."

Elena hung up. Peyton looked at the phone. *You're shitting me.*

*

"I spent last night and the whole day today looking at lesbian sites," Elena told Peyton as Peyton lounged in bed on her phone later that same night. It was near midnight. Everyone

153

had finally retired for the night and, Elena had told her, it was the only moment she'd had to herself to return to their earlier conversation.

"I'm not attracted to them, Peyton. Any of the *women* in them."

Peyton found herself laughing.

"But what does that *mean*?" Elena pleaded.

"I don't know. What does it mean to you?"

"I don't think I'm a lesbian, Peyton."

Peyton could hear the long sigh that accompanied Elena's assertion. Then heard knocking in the background accompanied by a low mumbling from a male voice.

"Yes…I'm fine. I'll be there in a second." Then to her, quickly, "I…I've got to go…I'm sorry."

*

The next night, right before dinner, Peyton's phone rang again.

"Can we just agree to call it a serious crush?"

Another long pause.

Elena continued, "I don't know why—or what it is about you—and the way we are together. I just want to be in it…I just want to be around you—all I can think about it…is…"

Elena stopped.

Barry stood in the doorway studying her. She quickly flipped her phone closed, horrified that she had just hung up on Peyton, horrified that her husband now stood before her, a questioning look in his eyes.

"Are you all right?" he queried.

"Yeah," she said breathlessly.

His eyes drilled into her own. "Something's burning."

He looked at his wife for another long moment, then left the room.

*

Peyton was just finishing a call with Emily about a possible new assignment that would present the opportunity to travel to

Paris. Paris! She had only visited this extraordinary city once with her mother, before she knew she was a lesbian and knew anything at all about the rich and textured universe of the Left Bank, the expatriates, the literati of Paris in the '20s and its unique lesbian subculture. Even though she hated traveling because her OCD made her flight-phobic, Paris was an adventure she would not let slip through her fingers.

She had just hung up when her doorbell rang.

Peyton walked to the door, still distracted by the call and when she opened it she was utterly taken aback to see Elena standing there.

"Hey—" she managed.

But Elena did not respond, nor did she wait to be invited in. She strode in, put a hand to Peyton's chest and gently pushed Peyton up against the wall. Their faces were inches apart. Before Peyton could even speak Elena's amazing brown eyes pierced her own until she could barely hold her gaze.

Elena's eyes continued to laser into Peyton's. A question lingered, momentarily. Elena slowly, agonizingly slowly, moved her lips closer to Peyton's, Elena's eyes still holding Peyton's, as her breathing became more ragged. Surprisingly it was Elena's eyes that gave Peyton strength, and before she could utter Elena's name, Elena's lips gently grazed her own.

Peyton buckled. Hands trembling she reached for Elena's shoulders to hold on for dear life as she succumbed to Elena's lips, the silky gentle questioning, the invitation, the exploration, the sensation blinding her, sinking her as she let Elena's lips own her and then, because she could not hold back a second longer, began to kiss Elena in return, answering the hunger, the need, the waiting, a thudding in her temples blotting out the world.

"Elena..."

"Oh...I knew you'd feel like this." Elena's voice was low, husky, murmuring the words against her lips. "Soft...so soft... like velvet..."

Peyton felt her knees go numb, but she managed to breathe, "Look, we can stop right now," still kissing her, "stop here before we go any further."

"Really?" Elena's lips continued to linger ever so gently

against her own, the vibrations of her voice as erotic as their touch. "Are you afraid to be alone here with me?"

"Yes..."

"Seriously?"

"Seriously," Peyton insisted, but the exquisite feeling was so present as Elena's lips continued to caress her own, the intensity of her gaze, the pureness of her want, until that was all she knew, Elena's lips on hers, her silky tongue now thrusting gently against her own, the seduction into a new world where nothing existed but Elena enveloping her, where thinking ceased and for the first time ever Peyton found herself engulfed, completely lost in a kiss.

Elena's hands found Peyton's hair as Peyton's hands snaked their way up Elena's back. Completely swept away, Peyton was aware of a frenzy of warning bells. They were heading to a place from which they could not return. But Elena was now master of their fates, holding Peyton fast in an embrace that neither could break, both fully absorbed in the kiss, their bodies pressing ever closer together as Elena, again the master choreographer, moved Peyton near her couch, and without parting, they tumbled upon it, the urgency and heat of the kiss creating more heat, more desire, more intimacy, more layers uncovered, stripping themselves bare. The desperation of that first entanglement easing into deeper exploration as they continued to taste and feel one another, hands softly exploring, a long sigh escaping them both, as Peyton tried one last feeble time to reason, even as Elena's mouth moved firmly upon her own, owning her, until Peyton, senses reeling, thought she could no longer breathe. Finally, a tenderness to the kisses, a sweet softness, the purity of desire sated for a moment.

They lay wiped out from the kiss, breathing deeply, then turned to one another.

"...that was so much better than I even thought it was going to be..." Elena said with conviction, then smiled and laughed.

They kissed for hours. Hours, an endless passage of time where they traveled to another place where Peyton knew only Elena and Elena knew only Peyton, a place where souls met—had to have met—and could not escape, their lips never sated, their hunger for one another growing stronger, more urgent, infinite.

"We...we've got to stop," Peyton begged at one point.

"Why?" Elena asked as her mouth kept ravaging Peyton who lay in disarray beneath her.

"I...I don't..."

"Shh..." And on they kissed until Peyton was only vaguely aware that the afternoon's sun had set and it was dark, and the darkness enveloped them into a time and place beyond Peyton's chaise lounge where their lips fed off one another as their bodies lay hungrily enwrapped, until sometime, hours and hours later, when Peyton glanced at the clock and it was after eleven p.m.

"Oh...my...God," Peyton moaned.

Elena gazed at her, her eyes searching for an answer...for what had just happened...

"Wow," Elena sighed, and put a gentle finger to Peyton's face. "How can this be? That I've gone my entire life without ever having been kissed?"

"Oh, my God...we've been kissing for seven hours."

Elena shook her head, amazed that such a thing could be true.

"I don't know, Elena... All I know is I think we've just kissed more today than I have all the rest of my kissing put together for my lifetime."

Elena smiled. "Well, it certainly is more kissing than I could possibly imagine ever taking place."

"Oh, my God." Peyton was incapable of any other words.

Elena leaned to her. The moment her lips touched Peyton's they both slipped into that other world again, where time and space did not exist, just their togetherness, stronger than any reality either had ever known.

*

The next day Elena and Diana were sharing tea at the church office. Elena was trying to keep pace as Diana, looking more frazzled than usual, reeled off every anguish she'd ever had about all her children and the troubles she was having with her current issue around getting pregnant yet again.

"...and then he said I wasn't the only one to make this decision. That it affected our entire family and that he had some say, but it's not his body carrying another baby and—" Diana stopped, looked sharply at her friend. "Elena, are you listening?"

"Oh...yes, I'm sorry Diana." Elena pointedly directed her attention to Diana. "Just a little distracted today. Didn't sleep much last night. I think you just need to put the brakes on. It's ridiculous for him to think you would want to have another baby."

"It doesn't make me selfish? Unloving?"

"It makes you sane." Elena assured her friend.

Diana stared at her squarely. "What...what's going on with you? You seem...so different."

Elena considered a moment. "I...I'm happy."

Diana created an uncertain smile for her friend. "Well, Barry is far more understanding than Rich. You're very lucky that way."

The smile slid from Elena's face. She nodded bleakly.

*

Back and forth Elena's emotions went all afternoon and into the evening. She would live in a cloud of bliss, remembering the day before, replaying Peyton's lips against her own, remembering the touch, taste, smell and feel of her, and with every recall, her body would surge with electric desire. She had never felt so little control over anything, the suddenness and intensity of the physical clamoring in her body—and just as suddenly those feelings would be dampened by her actually being in her day, picking up the dry cleaning, shopping for dinner, cooking dinner, half here, half there as somewhere in the background Nash and Tori attended to their homework, and she felt their presence as she always had but now it felt like two worlds overlaying one another.

As Elena was cooking dinner, she was planning the schedule in her head for the next couple of days and trying to find brilliant ways in which she could maneuver blocks of time around where she and Peyton could spend more than an hour at a time together.

"Mom, I said we needed green markers," Nash lamented. "This set has every color BUT green!"

"Can it possibly make that much difference?" Elena asked.

"It's a project about the green movement—ya think?"

"Nash!" Tori called him out on his boorish teen behavior.

"Sorry, Mom. It's just I told you right before you went to the store yesterday that this set didn't have green."

It was true. He had. But Elena hadn't gone back to return the set, as she would have once so dutifully done, as possibly the first errand she would run for the day—to get ones that had green markers—because she had been wrapped in Peyton's arms, kissing her, living inside her and everything else had completely vanished from her mind.

Barry walked in with three of the church congregants, whom he pointed on toward the living room. Elena frowned. Barry hadn't told her he was bringing company and she was trying to figure out how to leave the house—so that she could see Peyton, feel Peyton...feel those lips against her own again, even if only for minutes. She blushed, then shook her head.

"Hey, sorry, El," Barry responded to her crestfallen face. "I tried to call you earlier."

"I...I was actually going to go out tonight..."

"...but you didn't pick up," he ignored her words. "It's three more for dinner."

"...This project just proves how abject consumerism is total whack." Feeling the tension Nash hunched over his project and Tori began one of her rambles. "—it's like the more we have all this stuff, the less inside it we are."

Elena attempted to speak through Tori's chattering, "I don't have enough for everyone. Can't you just go out or order pizza?"

"I don't think so." Barry was looking a little peeved.

"—All kinds of food without fat, dessert without sugar, flavor—"

"Barry really—"

"—Our beliefs are without conviction—"

"It's the board members. I'm not serving pizza."

"—And who wants to read a book without pages?"

"Just defrost something please. We can wait. This is important, Elena."

"—Commitment without honor."

That stopped both Elena and Barry. They glanced from Tori back to each other.

"Can you just please..." Barry pleaded.

Elena shrugged. Of course she would. Didn't she always?

Barry ruffled Tori's hair. "Girls without manners." Now that he had his way he was in a better mood, and walked over to Elena and kissed her quickly on the cheek. "Guests without dinner."

"I just said I would do it!" Elena snapped. All three of them turned to her.

"I was just kidding, El!" Barry shook his head at the kids like, *What's up with her?* then exited.

"It's like we're the antithesis society," Tori pondered sadly. "Doesn't it strike you as the ultimate contradiction that we have ALL this stuff that is full of nothing?"

Elena felt them all, knew exactly where they sat, exactly what expressions would be on their faces. She knew precisely how Nash would turn to Tori now and remark, "Stop already. I get the point." He knew that Tori would return an adoring gaze and respond, "Just sayin'," and she knew that Barry would be enthroned on the La-Z-Boy as the congregants all sat staring at him with utter admiration from the couch. She knew it all. All of it she knew and she was sick of it. But she had no choice but to simply forge ahead, and she rotely pulled out steaks from the freezer. This was her life. How had she thought for a moment it was anything else?

*

The next afternoon Elena showed up again at Peyton's door, unexpectedly.

"Look, I literally only have fifteen minutes. I just...I just..." Elena moved inside the door and boldly kissed Peyton. "I just had to see you..."

Elena practically slammed Peyton against the wall, attacking, her lips bruising, aggressive, her hunger undeniable. And just like that, as quickly as they had become engulfed, they had to part.

"Ohhh, God," Peyton hissed, calming herself down.

"I'm sorry, Peyton..." Elena smiled sweetly at her. "I'm sorry—I know I should have called, but I was on my way to pick up the dry cleaning and I missed you so much. I miss you, Peyton, every minute I'm not with you."

Peyton smiled grimly, but nodded. "I know."

"Okay, then." Elena kissed her again. "I...I've got to run. But I'll call you later. Tonight."

Elena left as quickly as she had arrived and Peyton felt her head begin to buzz.

*

"Hey it's me..." It was around seven that night, and Elena's voice on the phone to Peyton was bubbling over. "I'm free."

Elena had walked into the house from finishing errands in record time and saw the note from Barry and the kids on the frig: *Gone to the movies—see you later, love Barry.*

Elena, who had been a whirling dervish trying to find any conceivable way to get out of the house, could not believe her good fortune. She put on her makeup, took a quick survey in the mirror, called Peyton to alert her this time, and just as she was heading out the door, Barry, Nash and Tori all plowed in.

"Hey Mom." Nash gave his mom a quick hug. "I'm starvin'."

"I–I thought you were all going to the movies?" Elena heard the strain in her voice.

"We missed you too much!" Tori giggled.

"It was sold out...Mom can we have burgers?"

Barry brushed her cheek with his lips. "Hey babe, grab me a beer, will ya? The game's about to start."

Elena felt stunned as her life hit her full-on and knew she was going to have to call to cancel Peyton.

*

I once was lost, but now I am found
Was blind, but now I see

The head of the Holy Light's chorus had just finished a beautiful a cappella of the song.

"Yes, now *I* see..." Barry nicely tied in as he stood tall and noble at the altar. "Yes, I see...but only because God's love heals and allows me to see the sin within myself, to purge the temptations, the desires that are the devil's work..."

Elena sat in the pew, thinking of her, thrilled at the prospect of seeing her in a few short hours. She had actually been able to carve out the entire afternoon and early evening for them to spend together, and getting to that moment was almost more than she could bear, so until the time when she could actually see her, she found herself thinking about her. Obsessively.

Never had she had these feelings, feelings that rushed over and through her like a brushfire, scorching one way, rippling with intensity the next, unstoppable, inextinguishable. Thinking of her skin, her lips, her eyes, how the touch of her sent a torrent of pleasure through her, how nothing in the world could have prepared her for the feelings that seemed to just involuntarily happen to her body the moment she was near her, how she wanted to feel her skin, lay her skin upon Peyton's skin. Swallowing hard, feeling the tingling pressure between her legs, another new sensation Elena had never ever experienced in her life. That her body had a mind of its own, swollen with feeling that ached every moment for expression—

"...And only with God's love...God's glorious love do we become whole. Pure... Reborn. How many of us want to push those terrible urges from within us, those base human impulses, those craven desires of the flesh..."

Elena bolted upright. The words burned in her mind. She felt naked, as if every parishioner could see her body was this heathenous monster that Barry spoke of...as if somehow Barry were channeling her every thought in his sermon— "...that push us to do things we know are wrong...God, help us to force the evil from within... Let us pray for God's guidance in moving beyond these desires that only lead to self loathing, that truly are not in our best interest..."

Elena swallowed hard, crossed her legs, felt the flame on her cheeks, felt Tori and Nash staring at her. She began to fidget, tapped her feet. Would this sermon never end?

Peyton paced about anxiously, then sat and reviewed the papers before her.

"Stop, stop, stop..." she whispered as she collected herself and carefully and deliberately made herself attend to the task at hand, organizing the photos from the archives to share with Elena.

"Stop, stop, stop..." Because if they just really focused on work, Peyton knew she could keep herself from straying, keep herself from wanting to ravish this woman who had come into her life like a thundering freight train.

"Stop, stop, stop..." All she had to do was just stay true to the work. She had amazing abilities to concentrate and become laser focused. That was one of the side effects of her OCD...she just needed to really tap into it.

Knock knock knock.

Elena stood at the door.

*

Seated on opposite ends of the couch in Peyton's living room, they both glanced at an array of archival photos from the June Mazer collection; with everyone from Gloria Steinem to Peyton's favorite mystery writer, Katherine V. Forrest. All the photos lay spread into varying categories of interest on the coffee table.

"I really love this one," Peyton suggested, focused on the photos, really concentrating on keeping on task. "You know these women gold miners—pioneers—no one ever talks about them. But look at the camaraderie—"

Peyton showed Elena the photo. Elena looked at it briefly, nodded.

Peyton's eyes caught Elena's but she literally could not meet the intensity of their gaze. Ever since Elena had walked into the house, and kissed her with strength of purpose, Peyton had pushed back. She couldn't allow herself to feel much more; if she did they were both going to go down a road for which neither of them were ready. She said to Elena, "It's just so…well, I don't know, shows a woman in a man's world, just as rough and tumble…I just….well, I love it."

"Hmmm," Elena responded, because at the moment she could care less about any of these photos. She could only feel her body, driving, hungry, intent, as she watched Peyton, the real Peyton so much better than in her imagination.

"And this one…" Peyton picked up another photo, and then realized there was one missing that she really had wanted to share with Elena and dug through several stacks. "Oh…here it is."

She turned to Elena but Elena wasn't looking at the photo. She was looking straight into her.

"Make love to me, Peyton," Elena said without a quiver of doubt.

Peyton's heart dropped to her stomach. Her mouth went dry.

"I thought…" Peyton let out a deep sigh, forced herself to look back at Elena who sat in a stillness of waiting. "I thought you wanted to wait—to see if—"

"Peyton, make love to me."

The air between them crackled.

"I…I…I want to, Elena, believe me…but once we go there… there is no going back."

Elena saw the fear in Peyton's face. She very slowly, and very deliberately picked up the file that lay between them on the couch. She tossed it to the floor, and slid herself up close to Peyton, her lips a breath away. In her eyes lived a force of certainty that helped to calm Peyton.

Elena said slowly, evenly, "I don't want to go back."

Elena took Peyton's hand, led her to the bedroom. As she closed the door, she realized she had no earthly idea what to do.

Peyton moved to Elena, trembling as she touched the beautiful woman before her, more nervous with desire than Elena, who was transfixed, taking it all in, like a grateful child. No nerves, simply an unyielding certainty and readiness to indulge in an exquisite new experience.

Peyton slowly began to undress Elena, her fingers nervously awkward until Elena bent to kiss them, one at a time, and then both of them removed the remainder of their clothing with swift dispatch.

As they leaned toward one another on the bed, their eyes held each other's in a tender embrace.

"Are you okay?" Peyton whispered.

"Yes," Elena answered, putting a gentle hand to Peyton's forearm. "Are you?"

Peyton nodded yes. Elena looked at Peyton, the strong lines in her arm, the gentle swell of her stomach, the, muscular thighs, her smooth skin. "You are so beautiful...so beyond my imagining..."

"As are you..." Peyton's voice was but a whisper.

They kissed.

Peyton tenderly lay Elena upon the bed, gently exploring every contour of Elena's beautifully shaped body, the long lines, the taut muscles the gentle plump of breasts, her fingers tracing every surface, leaving Elena breathless, enraptured, waiting, wanting. Peyton glanced up to Elena, asking for permission. Elena smiled, nodding her head at Peyton. *Yes, do as you will...I am yours...*

Peyton lay her body softly upon Elena's, gasping as their skin made contact. Even knowing the desire she felt for this woman, she could not have been prepared for her body to feel as if it would break from want, feeling desire beyond anything she had ever experienced, an agonizing want where nothing else mattered.

They kissed deeply, Elena's hands in Peyton's hair, her body moving in a rhythm suddenly as natural as anything she had ever known, even when Peyton was not supposed to be the kind of body on top of her, only used to Barry's rutting motion, feeling his penis break a barrier—and with Peyton there was no barrier because she so desperately wanted Peyton. Wanted Peyton inside her, wanted Peyton's mouth on her neck, loved feeling Peyton's lips eagerly tasting her skin, each grazing nip sending an intense searing need that Elena beckoned further, and the further it took her, the more Peyton wanted her, needed to be there, needed to taste what she had been waiting for so long, easing herself between Elena's legs, and smelling the deep richness of Elena, the scent of pure desire, her tongue now just barely taking Elena in, gently taking her in, then unable to hold back, now hungrily exploring, her mouth fully upon Elena.

Elena screamed as her hips bucked into Peyton's mouth, her desire to be had equal to Peyton's need, their mingling a coming together, Peyton feeling the sweet wet all over her face, rapturous in her need to please Elena, as Elena swelled into a smoothly pearly peak, Peyton feeling Elena's legs tightening, faster, urging Peyton into her, Peyton savoring every second of bringing this to Elena, this final moment, feeling her come, come hard in her mouth, the pulsing throbbing release as Elena rasped "Peyton," her beautiful neck arched in ecstasy.

And as she continued to come, Peyton quickly withdrew, thrust her fingers into her, climbing up beside her, fucking her, fucking her as deeply and as quickly as she could, then slowing the pace as she watched Elena's face, void of anything but sheer ecstasy, holding her at bay a second longer, the edge of her palm easing against Elena's clitoris as she continued to fuck Elena until she saw that she was going to come again.

"Stay with me!" Peyton's voice a ragged plea. "Stay with me, Elena!"

Elena's eyes opened as she came and she saw in Peyton's eyes the sheer intensity of Peyton's being, as she choked out something, she had no idea what, as she felt herself fall into a world where only she and Peyton existed, their bodies entwined, inside each other.

And Peyton, for the first time ever, felt her mind stop, as she joined Elena in this place that was not here but another place in time, and all she knew was the two of them, engaged, in union, in this most natural and perfect place.

*

Afterward, Elena's eyes opened briefly in the dark. She lay in Peyton's arms, her limbs liquid, her whole body feeling deliciously gratified, yet not quite sated...there could be no such place where desire wasn't just around the corner. She felt cherished in Peyton's arms, felt completely loved, and she knew, with complete certainty that giving herself over to Peyton had been the right thing.

She glanced at Peyton, watching her beautiful face as she slept, and she felt an immense swell of gratitude toward this amazing woman, and feeling tears, she closed her eyes, and allowed herself to feel this moment, completely, fully, owning this entirely new part of herself.

*

For the next week, while Barry was busy with a weeklong convention in town, and Nash was visiting some relatives of Barry's for Christmas break, Elena and Peyton stole every conceivable second to be together.

At moments it was a mere grappling at the door and Elena had to dash off, other times they had an hour or two where they would enwrap their bodies, unable to quell their need, both driven with more and more intensity to have what they craved.

"You're like air for me," Elena said at one moment. "I feel like I cannot breathe when I'm not with you."

Peyton could only nod. She understood in some depth of her that their hunger and need for each other was so huge it would consume them and everything in their path. And knew she should care but she did not care.

Two women, near fifty, sit across from each other, obviously still so very in love...

"...oh, my God," Nicole says, laughing, "at first I thought she was some kind of crazy stalker! She wanted to bring me dinner, she wanted to take me for a massage and I'm like—who is this straight housewife, and doesn't she know anything about lesbian etiquette?"

"After I saw her documentary about her premature son," Marina sighs, "and everything she had been through with him, I just wanted to do things for her. Make her feel good."

They kiss, deeply.

"Marina makes everything better."

"I'm glad you think so."

"I know so."

Chance Encounter at the Park.

Elena's Self-Portrait—when she shows Peyton her work.

Tyler tells his Youngblood Hawke Soul Mate Story.

Elena with her husband, Pastor Barry Winters.

Peyton runs into Elena at the Park.

Wave tells Peyton: "She's straight."

Impure Thoughts—Elena Can't Get Peyton out of her Mind.

Elena Falls in Love with Peyton.

The Morning After—Elena tells Peyton the family is going to Hawaii.

Elena Meets Peyton after Nash finds the letters.

Peyton swims off her anxiety.

Nash & Tori at the Park.

Barry at the Church.

Tyler asks Peyton to hear Elena out.

Happily In Love.

Elena came into Tyler's office while he was putting his finishing touches on this sweet little webisode.

Hearing her walk in, Tyler suggested, without turning around, "Just give me a second."

She walked in with a huge grin on her face, her usual fastidious braid gone. Her hair was almost a caricature of dishevelment, still sex-mussed from having just come from Peyton. She was radiant and ready to explode. If she didn't tell someone she didn't know what might happen to her, and, of course, the only person she could tell was this dear man who knew her so well.

Tyler looked at her then, and his head literally snapped into a vaudevillian double-take.

He jumped up and began to circle this new Elena, staring her up and down, his eyes virtually popping with surprise. He twirled her about, settled her, then stopped, shook his head.

"Okay, I'll bite." A big grin spread over his face. "So what's with the shimmering new and improved you?"

"Oh God, Tyler." She grabbed him in a deep and engulfing embrace, then walked him about his shop, gesturing all over his environment. "I just thought all this was a bunch of silly sappy—"

"Do tell." He smirked victoriously.

"I just had the most earth-shattering sex of my life."

Tyler looked impressed.

"With a woman!" Elena appeared as surprised as she did self-satisfied.

"Oh...baby girl!" Tyler literally burst into tears, so thrilled was he to hear that his friend, his dearest friend, finally had found some emotional nourishment.

"I'm in love for the first time—for the only time, Tyler, in my life."

He waited.

"With Peyton."

Tyler's eyes brightened with delight as he picked her up and twirled her around, shrieking in ecstasy, "You've found your Twin Flame, my sweet wonderful friend."

He held her in front of him, and emphatically stated it again: "Your Twin Flame."

"It's okay." Elena's smile was beyond containment. But a question of conscience flitted across her eyes. "Isn't it?"

"Yes, my beautiful angel." Tyler held her close. "It's okay."

*

It was late at night and Peyton was sitting in Wave's living room. Wave poured another shot of scotch for both of them.

"I guess I never knew what the phrase 'insanely in love' really meant," Peyton mooned. "Thank God she's not a controlled substance."

"Yeah, she's far more dangerous," Wave said, shaking her head at her friend. "You have clearly overlooked some patently obvious issues, my love, and I don't want to burst your love bubble—but what you are doing is the very definition of insanity: Gorgeous straight housewife, who's never had sex with a woman—thinks she's died and gone to heaven. Now what?"

Peyton sighed, again, pretty self-satisfied. "Oh my GOD. The way she tastes….smells, feels. You know me, Wave…I've always been a huge fan of…well, you know—"

"What—eating out, goin' down, eatin' pussy, chowin' on the Vjay-jay, snackin' on the kibbles & bits—you're doin' it for chrissakes and you can't say it—will it make it better if it's clinical? Oral sex?"

Peyton wasn't going to let her friend ruin this for her. "I'm just sayin'—this goes beyond the beyond. I have to say I thought men were the only ones that went insane over women—really. I know that sounds utterly antifeminist, but making love to her goes beyond anything I could have imagined."

"Brilliant. And now what? What about her husband? Her family? And forget the pressure she's going to feel from the church—not to mention culturally. If she thinks her parents disowned her before—blimey girlfriend, what do you think they'll do about all this?"

Peyton's smile faded. "Can I just stay in my happy place for another second?"

"Happy place—yeah, the one where you two walk off into the sunset? No dead bodies strewn behind?"

"Now who's Miss Gloom and Doom?" Peyton cracked. "What happened to me feeling good? Being happy?"

"Okay, my friend." Wave picked up a piece of licorice, gnawed off a bite. "Let's say she was brought into your life so you could know love is out there, to show you anything's better than Marg-e-RAT, to help you heal…or all of the above." Whipping the licorice about as a lectern prop, she became philosophical. "It's possible that's what this is. And that's all she is. A sort of connective tissue to the next step. But if you bloody think this is going to be anything else, well, Peyton, then you're just lying to yourself. And I can't do that with you because you are my very best friend. You're my acest pal. I can't lie to you, or allow you to do so to yourself."

"Okay now my happy place has a big foreclosure sign on it." Peyton glared at her friend. "You happy now?"

Peyton got up and left the house.

Wave stared at the piece of licorice, then addressed it. "Well I tried."

*

Peyton worked late into the night, keenly aware she was precariously close to missing her deadline. She realized that even though she spent half her time waiting for the brief moments of time she and Elena could steal away together, she had seriously let her work slide. She knew, if she were to be honest with herself, that she was being consumed not just by the time she spent submerged into that rich and textured world she now referred to as "the bubble," but worse yet, by all the many moments in which she unproductively waited for Elena to arrive to join her there. Lost moments, daydreaming, reliving, pondering the future—anything and everything but attending to her writing.

"I…I have just never had a moment when my head stops," she'd confessed to Elena.

"What?" Elena had asked.

Elena's beautiful hair cascaded over the length of Peyton's stomach while Peyton lightly stroked her fingers through it. As much as Elena relished the chills the caressing sent through her body, unused to being so utterly pampered and so lovingly taken care of, Peyton equally relished the exquisite sensation of touching Elena, the way it burned the edge of her fingertips. She could literally feel the energy between Elena's skin and her hand as she raised her palm just above the surface of Elena's skin, feeling the current of desire, need, want, passion all in that space, the explosive charge of a mere touch unlike anything she had ever experienced.

"My head...my brain...it never shuts off," Peyton mused, "except for when I'm with you. When we make love...it blots out. I've always wondered if that was even possible or what it might feel like—but with you, my mind literally goes blank, stops processing and my body takes over and feels. *Feels*, Elena." Peyton looked deeply into Elena's eyes. "You can't even imagine how that is for me."

Elena looked up into her lover's eyes. "Well, I can't say I entirely understand...all I know is that when I'm with you, I feel right. I feel absolutely right. Nothing has ever felt more right or certain to me."

Peyton smiled now, thinking about this. Was it yesterday, two days ago? She couldn't quite remember, as some of their hasty scramblings were beginning to mesh together in her mind. Every time it was a variation on the same theme. The moment they were in contact, they were unclothed, crazy greedy to get more of what neither of them could get enough of, tearing at each other, hunger, need, desire all overcoming anything in their path.

Last week Peyton had jumped when her phone rang, jarring her from her reminiscing.

"Hi, it's me."

"Hi..." Peyton had smiled.

"Is it...is it okay if I come over?"

"Of course!"

"Great, then let me in."

"What?"

"I'm at the door."

Peyton had dashed to the front door, and from the moment Elena forcefully made her way in, taking Peyton's face in her hands, hungrily kissing her as she maneuvered her to the chaise lounge, everything turned into this new place for Peyton, this place of sheer feeling.

And for Elena, the moment she laid eyes on Peyton, smelled Peyton's cologne, touched her fingers to the soft skin of Peyton's cheek, grasped the sinewy muscles of Peyton's arms, Elena's old life, her entire universe faded...all of it disappeared the moment she was in Peyton's arms.

*

"...yeah, because Martin Luther was so blown away by the stars in the sky he decided to mimic those stars by bringing the 'lights of the stars' right into his own home. And that was like in the sixteenth century. I always wondered how this all started," Tori mused as she and Nash, Barry and Elena were all trimming the Christmas tree. As usual, Tori was festively decked out; green skirt, green and red polka-dotted sweater and a Christmas tie, full of large "obnoxious Santas" Nash had groaned when he saw her. She had stuck out her tongue and put a Santa hat on Nash insisting he get into the spirit.

"You did, eh?" Barry asked her, helping the kids string the lights.

"Yeah, and while I was digging into it I found some other cool things, you might like to know."

"Here we go," Nash sighed, but good naturedly.

Elena went to the kitchen, still listening to their banter as she prepared their annual eggnog. Every year they played out this family ritual. They all had Elena's famous eggnog while they trimmed the tree and then they would discuss the holidays and try to find the most interesting place they could plan to travel to for Barry's annual vacation, which took place in late February.

As Elena brought the tray out she stopped. She watched the three of them, giggling, nudging one another playfully, and she suddenly felt terrified to hurt this family that she loved with every fiber of her being.

"Yeah, bet you don't know what other amazing things happened on Christmas Day."

"What's more amazing than Santa?" Nash teased.

"Well, snooty face, tell me this...what do the twelve days of Christmas even stand for?"

"Shopping at the mall, wrapping presents, eating the best food of the year," Nash answered unequivocally.

"Uh, not so much. So the song was created to help kids learn to count, ergo, counting down from twelve. But what it was originally about was the Christian tradition honoring the time the Wise Men arrived twelve days after Jesus was born, which made it all official like. And speaking of food, since that's all you ever think about, plum pudding used to be a soup with, like, mutton, dried plums and beef all gooped up together."

Nash rubbed his belly. "Ohh, tell me more."

Tori nabbed a candy cane, unwrapped it, and taunted Nash with it. "And the candy cane was created by a German choirmaster all the way back in the sixteen hundreds—you know why?"

"Nope."

"To keep young toddlers quiet," she gently poked it into his mouth, "during services. First they were just straight stick candy. Only later did they curve them to mimic the shepherd's staff in honor of the season. I know all you care about is getting out of school and getting a bunch of presents, but quite a few other things happened on Christmas Day. It also happened to be the same day King Arthur pulled Excalibur from the Stone, Hong Kong fell to the Japanese during World War Two and Charlemagne was crowned the Holy Roman Emperor."

"Whoop-de-doo." Laughing, Nash and Tori leaned into one another. "Only one important thing happens at Christmas and it's this." He grabbed Tori's hand, led her to the mistletoe and gave her a sweet kiss.

Barry smiled, genuinely pleased.

She watched them, so happy, so completely content with their lives. This was her family. She was here. But not here. A chill ran up her spine in spite of the heavy red Christmas sweater she was wearing. She suddenly had never felt so empty or lonely in her life.

*

Peyton sat bundled in a deep teal sweater reading outside by the gazebo when her cell phone rang. She picked it up eagerly.

"Peyton I'm so sorry...I cannot believe this. Nash and Barry aren't going to go golfing after all. I've...I can't really leave. It would seem really strange that I'm not here. I'm..."

"Sure," Peyton replied in disappointment, her voice tight. "Sure. No problem."

Elena had rushed into the bedroom in her nightgown, sat at the far end of the bed to find some privacy to reach Peyton.

Peyton sat at the other end of the line, in the middle of an assignment, trying to sound casual. "Look, Elena, I know you have a crazy busy life. I do too. Don't worry. It's okay."

"No, it is not okay," Elena replied emphatically. "I know this is the third time I've had to cancel...but please know that it's not okay. I want..." Elena looked around the small room, feeling like a caged animal. "I need to see you."

Elena jumped when Barry opened the door, came up behind her.

"Yes, Millie, well I'll talk to you about it tomorrow. 'Bye." Elena quickly got off the call, tried to regain her composure as she nonchalantly set the phone on the dresser. Barry came over, leaned up against her. She moved out of his range, trying to put a couple of pieces of laundry away when he grabbed her by the arm and playfully toppled her upon the bed.

Their faces were very close. He leaned to kiss her, which she allowed to happen, because she could not think fast enough. But as she felt his lips, so unlike Peyton's, so hard, nothing more than a mashing of skin that felt dead to her now, so unfeeling, and then Barry trying to pry her own open with his tongue, she had to push him away. She thought she might become physically sick, her heart racing. She abruptly sat up.

"Whoa..."

"I...I'm sorry—"

"What's with you?"

"I...I'm just tired. It's been a long day."

"Long day, right. You know what? We're both busy—and we're both tired." His voice grew tight. "Maybe I've had a *long day too*."

175

"I...I just really don't feel very well."

Barry looked at Elena and then gently put a hand to her forehead as if to see if she were running a fever, then let his hand rest on her shoulder. He smiled sweetly. "Hey, don't worry about it. You have been doing too much. You need to get some rest."

She smiled bleakly.

"Good thing I'm not the jealous type." Barry grinned. "Yep. That's one thing I've never had to worry about."

Barry rubbed her arm absently, as if already thinking about something else. "Hey babe, I really need for you to look over my speech for the fundraiser. Do you think you could do that a little later? Or even first thing tomorrow morning? And don't forget, you're meeting with Millie Tuesday." He mindlessly kissed her arm. "You know what? I'm really bushed too."

Barry got up, walked into the bathroom. "And make sure you get my blue suit into the dry cleaners tomorrow," he called. "You keep forgetting it," he yelled and then closed the door.

Elena sighed, rubbing her forehead. She glanced around the room. It could have been a locked cage. She was trapped.

*

The next day, the very first moment she could, Elena sped to Peyton's.

Peyton opened the door, they fell into one another's arms, Peyton took her to the bedroom and made love to her quickly, aggressively, Elena matching Peyton's ardor, each kiss rougher, more agonizing than the next.

Elena rasped Peyton's name as she came, hard, as hard as she had ever come, more intensely than she ever had, and pulling Peyton to her, she tried to return this pleasure, this unbridled pleasure she could not believe she had not known could exist until this late in life. But as she attempted to do go down on her, Peyton moved on top of her, holding her down, grinding the gorgeous swell of flesh, feeling the softness of her hair against her own, Peyton's body, sweaty, entwined with her own as she ground into her, bruising, a rhythm aggressive and exotic, Elena feeling her desire grow as Peyton's breath became more ragged.

"Elena...ohh...fuck..." A whisper plaintive in her ear, as Peyton's neck strained into an arch with the pleasure of coming, her throaty voice strangled in ecstasy as she came, and then came again, riding her as Elena held her with one arm, teased her nipple with her other hand, willing Peyton to come again, and when Peyton did she felt her release, felt her body seizing in pleasure, rippling over her, as Peyton choked out a final orgasm, her arms trembling as she collapsed upon her, sobbing in a sort of liberated aftermath, as Elena heard Peyton whisper her name over and over again, and Elena lived for that voice...that tender love-wracked voice in her ear...

An hour later, Peyton's face was buried between Elena's legs, trying to hold Elena off for as long as she could, teasing her, taunting her, Elena finally screaming, "Now...please....please, Peyton," and as Peyton moved up to her, and began thrusting into her, slowly at first and then with deeper strokes Elena began to come in a way she never could have imagined, from every source imaginable, her body moving into a kind of rapture she could not have conceived of before.

When Elena could open her eyes, when she could focus on light, and shadow, and depth, when she was fully back in a three-dimensional world, she gazed at Peyton, her eyes filled with love, gratitude, wonder...the emotions raw and exposed.

"How can your fingers feel so goddamn much better than a penis?"

Peyton rolled over, taking Elena in. She arched an eyebrow and then responded very slowly and sexily, "And how can you taste so fucking good?"

Elena smiled.

"Cunt," Peyton purred...and then with real desire, "cunt...." And then lacing it with an even raspier sexuality, "Cuuuuunnnnt."

"Honestly." Elena giggled, but blushed, a bit embarrassed.

"Elena, I know you have no frame of reference for this..." Peyton adjusted her body so that they were still as entwined as possible, but so that she could see clearly into Elena's face, "and while I hate to admit that I've been around the block a few more times than I should have been...I just have to tell you—the

177

way you taste, feel, smell—you make the term cunt beautiful. I've always loathed that word and felt it belonged right up there with all the other pejorative terms men use to demean women. But, seriously, Elena...there is nothing more delicious, more delectable, more exquisite than your cunt—which has in and of itself, removed years of damage from my psyche...and restored this much maligned word to a place of honor!"

As Peyton proceeded to go down on her lover, Elena laughed so freely at an idea and concept that had always caused her such intense shame, laughed with abandon and celebration.

*

"So, how's that whole adoption thing going for you?" Wave asked as they shared a glass of wine outside under Peyton's gazebo.

"Oh...well, you know," Peyton answered, evasively.

"I know what? That you've turned into a love zombie and nothing else in the world seems to matter, not me, your dearest friend, your work—or the fact that the only thing you've pined for the past few years is a child?"

"Okay." Peyton nodded, defenseless. "The truth is, both Elena and I discussed the whole notion of adopting right now and felt it was better to put baby plans on hold while...while this is—"

"—is going where?" Wave asked. "Until you've burnt one another to a crisp with passion and you are no longer capable of tending children? Or until you've run off to have children together? Or..."

"You know what? It'll happen when it happens, Wave." Peyton knew her tone had grown testy, but the fact of the matter was that it was Peyton whose plans had been put on hold. She really had no idea what Elena was going to do. While she hadn't lied to Wave about the fact that they had discussed the bizarre coincidence of meeting at the adoption center, and that neither of them had made great headway down that path, the reality was that Peyton had no idea what Elena's plans were for children in the future. Any conversation along those lines had been cut short by more pressing needs, meaning being with one another.

Now Peyton sat reading. Wave had left and Peyton could not help but replay the conversation over and over, her OCD rearing its omnipresent head and only reprieved when her phone rang. She picked it up right away, expectant. But as she heard the tone in Elena's voice, the joy quickly faded.

"...God, I so badly want to see you." Elena sounded distraught.

"Hey it's okay...it's okay."

"No. It isn't."

Long silence.

"Nash is coming."

Click.

Peyton looked at the phone. This had now become a way of life.

*

Elena tuned out Barry's sermon, as she had every sermon for the past several months, the sermons seeming more and more interminable. At first all she did was obsess about how to manipulate every minute of her day to get to Peyton. All that mattered was being with Peyton. If she could not be with this woman for whom she created contortion upon contortion, racking up white lies a mile long, letting so many things slip through the cracks to make it happen, she feared that someone could put a gun to her head and she would gladly have the trigger pulled. She used the lie that was easiest, constantly telling Barry and the kids that she was "working." Working on the project. Having meetings for the project. Long brainstorming sessions, and because they had done enough research before they had come together like a thunderous collision, Elena had enough interesting information to make most of her deceitfulness ring true. She had one goal and only one goal. Finding time to be with Peyton. And when that happened, all that mattered to her was being inside their bubble, being completely wrapped up in her. And afterward to relive over and over every moment,

179

her mind replaying lovemaking as Barry droned on in the background.

But for the past few weeks, her mind had gone to a darker place. The world in which she lived was no longer orderly and predictable, it was fissured and full of semitruths; the falsehoods that so easily tumbled from her lips could no longer be counted as white lies. She was telling bolder untruths about where she had been and what she was up to. She hadn't allowed this element—the fact that she was committing adultery—play into what she was doing until a couple of weeks ago when she had walked into the house, just moments after having the most extremely intense sex with Peyton, and as she opened the door, still smelling of Peyton, she ran headlong into her son. The look of surprise, not just at their near collision, but the confusion in his eyes as he studied his mother, completely undid her.

"Where…where have you been? I've been waiting for you for the past hour."

"What…"

"My coach's retirement party?"

It had completely slipped her mind.

"Where have you *been?*" Nash demanded. "And why do you look like that? You look like you've…fallen down a hill or something."

"I…I got in a bit of scrape…caught my skirt in the car door," Elena replied lamely.

"Well, can you pull yourself together so I don't miss the whole party?" Nash's voice was full of hurt and at the same time held the demanding tones of someone who knew he was in the right.

"Yes, of course sweetie…just give me a moment…I'll get…put some makeup on. Get in the car—I'll be there in five minutes."

"God, Mom," Nash sighed as she darted to the bedroom, "what's with you lately?"

*

"I'm sorry I couldn't call you earlier," Elena grieved. It was much later and she was calling from the living room. Everyone was asleep. "Look...I know I told you I would find a way to get over there tomorrow, but I think I need to lie low for a few days. Nash is starting to watch my every move...and...well..." Elena didn't know what else to say.

Peyton waited and then asked what both lived inside their minds, daily.

"How long do you think we can keep doing this, Elena?"

*

Elena fussed with Nash's collar, under his blue crew neck jersey. He kept pushing her away, grumpy, as they stood outside, Barry loading the car with duffel bags and a suitcase. Tori pulled out a beautiful origami Valentine heart for Elena, and presented it to her.

"I'm too old for youth camp," Nash muttered. "Really, I'm not a kid anymore."

"Okay, we'll send you over to the seniors while Tori and I whoop it up," Barry jibed good-naturedly.

"Come on, sweetie." Elena put an arm about her son, but he shrugged it off. "You know you always have fun."

"Whatever." Nash rolled his eyes. "And what are you going to be doing? While we're gone?"

They all turned to her, waiting for her answer. "Well, I...I'll be catching up on the housework—you know how it's always easier to get things done when you're not around. Nothing terribly fascinating." She swiveled to Tori. "Thank you sweetie. This is beautiful. I didn't know you did origami."

"Yeah...it's so amazing. I just got into it a couple of days ago. It's such a fascinating and beautiful art form." She cocked her head to inspect Elena. "You know, Japanese lovers used to hide secret messages within the folds. Pretty cool huh?"

Elena blanched.

They all stood there, shuffling about, a bit uncomfortable.

"Well, thank you, Tori," Barry concluded blithely. "Now in you go."

Tori turned to Elena, hugged her. Elena convinced Nash to give her a solid hug goodbye, and when Barry came to get his, she moved to the car, patting him gently on the arm and pecking him on the cheek. "Drive safely."

"We should be back tomorrow afternoon. I'll call you when we hit the road."

"Sure...but just in case I'm out running errands...call my cell, okay?"

"Yeah." Barry looked at his wife.

She smiled, gently, then turned to the kids. "Have fun you two!"

She stepped aside from the car, and waved as they pulled out, all the while the ticking time bomb going off inside her, waiting to move as quickly as she could to get to Peyton. She hadn't seen her in a week, and the wait had been interminable, unbearable.

*

Peyton's palm just barely touched Elena, skimming the surface of her fine, smooth stomach. Touching her, stroking her like this, had now become a most favored pastime. Each time, Peyton found herself amazed by the extremes of physical sensation that actually could occur in her by simply caressing Elena's skin.

"...when I touch your skin...it's..." Peyton's breath caught as she felt the ecstasy of this simple new phenomena. "God, with you...everything's so different...so..."

Elena took Peyton's hand, allowed her to trace her body, feeling every graze, then guided Peyton's hand slowly over the mound of softness to the core of her pleasure, and just as Peyton began stroking Elena, Elena nabbed Peyton's hand and flipped Peyton over.

"What are you doing?" Peyton giggled nervously.

But Elena pinned Peyton's arms beside her, teased her tongue up the ridge of Peyton's neck to behind her ear, then gently nibbled her way over the lobe, kissing her forehead, tracing kisses over her eyebrows and down the ridge of her nose, stopping for a generous kiss at Peyton's mouth and then Elena stopped, looked closely at Peyton, her eyes questioning.

"What…what….Elena?"

Elena had begun to move downward, and Peyton panicked.

"Elena, what do you…"

"I'm doing what *I* want," Elena proclaimed and continued to kiss her way down the length of Peyton's body, gently biting the soft edge at Peyton's pelvic bone, Peyton's hips jumping in delight.

Peyton made one last effort to move from Elena's command, but Elena was deftly removing control from her as she began to make love to Peyton, confident and in command.

Peyton trembled, terrified to let go, but Elena did not let up, and would not allow Peyton to hide. Elena slowly, deliberately, and certainly began to fuck Peyton, and as Peyton felt more and more, the delirious sensation not only of being made love to, but being made love to by someone who so desired her, so completely wanted her, heightened every sensation exponentially, beyond her comprehension.

Elena never hesitated. She had wanted to do this for so long. The only thing stopping her before had been fear that she could not please Peyton nearly as much as Peyton pleased her, but as with everything else that happened with Peyton, going down on her was the most natural thing in the world.

Elena's mouth found Peyton, tasting the female of her, her musky sweet desire, luxuriating in Peyton's craving, knowing that as she trailed her tongue along the folds and fullness, she could feel Peyton harden, and finally knew the power in owning another so completely, indulging herself in taking Peyton to a place she somehow instinctually knew.

And Peyton stopped trying to understand, and just let herself feel, relinquishing control, she stopped pushing Elena away, finally succumbing to someone loving her, her eyes filling with gratitude and then ecstasy.

*

Peyton and Elena kissed inside another endless moment of time, their bodies entwined, their features highlighted by the moonlight streaming through the open doors that led to Peyton's pool. The night was warm and Peyton had opened both doors before they had entered and now, after having made love, they pulled the mattress out by the pool, in the luxuriant air, their naked bodies glistening in the pale candescence, steam shimmering from the pool, an exotic setting for their endless embrace.

"...the pain of too much tenderness..." Peyton sighed.

"Isn't that Gibran?"

Peyton nodded. "That's how it feels when you make love to me..."

They lay in silent repose, each deep within her thoughts. Peyton cleared her throat. "That...that's never happened before."

"What do you mean?"

"I'm always the top." Peyton's jaw tightened. Vulnerable, she tried for bravado. "You know, more butch."

"You're not butch," Elena sputtered, "I didn't even know you were a—"

"No, no...not like that...it's more about the energy. More male, top, in control. I've been that way my whole life." Peyton stopped, thinking over all the ways in which she had made certain she never gave over anything too precious. "I'm the top, I initiate—no surprises—I stay safe."

"It's a whole new lexicon," Elena said with a grin, shaking her head. "You know I'm clueless about all this."

Elena traced a finger down the side of Peyton's face, covered her chest gently with her hand, pressing it against her heart.

"How do you know to touch me like that?" Peyton's voice was but a whisper.

Elena could see how exposed Peyton felt. "Instinct." Elena continued to touch her.

"I can't believe...how much of me I've given over..." Peyton felt everything, every caress, every grace, every brush of Elena's fingers upon her skin, and Elena saw in Peyton's eyes her willingness to trust.

"Peyton..." Elena kissed the swell of Peyton's breast tenderly, "I'm kissing you...a woman... touching your breast, loving the smell and feel of you as if it's the only thing that can make me whole. I want so much to please you."

Peyton's eyes brimmed with tears.

Elena pulled her close, empowered. "Peyton...I love you." She embraced her tenderly. "... I'm crazy in love with you..."

Peyton pulled Elena to her, moved her body atop Elena, kissing her thoroughly, aggressively, riding her, and suddenly stopped, grabbed her hand, pulled her up and propelled her to the edge of the pool.

Together they took the plunge.

*

After their swim, Peyton brought several different cartons of ice cream, along with a healthy piece of decadent chocolate cake Wave had dropped by earlier, along with some other nibbles she had grabbed on the way back to their picnic mattress, lit by numerous outside candles. The air was still balmy. They could have been in Hawaii, it was that warm, the shimmering mist above the pool heralding the mystical evening.

"It's really shocking that you have never been with a woman before," Peyton said between bites of decadent chocolate cake smothered in icecream.

Elena took one last bite. "I'm stuffed, filled up, overflowing," she remarked to the moon. She stretched like a cat, found a comfortable spot half inside the curve of Peyton's body, half slung upon the mattress.

"I...I had no idea people could make love over and over again," Elena stated. "Or why they'd even want to. I just never got what the fuss was all about...why in the movies people were 'doing it' all day long...how boring, I thought—and now, it's like sex is soooo much fun. It feels so good. I just don't want to stop. Ever."

Peyton leaned over, kissed her, spoon-fed her another bite.

"I thought I was full..." Elena smiled. "Do you think I ever will be?"

"I guess that depends..."

"On what..."

"Well, a lot of things, I still don't know how you are able to be so sensually gifted. If I didn't know better I would think you had been with women all your life."

"Well you do know better."

"It's just that…truthfully, Elena…and you know I hate bringing up my past and the fact that I did go through a phase of fairly relentless serial monogamy."

"Yes?" Elena cocked a *tell-me-more* eyebrow to Peyton.

"I guess you could simply call it dating, it's just that women feel so compelled to be monogamous that you make a relationship out of it, rather than just calling it what it is…which is, you meet, you date, you do it, it grows old, you go on."

"Sounds like most of the relationships I know about." Elena thought back to the few friends who had shared something approaching this kind of intimacy, and this story sounded very familiar.

"Yeah, only with lesbians it usually only lasts for six to eighteen months…you know, up until the time they hit lesbian 'bed death.'"

"Oh, for goodness sake."

"It's true…it's not in our DNA to procreate—to be driven to fuck as a means to survive. We're programmed to nest and nurture. The nurturing we have down great—I mean we're all flipping codependent. Our problem is, instead of just dating and having a good time, we insist on making it something more serious, or maybe we have to make it more serious because we simply don't know how to do it in any other way…Whatever it is, I've done way too much of it. The point is, I love sex, I've had way more than my fair share of partners, and yet I have never been made love to by anyone, the way you make love to me."

Elena smiled, gratified. "I hope so… you know I don't really know what I'm doing—"

"Well, you do a damn good imitation then."

"I love giving you pleasure…in fact, I don't think I've ever known anything to be so absolutely gratifying. I love seeing you…when you come—see your eyes, full of joy…I just love your face, Peyton."

Peyton glanced away, then started giggling. "And why the hell am I the shy one?"

"Yes, what kind of top are you anyway?" Elena teased.

They lay there a moment giggling, caressing one another.

"So do you…do you hate penises—or men, or—"

"No, I love men…and I have always had a healthy case of penis envy." Peyton glanced at Elena. "Although I've never been much into penetration. What about you?"

"Well, Peyton, I've only had experience with one penis, one man. And, trust me, it has just never been something I've found any fondness for."

"You sound like you're talking about cashews or something."

"I'm sure it sounds silly, and maybe I'm terribly unsophisticated, but it's never been about the penis for me—I don't enjoy it, I don't think about it. It just is. Take it or leave it, only there happened to be one attached to the man I'm married to."

Peyton shivered. Elena wrapped her arms about her, and her hand found Peyton's. She touched the ornate blue ring that Peyton's mother had given to her.

"It's beautiful. Whenever I see it, it just reminds me of you."

"Does it?" Peyton slowly took the ring off, moving it from her finger, and took Elena's hand, and gently pushed the exquisite sapphire onto the ring finger of Elena's right hand.

"Peyton, you said your mother gave this to you."

"She did. But I want you to have it."

"I can't."

"Are you afraid you'd have to explain it?"

"No. It's not that." Elena knew she could easily say she had bought it for herself.

She was worried it was too precious for Peyton to part with. "It's just it was from your mother and I don't want you to regret—"

"If this reminds you of me…I want you to have it. Please. It will make me happy knowing when we can't be together that I'm always a part of you."

Elena turned to her then, gently pushed her to the mattress and slowly but very assuredly began to make love to Peyton again. Elena had found her way as a top and made love to Peyton now with such confidence and grace, beyond all expectation, taking Peyton in her arms, knowing her body now, devoted to pleasing every part of it, operating on instinct, loving her so tenderly, so exquisitely, so completely.

And now, Peyton was getting more used to being made love to, something she had never really felt before, not like this, not this absolutely enthralled concentration on pleasing her with every touch. The more Peyton allowed Elena to take the lead, the more assertive Elena became, kissing her deeply, thoroughly, finding her, feeling her wetness, teasing Peyton with it and then confidently and with full ownership thrusting her fingers into Peyton, fucking her as if she had done this her whole life, taking this woman who most assuredly belonged to her.

Peyton lay back, a high thin vibrato breaking from her throat as she lay, splayed out, utterly at Elena's whim and desire, Elena thrusting her fingers further into Peyton, faster, Peyton succumbing to it in a way that felt real and natural and for the first time in her life, Peyton letting herself be taken, laid out, in total submission.

And for the first time in her life, Peyton felt the deliciousness of what it meant to be female.

*

It was very early morning. The sun was just beginning to rise and they still lay beside the pool cuddled beneath a comforter, feeling the fresh chill of a new day.

"I know you said you didn't care for pene—well, for that." Elena waited a moment, suddenly scared she had gone too far, because before they slept, as Peyton had come with Elena deep inside her, she had screamed into the pitch of night, and soon afterward began to sob, exhausted with what seemed to Elena perhaps like being relieved of a weighty burden. But then she had cried for some time, and Elena was not sure if she had read it right and had perhaps gone too far in her eagerness. Hell, she couldn't hold back—something had taken over her and she had to have Peyton in that way, had to own her, mark her, make Peyton feel Elena's entire being so inside of her that she could never let go. But when it was over Peyton seemed almost bereft and, except for her sobs, silent, falling asleep in Elena's arms whimpering.

"Yes..." A trace of a smile lit Peyton's face but something else, a sort of wisdom as if Peyton had learned a secret.

Elena held her closely as she said, "But you seem to like it... with me?"

"I like things with you I never thought were possible...I cannot...I can't believe how opened up you make me...how much I allow myself to feel. Especially given our circumstances."

Peyton sat up, then looked carefully at Elena. "Please don't think I'm crazy."

"What?" Elena asked.

"Well...I don't really know how to tell you this...but sometimes, when we're deep inside...well, being together, I almost feel like I'm in another place...another time, even. Like we have been together before. And I can't even tell you how out there I think past lives are, and I didn't even think I would ever consider believing in such improvable stuff, but when I'm with you, I often feel us in...a completely different way. And it's like I know this other essence of who we are to one another as well as I know ourselves. But they aren't us. They're from a time before."

It took a long moment, but when Elena finally glanced up at Peyton she was smiling. "So it isn't just me? Because I feel that too...like there is something from before. It's the strangest thing, but it doesn't scare me."

"Pheww." Peyton then grinned. "Didn't want you bolting for the door."

Another silence, but this one was much heavier, weighted with many unspoken feelings.

"I know how difficult it is for you to trust, Peyton, but I will never take advantage of you. Never."

*

"Good Moooorning." Elena waltzed to Peyton, who sat waiting on the gazebo couch outside as if she were Donna Reed, presenting a fully prepared breakfast for her mate—toast, eggs, pancakes, a bowl of fruit and steaming hot coffee she had quickly whipped together while Peyton had showered.

189

It was a gorgeous morning, the sun just warming the earth, birds chirping sweetly in the background. It was an idyllic setting, Peyton thought as she sat, blown away by how beautifully Elena had set everything up and how well she attended every detail.

"Hell, I didn't even know half this stuff existed in my kitchen!"

Peyton sat in her robe, hair still drying, and pulled Elena to her and kissed her, and Elena kissed her back ardently. Peyton pulled away. "Better not start—if we do, all this lovely food will go to waste…and I kind of need some fuel."

"Eat, please." Elena poured coffee, handed Peyton some toast and buttered a slice for herself.

Peyton's phone rang. She checked her watch. "Wow. I didn't realize how late it was."

"Well, we didn't get much sleep." Elena grinned as she sipped her tea.

"Hello?" Peyton's face blanched a bit as she rushed to say, "Uhmmm no, maybe a little later. Yeah, let me, uhmm, finish my swim and then we can go…"

A pause as Elena heard Wave's raised voice in the background, apparently miffed about something.

"No, I didn't forget…it's just that time got away from me… yes, it did…" Then a longer pause followed by a surreptitious whisper. "Yeah…mmhmm… yep…okay 'bye."

Peyton hung up, tried not to catch Elena's eyes.

"I take it she realizes I'm here."

Peyton nodded.

"She doesn't like me, does she?"

"Really, it's not you," Peyton insisted. "I think it's more about not trusting you. You know, being married and all."

"If I cheat on my husband how can I possibly be honorable?"

Peyton did not respond. She looked down at the table, stiffened a bit. "Well, I suppose it does sort of beg the question…"

Peyton's words floated out before them for some time, until Elena turned to her.

"What?"

"Well…like, do you make breakfast for him like this?"

"He doesn't eat breakfast." Elena smirked. "Anything else you'd like to know?"

"He doesn't eat breakfast…but well, do you have coffee together? Discuss your day?"

"Not really. He usually runs, showers, grabs a coffee on his way to the church."

Elena moved to hold Peyton's hand, but Peyton removed it, assessed her. "So…what about you and…him."

"It is what it is," Elena stated flatly.

"I want to know."

"Don't, Peyton." She remembered all those times in her bedroom calling Peyton, and feeling locked in a cage.

"Well…do you like it? Is it even mildly enjoyable?"

Elena refused to answer.

"So…" Peyton couldn't stop herself. "Well, like what…what happens…how does he make his move?"

"Good God, Peyton." Elena clearly had not planned on having this conversation.

"I asked you not—"

"Tell me?" Peyton asked and then more assertively, "I want to know."

"Well…" Elena put down her toast, swallowed and leaned back. A sadness filled her eyes and Peyton felt immediately guilty. "We have date night on Saturdays."

"You have sex every *week*?"

"Oh my God, no…every few Saturday nights he likes to take me to some fancy dinner. We sit there, eat. As I told you before, we talk very little, only discuss whatever happens to be going on with either Nash or the church, and we head home. That's it. Why are we talking about this?"

"That's it. Well that can't be all there is to it. You have to have sex some time."

Elena looked as if Peyton had slapped her.

"Every now and again he'll let me know that we should…you know."

"Does he say it?"

Elena closed her eyes.

But Peyton couldn't let it go. "Well, like what, does he say, 'dinner's over, we've gotten the preliminaries out of the way, and now let's fuck?'"

Elena's jaw squared and she narrowed her eyes in displeasure, shot a warning glance at Peyton, but Peyton was too far into it now.

"No, he'll just say something like, 'why don't we go to bed early' or 'let's work on the baby.'"

"You're kidding...and then what?"

"It is what it is. When it happens...which I've told you before is extremely rare."

"Come on. I want to know."

"I don't know what you're hunting for here. Do you want to hear that he's always considerate, always very good about taking care of my needs?"

Peyton's body tensed. Now that she was hearing it, she really didn't want to know after all.

"Look, Peyton, I wouldn't be here if I was having great sex with my husband," Elena exclaimed sadly. "I...we just have never connected in that way."

"And then what, does he—"

"My God, you ask a lot of questions."

"*What?*" Peyton's voice was sharper than she wanted. She put out her hands as if to explain. "Well, I'm a *woman*."

They sat awkwardly for a moment.

"I thought it would be easier for me to hear it was nothing... but it's not." Peyton leaned back from the table, suddenly exhausted. "Just thinking of you lying there...submissive...when you're—well, the way you are...it's so antithetical to how I see you."

"Peyton, listen to me. Look at me."

But Peyton's face, her eyes, were impenetrable. Elena got up, moved to her, leaned down and gently but deliberately took Peyton's face, kissed her fervently.

"Peyton..." Elena's voice was quiet but firm, "there is nothing here with Barry..." She put her hand over Peyton's heart. "Don't you know that by now? It's you. And only you."

Peyton looked up into Elena's eyes, feeling small and ridiculous.

"I love you..."

It had not been the first time Peyton had heard these words, but it was the first time she truly believed them.

Elena touched Peyton's face gently, briefly. "I don't want to fight, Peyton...I...I do have to tell you something, though." Her voice was somber.

Peyton sighed. *Now what?*

"We're taking a trip...to Hawaii." She continued before Peyton could explode, "It's our annual vacation and I would have told you sooner, but I didn't want it to put a damper on this time together. Our first night together."

Peyton's body grew stiff and ungiving.

"I...I knew it would upset you and I didn't want you to worry about...about any of it."

"You mean the fact that you're going to be in romantic Hawaii with your *husband?*"

"I know...I... Peyton," Elena replied soothingly, "nothing's happened with Barry...he hasn't touched me since we've been together. You know that right?"

Peyton nodded, staring out at the pool.

"God what was I thinking?" Peyton asked of herself and then, as if talking to anyone but Elena, "What in the hell was I thinking? Who could think?"

"Peyton—"

"At some point you're going to have to...well, you are going to have to do it again."

"But I've told you it's nothing," Elena snapped. "It means nothing."

Peyton pulled her body away from Elena, sat looking squarely ahead, her eyes deadly serious. "No. It will make us mean nothing."

Elena's cell phone rang.

"Great," Peyton hissed under her breath.

"It's Barry."

Peyton looked away.

Elena answered the phone, got up from the couch and walked toward the pool to remove herself to a respectable distance, but Peyton could still hear her. "Yes...when will you be home? Oh... you left early... Okay, yes... No. I'll be home. I'll see you then."

Elena returned to Peyton "I'm so sorry, but I've got to..."

"Go," Peyton finished for her. "Yeah."

Elena slowly walked back to Peyton and leaned over the patio couch where she was sitting, her beautiful hair cascading down beside her. "Aren't you at least going to kiss me goodbye?"

Peyton stared out for a very long moment, then turned to Elena. She grabbed her hand, touched Elena's wedding ring, twirled it about, and then gave her a brief peck on the hand.

Elena watched, almost dazzled by hurt, but realized there was nothing else that could be done now. She was already running late.

"I'll call you," she said as she walked from the patio into Peyton's living room.

Peyton's eyes followed Elena as she left. She felt angry, hurt, disappointed and absolutely frustrated with herself. *What did you expect?* She confronted her own appalled realization. *You have only yourself to blame.*

*

It had been almost a week since they had seen one another. Even when Elena had tried to figure out a way for them to spend at least an afternoon together before she was going to board a plane to Hawaii, every plan she spun had derailed.

Today Peyton had asked if there was any way she could quickly drive to Pinot Latte to see her before she left, and Elena had made that happen.

Peyton now waited in the booth, nervous, feeling silly one moment, longing the next, wondering if this was dumb. But the insecure part of her and that part of her that absolutely needed Elena to know how she felt still wanted to give herself this before Elena left on her trip.

Elena dashed in the door, and Peyton was again shocked by how drop-dead stunning she was with confidence blazing, her hair falling softly about her shoulders, her features highlighted by a deep lavender summer dress. Peyton's breath was knocked from her.

Elena saw Peyton sitting in the booth, Peyton's face so

exquisite to her—how she would miss those beautiful eyes, the dimples, Peyton's engaging smile. She slipped in beside her, and while she did not feel bold enough to kiss her, leaned her head against Peyton's shoulder, taking in the familiar smell of her, her woman smell, the musky cologne she always wore that Elena would breathe in long after they had been together, and never get enough of.

"I'm so sorry—I only have a few moments…I said I had to dash out to get some female supplies for the trip."

"Baby, it's fine. I just wanted to give this to you." Peyton shyly presented a small present wrapped in beautifully handmade paper gift wrapping.

"Oh Peyton," Elena was truly touched.

"The only thing is, you can't open it until you're in the air—in the plane—and then just promise me you'll follow the rules!"

Elena frowned at her, at the same time grinning. "Very mysterious."

"Yeah that's me…so mysterious…so in love I can't think of not seeing you a whole two weeks."

"Walk me to my car?" Elena asked with a sad plea in her voice.

"Sure."

Peyton climbed into the passenger seat. They looked at one another and a second later their mouths met, hungrily, desperately, both of them knowing it would be days before they could touch again, feel, wrap their souls about one another, know the other was truly there.

"I…I actually have something for you too." Elena leaned over and extracted a small square box from the glove compartment. "Wait until I'm gone. I feel entirely too self conscious."

Peyton smiled. They turned to one another, their eyes became serious.

"It's only two weeks," Elena whispered between kisses. "Nothing can change in that time except that I will miss you more and more every day."

*

Only after several hours, when Barry was asleep and Nash

and Tori were playing DES games in the seats ahead of them, so Elena could see if they were to turn around, did she dare to remove the package, which she had put in her small carry-on. She had thought of nothing else since they boarded the plane, waiting, waiting, what seemed an interminable time to simply see what it was that Peyton had gotten for her.

She double-checked Barry, who was snoring, and extracted the package, unwrapping it to reveal a beautiful black satin cloth with a lace ribbon that bundled a packet of cards/letters with a business card-sized note on the front that stated: *Do not open it until you're high in the sky...*

Well, Elena had waited, so she breathed in deeply, could smell the cologne which Peyton must have spritzed over the satin and opened the first letter on top that was sealed in an envelope, deep red, and could hear Peyton's voice, soft and intimate in her ear as she read: *I miss you. I missed you before our last kiss was finished...I want you to know that I am with you...every single day. In heart. Soul. Spirit.*

Elena flipped through the cards and letters. They were all exquisite. Some were notecards, some were sealed envelopes, all gorgeous, handpicked. Clearly Peyton had taken her time to create this wonderful gift so that she could have her by her side, no matter where Elena might travel. Each love letter Peyton had written had a date and a number—fourteen altogether, for the days they would be separated, and the one she held now, with the lovely words:

So the only way I can be with you right now is to touch you each day, with a moment that I hope you can steal away to have just for yourself—that is just for you, baby...here's only one rule: You have to read them as they are numbered...no skipping ahead like you did with my book!! This way I will know you and I will have a little shared space every single day that you are gone...and you will know how much I love you each and every day—

A tear fell on the paper. Elena felt herself let go, missing Peyton so completely she felt swallowed up by sorrow. How she could miss this person, more than anything...anything other than...oh, if she thought about Sarah now, she would completely lose it.

Elena quickly dried her tears, sniffling quietly, afraid that Nash or Tori might catch on. She simply folded the top letter and held it tightly to her breasts for a moment, then returned it to the others and placed them all back in her carry-on, taking comfort and delight in the fact that she would have Peyton with her in this entirely different way, excited and looking forward to reading her first letter.

*

Peyton waited until she returned home to open the box Elena had given her. She took off her jacket, hung it up, arranged herself on the couch, and only then touched the box, gently, as if in some way she could link herself to Elena. She shook her head. This was insane, missing another person like this. It made her feel a little out of control. Always dangerous. Because now it made her wonder what would happen if she were to lose Elena, and the likelihood that their circumstances would never work out.

Stop it. Stop it. Stop it.

She swiftly unwrapped the box to reveal a framed photo. It was a shot she must have set up herself in her studio. Peyton smiled, thinking about who Elena had been and who she had become. In the photo she was wearing nothing more than a white shirt, left undone, her hair full and thick about her shoulders, and she was looking directly into the camera with absolute love and a very sexy twinkle in her eye

Peyton could not stop grinning. It was such a metamorphosis. This woman bore no resemblance to the woman she had met at the adoption center. As Peyton looked into Elena's eyes, she felt as if she were there with her. It was the best gift she could have given her, so that she would not feel so alone.

*

February 27th
When you walked in from the kitchen, dressed for the outside world in your jeans and that dusky teal tank top—it struck me, Elena, how

absolutely beautiful you are…and it's because your beauty radiates from your soul…sensual, deliberate, graceful…

Yours is the kind of femininity that beguiles all the more because of the sheer strength of you behind it…so indelibly female, a handsome beauty that carries your power and the confidence to know how to use it…you are the best of woman…the most enticing because you are not afraid to love with all of your being, not afraid to follow your instincts, feel the searing intensity of your own passions and bring them out in me…the sheer attraction in that, Elena, leaves me breathless…I finally understand the clichéd term "take my breath away"….Elena you take my breath away—simply by the power of who you are…

*

Peyton thought of her, in just that moment, as Elena was reading the first of her letters that night. Peyton sat out at the pool, thinking how she loved watching the way she moved, simply walking across the room, or as she made her tea. It was these prosaic moments that made up an epic beauty, the way she so very slowly twirled the spoon in the cup with her long fingers, the way she drank her tea, so gracefully. Elena was the most elegant and alluring woman Peyton had ever laid eyes on, and it gave her great aesthetic enjoyment to just watch her.

Peyton smiled, thinking all this as she sat with her own tea by the pool. And then she sighed, long and hard. Thirteen more days to go. Already today had seemed like an eternity. She was going to have to really think of ways in which to fill the days to make the time pass. Sure, she had plenty of work she was behind on. Dammit, that's what she was going to do…she would catch up, so that when Elena returned she would be able to spend with her whatever time Elena might have free. Because if she didn't meet deadline on the huge Women in the Arts piece for *Vogue*, there was no way she was going to make her Paris trip. Paris. She wondered, if there would be any possibility that Elena could share—*stop it, Peyton. That won't happen. She can't leave her family for an entire week. But she can so easily leave me. Stay focused.*

Simple. She would just grind the work out while Elena was gone. But the moment she concluded this was the best use of her time and the best way in which to make the time speed by, the niggling irritation intruded that her life and how she filled her hours were always going to be determined by the time Elena was available. This was always going to be on Elena's timetable. And it began to irk her.

Stop it, she chided herself. She'd known from the start what she had walked into. It was worth it. Even if it ended tomorrow, loving Elena was the most incredible thing she had ever done, and she would never allow herself to regret it.

*

March 2nd…Oh but when you kiss me…oh…fuck, when you kiss me…that bottom lip—no earthly experience could prepare me for your bottom lip, your tongue, your mouth, the way you kiss me with your entire body, soul and being…when you kiss me and hold my head with your hands, with those long tapered fingers gently caressing my face as you kiss me…and continue to kiss me until nothing else exists but your mouth, pearly tongue, soft as silk lips…oh, fuck when you kiss me…

March 5th… After I make love to you, you tell me "Lay on your back!" and those fingers of yours glide over my body, teasing me, owning me…slipping inside me now and then fucking me…fucking gently at first, then firmer, fucking me until I cannot breathe, and before I can even catch my breath, you tease me, touch me as I have never been touched, playing out the rhythm of your ownership, taking me deeper as I grow tighter about your fingers, ever deeper until all feeling begins and ends with those fingers…I remember the night you showed up so unexpectedly after our first fight…when you made love to me with no words…

*

Elena remembered now as she sat out at the beach with her book. But inside her book was her "letter of the day" and as she read it, it immediately brought her back to her entering Peyton's house, putting fingers to Peyton's mouth so that she wouldn't say a word and moving her swiftly to the chaise lounge, slowly but

199

deftly unbuttoning Peyton's jeans, teasing her fingers into the open pants and then she began to gently stroke her.

I've never let anyone have me, let anyone take me, ravage me...

Elena's eyes were closed as she remembered now, as she watched Peyton's face, Peyton coming...

...you have given me such a gift...the other side of myself...you have made me whole...

*

"*Christ!*"

Nash sat on his bed, back from vacation, luggage strewn all about along with Peyton's letters spread out before him on his bed, as Tori read, as rapidly as she could, so she could catch up on what Nash already knew. She glanced at Nash, whose face showed a spectrum of emotion: disgust, sadness, anger, confusion, shame.

"Wow..." Tori said, speechless possibly for the first time in her life. She had never actually read anything quite like this. Not that she hadn't been exposed to it. It came with being a research assistant. You were bound to find some pretty skanky sites on the Internet, no matter what you were looking up. But something so intense, so raw, so clearly personal and intimate? Not on your life. She couldn't think of what to say and out popped, "Can anyone say outed in Maui?"

Nash found no humor in Tori's quip and looked at her sourly, despairingly.

"I'm sorry, baby." Tori quickly followed up. She watched Nash as he tried to grapple with all the implications these letters presented. "So you found these letters right before we came home?"

"I had a headache so I went to find an aspirin in Mom's suitcase—and I was digging around and I saw..." he gestured helplessly to the letters before him, "...these."

"Well, this puts a whole new spin on 'The only way to get rid of a temptation is to yield to it.'" Tori picked up one of the letters. "On the other hand...these are decidedly erotic and...well, hot."

"Yeah...great." Nash snorted.

"I'm sorry," Tori offered. "God, I just keep putting my foot in it. I...you know, I just really don't know what to say, Nash...I mean it's Momma Bear—it's your mom for gosh sakes."

"I got that," Nash replied sullenly.

"I guess this isn't really the best way to find out your mom's fucking another woman."

"You think?"

"Maybe we aren't getting the entire picture here. You know, if I've learned nothing else, don't jump to conclusions until you've done all your research."

"What are you suggesting, that we spy on my mother?"

"No. Of course not." Tori pondered, saw the tears begin to slip from Nash's eyes. "Oh baby, come here."

He fell into her arms, sobbing deeply, holding onto the only true thing he knew.

*

Barry had discovered when they returned from their trip that his car battery had died while they were gone. He had asked Elena to drive him to the church and also asked if they could "have a talk."

"I can drive you over, Barry, but really, I don't have time for—"

"Look, I'd really like to talk, and the shop said it would only take a couple of hours to get over and get the car up and running—"

"I can't!" Explosive.

Barry literally jumped.

"I'm sorry..." Elena made herself calm down. "I've just got so much catching up to do, unpacking, the laundry, I have to go shopping—" Elena could hear her voice rising in hysteria, tried to control herself. "I have too many damn errands...I'll be back, don't worry."

"You've been jumpy all morning. And don't even get me started about our trip."

"I told you...I'm sorry. It's the new medication."

"It's the medication, you're tired, it's this, it's that... Come on, Elena, I don't pressure you...and I know a lot of husbands who wouldn't put up with this kind of bullshit for as long as I have—do you even realize how long it's been? Since we've...? You said you didn't want to talk during the vacation—just wanted everyone to have a nice family outing, and I agreed, it wasn't the place for anything heavy, but now we're home, dammit. And we're going to talk."

Elena sat stoically, waiting for Barry to get out of the car, but he wasn't moving.

"Barry, I know you want...that we need to talk, okay? I understand that. But please, I just have so much to take care of before Nash gets back to school, I've got to go to the store—"

"Elena, what the hell is going on?!"

"Nothing, Barry. Haven't you ever noticed before that when we go away for vacation, I do all the travel plans, the packing, I schedule all the outings on the trip, budget everything out—all the planning, and when we return I need to get everything put back as if we'd never left and all that falls on my shoulders. Would you like to have dinner tonight?" Elena put the car into first gear.

He looked at her. "Go ahead...but we ARE going to talk... something's going on and I want to know what the heck it is."

"Barry, I'm just...just—Look." Elena knew if she started, it would not stop and she still could not quite get there. Yes, she knew things were bad. Yes, she knew she was in love with Peyton, a woman. But when she looked at this man with whom she had shared almost half of her life, all the history of Nash and the tragedies they had overcome together, she couldn't quite come to terms with telling him it was over. Just like that.

He leaned to kiss her. She offered him her cheek.

"Fuck!"

He leaped out of the car and before he could slam the door, Elena had already pulled away.

*

Peyton paced, anxious, hopeful, terrified, barely able to contain the jumble of feelings.

Elena finally walked through the door.

Peyton could barely breathe. Somehow Elena's beauty always struck her as if she were seeing her for the first time. She almost looked ethereal in a white blouse, the top buttons open, her hair a wild thrill of waves. The moment she saw Peyton, her face burst into a huge smile.

Elena felt like her heart was going to pound from her chest when she saw Peyton. *Her lover.* This woman, standing there, at once looking masculine with her defined swimmer's arms in a forest green muscle tank top, and yet so beautiful in the same breath. It was that mix of handsome and feminine that was so compelling.

"Oh God, I've missed you!" She rushed headlong into Peyton's arms, began to kiss her, but Peyton, while yearning to do nothing more than throw Elena down upon the chaise beside them and ravage her, could not break away from how shut down she felt, and Elena could feel Peyton's restraint.

"What is it?" Trying physical seduction, unable to keep her hands off Peyton, again Elena tried to kiss her, then stopped, exasperated. "I...only have an hour..."

But as much as Peyton wanted Elena, she slowly pushed her away and looked directly into her eyes, asking the question she did not necessarily want the answer to.

"He didn't touch me." Elena's eyes seared into Peyton's. "He didn't."

Peyton felt her anxiety ease, and trembling with relief and desire, pulled Elena into her, kissing her as if they would never kiss again, picking her up enveloping her in her arms, owning this woman who belonged to her by a right that was stronger than any other.

They consumed one another, starved for each other after weeks of separation.

Finally, Elena tried to catch her breath, and pulling free she looked into Peyton's eyes, and began to laugh from sheer giddiness.

"Oh Peyton..." and kissed her again. "I've missed you in a way I didn't even know was possible."

Peyton let her eyes linger on Elena's beautiful face, then she broke out into a grin.

They smiled, then, both of them, and Elena, holding Peyton closer, said, "Oh, yes…" and began to move Peyton toward the bedroom.

*

Elena came, hard, intense, a tear escaping down her cheek.

Peyton looked at her, breathless as she witnessed the raw beauty of exposure, seeing Elena's face as she probably looked ten years earlier, not a line upon her tender face, a youthfulness to her eyes, an elegant purity to her beauty that she had never seen before.

"My God…you are so beautiful."

"You are…Peyton…" Elena could barely breathe from how deeply she felt her love for Peyton, almost a physical pain. "You are beautiful…"

*

As the Winters family sat at the dinner table, there was a tension in the air that everyone seemed to feel. They were picking at their meals, accompanied by very little conversation, which was unusual. Elena glanced at Nash, pale and turned inward.

"Are you okay, honey?"

He nodded yes.

"You look so pale, are you sure you feel well?"

Again a brief nod.

"You've barely touched your hamburger—"

"He's just not hungry!" Tori snapped.

They all looked at her. And then Barry, frowning, asked her to pass the salt. "Come on buddy, you need to eat. Soccer practice tomorrow," Barry added, handing the salt to his son.

"Look, I'm just not that hungry." Nash tapped his fork against his plate. "Is that a federal crime or something?"

Everyone backed off.

"You know it was the Germans that first got the idea to soften meat." Tori cleared her throat and attempted to ease the tension with the normalcy of one of her riffs. This was conversation they understood and could handle. "Sorta came to them when they noticed the Tartars, a nomadic breed, storing their meat under their saddles while riding—yeah, it just pounded the meat to smithereens. Talk about your tenderizing!"

"Great." Nash shoved his plate aside. "Now I've lost what little of my appetite I had left."

Elena glanced from her son. To Tori. To Barry. The silence was deafening.

*

Barry dashed into the house, looking for his wallet. He knew he had left it behind, had taken out the Blockbuster card for Nash the night before, and now had no idea where he'd left it. He glanced through the living room, tore through the kitchen, began rifling through Elena's papers seeing if his wallet got stuck underneath the piles of papers she always kept in heap when she was paying bills.

He stopped suddenly. Heard something. But no one was supposed to be home.

There it was again.

He slowly looked around, began to stealthily make his way down the hall.

The sound came from Nash's room. The door was closed. Barry leaned in, thought he heard jagged breathing. Now it sounded like bad porn.

Barry thrust open the door.

Nash jumped as if he'd seen a ghost. He quickly mashed the *Lesbian Heat* porn DVD under a pillow at the same time as he reached for but failed to slam his mother's computer shut.

Barry almost smiled, but returned to the gravity of the situation and without a lot of tone demanded, "What are you doing home?"

But Nash was too busy blushing to respond. Barry walked to the bed, pulled out the DVD. Again he had to suppress a smile, had to concentrate hard to remain serious and reminded himself it was important for Nash to learn proper morals.

"Really! Couldn't wait until school was out?"

205

"Didn't feel well," Nash mumbled, then jumped as he saw an e-mail from Peyton announce itself.

The ping stopped both of them.

"And what are you doing with your mom's computer?"

Nash slammed the laptop shut. "I told you. I don't feel well. Can you just—"

"Yeah, you look really sick, buddy." Barry smirked. "What the heck is going on with you? You know better than to cut school. And for something like this?"

"Oh, is this the pot calling the kettle black, Father God Knows All?" Nash lashed back, then stood to confront his father. "And your hypocrisy about all things that keep you in good standing with that stupid church instead of paying attention to what's going on around here?"

"What the hell does that mean?"

"Strike a nerve Dad? Do you even have a clue?"

"You will not talk to me this way."

"Get out of my face!"

"I will not get out of your face. Whatever else I may be or do, I am still your father." Barry was angry. "And since your mother's gone half the goddamn time these days, you need someone in your face!"

Barry looked his son in the eye. Nash's lips were tight, his eyes boldly challenging his dad. "I assume I don't need to tell you—"

"Oh…*what?*" Nash mouthed the words *You're grounded.*

"You're damn right. You're grounded. You can just stay in here and think about missing the ball game this weekend."

"Whatever…" Nash slumped back on his bed as if nothing in the world mattered.

Barry nabbed Elena's computer, walked from the room, shut the door loudly enough for impact, but not so loud that Nash would think he'd really lost his temper. He stopped, opened up Elena's laptop and saw her in-box, but nothing was on the screen. Barry shook his head, confused, trying to figure out why Nash would be using his mom's computer instead of his own.

He thought about pulling up Elena's e-mails. Then stopped, considering what that meant. He had to trust her. He had to. If he didn't—and it was at that moment that he spotted his wallet beneath the folded newspaper he had been reading.

He closed Elena's laptop, returned it to her little makeshift desk in the dining room, plugged in the power and walked from the house.

*

Elena walked into the house much later than she had intended. This wasn't the first time she'd ended up coming home after everyone had gone to sleep. She knew she had to stop. Stop pushing the boundaries, but when she was with Peyton, the world ceased, and with Peyton she was happy. Not just happy, but blissfully alive. Being with her was such an intoxicant, Elena found herself strangling her schedule to figure every free moment she could squeeze out, knowing that as she did so, she was getting sloppy, missing appointments, cancelling things that were important. She shook her head. Every time she made mistakes like this, she promised herself she'd be more careful. She had to be. Being discovered was not an option, she declared to herself as she tried to get her bearings in the darkened room.

The light came on as she was stuck in this very thought.

Barry sat in the living room chair, and it appeared he had been sitting there for some time. Waiting.

Thunderstruck, Elena hoped that she looked herself, not like the sex-mussed adulterer she most certainly was.

"While you've been out finding yourself with your new BFF your son's on his way to becoming completely unmanageable."

"Barry—what are you doing up?"

"What were you doing out so late?" He stood up, walked to her.

"We went to a movie...then caught a bite after."

"A bite? This late? Are you kidding me?"

"No...the movie was longer than we thought...I was starving..." She let her weak lie float between them as Barry, apparently contemplating how to handle this situation, opted for reasonable tones.

"I've always let you have a pretty free rein, El...but whatever's

207

going on, deal with it. Our son's at a crossroads and I need you to get your head back in the game."

He stared her down, but Elena had nothing to say.

"I'm going to bed." He turned, left her in the room.

*

Elena paced quietly in the very early morning hours. She picked up the phone to call Peyton. Stopped and instead headed to her computer.

> Peyton...I need some time to get things settled with Nash—I won't be able to see you tomorrow afternoon...just know how much I love you...E

She sent it and then sat, stared out at the moonlight. But no answers came to her. Except one. She could not continue to do this indefinitely.

The next day Elena was furiously dashing through all the church bills in the church office when Diana popped her head in.

"I'm getting ready to head home, but I wonder if you have a moment."

"Sure." Elena put down her pen. "Everything okay?"

"I don't know." Diana looked at her strangely. "Is it?"

At that moment Millie walked by with several of her minions. Diana motioned for Elena to follow her. They poured themselves coffee, went down the hall, out of the church, and then headed to a table under a tree not far from the parking lot.

Elena and Diana sat not speaking for quite some moments. Elena felt stiff, totally unnatural and she had never been uncomfortable with Diana before now.

"I haven't seen you and I...I feel like you're keeping something from me." Diana played with the Styrofoam on her cup.

"Oh, Diana, I've just been really busy lately."

"Elena, you've always been one of the busiest people I know. But something is going on. I can feel it."

Elena's jaw tightened.

"Look, I'm constantly badgering you with all my problems, complaining endlessly about Rich, and not being a very gracious friend," Diana continued. "Heck—you know you can trust me, don't you?"

Elena studied the woman before her for a long moment, glanced back at the church, uncertain.

"Elena, it's me. We've known each other since Barry started here...what, over ten years now. Whatever it is, I am your friend and we'll get through it."

Diana put a hand over Elena's, smiled at her with conviction and encouragement.

"Okay. Diana...I've—I've—" Elena suddenly realized this was not at all easy to share, but she wanted to hear herself say it to someone other than Tyler. "I've fallen in love."

Diana almost fell from the bench, toppling the remainder of her coffee.

"*Whaaat?*" she screamed, tossing the cup on the ground. To hell with the spilled coffee.

Elena nodded sadly.

"Oh my gosh —I knew there was something wrong between you and Barry." Elena could see Diana trying to put together all the pieces. "You've seemed so distant with one another and I know you've got your problems like Rich and I. But, Elena, you've been married for *fifteen* years. You've got the most wonderful son. You're so well regarded in our community. You can't let a crush on—"

Diana stopped. Looked straight at Elena, shaking her head. "It's not Phil...no, it wouldn't be someone at the church. Who is he? Where'dya meet him? Is he married?"

Elena shook her head furiously.

"No...no. It's none of the above."

"So he's not from the church. Is it another town? Did you meet him while you were on your trip?"

"I...it's not like that."

"Oh, this is serious, isn't it?" Diana said, clearly eager to hear more. "It's okay, Elena. You've got to tell someone. It's not good to keep it bottled up inside. And I suppose he's taking advantage of the situation. No wait. Is he married too?'"

"No...it's—"

"Oh, well at least that's a silver lining. What does he do? Where is he from? How did you meet him?"

"It...it's not a man."

Diana simply could not register what her friend was saying.

"I've fallen in love with a...woman."

Diana's face turned crimson. She began fanning herself with her hand, shaking her head, then stopped, glanced at her friend as if to see if she was pulling her leg.

"No...Elena, no." Diana kept shaking her head. "You must be mistaken..."

The mistake was in telling Diana. Elena knew immediately she had made a huge error in judgment.

"Oh, Elena...I am so...sorry." Diana's voice descended from surprised to calm and pragmatic. "No, no no...you cannot do this. You cannot do this to your marriage."

Elena wilted as Diana's voice got stronger and her countenance more certain—virtually becoming a new woman, the woman Elena wished Diana could be with her husband when he hounded her endlessly for more children.

"It's against everything we believe in." Diana stopped, smiled sympathetically. "Look, Elena I don't mean to sound pedantic, and I'm not crazy like Millie—you know that. I have an uncle who is gay, but this...this, Elena, is wrong. Dead wrong. This isn't you. Your life. Your world will not fit into their world. Not to mention, you owe Barry, your marriage and your family the benefit of not acting out on what most certainly must be a...crisis in faith. You must learn from it. Don't make it any worse."

"Diana, it is not that simple."

"No, what you mean is that it's not easy. But it is very simple. What you are doing is wrong. A sin and you know it."

"But I lo—"

"Stop it!" Diana's voice was more stern than Elena had ever heard it. "Elena. You're not seventeen. You do have control over your actions. And you're certainly old enough to know the difference between right and wrong. Whatever has happened is over. I'll help you. I'll be there every step of the way. But you must stop it now. Right away."

Elena came up from behind Peyton who was working, having let herself in. She put her hands over Peyton's shoulder, down to her breasts, let them linger there, and began to kiss Peyton's neck.

Peyton turned, pushed Elena from her.

"I'm only here for a few moments…I only have time to kiss you." Elena took Peyton's face in her hands.

Peyton stood then, grabbed Elena to her, began to kiss her deeply, assertively.

Elena tried to catch her breath as Peyton's aggressiveness was as seductive as it was frustrating. "I've got to go…"

"Where you headed?"

But before Elena could answer, Peyton pushed her up against the wall, pinning her, and began to kiss her, even more aggressively.

"Peyton, I don't have time—"

But Peyton didn't hear, or if she did, didn't care, grabbing Elena by her wrist, yanking her down on the couch, and toppling above her, her knee thrust between Elena's legs, her hands pinning her down.

Peyton wrestled Elena and kissed her even more demandingly. It was the only time Elena had ever felt resistant, and holding back did not last long because as Peyton continued to overpower her, every fiber in Elena's being answered back, even when she did not care for Peyton's aggression, she could not deny how much she wanted her and wanted Peyton to take her, Peyton's manipulation finally overwhelmed her. Between Peyton's mouth on her and Peyton's fingers inside her, Elena felt herself beginning to come, and nothing was going to stop it.

She screamed Peyton's name, Peyton fucked her a moment longer and then breathless, withdrew, fell to the side of her. They both lay there momentarily looking at the ceiling.

"Was that for me…or for you?"

"I don't want him to…touch you."

"So was that your way of marking your territory?"

Elena began to rearrange her clothing, adjusted her hair and began to get up.

"Well, it is your anniversary tonight, isn't it?"

*

"So that's how you attempt to put a rein on your feelin's?" Wave asked, half soused. "By fuckin' the lady like a bloody hound dog?"

Peyton too was getting soused, flanked by Emily and Wave, the three of them drinking lemon drop shots for hours at a local bar in Silverlake.

"I…I was just trying to see if there was anything that would help."

"Well, that, my love, kind of sounded like bungee jumping without a bungee. Like holding back the Red Sea, like—what was I sayin'…" Wave meandered off in the middle of her sentence.

"…and how in the hell do I know if they're not fucking right this minute? I mean really, how could they not on their anniversary? It's like…FUCK!" Peyton moaned more than shouted, having felt the inevitability of this night for so long now.

"You are soooo shit-faced, my dear friend," Wave replied.

"Yes, Wave, I am. It's the only way I can get through tonight."

"Well, maybe you shouldn't jump to—"

"This isn't a conclusion…it's a denouement…" Peyton was going somewhere with her literary logic, but she was damned if she knew where.

"I hate to say it, Peyton, but I'm not at all certain that you have the right to be jealous," Emily countered.

"Jealousy will not be inhibited by rights…trust me on this one," Wave pointed out.

"I really thought I could do this," Peyton sighed. "You know, just make it about awesome unforgettable sex. I can do my life, my work, find a baby and she could do hers. Meet in the middle because I know she's never going to leave him…"

"Well, as a matter of fact, you don't know that," Emily countered.

"Oh, don't feed her any more rubbish, Em," Wave snapped.

"Why should she leave 'im? She's got her entire life wrapped up in her kid, her pastor husband, their church...not to mention the big enchilada for all women hitting midlife—security. It's one thing for a straight woman to have a wild fling during a midlife crisis and quite another for her to trash her world to enter the insane universe of lesbiana-ville."

"That's just it. She's not a lesbian...she's nothing like a lesbian," Peyton declared.

"Well...you do live in entirely different universes. Not to mention you're both doing to her husband what Margaret did to you."

Emily's remark sobered Peyton up. "Oh...thanks for making me feel so much better."

"Well, honestly, Peyton." Emily shook her head. "Don't you think this has gone on long enough?"

"Well," Peyton mused, "apparently so, because this is clearly the part where I get destroyed. There's not much more to go to from here."

"Maybe she was brought into your life for you to remember your priorities," Emily suggested. "You know. Like writing, getting your assignments in on time. Realizing what a brilliant agent you have who you don't want to lose because you're acting like a teenager."

"Personally, I think you're both going to go down in flames." Wave belched.

"Thank you for the fatalism."

"Hear, hear." Emily raised her glass. "I'm all for telling it like it is."

"Oh...so that's how I sound being such a damn downer, do I?" Wave glanced from Emily to Peyton. "Okay, let me put my kinder, gentler hat on. Let's say we stop lookin' at it in terms of black and white. You know, where chicks like us live so we can deal with all our endless insecurities. If I were to shed my cynicism—which is no small feat—I suppose there is an infinite array of possible outcomes here. Maybe the secret is to be really smart about the way you approach this—don't fall into the old clichéd traps—and just maybe you can land somewhere in the middle of the rainbow. Well, metaphorically speaking."

"That was quite literary."

"It was a thing of beauty," Emily concurred. "Maybe you're the one that needs an agent."

"Well, they don't call me summa cum barrista for nothing!"

*

That night, Barry walked in to see that Nash had fallen asleep against Tori's shoulder as Tori eagerly watched the end of a movie.

"I just want to know why there are so many wretched romantic comedies? I mean, even when they have great actors, they all seem so ridiculous. And you always know how it's going to end up. You always know the guy's going to get the girl, or the girl's going to get the guy—or whatever variation, but you all know how it's going to end, so why in the heck do we bother sitting through it—even though that's not how it ends in real life. The guy doesn't suddenly get that he's been a rude overbearing jerk and turn into a sensitive guy who can cry, and the bitchy shallow girl was bred that way, and we all will still kowtow to her, so she's not suddenly going to become less aloof and approachable...and the worst part is that Hollywood knows they can make a bundle because we'll watch these stupid movies and pay good money to do so, so on and on it goes."

"Are you finished?" Barry was irritated as he leafed through the mail.

"Yeah...pretty much."

"Where the hell is Elena? Working on her 'project' again? Out with that...that...that woman?"

Nash's head popped up, startled.

Barry glanced at the two of them, disgusted. "You both should be in bed. Tori, I'm too tired to drive you home...you do have a home, don't you?"

"Yes, Poppa Bear, I do indeed," she replied, small and hurt. She got up and exited with what flair she could but it was not very successful.

Nash, pissed, got up, straightened his sweatshirt and began to head out of the room.

"Get your butt back in that chair, Nash," Barry demanded.

Nash hesitated a moment, then realized his father meant business.

"Your school counselor called me today. Said you skipped the afternoon altogether. And when you did show up you were smoking a cigarette. You're an athlete. Why would you do something so foul, so stupid?"

"It's my body not yours!" he shouted annoyed, then mumbled, "And all I did was try it."

"You're too smart for peer pressure, Nash."

"Oh, that's sweet. Peer pressure, from the man who spews whatever crap shoved under his nose for a bunch of people who don't know how to think for themselves!"

Barry walked right up to his son. "You will not talk to me this way."

"You know what Dad?" Nash taunted him. "I will do whatever the hell I want. And I think we both know. You can't stop me."

"GO TO YOUR ROOM!" Barry exploded.

Nash cowered. Swallowing hard, and appearing as if he might cry, Nash made a beeline for his room.

"Shit!" Barry cursed at himself, slammed his hand against the wall.

What was happening to his world?

*

Elena came home late, for the first time, perhaps the only time in months, not because she was with Peyton but because she had gotten tied up at the church. When she walked in the door, she felt an odd stillness, wondering where everyone was, and then had the nagging feeling she had forgotten something.

She wandered to the kitchen and saw the large bag of Farfalla takeout, her favorite Italian restaurant, and in that moment, it hit her. Their anniversary. But Barry had suggested they celebrate over the weekend, and she had been trying to figure out a way for the past week to keep him from attempting to sleep with her—hadn't planned on dealing with this issue tonight. Not even remotely.

She walked to the bag and jumped.

Barry stood in the opposite archway that led to the kids' room.

"You...you scared me."

"Seems to be a habit."

"Barry," Elena glanced at the bag. "I'm sorry. Did we get our wires crossed? I thought you had a meeting with the chamber, and I had to meet Millie to go over all the budget numbers and it took forever."

"I know."

"What?"

"I called."

"I...I don't understand—"

"I'm sorry. I thought you were with that...your friend. But then I remembered you were *supposed* to meet with Millie and I called her to let her know I was going to be home after all, so that we could have a nice dinner. You know, maybe celebrate our anniversary today—the actual day, you know? But she was on another call, and they told me you had gone out to get some copy paper."

Elena couldn't tell by Barry's tenor if he had been checking out her story, or simply upset that things hadn't worked out.

"Barry, I'm sorry. Really."

Elena went to the bag, pulled out the food. "We could have a bite now?"

Barry thought about it. "Sure. Why not."

The next half hour they sat in uncomfortable silence, eating the dinner that Elena had reheated. They made small talk, he told her about Nash and the call from the counselor and made a pointed comment about his recent acting out. "I think it has to do with all the changes around here, Elena. Look I'm the first to support you in doing stuff that you like. But not when it comes at the expense of the family."

Elena treaded lightly and turned to less dangerous topics, discussing the church budget and how Millie was very gratified with how much money they had raised the past quarter.

The moment they had finished eating, Elena jumped up to

clean the dishes. As she ran the water, Barry grabbed a beer from the refrigerator and left the room. She thought she was in the clear, but within a few moments she heard him return.

She felt him. From behind her. He placed his hands upon her arms, pressed his body close and nuzzled her neck. "I miss you."

Elena froze.

"Baby...I really need you," Barry whispered, moving against her. She could feel him, felt him grow hard through her skirt. "The dishes can wait."

"I...I just got my period, Barry," she choked out.

A long moment passed.

"God damn it, Elena." Barry did not move. "What the hell is going on? You can't keep doing this."

"Barry —"

"I don't know who/what the hell she is to you. She's just some stranger. We're your family. And you're not here anymore, Elena. You're just never here! You've changed...even your clothes have changed." She could feel the anger seeping from him. "I don't even know you anymore."

"It's late, Barry. And I know you're upset. I know this night didn't turn out the way you planned, but for now, I think it's best if we just go...to bed."

"Come on, El." She could feel the frustration in his body, as he pleaded with her.

She didn't answer, hoping he would leave. When the silence became resounding, his hands gripped tighter upon her arms.

"Barry," she stated very calmly, "you're hurting me."

"Christ!"

He left her standing there. Elena didn't move for several moments, then crumpled against the sink, tears dropping into the dishwater before her.

*

P...I want you to know, nothing happened last night

I will see you at three. I cannot wait to be in your arms.

217

Peyton got the text when she woke the next morning, hung over. Relief flooded through her body. She felt embarrassed. She had overreacted. And now what did she have to show for it? A monstrous hangover. Served her right. But still, how long could they keep this up, and how long would Elena be able to keep him at bay?

*

Nash skulked into a small hole-in-the-wall convenience store in a scraggly part of the city. He walked through the aisles, staring aimlessly, mad one moment, indifferent the next, then terrified. How could his mother do this? To him? To them all? Who was she? Did he even know her? He was disgusted.

He spied something upon the shelf. He stopped. Debated his next move, then nodded. Yes. Just the ticket.

He nabbed the bottle very quickly, thrust it beneath his coat.

*

Elena and Peyton lay together, having made love quickly that afternoon, and were going over the events of the night before, both feeling as if they had escaped a calamity, both knowing their happiness was still a moving target. But neither wanted to deal with reality for the time being, snuggling close together, safe within each other's arms.

"Tell me an Elena story..." Peyton whispered.

*

Nash ran as fast as he could, his lungs burning, scorching, he was so out of breath. He'd run laps faster than anyone on his soccer team, but this was running for his life. He stopped the second he felt he was out of danger, turned to see if anyone had followed, then continued to jog a little more slowly up a hill.

As Elena spoke she had become very still, as if the quieter she became, the less her words could damage her.

"...and we lost her...she was only six weeks old. Six weeks. I couldn't stand it. I couldn't live with the reality of losing her. My dear sweet Sarah. My life was over..." Elena choked back tears. "When I lost her...I felt I lost everything. Even if Nash still needed me, he was three at the time, I knew I could take care of him, be a wonderful mother, try to be a good wife. Do what I could at the church. It didn't matter if I didn't have love... it didn't matter...because I didn't deserve it. How can a mother let her baby...just disappear in the night..."

Elena remained so still Peyton could not even feel her breathing. She did not cry, but Peyton could feel the complete depth of her despair.

"...nothing else mattered, but being the best mom I could be, and to give back to the world through the church... Nothing else mattered," Elena turned to her, "until...you."

Elena saw that Peyton's face was etched with pain.

Peyton said, "Every time I don't think it's possible to fall more in love with you...I do..." She leaned to kiss Elena. "...Ever deeper..."

*

Nash sat up on a huge cliff, overlooking the skyline of the city. He looked straight out, the wind drying the tears on his face. He picked up his stash, opened the bottle of sour mash whiskey and took another slug, gasping as he had every time before. He found it a little difficult to believe people drank this stuff for enjoyment, and held the bottle out before him. Half gone. Took another swig. He was going to finish this damn thing, but he was getting awfully hungry, felt the burn in his gut from the varnish-like liquid.

*

Peyton had just finished making love to Elena, serious, deep and intense, Peyton trying to soothe the pain in a shared raw intimacy, wanting somehow to make it okay, to make Elena feel that she was safe, and that sharing such information was not only natural, but that nothing from this point forward could break their bond. They were in this together, no matter the outcome. They had to be.

Elena smiled, pulled Peyton closer as Peyton ran fingers through Elena's hair, lying there in stillness and bliss.

A loud rapid knock on the door caught them both completely unaware. They both bolted upright.

"Are you expecting someone?" Elena whispered.

Peyton shook her head. "Wave would just barge in. Let's see if they go away."

The pounding returned only with increasing velocity and then a voice shouting urgently, words neither of them could make out.

Peyton jumped into her jeans, threw on a shirt.

She dashed out of the bedroom, opened the front door to reveal Tori, cell phone in hand.

"Yeah, it's nothing like all those people standing around in those stupid commercials is it—you know like they're really all going to help you during a crisis of no connectivity!"

Peyton was trying to follow Tori's stream while at the same time wondering what the hell she was doing at her house and how she knew to find them here.

"So, where is she? I've been calling nonstop for the past two hours?"

"Uhmm..." Peyton shuffled her feet.

"Look, I'm on your side, so you can drop the pretense." Tori barged in without being invited, glancing about for Elena. "I need to find Elena. Now. Nash is in trouble. He lifted some really nasty booze—got snockered and then returned to the scene of the crime for some Doritos of all things."

Elena now appeared dressed, and frazzled.

"Where is he! Is he okay? Is he safe?"

"I guess it's the typical acting out with teens. You know their frontal lobe doesn't take into consideration the consequences of their actions...they're just not wired to understand stuff like—well like," Tori spread her hands to indicate the situation, "this!"

"Dammit! Where is he, Tori!"

"He was at some juvie center, but not to worry—when they learned Poppa Bear was a pastor, they let him out right away."

Elena momentarily stopped shaking, relieved that Nash was safe, and then had to take into consideration their current situation, but before she could even think about that Tori added, "Now they're both at home. Wondering where you are."

Elena looked at Peyton in self-recrimination, then walked out the door.

Tori shrugged, followed Elena.

*

Much later in the evening, as Elena was finishing cleaning up the dishes after what had been a very silent and tense dinner, Barry walked in. Elena felt her entire body stiffen. She had no idea who knew what. But to her surprise, Barry picked up a dish towel and began to help dry the dishes.

"I guess it's rather pointless to ask where you were?" He put a glass away.

Elena removed herself to the opposite shelves. "I already told you. I stopped at the park—"

"You were there all afternoon—" Barry didn't turn, but his voice was full of doubt.

"No, I was shopping and I guess..." Elena sighed. She hated having to lie. She wondered if she should just tell him. Tell him now. But the thought of everything going up in smoke at once was too much for her to bear. "I...I must have left my cell phone in the car—I've told you this. Do you want an exact timeline?"

Barry laughed. Elena turned to him, surprised.

"Gotta say, it took some guts for Nash to pull that off."

Elena realized as she looked at Barry that he was thinking about the past, when they were young and free to do stupid things like their son had just done.

"Reminds me of the day," he stated wistfully.

"That day is better off buried." Elena would not have him romanticize his own drinking, how he used to sit night after night when he couldn't get a gig, and would get drunk instead. Not that Barry was ever even a mean drunk. He'd just sit and get wasted. But since he'd been in his job as the pastor, Barry drank only in moderation. He had left those behaviors behind, and in that and so many other ways, Elena felt like Barry's position as pastor was all to the good.

"You're right. I know we have our problems Elena—well, what couple doesn't?—and we may have a few cracks here and there...but we also have it so good."

Barry put down the dish towel, walked to Elena, pulled her to him. She bristled as she had the other night, again amazed to feel her body's defensiveness, now so used to Peyton's skin, Peyton's gentle touch, and she felt repulsed, but held herself in check, and allowed him to hold her.

"I don't know what the hell's going on with him, El." Barry's voice was low and thoughtful and Elena knew she owed him this. "But we've got to—I don't know, maybe spend some more family time together."

Then he chuckled. "Yeah...I always think of him as your boy...but he's got a bit of the ol' man in him."

Elena felt badly now as she watched Barry try to deflect the ongoing rejection by Nash of his father. They had never been close and she knew it killed him.

"He has a lot of you, Barry. He's kind. Generous. And he's got your wonderful smile."

He glanced up to Elena. They shared a moment.

"That's one thing we didn't mess up." Barry sighed and then his voice became sharper. "And it's gotta stay that way. You got it?"

She nodded, obediently.

"I'm gonna get ready for bed." He waited for her expectantly.

"I'll be in, in a sec. I'm going to check on him first."

*

222

Elena stopped before Nash's closed door, trying to figure out the best way to approach discussing the day's events, wondering if she should be harsh and serious, when all she wanted to do was scoop him up in her arms and hold her baby close. But he wasn't a baby. He was nearly sixteen. And she wanted—no, needed—for him to understand the difference between right and wrong.

She slowly opened the door, and whispered, "Nash?"

No answer. She walked further into the darkened room and could tell by Nash's body language and the way he was breathing that he was awake and trying to pretend she wasn't there.

"Nash."

She sat next to him, put a hand through her son's curly hair and as she touched him, he flinched away from her.

"Honestly, Nash...what were you thinking? You know better than—"

"NO! What the hell were YOU thinking!" The vehemence and bitterness caught her off guard.

"I'm sorry?" Elena tried to get her bearings. "What...what are we talking about here?"

"You." He turned to her then, slammed the light on in the room, exposing his tear-stained face. He spat, "You and your dirty little secret!"

The air was sucked from Elena's lungs. She closed her eyes. Of course he knew.

"I read her letters."

"What...what letters?"

"Your girlfriend's oh-so-pornographic letters." Nash sat up in an accusatory posture. "God, I even liked her."

It took a moment to register for Elena, but when she realized he was referring to the letters Peyton had written her while they were in Hawaii, she blanched, her mind racing back to the contents, trying to remember how graphic they actually were... knowing they were terribly graphic.

"Nash."

"Yeah...that was a thrill ride."

"What were you doing going through my things?" Her voice was shrill.

"Hey, don't turn this around on me. It's like Tori said, it's almost as if you wanted us to find out."

"Don't be ridiculous. I would never want either you or your dad to find out in such a painful way."

"So now the question is, how are you going to tell *him*? Because let me tell you, Dad would never get over reading something like that."

Elena sat there stunned. In a moment her idyllic love affair with Peyton suddenly seemed petty and ugly and all wrong. But she loved Peyton, how could it be wrong? She wasn't quite certain what tack to take with her son. She looked at him then, put a gentle hand upon the blanket where his thigh rested.

"Nash...sweetie, I wasn't looking for this. God knows, I don't really understand it. And I certainly didn't realize what was happening until it was too late..."

"You *are* going to tell Dad!"

"Yes, well, I certainly had planned on him knowing before you."

"So, then, what?" Nash started tearing up again, and Elena could see not just the pain but the terror written all over his face. "Are you're going to get a divorce?"

"I...I'm not sure, Nash. I'm not sure what I'm doing."

"Then stop. I think he's an asshole half the time, but this'll kill him. It'll blow his whole ridiculous facade. How's he supposed to guide his fawning flock when his wife's sleeping with the enemy?"

Elena shook her head beginning to tear up herself.

"Nash, I need for you to understand something. I have never cheated or been dishonest with your father before...this." Elena looked Nash directly in the eyes so that he could see her truth. "But, I've never been in love with him, either."

He greeted this statement with bewilderment. "Then why, Mom, why stay with him all this time?"

She held him close, placed his head upon her shoulder.

"Why do you think?"

He lunged for his mom, holding onto her for dear life. The minute he began to sob, she began to cry as well. She held him, her little boy, her sweet tenderhearted boy whose life she was now disintegrating in front of them both...and knew that she had to protect him, no matter what, that she had to find a way to resolve things without causing him pain.

As he calmed, she kissed his forehead, and then rubbed his head until she heard his breathing calm. She held him long after he had fallen asleep.

"My son has severe autism and my wife left us when Julian was three." A slender man in his early forties, Anthony sits thinking back to this painful time.

"And my husband couldn't deal with our daughter's Down syndrome," says Julie, a frail beauty, whose life of hard knocks has certainly taken its toll.

"Shane's Inspiration is a full access park for kids with disabilities and my son loves to go and swing, but he also has seizures, so he has to be in one of the belted swings at all times. He'd go for hours if you'd let him." Anthony turns to Julie. "That's where we met."

"Angelina, my daughter, also loves to swing—anything with motion makes her giggle with delight, so I put her on the swing next to Julian, Anthony's son. Julian started singing 'Down by the Bay.' Julie begins to get emotional, "And I couldn't believe it…my daughter, who has never sung, joined in—not in tune or anything, but began singing—for the first time in her life at five. And she just kept on singing—wildly off-key, but kept up with him for a good forty-five minutes."

Anthony is beaming at his wife. "And that's how we met. Our kids. Their connection is so incredible. They can lay snuggled and cozy like puppies the whole day. They are the soul mates, and we're—well, we're the lucky beneficiaries."

"You don't know," Julie sighs. "How it is to be with someone who loves your child and accepts them for exactly who they are. No more walking on eggshells or apologizing. My ex…well, he was just plain embarrassed by our daughter. You just don't know how amazing Anthony is. He plays with the kids all the time, eats them up like candy. He just completely gets it. Gets them. I couldn't have asked for a better partner."

Anthony looks at his wife. A tear rolls down his cheek.

After the longest night of her life, Elena walked in to see Tyler at his editing bay. Long after Nash had gone to sleep she had paced, and then would intermittently stop in her tracks, sit in the darkness, hoping stillness would bring an answer, and then despairingly return to pacing. She couldn't hurt her son, she didn't want to destroy her family, she couldn't bear the thought of leaving Peyton. No answer came without deep pain and anguish to any one of the people she most dearly loved.

She had put on a brave face in the morning, made a special breakfast for everyone and sent them about their day. Then she jumped into her van as fast as she could, dashing to Tyler's.

Tyler was in the middle of editing what she could see was a very poignant Soulemetry webisode, but when he realized she was standing there, he hit the pause button on his Final Cut editing system.

"Gotta tell ya, there's a reason that that's one deeply meaningful cliché..." Tyler got up and took his friend in his arms, "...love truly can conquer pretty much any situation out there."

"Do you really think so?" Elena sniped. "I feel like it's about to devastate everything I know."

Elena withdrew herself from Tyler's arms, paced around his room, arms akimbo. "What am I doing? Look at all the people I'm hurting."

"Oh, sweetheart, the sad truth is, life happens, and you should only be so grateful life decided to send a thunderbolt down between your eyes or you might never have lived it!"

Elena sighed, and Tyler stopped his friend from continuing to pace.

"Listen, my angel. Barry knows without your guilt you would have left him ages ago. It's made me crazy ever since it happened. I don't mean right after, but when he could see the writing on the wall. And he has, believe you me. He just never mans up and gives you an out. Enough is enough."

"I...I..." She didn't want to cry again. She wanted to be strong. To find a workable solution. Not to feel impending doom heading her way. "I...I don't want to talk about it."

Elena remained shut down, angry, but Tyler wasn't having it, made her turn to face him.

"I'm so, so sorry, Elena. No one wants to talk about it! But we're going to talk about it here and now!" He was implacable.

"Tyler—"

"No, Elena. There is nothing that's right or just about any baby dying from SIDS." He put his hands to her arms. "I'm sure there isn't a parent alive who wouldn't blame themselves—and you're such a momma bear I'm sure you believe there must have been something you could have done differently to save Sarah. But there wasn't. I know you've beaten yourself senseless with blame—punishing yourself endlessly by staying with preacher man. Nothing...nothing you could do could prevent what happened. It was your little girl's time. But make no mistake, for however little time she was here with you, she was here for a reason and to make you the person you are today."

He took her by the hand, sat her down, his voice gentle, soothing. "So you commit to Barry, and you do all these awesome things at the church to balance the scales. And maybe that's part of your journey—whether you want to believe in this stuff or not."

Elena finally allowed the tears to come that she didn't dare let surface when she had told Peyton about Sarah. Now, after Nash, after her life blowing up in her face, she couldn't have kept them from coming anyway.

"I loved her...God, I loved her so much, Ty..."

Elena then broke down completely, sobbing, releasing, finally allowing all of it to come tumbling out, her grief at holding it all in, at keeping Peyton a secret, all the clandestine meetings that were wearing her to a frazzle, betraying her family, feeling guilty, but still loving Peyton with every breath in her body. All of it came out.

She took the tissue Tyler offered her. Blew her nose and tried to reassemble her face.

"We all have our destiny," Tyler stated gently. "She is part of yours."

"But...I didn't have a choice in some of that," she stated, nearing a point of no return. "I do here. How can I do this to my family?"

She could barely take in the events of her life. If she left Barry she would break Nash's heart and ruin his entire world. If she didn't, she was going to have to leave Peyton, something she simply couldn't bear. Losing Sarah suddenly felt so fresh, and she didn't think she could survive another such loss. How could she ever recover from the pain of losing the only adult she had ever loved? She began to cry again, unable to stop for several long minutes.

Tyler simply held her, rocking Elena in his arms. "There there, beautiful woman." He spoke with love and tenderness, "You can't rewrite history. But you know what you can do? You can reframe the present: Barry's let off the hook—I'm sure even he has a soul mate somewhere out there. Nash wouldn't have to constantly face the schizophrenia of your marriage. And you— what a gift you've been given. I've never seen you like this." Tyler put a hand to her chest. "Alive, joyous, full of passion. Peyton makes you breathe."

At that very moment Lily popped in, her glasses crimped on her nose, reviewing contracts, so involved in what she was doing that she didn't even see Elena at first. She was mumbling, "Tyler, doll, I told you this morning, these papers had to be signed by five o'clock sharp! Oh!"

Lily stopped, glancing from Elena's tear-stained face to Tyler kneeling at his friend's knees. "Oh God, I'm so sorry."

"Lily, as you can see, Elena's having a rough day."

"Hi, Elena..." Lily wasn't the most graceful person in these situations, tending to stay away from negotiating anything that involved actual contact with emotion. She was very good at what she did because she remained detached and disconnected to the situation so that she could remain focused. "Ty, I'm so sorry but I just need your signature on this merger."

Elena blew her nose.

"I know my timing sucks, but if Tyler had just taken care of this, this morning, I wouldn't be interrupting your—well, this. It'll only take a minute."

Tyler shook his head. That was his Lily, all high-powered and vogue elite, but without an ounce of social grace when it came to the plight of human frailty. Tyler rose, but then turned Elena's chair to the monitor before her. He kissed her forehead, hit the play button and exited.

Elena barely glanced at the familiar face of Tyler as he sat in his homemade studio speaking directly to the camera in his "host" role.

"And for those of you debating the Soulemetry qualities of that special someone, let's just run down the ol' soul mate criteria that must exist for this person to be a true Twin Flame.

"Remember, first, sometimes this person comes in an unusual package—maybe not your usual type. Secondly, you met under unusual circumstances, perhaps freakish randomness. Third, you are desperate to be with that person."

By this time Elena was not only listening she was ticking off all the qualities she knew existed in her relationship with Peyton. "Fourth, and this one's key, everything feels completely brand new, yet absolutely familiar. Yes, that person's eyes really are a window into your soul."

Tyler took a dramatic pause. "And, finally, this connection has fundamentally changed you. Significantly, altered you to the core."

Even through her tears, Elena smiled. Everything on Tyler's list was true.

*

Elena walked as briskly as she could, knowing she was already late to meet Peyton at the park after she had had to cancel yesterday because Nash kept dogging her, following her every movement. If she stood up, he'd interrogate her. "Where are you going? Are you going to see *her*? Is that what you're doing? Just tell me. Tell me the truth!" Until Elena thought she would lose her mind.

The day before, when she had set up this meeting with Peyton, she had made it into her car and begun to back up and there he stood behind her at the end of the driveway, arms folded. He terrified her. Shook her to her very foundations. Like her son was now her judge, jury and executioner. But finally, finally, he had left with a friend to go to the movies. After he had safely been gone for ten minutes she had phoned Peyton and asked her, rather desperately, if they could meet at the park.

She stopped when she saw her, standing at the bridge that overlooked the brook. So handsome. So beautiful. Once again Elena was struck by Peyton's entire being, and couldn't resist running to her, wrapping her arms about her, finding Peyton's lips, and the moment she did she felt safe, on solid ground, and could feel the rightness of who they were together and the exquisite warmth and feeling of being alive, startlingly alive when she was with her, all of it flooding back over her in the same breath.

Peyton gently but firmly tried to push Elena aside, but Elena held her close and Peyton too sank into the smells, the silky softness of Elena's lips, the ungluing that always happened the moment Elena touched her.

*

Millie was powerwalking, up to six miles a day, which was really great because it also meant she could jam in all her afternoon calls on her headset as she plowed through her miles, checking her BlackBerry, steady as she goes, walking her pink-bowed Chow, Snowflake Angel, managing the universe according to Millie with precision and efficiency. She was proud that she could literally handle anything. Everything. The more she had to do the better off she was. She was going to change the world. And they were going to be good changes. Changes that not only needed to happen to save the very fabric of marriage, but would put her in position to pen her memoirs. She'd tie it up and promote the heck out of it, take part and delight in every talk show from Oprah to her absolute favorite, Glenn Beck—okay so she had a little crush on him, but it was nothing. Nothing, really. She really could begin to position herself as the next Dr. Laura—helping all those poor unfortunate misguided fools who had lost their way—

What was she seeing?

No.

NO. It couldn't be.

Two women kissing. At this park. A *family* park.

Millie almost tripped over Snowflake Angel as she gaped,

231

watching these two women really going at it. *I mean get a room already!* Millie was beyond incensed that these two people had the audacity to exploit their filth at this park, this park where kids, children and her innocent Snowflake Angel roamed. If people weren't safe here, where were they safe?

Elena!

Her horror soon turned to fascinated repulsion. She scrambled to collect herself. She could barely breathe. Barely could catch her breath as she lunged for her cell phone.

Elena Winters. In the park. Kissing.

Kissing a...a WOMAN shrieked in her brain.

She dropped her phone.

She scrambled to pick it up, tangling her feet up with Snowflake Angel, tripping to her knees, but jumped back up as she nabbed her BlackBerry and began to dial.

*

Peyton gently but firmly pushed Elena from her.

"Is he...is he okay?"

Elena nodded yes, not with great confidence, but enough so that Peyton felt relieved. She took Elena's hand, smiled weakly, and then led Elena to several large flat boulders below a huge oak tree.

As they sat, Elena studied Peyton, traced a finger over her face.

"I'm in love with a woman." Elena's voice was filled with wonder and awe. "It still amazes me. At times I feel it's all been a dream. But then when I'm with you...it's all so real."

Peyton tossed Elena a bleak smile.

"Look, Peyton...I know this last week has been rough..."

"Yeah." Peyton sighed long and hard, then said, without looking at Elena. "Maybe we should pull back a bit. Until...you know—things settle down."

*

"I tell you I just saw her kissing a woman!" Millie yattered

232

on the phone as fast as her lips could form words. "In the plain light of day!"

Millie summarily tossed her Snowflake Angel into the car as she frenetically tried to keep pace with her own gossip. "I knew something was up with her. Not wanting to protest, missing services. But *this!*" She barely gave the poor dog another moment as she jumped into the front seat and began driving without having fastened her seatbelt.

"She's turned into...into a GAY! And what about poor Pastor Barry? How could she *do* this to him?"

Millie, now on a mission, sped through the streets of the city.

*

Elena glanced sharply back to Peyton, could see the raw pain etched in her exhausted face.

"You wouldn't have to feel so guilty," Peyton continued softly. "I could dial this back and get my head screwed back on right."

Elena bolted to her feet, alarmed.

"Where...where is all this coming from?"

"I...I just think we need to pull back and get some perspective."

"Do you really believe if you rearrange the psychic furniture that will fix it? If you act like you're not as in love with me as I am with you that—that—" Elena stopped. She could see that escalating this debate was getting nowhere, and tried to calm herself.

"I understand all the reasons you can't trust. Your mom, Margaret cheating on you...but Peyton, I've never lied to you and I never will."

"I guess at this point I really don't know that, Elena."

Elena shook her head, now getting upset.

"I spent the last day and half with my guts skewered inside out wondering whether you were having sex with your husband." Peyton's jaw clenched as she took a deep breath, "and last week I did the same thing because of your anniversary— getting shit-

233

faced over it because I can't bear the idea of him touching you. But also because I have no right to these feelings—"

"Oh Peyton...nothing happened. We didn't even go...Barry had an emergency at the church."

Peyton looked at Elena. She didn't get it. It seemed to Peyton that as long as Elena felt she could dodge one bullet after another, the end still wasn't going to be global destruction—for both of them.

"I knew what I was getting into...it is what it is." Peyton bowed her head, then looked out at nothing in particular. "I just don't think I can do it."

"Peyton, don't you see a future with us?"

"So this date night nothing happened. What about the next one and the one after that? At some point...something will happen."

Elena was about to defend this last, but how could she really? How could she say she and Barry would never sleep with one another again? Not because she would want that—the thought made her stomach lurch with dread, but the reality was that they were still married.

"After all, Peyton...I have been married for fifteen years." She stopped thinking about how she had been able to hold Barry off for nearly eight months. But without telling him why and it had already become such a huge issue—and she wasn't quite certain she was prepared to do that yet—she knew that sleeping with him again was, in all reality, a likely possibility. "I...Nash, my family—they don't—they can't understand this...and I, I've already told you—it would mean absolutely nothing—"

"Don't you get it?" Peyton turned to her, the agony plain in her eyes. "I'm...I'm too damn far in."

Elena reached for Peyton, but Peyton's face and body were stone.

"Please if you can give me some time, I'll..."

"You'll *what?*"

"I'll...I'll work it out." Elena felt like the ground was disappearing from beneath her. "But I need to know you're right there with me."

Peyton clenched her jaw as she stared ahead, felt herself withdrawing, farther and farther away. When she looked at

Elena, even though she loved her with all of her being, she also saw a woman willing to sleep with *him* in order to keep both lives. She felt herself hardening. "I believe they call that having your cake and eating it too."

Peyton saw that she had gone too far. Saw the surprise in Elena's eyes. She was not used to Peyton causing her pain.

"I don't think I can do this halfway," Elena countered.

Peyton shook her head. The tone in her voice wasn't accusatory, merely bleak and pragmatic. "You *are* doing it halfway."

Peyton saw the tears in Elena's eyes, knew she would begin crying soon herself and wanted to finish this business. Be done with it. "Maybe I'm limited, but no, I don't see a future with... this."

Elena could not believe what she was hearing. Confused, angry, terrified and completely overwhelmed she shook her head, and walked away.

*

"I can't even say the word." On her seventh call now, heading from her home to the church, Millie sucked in her breath. She had dashed home in a panic, knowing when she went to see Barry she was not going to present her news in a Martha Stewart jogging suit. She'd flown into the house, jumped into her sexiest Ann Taylor skirt and blouse ensemble, hastily putting on her makeup, letting her hair down as she jabbered furiously with one lead congregant after another.

"...lesbian!" Oh, Millie said it after all, shocked by the titillating jolt that ran through her body. "A...lesbian. That's what they call them. That's what she is."

"Don't call her that," Diana said on the other end. "Look, Millie. I know."

"What? You knew this was going on?"

"I...Elena told me a few weeks ago. I thought it was a phase. That it would pass. That she would do the right thing." Diana sighed. "And I think we owe it to her and her years of service to the church to come to the right decision. Millie, please tell me you haven't said a word to anyone else."

235

"Of course not!" Millie lied easily. "But has it occurred to you that maybe Elena's been like this all along?"

"No."

"Well, you would know," Millie suggested. "I know how close the two of *you* have always been."

"Millie—"

"Don't be silly," Millie recouped, "you think I don't know how full your hands are with those kids of yours? I'm just saying, if she would have told anyone, she would have told you...and apparently she has. Now, the question is, who is going to tell Pastor Barry?"

"No one," Diana snapped, shocked that Millie would ask. "It's their business, Millie—"

"I'm afraid that's simply not the case. This is Pastor Barry we're talking about here. How is he supposed to lead this charge when his wife is sleeping with one of *them*? He can't do an effective job. He'll be laughed out of the pulpit. Someone has to protect him," Millie proffered indignantly. "Someone has to take care of this. And I'm the one to do it."

*

Barry walked to the altar, his face ashen. He slammed his hands on the pulpit that he stood before every Sunday, then burrowed into his head into palms, trying to blot the vision from his head of his wife, kissing...*NO...it can't be true!* He swiped his sermon papers before him to the ground.

Millie watched his rage. A smile curled at the edges of her mouth. Yes, this was causing her no end of satisfaction, but she couldn't be having Barry tear the place apart. She had put too much money into the spring renovations. She allowed another moment of sweet solace, then, righting her shoulders, she calmly walked to Barry and put her arms about him.

"There, there," she held him, soothing him.

Barry bristled at her touch. He wanted to throw her against the pews, break her slimy little neck. How dare she!

"How could she?" he hissed. "No. You must be mistaken. Not Elena."

"Barry, I know how difficult it is to accept this—"

"How do you even know it was her?"

Millie cocked her head with a patronizing shake of the head, feigning pain.

"Barry, Barry, Barry...I've got the good eyes the Lord gave me. And while others have difficulty embracing the evils of the world, God gave me the gift to stare it straight in the eye...to call it for what it is. And this is not just adultery, Barry. She hasn't just wronged you by sins of the flesh, she has gone out of her way to insult you—to tear at the very foundation of your greatest battle."

Millie put her arms about his broad shoulders. But he no longer could bear her touch and shrugged out of her cloying tentacles. The idea of his wife, of Elena with anyone, sent him reeling, but with that woman, *that woman who'd robbed his family of so much time*...he wanted to strangle her. He wanted to crush that bitch—that lesbian who had turned his wife. How? How in the hell was it even possible? Didn't you have to be born that way? And if that was the case, had Elena been a lesbian all this time? NO! NO!

He stormed from the altar, unable to tune out his thoughts, but unable to answer any of these mounting questions. Frustrated as he had never been before he charged out of the church to the archway, pacing, kicking at the bench. Millie dutifully followed her lost lamb, let him rail for a few moments longer.

When he turned she was in front of him. And her eyes no longer carried the gentle care when she first gleefully informed him of Elena's "transgressions" but a brittle and steely edge that warned him. He stood there a long moment, taking in the ugliness that had come from her mouth, the satisfaction she had taken in delivering this news that he now knew beyond a shadow of a doubt was true.

It was true. That was just it. He had known it was something... how the hell could he not. But this? *That fuckin' lezzie? Going down on my wife?* He saw black. Infuriated. Humiliated. Sickened. She wasn't even attractive...she was—she was sick. All of this was sick. He knew, deep down, he didn't give a rat's ass what the gays and lesbians did in their own time, in the shadows where they belonged. He didn't need to save their souls. It just was the fact that they threw it in your face. That's what he objected to. And now...now it was personal.

"God damn it!" he roared.

Millie let out yelp, shocked by Barry's outburst. "Pastor Barry!" She maintained her steely resolve and lost the feigned sympathy.

"I...I'm sorry, Millie, I..."

He glanced at her. He was keenly aware that how he handled this could affect the rest of his career. His livelihood.

Their eyes met. He lifted his hands, although they felt like they weighed a thousand pounds. "What...what do I do?"

Millie walked to him. Got very close. Looked deeply into his eyes.

"You are going to use your anger to pray with me, Barry. And then you are going to march home and tell your wife to stop this madness. That she not only owes it to the church, but to you and your son. Elena is not a stupid woman, Barry. She will do what she knows is right."

They stood close for a long moment. What they both knew was that they lived lies, shadowy furtive lies, full of the pretense of good bidding.

"Pray with me." Millie didn't ask. She demanded.

Barry was now caught in his own farce, impotent on every level, but they both knew he had no other choice but to continue in his spiritual sham. So he bowed his head and prayed.

*

Elena heard Barry's car drive up the driveway, heard the car door slam fiercely. Listened as he headed to her studio with stomping footsteps and sat still as she heard him throw a frame against the wall. Shattering glass, followed by a thunderous clamor of destruction, Barry tearing apart Elena's studio with all the anger he had felt at the church, free now to purge his rage.

She waited. But all she heard for a long time was silence. Then the car starting and backing up in a screech of tires.

Hours later, long after she had put Nash to bed, she sat out on the back porch.

She had moved through every minute since Peyton had broken off with her in a sort of hyper surreal calmness. She walked slowly, gracefully, attending to each and every task with deliberation and care. She came home, cleaned up the house, did the laundry and heard the calls on the answering machine from Diana, scrambling to find her, Millie scrambling to find Barry, then Diana telling her she had to call, that Millie had seen her with "that woman" in the park. Even when she felt her heart drop to the floor, knowing what Millie had seen, she continued to move in the same way, step by careful step, because she knew if she did not, she would lose her mind. Completely.

She fed Nash and Tori when they arrived from hanging with some friends at the mall. She sat with them in the living room, waiting second by second for Barry to rage through the house, and when that did not happen, she put the kids to bed, and sat. She made tea she did not drink.

She sat. And felt absolutely dead.

And that's when she knew what she had to do.

And so she sat and waited until two in the morning when she heard the car pull up, this time its door closing quietly. She sensed more than heard Barry trying to find her, and that when he didn't find her in the house he would find her where she sat when she wanted peace and quiet, in the garden in the backyard.

And then he was there. Standing in front of her, then falling to his knees.

He looked up into her face.

A single tear fell from her eyes. He slumped over her knees, his shoulders began to quake, his body sobbing wildly out of control, wracking cries of anger turned to grief, of anguish, confusion. In his torment, the only words she could make out were a wretched, "Don't do this to us."

Elena watched him, no longer detached, aching for his loss, their loss, and put a hand to his back, soothing his broken heart, then lay her head upon his. She held him for hours, as the dark turned to dawn. She held him until he could cry no longer.

*

Elena later walked into the studio that was now in complete shambles. Everything ruined. She didn't care as she began to quietly weave through the shards of glass, the mangled frames, and then stopped.

Her shoulders began to quake. Her heart began to race.

She slumped to the floor and began to cry, sob, let go of every second she had waited for Barry to return, and she mourned them all as she picked up the broken frame of their baby daughter.

She cried until there were no tears left, curled into a ball and fell asleep among the ruins of her life.

*

Peyton did not return home until sometime after three in the morning. Utterly plastered, she had stumbled to her couch and passed out before she even hit it.

The next morning when she tried to open her eyes, she wondered why they hurt so much and then remembered. The crying. All the endless tears. The only thing that had stopped them was drinking, which she had done on her own in her car, overlooking the majestic sweep of the valley, off a lone ridge on the Angeles Crest Highway. Slugging from a bottle of Cuervo— she didn't even like tequila, but that was all the better. It all felt like castigation, one way or another. She only stopped crying when she had drunk enough to become numb, and then she had passed out briefly.

She didn't want to drive home, had called Wave who picked her up and insisted she stay with her, but she had said no, absolutely not. Yet there were Wave's feet she was looking at across from her as her eyes tried to focus.

She slowly lifted her head. Yeah, it was Wave. With a mug of coffee in hand.

"Up you go then," Wave suggested softly. "Don't want all that mush in yer brain to flow out yer ears."

Peyton sat up slowly. Wave handed her the coffee, sat

240

beside her and read the paper. Wave knew her so well. Knew she wouldn't—couldn't talk yet. Knew her better than she probably knew herself. Why the hell couldn't she just fall in love with her?

"Up you get when you've got your sea legs," Wave added, continuing to read her paper. "A shower would make you a new woman and since I'm sittin' downwind sooner than later would be appreciated."

Later, after Peyton had showered, the water hurting her throbbing head, she had finally come back to life. Wave had made some scrambled eggs and toast, "somethin' light on that bludgeoned tummy of yours," which she ate without tasting, not daring to protest. When Wave had inspected Peyton to her satisfaction, she told her she had to get home to walk her dog, but "don't be runnin' off for any more escapades like last night—unless of course I'm invited along with you!"

Peyton sat in her living room now, feeling utterly helpless, fatigued, hung over and hopeless. She sat for an hour before she checked her e-mails.

A message from Elena glowed brightly from the screen.

Peyton's heart began to race. She got up, walked away from the computer. Paced. Sat, tapped a pen until it was going to drill a hole to China, and did every conceivable toying with every object on her desk before she caved.

> I didn't want to do this in an e-mail, but you won't see me, or answer my calls. Peyton, of all the things I came to realize last night, the one that overrides everything is that you deserve to be in a balanced relationship where ALL your needs are being met. As you pointed out, I can't give that to you. I can give a lot, but not without more heartache. You were right about the fact that I wasn't thinking or looking beyond the moment I was in. Not fair of me at all.

*

"'You have so many pieces of your life that you are trying to put together and I didn't fully understand how damaging this relationship could be to you,'" Wave now read the rest of the e-mail out loud to them both as she and Peyton sat in a corner booth at Pinot Latte. Peyton had tried, unsuccessfully, to read between every line, more and more engaged with each pass until she had to get out of her home, her head, her heart, and dashed to the coffee shop so that Wave could confirm what she felt—that the e-mail was utter bullshit.

"'I just wanted to love you and make you happy,'" Wave continued, "'but it wasn't quite that simple. You would never be able to trust, or feel strong or complete with me, and I'm so sorry for that, but I'm not sorry I fell in love with you so completely.'"

Wave gently placed the printed e-mail between them on the countertop, glanced at her friend. "Are you okay?"

"No. I'm not okay. I'm pissed as hell."

"Well," Wave considered having just read the e-mail, "you might just have a point. Sounds a bit like she's dodgering off the hook. But look, I can tell she really means well."

"Means well?" Peyton snorted "*Means well*? She has just reduced us to the most boring cliché in the lesbian universe."

"I'm not trying to get all Hallmark on you, Peyton, really I'm not, but you knew from the start this was sort of straight out from the top of the lesbian ten commandments: Thou shalt not sleep with straight married chick."

Peyton couldn't even summon a smile. Wave sighed. "My point being, maybe—just maybe, if you can let this go gracefully, it will, in the future—and maybe not too far in the future—become, well, a beautiful memory."

"Yeah, well, that's not going to happen. How can this be a beautiful memory when I know that she's living a complete lie? She's just going to continue on living in this sham of a marriage?"

"Maybe it's not as much of a sham as we think. You know some people are fine with status quo and she does have a son, after all, and we've already gone over her parents and all that malarkey. Maybe this is what's truly best for her, and she's actually doin' the right thing for you, by letting you go...so you can get on with your life."

"Whose side are you on?"

"Yours, my love. Always yours and that's why, I gotta tell ya, I think she's doing you a huge favor."

*

On the same Sunday, across town, the congregation of the Holy Church of Light sat in electrified anticipation of what they might see at services that morning. The buzz from member to member grew with each retelling of the story and with each retelling more erroneous facts were attached and embellished upon until the party line of gossip had hit a furious apex.

As Barry entered the church from its front door the entire room turned in unison, all eyes swiveling to the very picture they had all been waiting for for days—was the good pastor going to show up with his fallen wife or not?

Barry walked in first, followed by Nash and Tori and, yes, a stunned gasp emitted from the congregation, there was Elena, bringing up the rear as they all entered the church in a unified front.

"Really, Pastor Barry." Millie rushed to Barry, leaned to him and whispered, "Do you think it's a good idea..."

Diana jumped in to shore up Elena, making her voice heard loud and clear, "Good morning, Millie. Turned out to be a lovely day, didn't it? They said it was going to rain. Come on, Elena, let's set up the coffee for after service."

Elena accepted both Barry's brave show of the loving husband as well as Diana's intervention while Barry headed Millie off.

He said, "Why don't we all thank God for this glorious day... and consider how fortunate we are."

Millie glanced about. Saw that she was outnumbered. Backed down.

*

Wave refilled both of their coffee cups and sat down once

again, now that the first flood of morning customers was settled.

"Well, hell, it's not like she's married to an accountant. Think of what this will do to his world. Their family. You know I think you did the right thing for Elena, and for her family, by putting the decision squarely on her shoulders. If you hadn't backed out Peyton, where do you think this would go? It would still have the same ending, only now you've gotten out with some sense of honor and grace."

"Yeah, bully for me."

*

Elena sat stoically as Barry preached, and again she vaguely heard the cadence of his voice full of words that did not register, until, he, of course, had to explain their circumstances and create an avenue to patch up this horrible mess she had made of things.

"...and sometimes a person gets lost on a path they never meant to take in the first place. We don't punish them. We open up our arms, embrace them back into the fold."

The congregants were very receptive to this offering, happy to be able to put this shameful and embarrassing event behind them, even if it would be the center of gossip for months to come. Tori raised her eyebrows, in a "whatever you wanna think" expression.

Nash took his mother's hand, and gently held it through the remainder of the service.

A September Sunday two months later

Elena sat, looking uncomfortable and a little queasy as she tried to finish making dinner. Barry walked in, kissed Elena on the forehead, put his arms about her shoulders.

"How are you feeling?"

"Ohh...you know."

Barry nabbed the boiling tea water, whistled while he made her tea and sat with her.

Silence.

"Elena..." Barry searched.

"I...I don't want to talk. Really."

"I know you need time. I'm not pushing you. It's just that they're beginning to...you know how they get—"

"Tell them I'm not feeling well," she snapped. "Tell them I've got a headache. Tell them—I don't care what you tell them."

"Do you think you could at least try to put in an appearance—"

"So we can continue to play out this farce? No. I at least cannot do that. Please leave me alone."

Barry got up, walked to her as if they never had this discussion. "Just think about it. I know everyone would love to see you."

He took his tea and left the room.

A huge sigh filled the room. But it wasn't from Elena. It was from Nash.

A Thursday in October

Peyton worked desultorily on an article about illegal immigration, unable to concentrate. Her OCD had flared up again, with all the stress she was under, and she had had to up her medication a bit to handle it. She had to get this article completed by the end of the day. But she had gotten a call from Elena's number earlier that morning. She had seen it when she had gone to check her messages. Nothing had been said. Elena had clearly hung up before the machine even picked up, but now, two hours later, Peyton could not stop wondering about the call. Had Elena meant to call? Had it been an accidental dial off her cell phone? Had she been trying to call her before? If so, why? And how the hell dare she?

No. She was not going to do this.

Peyton got up, disconnected the phone.

Now maybe she would actually get some work done.

*

Nash sat across from both his father and mother in the small trinket-filled waiting room. Elena glanced from Nash to Barry and back again. They waited. Tension filled the silence

245

as Nash tapped long nervous fingers against his skinny-leg Levi jeans.

They waited some more.

Finally the therapist entered the room.

*

"We'll get through this Peyton," Wave encouraged Peyton. "We always do."

But both of them could hear the different tone in Wave's voice. Not as certain now that it was three months later. This *was* different from anything they had encountered. Before this, neither of them had ever truly been in love. But this time, Peyton had been and they both knew it.

"Sure." Peyton pretended to smile. "We'll get through it."

*

Elena moved through the house, picking up, organizing. As she was rearranging the photos and frames on the shelf in the living room, she picked up one in sterling silver.

Sarah. Her daughter. The picture they had always kept in their bedroom and nowhere else as if somehow by keeping her tucked away they wouldn't have to think of her. But this simply wasn't the case. And it made no sense in the world, Elena now thought, for their daughter not to reside with the rest of the family photos she had chosen to signify hearth and home.

With a sad, but resigned smile, Elena set the photo in the center of the hearth.

A Friday in November

Elena walked up to the church and had to stop and look at this structure which had been such a huge part of her life for the past almost twelve years now. She and Barry had really started their little family here, baptizing Nash, sharing their grief during funeral services for Sarah. Barry's first couple of years here, when he had been the assistant pastor, until that third year when he had taken the reins. She remembered how thrilled they had been for his success, even if they both knew part of that was about Barry taking his performance to a new level.

This church had been a mainstay of her life all of these many years. She had devoted countless hours to its care, the meetings, fundraisers, fixing the back meeting room, refurbishing the pews, all the endless committees she had been involved with and the people who had become her family. Even if the Kinder program had allowed for her to be able to take care of the children away from the adults and their endless conversations about things she really didn't care about, she was so proud of the great strides she had made in the program. Everyone had commented on the quality of care, the wonderful activities she had provided for the children, the high standards it set for other programs of its kind. She had been thrilled with its success, and this was the one part of the church which she found difficult to let go.

But she knew she had simply been walking through life, not living it. Not being inside the experience of it, because now she knew with absolute clarity that she would not miss any other part of this church and its inhabitants. Maybe Diana. But she couldn't think of one other thing she would regret leaving. Not in the least.

Elena continued to walk into the empty church with a box, overflowing with toiletries, books, clothes.

She saw Barry at the altar, practicing, as he always did on Thursday and Friday evenings, his sermon. His "rehearsal hours."

She walked up, set the box on the front pew and turned to him. He took a long moment sizing her up.

"Do you have any idea what you're doing?"

"I didn't come to fight. I knew you would need this," she said calmly, and gestured toward the box.

A mixture of emotion crossed his face, dominated by despair and resignation. "Don't know what the therapy was all about when you knew all along this was the outcome."

"The therapy was for Nash, Barry."

Barry looked chastised a moment, then moved toward her.

"Elena, you know, maybe Nash was right...maybe I am

247

clueless...but I know one thing if I know nothing else. You are *not* a lesbian."

"I don't know. Perhaps I am. After all, I fell in love with a woman." Elena claimed this moment as her truth. "Doesn't that make me one? Does it really matter, Barry? Really. If you put a label on it, will it make the outcome any different, any easier for either of us to deal with?"

"I still don't understand. You're not with *her*. Why the hell would you do this? To us. To Nash. This is so senseless—not to mention singularly selfish. Nash needs us."

"Yes. He does. He needs the real us. The best of us." Elena looked right up at him, kindness in her voice along with strength and conviction. "I'm done lying to him, to you. To me. This has nothing to do with Peyton. This is my decision about our son and my life —"

' "Your life,' and 'your son.' God, Elena you are selfish."

"If it's selfish—so be it." Elena embraced this last with an edge of fury. "I should have been done with this charade years ago."

"Charade! Don't you dare—Look you...you went right along with—"

"You're right. You're right. That's what was selfish, staying here and not being inside it, really inside it *with* you!" Elena placed a hand to his chest. "I'm done with this, Barry..."

"Elena…" His eyes pleaded with her.

"I'm done."

Their eyes met. A final recognition of who they had been to one another. Elena's eyes filled with a glimmer of hope, for him, for her. For all their futures.

"Be well, Barry."

She turned and walked from the church.

Barry walked to a pew in his church and slumped down into it, put his head in his hands. When he glanced up his eyes ran into a picture that had lived in the church for all these years and he hadn't actually looked at. It was Jesus, herding his lost little lambs.

A Saturday in November

Peyton sat in the same room she had sat in almost a year ago now, in the same adoption orientation, listening intently to every word the instructor was saying. This time every word was essential and Peyton listened with full attention to putting her life back in order and on track. She made herself forget the shadowy memory of Elena, sitting right in that seat across from her, and how everything had started between them because she had lost her keys.

Later, after the class had dispersed, Peyton walked up to speak with the tall angular instructor, and responded to a question she had asked Peyton about where she had run off to for so long.

"I guess my life got a little carried away," Peyton sighed, then smiled firmly. "But this time I'm not going to let anything get in the way."

"Well, you certainly have a great application. I don't think it will take long to find a placement for you."

Peyton couldn't wait to get to Pinot Latte to fill Wave in on the details. She dashed in, set herself up at her regular booth, waiting for Wave, who seemed nowhere to be seen until she realized that Wave was in the booth behind her with a beautiful African American woman. She was clearly an intellectual, the last kind of person Peyton would expect with Wave, closely cropped afro, sporting a vest, loose tie, oxford shirt. Since she must surely be a business associate, Peyton didn't think twice about interrupting.

"Hey!" Peyton announced herself.

"Oh, Pey!" Wave jumped up and hugged her dearest friend, and then, turning to the stunning woman across from her, Wave's voice fell into love octave. "And this is Tea Warrington."

"T?" Peyton couldn't help but ask.

"Yeah, as in iced tea."

"Oh." Peyton smiled, leaned over and shook Tea's hand. "How did you two meet?"

"Very indirectly," Tea answered.

"Well, it's the daftest thing ever," Wave started, pulling

Peyton into the booth and down next to her. "You know how I've been e-mailing back and forth for the past few years with this chicklet in India—just sort of as a virtual pen pal. I mean, isn't that what Facebook is all about when you get right down to it? Just a bunch of pen pals with nothin' better to do with their time than to nose into the business of others thousands of miles away?" Peyton was trying to follow Wave's story. Wave smiled and shook her head. "Right then—back on track. Anyway, the Indian chicklet happened to have a friend visiting who was there training some of her horses. This friend was none other than *Tea!* Yeah, I mean a regular horse-whisperer this one."

Tea grinned modestly. "I've been training show horses since I was sixteen. I'm not a whisperer but I do have a great respect for their grace, their simplicity and strength."

Peyton was already impressed.

"Anyway Shaline, the Indian chick, told me it was weird because her friend Tea actually lived in the same city I did— Silverlake. Now how random is that? And when she came back, Shaline wanted Tea to deliver me a sari because I'd helped with some online donations they were running for one of the children's clinics that Shaline works for. Turns out Tea works with the kids, helping the disabled ones by putting them on the horses, and the contact with the horses helps the kids, and the kid I'm sponsoring asked if Tea could hand deliver a thank you card because she had had so much fun riding." Wave was breathless from her eagerness to tell the story.

"These kids get so much out of it." Tea sighed in appreciation, then, winking at Wave, said, "And apparently so did I."

Peyton cocked an eyebrow.

"Yeah, so Tea delivers the sari and thank you note, arrived here last week, and I don't think we've spent more than a few minutes apart since?" Wave looked at Tea to see if that was correct.

"What can I say...I can't be away from you," Tea stated matter of factly. No hyperbole, just a simple truth for her.

Peyton couldn't believe it. Tea was nothing like the rest of the women Wave had serially dated. Tea had such a groundedness to her that it appeared to be rubbing off on Wave. Peyton couldn't remember the last time she had seen

Wave this calm and, she realized, so utterly graceful. As if Tea had put a spell on her.

"Anyway, I'm a bloody believer in fate, because you know, this is what Tyler told me was going to happen."

Peyton's smile faded, momentarily.

"Yeah, when I had that first reading with him, he told me a woman would 'saddle up to me in during a harvest moon.' Now at the time I thought that was the strangest wording and strangest way to predict finding a lover, but can you get over how accurate he actually was? The day Tea arrived, was harvest moon!"

Tea again bowed modestly.

"That's great." Peyton smiled, genuinely happy for her friend. "Tea, it's so good to meet you—you don't even know."

"I think I might have an idea," Tea responded as if she had known both of them their entire lives. Whatever it was about this woman, Peyton decided, it was the best of all possible energies for Wave's wild and radical bohemian lifestyle. Tea seemed like a spiritual healer, with calm and serene energy and a gentleness to her that might possibly heal the lost soul in Wave.

"I've got to take off now, jump on this paperwork."

"Yeah, and I'm going to be here to make sure nothing gets in your way!" Wave remarked.

"No worries...trust me, I have one focus and one focus only. Nothing's going to shake that." Peyton glanced from Tea to Wave and it suddenly hit her. She blurted, "...I'm going to be a... a mom, Wave. Get that!"

"Yeah, well, I'll be 'round for auntie duty right after that screaming infant, oogie diaper stage." Wave sputtered, then winked and snuggled closely to Peyton, her eyes gleaming across the counter at Tea. Wave turned her attention back to Peyton.

"Hey." Wave took Peyton's hand. "I know it's taken a few months, but you finally look like you're among the living."

"Well, that would be the spray tan," Peyton demurred.

*

Several hours later, Peyton hugged her dear friend and said goodbye to Tea, and decided to just walk for a bit, up and

251

down streets of storefronts near Pinot Latte, vaguely window-shopping and feeling so much better than she had for so long. Just finally feeling good, inside her bones. Because she ultimately knew that every moment she lived wasn't going to be always filled with heartache and missing...missing her. But, instead, it would be filled with a hope for the future, like that one woman had said at the first orientation. That's what they were all looking for. A hope for a better tomorrow. And this time, Peyton was laser focused and as she had promised Wave, nothing, NOTHING was going to get in the way of finding the child she was supposed to be raising, lifting up into the world and giving every opportunity to be the best he or she could be.

Excitement. That was what she felt. For the first time in months. For the first time since...

And there, as if ordained, was a baby boutique right in her path. What the hell. So it was early, but why not go in and look at the clothes and all the fun little toys?

Peyton meandered through the rather large but fully stocked store. There were so many racks of clothing—she had to smile, there were oodles of things to select from. She had had no idea how huge the baby market was.

She rounded a rack of discounted summer clothes and knocked forcefully into another customer who she was profusely apologizing to when she realized it was Tori.

"Hey," Peyton finally said, when she caught her breath and bearings.

"Hey...uhmm...hi there..." Tori returned, just as stunned and even more flabbergasted when Nash joined them.

Nash simply stared, then muttered. "Uh...hey."

The three stood paralyzed for a long moment.

Tori finally broke the silence. "Wow. Oddly enough I was just reading this morning about the correlation of coincidence to the concept of fatalism—that all things occur as the result of a predetermined path, plan or formula..."

"Tori, what are you talking about?"

Peyton and Nash exchanged nervous glances.

"...which would—you know—really sort of throw a good

deal of weight to the premise that the three of us running into one another was probably inevitable."

"What...what are you doing?" Peyton indicated the baby store, "...here?"

And then she realized she had probably put her foot in it. "Oh my God, Tori, are you expecting?"

"I may spout statistics, but trust me, I most assuredly have no intention of becoming one!"

Nash glanced away and Tori still had no clue how quickly she was running her foot into her mouth. "I'm much smarter than that. Plus, Nash and I still belong to the narrow majority of the teen population who practice abstinence. Not because we too won't be an 'inevitable probability'—but because we love one another without all that sorta thing. No, we're getting stuff for the new baby."

"Ohhh...is Elena...are you all finally adopting?"

"Mom's pregnant," Nash stated in a sort of attitudinal "duh."

Peyton's face dropped and her stomach plummeted. It took her a moment to wrap her mind around this.

Nash stuttered, "I...I thought you knew—"

"How...why would I know that?"

"I thought that's why...well...you left her alone."

Peyton could not speak. She couldn't breathe. She didn't even try to say goodbye. She felt the room closing in on her, was vaguely aware she muttered something about missing a conference call, and ran from the store. The minute she rounded the corner of the block, she fell against a brick wall and vomited.

"You know, Nash," Tori informed her boyfriend, "being subtle really isn't your strong suit."

They both stood a moment, staring at one another. Nash shook his head and muttered, "Now what in the hell am I supposed to do?"

Tori waited a long moment, then put a hand in his, leaned her head against his chest and softly patted it where his heart lay beneath. "Follow this."

*

Peyton and Wave sat in the dark, after hours, killing a bottle of wine. They had been at it for some time, both sunken in their seats. Peyton's eyes were rimmed with agony…

"You know what rips my craw?" Wave blurted. "On some level, I had, you know, begun to believe in her…that she had done the noble thing."

"Yeah…I thought she had reduced us to the most boring cliché in the lesbian universe. But I had no earthly idea how duplicitous a person she could be. Me. The person who doesn't trust…trusting the worst person I could."

Peyton shook her head, trying to focus, but she was almost so drunk she was sober. "I…I still can't believe I fell for it…what a schmuck…"

"Had me fooled. I mean, she's good. Really good."

"She had to have been fucking him the entire time."

"You know…she could have…I mean, technically, she could have gotten pregnant after you broke up."

"That makes me feel so much better."

"Well, it would be possible and it would make this a whole lot more tolerable."

"What—to think that to get over us, she had to jump into bed with him?"

"No, sweetie," Wave suggested softly. Since she had been with Tea, she was so much gentler, so less prone to go into a tirade against things she felt were unfair in the universe. "Maybe the pain was so much for her, she decided to continue to do what she had been doing all along. You know, the same thing you're doing. Trying to have a baby. And maybe since she didn't care, it took. She stopped being desperate."

"Great."

"I just think you have to give her the benefit of the doubt…" Wave hiccupped, "because to tell you the God's bloody truth, since Tea, I've become a believer. Maybe you should go and see Tyler. Get a reading—"

"He is the last person I want to see. I want nothing more to do with her world. Ever."

Peyton slammed her wineglass down and left the room.

*

Elena walked through the park, along the same path she and Peyton had grown so fond of as their relationship had deepened, the one with the winding curve by the brook, that ended at a breathtaking and panoramic view of the city.

She sighed. Yes, there was an undeniable specialness to this place that somehow gave her sustenance.

She eased herself down upon a bench. Touched the gentle swell of her stomach.

Tyler joined Elena, sat and leaned to kiss her cheek. "Hi beautiful beyond beautiful mom."

He put his hands to her stomach. "How's our little one doing?" He added, "Was that a kick?"

Elena glanced at Tyler, smiled in the affirmative.

"Oh, Elena, I never knew this could be so amazing. You know, I've always wanted this to happen, but to actually be a part of something so wonderful…" He bent to her stomach and cooed, "Tyler's going to take such good care of you and teach you all about Soulemetry and convince your mom to give it another go someday."

Elena shook her head, and leaned into him. "You!"

"Well, I've got to have the baby growing up with the right set of beliefs!"

She moved closer to Tyler, feeling a bit of the chill from the breeze. He took off his brown corduroy jacket and covered her shoulders, put an arm about her to warm her.

"I…I thought somehow, this would make it okay." Elena glanced at her stomach and then back out at the view. "And, of course, I know once the baby comes it will be okay… but I feel like I'm walking through this pregnancy like a mindless drone."

"Perhaps not mindless…perhaps just lonely, feeling a bit soulless."

"Oh Tyler—"

"So, my beautiful woman," Tyler sighed, and looked out at the vast expanse before them. "Why don't you call her?"

"I tried. You know that."

"That was months ago." Tyler hooked Elena's hand to his arm. "Maybe she just needed some time."

"I don't know. I…I just feel like I hurt her so badly."

"I'm not swagging from one of my webisodes, sweetheart, but let me tell you a story."

Tyler got her all set up, relaxed her into a calming position against him. "I don't ever think I told you about how Lily and I really got together."

Elena's head swiveled to Tyler, in surprise. "What do you mean?"

"Well, you know I met her in Paris. But you don't know how we actually came together, the circumstances over which we fully realized we were meant to be with one another."

"I thought you met at a wedding?"

"Yes, but you never knew it was *her* wedding."

"*What?*" Elena bolted upright, shook Tyler by the arm. "What are you talking about?"

"Lily and I actually first met during a phase in my life you aren't aware of. I'd been living in Paris, working on a play. At the time I had fallen hard. For the lead. It was a man, by the name of Louis. And Louis Jordan he was—all the way. He had that full thick head of hair, fine features, that same insanely enticing accent. I'd dabbled with both sexes at the academy and I was just in the process of coming out. But when I found Louis I thought, that's it. I'm gay, I know it now. This is the man for me. But I wasn't the man for him. Although we had a torrid affair that lasted six months, he told me early on he was engaged to be married to a very distant relative, a setup from his family. Sort of a business merger."

"Lily?"

"Yes. He'd told me about her, showed me pictures, but I didn't believe it. I remembered when I looked at her thinking, what a striking woman and all wrong for Louis. I didn't think he'd actually be able to pull it off, and he'd realize before it was too late that we belonged together. He told me he valued my friendship immensely, but what we had was over. He came from a family so lofty among the Paris elite, being gay wasn't an

256

option—even if the French are known to be open-minded. He broke it off, but he invited me to the wedding."

"I can't believe you even considered going."

"Well, I didn't." Tyler paused and thought back. "But I received a letter, written so beautifully, so eloquently from his fiancée, telling me he had been honest about our relationship and she so wanted me to share their day, and she also wanted me to know if his happiness was in any way sacrificed, she was more than open to him having a lover. Can you get over it?"

"Lily negotiating." Elena had to shake her head. "The woman has balls of steel."

"It truly came from her heart. I happened to get drunk the day of the wedding, with no intention of going, when a car arrived for me, again, arranged by Lily, and by then, I was so stinking, I thought, what the hell, I'll go and have some closure."

"The wedding was beautiful, ornate, ostentatious, done with class and all out from here to Sunday. And the strangest thing happened. When I watched the two of them, watched them exchange nuptials, something in me clicked. I knew he was gone. Afterward, at the reception, when I met Lily, she was nothing but lovely and warm, and toward the end of the evening, she pulled me aside, and again told me she had no intention of keeping Louis from anything that made him happy."

Tyler turned to Elena and she could see the love shining brightly in his eyes thinking back to how he and Lily had started. "I had to ask her if she was really that selfless, and she answered in these exact words: 'I don't look at it in terms of selflessness. I know this was an arranged marriage more for business than anything else, and while I'm fond of Louis, I'm no more in love with him than he with me. And even if I was, I believe in freedom. I believe a person needs to be who they are. And I also believe a person can only love who they love. If it's meant to be, it will work out.'"

"A few months later, I heard they had separated. The following spring, I was packing up to leave, getting ready to head to New York, when I got a phone call. It was from Louis. He said he was in town, heard I was leaving and wanted to have drinks for old time's sake. When I showed up at the bar, my hope, my intention had been to win him back. Now that he was free, what was to stop him? But when I was shown to his table, Lily was sitting there, reading some contract or other. I saw Louis at the bar ordering drinks. I swear to God, I don't know what happened, because when I sat to join them, I could have cared less about Louis. But Lily? Oh my heavens! I couldn't take my eyes off her. Louis made small talk and all Lily and I did was gaze into one another's eyes, until finally I didn't know what to think."

Elena couldn't help but laugh. "This is too crazy."

"Isn't it?" Tyler laughed. "So there I am, over my man crush and here is this woman, that to me is now the only person on the planet. Lily finally turns to Louis and says, 'You know, sweetie, I think we can take it from here.'"

"Louis was flabbergasted. He'd come for the same reason I had. To hook up with me—even if it was only for a bon voyage f— oops." Tyler remembered the baby and whispered to Elena's stomach, "Sorry. Anyway, he glances from Lily to me, and could see the cards on the table. When he left, Lily looked me straight in the eye and said, 'Goddamn it man, you have wasted so much of my time! I haven't stopped thinking about you since my wedding day. And I have a lot to do. I can't be spending all my time daydreaming when I have work to do.' And that was all she wrote."

"Tyler—why haven't you ever told me this before?" Elena was still mystified by this whole new side of Tyler and Lily.

"Because I knew you wouldn't get it, couldn't relate to it. Until now. You have to go find out if Peyton's the one. And, trust me, you'll know when you see her. If she's not, no harm no foul. If she is, then by God, Elena, you've got to stop wasting *your* time."

*

Peyton packed boxes with a vengeance. She had made up her mind, and now she was going to get this done. She had kept all her mom's old books, papers and antiquities for the past year and a half, but now it was time. Time to clear everything out. Time to start anew. Everything had to go. She moved with efficiency and speed, walked out with one of the boxes.

As she opened the door, Elena moved surreptitiously through the maze of boxes and clutter and when she turned Peyton was cleaning off some dust from her sleeveless T-shirt.

Peyton stopped, dead in her tracks.

"Elena..."

"Peyton...I—"

"Elena...what are you doing here?"

Elena glanced about the boxes, and panicked. "What are you doing? Are you moving?"

"No. I just finally went through all my mother's stuff to go to the women's shelter."

"Oh...oh, I see." Elena could not catch her breath, feeling dizzy suddenly. Why had she come here?

"Yeah, the social worker's coming next week, and I'd like for things to look tidy...up to..." she said, and then wondered why in the hell she was explaining anything to this woman.

"Oh...yes, for the adoption, right?"

"Yes." Peyton's voice tightened. "Look, I'm sort of in a hurry. I've got to get all this stuff out of here by the end of the day."

"Oh...okay. Can I help you with anything?"

"*No!*"

They both stopped short at her vehemence.

"I...I don't think you should be lifting at this point."

Elena was confused.

"What do you want, Elena?"

Elena stood there, empty-handed. "I just wanted to see you."

"Why?"

Elena was hurt, not sure where to take the conversation, feeling more and more dizzy by the moment.

"Can we, at least, talk for a few moments?"

"I don't think there's really anything for us to talk about," Peyton said as she returned to her packing, shoving books inside a box with vigor. "I think you should go."

Elena walked up to her, took the books from Peyton's hands and put them aside.

"I know you're hurt. So am I. I just want to explain—"

"Elena. I don't want to talk with you."

259

"Pey—"

"Save it!" Peyton stood there, trembling as confusion turned to anger.

"Please, listen to me—"

But Peyton could only feel her rage. "*Listen to you? Oh my God. Why?* You lied to me the entire time we were together."

Elena had to sit. Peyton was standing there so angry and everything had gotten so twisted. She wanted to explain, but her senses were reeling, she felt as if she were in a dream, as if she could not control what came out, "I told you, I...would never lie—"

"You were fucking him this whole time to get pregnant? God, you played me—"

"Peyton—" Elena was growing more disoriented by the second, her body suddenly feeling so heavy...

"You played me. Good for you. So maybe I'm stupid as sin, but you know what you are? You're nothing but a whore!"

Her head spinning, she felt pummeled, assaulted. As Elena began to reach for a chair, Wave walked in.

Stopped in her tracks. "Oh, bloody hell! What are you doing here?"

Wave approached her like an attack dog. Elena could see how much the woman despised her.

Everything began to spin. And then it all went black.

"Elena!" Peyton screamed.

*

Peyton paced the hospital waiting room as Wave tried to calm her. She felt terrible, horrified to think she had caused Elena to faint. What if something happened to the baby? At the same time she was so angry with her she could not stop shaking. And then she was wondering why the hell she didn't just leave the hospital. This wasn't her problem. This was none of her business.

Nash and Tori dashed in at that moment. When they saw Wave and Peyton, no one knew quite what to do.

"My mom!" Nash croaked.

"She's all right," Wave informed them, her arms crossed.

"She's resting quietly. But her blood pressure is out of whack."

"What happened?"

"She fainted." Peyton spoke like a woman who deserved to be hung.

"What did you do to her?"

"She didn't do *anything*," Wave insisted. "I was there. The doctor's going to come and talk with us in a few moments and I'm sure you'll be able to see her then. But right now, we have to all remain calm."

"Wave's right, Nash." Tori shook her head. "Fighting only proves to make situations like these even more gnarly than they already are."

Convinced or not, they backed into their separate quarters of the waiting room.

"I've left like a kabillion messages for Poppa Bear...I have no idea where he is. No one can find him."

Peyton shook her head. Great.

What seemed hours later, a doctor came out to speak with them at nearly the same time that Tyler and Lily arrived.

"Everyone, she's going to be fine. Her blood pressure's dangerously low. But we're running an IV...giving her plenty of fluids and some extra vitamins for the baby."

The doctor looked at his lab report, then at all of them as if trying to configure the relations within their highly diverse group. "She says she wants to speak to a...someone named Peyton and the baby's father."

Peyton glanced around. Barry wasn't present.

"Bloody hell," Wave muttered under her breath.

Tyler walked to Peyton's aid, offered his arm.

"I'll take you in."

"Uhmm...thanks," Peyton agreed in a daze as Tyler escorted them into Elena's hospital room.

When they entered, Elena turned to face them.

"Sweetie pie," Tyler said, "you can't be scaring Tyler like that again, you got that?"

Elena forced a bleak smile.

"Elena...I'm...I'm sorry." Peyton spoke up. "I was...but I shouldn't have upset you."

"You had every right." Elena's voice was soft and low. "But please, just give me a chance to set the record straight."

Peyton glanced at her, confused. What was there to explain?

"I *am* pregnant," Elena confirmed, "but it's not because I was sleeping with Barry."

Peyton glanced from Elena to Tyler to see if she had heard correctly.

"Barry has still never touched me since...since you and I began."

Peyton was now completely mystified.

"It's Tyler."

Peyton was now even more baffled.

"Tyler is the father."

"And trust me, we weren't sleeping together either!" Tyler insisted. "Lily wouldn't stand for that!"

"But I don't understand." Peyton was entirely lost.

"After all those years of infertility hell, Tyler offered, and I accepted."

"My greatest contribution to mankind," Tyler proclaimed.

"I'm sorry I couldn't tell you. But Tyler, Lily and I agreed that no one would know about this unless and until it took and the pregnancy was safe."

It was finally seeping in. Peyton was finally beginning to feel the heaviness lift from her chest, feel the depression edging away, and to suddenly realize all this had been a terrible misunderstanding.

"Ty...can you give us a few minutes..." Elena asked. "And then send Nash in."

Tyler made a graceful bow.

Peyton got a chair, moved to Elena. Peyton dropped her head. She felt nauseous thinking of all the terrible things she had said to Elena that had caused her to be here.

"Why...why didn't you tell me?"

Elena shook her head as if trying to make sense of it all.

"I had so many things to take care of. Ending my marriage of fifteen years. Nash and I had to go to therapy, we had to deal with Barry and I had to make changes. After I started my divorce, I was so sick my first trimester that I really couldn't cope well.

And, Peyton, I must have called you a thousand times…and after a certain point, even I knew that I had hit a wall."

Peyton nodded. "Elena…I just couldn't do it anymore. I shut down at the end. And after you sent the e-mail that said you knew the relationship wasn't fair to me, well, I just had to cut every tie to you I had. For me it had to be black and white. I couldn't risk going any further than I had already gone."

"Look, I don't blame you." Elena looked into Peyton's eyes. "I needed some time to pull myself back together. But there was never any question in my mind about how I felt about you. How I still feel about you, Peyton."

Elena reached a hand to Peyton's arm. The ring. Peyton saw the ring she had given Elena, saw that she had been wearing it all this time, and realized how she had completely misjudged the time they had been apart.

Peyton touched the ring, looked at Elena, and tears began to fill her eyes. "God, Elena, I've been such a fool…I said such hateful things. I…I'm so sorry, Elena."

"I would have said them too if I had been in your place." Elena felt Peyton's guilt and humiliation and needed to stop it. "Peyton. Look at me."

Peyton slowly lifted her eyes.

"I need for you to know…none of it…not one second of what we had together was a lie… It is the truest thing I have ever known."

Peyton smiled. A tear fell from Elena's eyes.

At that moment, Nash walked in.

Peyton glanced at Elena. "I…I guess I should…"

Nash walked over to them both, turned to Peyton. "It's okay. You don't need to leave." He smiled at Peyton.

Peyton looked from son to mother and placed a hand on Nash's shoulder. "That's okay. I'll give you a few moments with your mom."

Nash, unable to hold back a second longer, dove into his mother's arms. She held him tight. He held her just as tightly, crying…

"It's all going to be okay," Elena said with solid assurance. "Don't worry, baby. It's all going to be okay."

Nash finally got up, walked around the hospital room, and then returned to his mom's side. "You know I'm okay with this, don't you?"

"Yes, sweetie. I do."

"Good, because I want you to be happy, Mom."

She held out her arms. This was the last piece she needed. Now everything would be okay.

Epilogue

A Sunday a year later.

A glowing peach-hue sunset dappled the beautiful grounds of the park where a picnic lunch was laid out on a blanket on the grass. Tori was curled up against Nash, Lily's head lay on Tyler's lap, Wave was happily ensconced in Tea's arms and between Elena and Peyton the adorable Alexandra bumped her way on a baby blanket.

Elena picked her sweet little girl up into her arms, and Peyton offered her the teething biscuit, over which Alexandra made a screwed up face. Everyone laughed.

This was a family that was meant to be, every part of it belonged. Elena looked into Peyton's smiling face, so deeply in love with her it almost hurt, and when Peyton caught Elena's eyes, the unwavering love between them coursed across the picnic blanket like an electric wire.

Peyton leaned over, kissed Elena softly, lingeringly, deeply, until Nash began to groan.

"Okay, okay." Peyton looked into Elena's eyes. "Just when I think I cannot fall in love with you more—I do...every day... it's..."

Elena finished for her, "...ever deeper..."

"Blimey, you two get any more dopey, darlings, I may have to leave the country," Wave suggested. "Oh wait, I don't have to because you're leaving the country for me—and we get to take care of that beautiful little baby."

"Speaking of Paris," Tori interjected easily, "everyone refers to the city of love as the city of lights—and many people think that's due to all that massive wattage beaming from the Eiffel Tower, but it's actually a reference to those artists, the painters, writers, sculptors that were the lights of the city."

Nash shook his head. "Of course we knew that!"

"So the two of you should feel right at home!" Tori stated, ignoring Nash.

"I'm sure we will." Elena smiled back at Tori.

"Only a week left," Peyton sighed. "Until our honeymoon."

"Did you know that some believe the term honeymoon was first noted around the sixteenth century—honey, naturally, to indicate the sweetness of a newly married couple and moon, sadly, reflected that like a full moon, it was inevitable for that sweetness to fade and—"

"Tori, how 'bout some backgammon?" Lily asked. Tori was game.

Tyler looked about him at this tightknit and happy group of people. He smiled, watching Lily as she began to set up the backgammon set as Tori pummeled her with backgammon trivia, then glanced at Tea who kissed Wave as they unpacked the picnic basket together. Nash had began to bump his soccer ball against his knee and Tyler's eyes glowed as he watched Peyton and Elena tending to Alexandra. Yes, this was one big, beautiful family.

"All is as it should be," he sighed, quite happy with the state of things. "It's Soulemetry..."

Publications from
Bella Books, Inc.
Women. Books. Even Better Together.
P.O. Box 10543
Tallahassee, FL 32302
Phone: 800-729-4992
www.bellabooks.com

THE GRASS WIDOW by Nanci Little. Aidan Blackstone is nineteen, unmarried and pregnant, and has no reason to think that the year 1876 won't be her last. Joss Bodett has lost her family but desperately clings to their land. A richly told story of frontier survival that picks up with the generation of women where Patience and Sarah left off.
978-1-59493-189-5 $12.95

SMOKEY O by Celia Cohen. Insult "Mac" MacDonnell and insult the entire Delaware Blue Diamond team. Smokey O'Neill has just insulted Mac, and then finds she's been traded to Delaware. The games are not limited to the baseball field!
978-1-59493-198-7 $12.95

WICKED GAMES by Ellen Hart. Never have mysteries and secrets been closer to home in this eighth installment of this award-winning lesbian cozy mystery series. Jane Lawless's neighbors bring puzzles and peril--and that's just the beginning.
978-1-59493-185-7 $14.95

NOT EVERY RIVER by Robbi McCoy. It's the hottest city in the U.S., and it's not just the weather that's heating up. For Kim and Randi are forced to question everything they thought they knew about themselves before they can risk their fiery hearts on the biggest gamble of all.
978-1-59493-182-6 $14.95

HOUSE OF CARDS by Nat Burns. Cards are played, but the game is gossip. Kaylen Strauder has never wanted it to be about her. But the time is fast-approaching when she must decide which she needs more: her community of Eda Byrne.
978-1-59493-203-8 $14.95

RETURN TO ISIS by Jean Stewart. The award-winning Isis sci-fi series features Jean Stewart's vision of a committed colony of women dedicated to preserving their way of life, even after the apocalypse. Mysteries have been forgotten, but survival depends on remembering. Book one in series.
978-1-59493-193-2 $12.95

1ST IMPRESSIONS by Kate Calloway. Rookie PI Cassidy James has her first case. Her investigation into the murder of Erica Trinidad's uncle isn't welcomed by the local sheriff, especially since the delicious, seductive Erica is their prime suspect. 1st in series. Author's augmented and expanded edition.
978-1-59493-192-5 $12.95

BEACON OF LOVE by Ann Roberts. Twenty-five years after their families put an end to a relationship that hadn't even begun, Stephanie returns to Oregon to find many things have changed... except her feelings for Paula.
978-1-59493-180-2 $14.95

ABOVE TEMPTATION by Karin Kallmaker. It's supposed to be like any other case, except this time they're chasing one of their own. As fraud investigators Tamara Sterling and Kip Barrett try to catch a thief, they realize they can have anything they want--except each other.
978-1-59493-179-6 $14.95

AN EMERGENCE OF GREEN by Katherine V. Forrest. Carolyn had no idea her new neighbor jumped the fence to enjoy her swimming pool. The discovery leads to choices she never anticipated in an intense, sensual story of discovery and risk, consequences and triumph. Originally released in 1986.
978-1-59493-217-5 $14.95

CRAZY FOR LOVING by Jaye Maiman. Officially hanging out her shingle as a private investigator, Robin Miller is getting her life on track. Just as Robin discovers it's hard to follow a dead man, She walks in. KT Bellflower, sultry and devastating... Lammy winner and second in series.
978-1-59493-195-6 $14.95

LOVE WAITS by Gerri Hill. The All-American girl and the love she left behind--it's been twenty years since Ashleigh and Gina parted, and now they're back to the place where nothing was simple and love didn't wait.
978-1-59493-186-4 $14.95

HANNAH FREE: THE BOOK by Claudia Allen. Based on the film festival hit movie starring Sharon Gless. Hannah's story is funny, scathing and witty as she navigates life with aplomb -- but always comes home to Rachel. 32 pages of color photographs plus bonus behind-the-scenes movie information.
978-1-59493-172-7 $19.95

END OF THE ROPE by Jackie Calhoun. Meg Klein has two enduring loves— horses and Nicky Hennessey. Nicky is there for her when she most needs help, but then an attractive vet throws Meg's carefully balanced world out of kilter.
978-1-59493-176-5 $14.95

THE LONG TRAIL by Penny Hayes. When schoolteacher Blanche Bartholomew and dance hall girl Teresa Stark meet their feelings are powerful--and completely forbidden--in Starcross Texas. In search of a safe future, they flee, daring to take a covered wagon across the forbidding prairie.
978-1-59493-196-3 $12.95

UP UP AND AWAY by Catherine Ennis. Sarah and Margaret have a video. The mob wants it. Flying for their lives, two women discover more than secrets.
978-1-59493-215-1 $12.95

CITY OF STRANGERS by Diana Rivers. A captive in a gilded cage, young Solene plots her escape, but the rulers of Hernorium have other plans for Solene--and her people. Breathless lesbian fantasy story also perfect for teen readers.
978-1-59493-183-3 $14.95

ROBBER'S WINE by Ellen Hart. Belle Dumont is the first dead of summer. Jane Lawless, Belle's old friend, suspects coldhearted murder. Lammy-winning seventh novel in critically acclaimed cozy mystery series.
978-1-59493-184-0 $14.95

APPARITION ALLEY by Katherine V. Forrest. Kate Delafield has solved hundreds of cases, but the one that baffles her most is her own shooting. Book six in series.
978-1-883523-65-7 $14.95

STERLING ROAD BLUES by Ruth Perkinson. It was a simple declaration of love. But the entire state of Virginia wants to weigh in, leaving teachers Carrie Tomlinson and Audra Malone caught in the crossfire--and with love troubles of their own.
978-1-59493-187-1 $14.95

LILY OF THE TOWER by Elizabeth Hart. Agnes Headey, taking refuge from a storm at the Netherfield estate, stumbles into dark family secrets and something more… Meticulously researched historical romance.
978-1-59493-177-2 $14.95

LETTING GO by Ann O'Leary. Kelly has decided that luscious, successful Laura should be hers. For now. Laura might even be agreeable. But where does that leave Kate?
978-1-59493-194-9 $12.95

MURDER TAKES TO THE HILLS by Jessica Thomas. Renovations, shady business deals, a stalker--and it's not even tourist season yet for PI Alex Peres and her best four-legged pal Fargo. Sixth in this cozy Provincetown-based series.
978-1-59493-178-9 $14.95

SOLSTICE by Kate Christie. It's Emily Mackenzie's last college summer and meeting her soccer idol Sam Delaney seems like a dream come true. But Sam's passion seems reserved for the field of play…
978-1-59493-175-8 $14.95

FORTY LOVE by Diana Simmonds. Lush, romantic story of love and tennis with two women playing to win the ultimate prize. Revised and updated author's edition.
978-1-59493-190-1 $14.95

I LEFT MY HEART by Jaye Maiman. The only women she ever loved is dead, and sleuth Robin Miller goes looking for answers. First book in Lammy-winning series.
978-1-59493-188-8 $14.95

TWO WEEKS IN AUGUST by Nat Burns. Her return to Chincoteague Island is a delight to Nina Christie until she gets her dose of Hazy Duncan's renown ill-humor. She's not going to let it bother her, though…
978-1-59493-173-4 $14.95